Mystic Montana Sky

BOOK SIX OF THE MONTANA SKY SERIES

Books by Debra Holland

Montana Sky Series

1892

Beneath Montana's Sky

1886

Mail-Order Brides of the
West: Trudy
Mail-Order Brides of the
West: Lina
Mail-Order Brides of the
West: Darcy
Mail-Order Brides of the
West: Prudence
Mail-Order Brides of the
West: Bertha

1890s

Grace: Bride of Montana
Wild Montana Sky
Starry Montana Sky
Stormy Montana Sky
Montana Sky Christmas
A Valentine's Choice
Irish Blessing
Painted Montana Sky

Glorious Montana Sky
Healing Montana Sky
Sweetwater Springs Scrooge
Sweetwater Springs Christmas
Mystic Montana Sky

2015

Angel in Paradise

The Gods' Dream Trilogy

Fantasy Romance
Sower of Dreams
Reaper of Dreams
Harvest of Dreams
Season of Renewal

Twinborne Trilogy

Lywin's Quest

Nonfiction

The Essential Guide to Grief and
Grieving
Surmounting Shame: A Ten
Minute Ebook
Cultivating an Attitude of
Gratitude: A Ten Minute Ebook

Mystic Montana Sky

BOOK SIX OF THE MONTANA SKY SERIES

DEBRA HOLLAND

Montlake
Romance

Text copyright © 2016 Debra Holland
All rights reserved.

Published by Montlake Romance, Seattle

www.apub.com

Amazon, the Amazon logo, and Montlake Romance are trademarks of Amazon.com, Inc., or its affiliates.

ISBN-13: 9781503936751
ISBN-10: 1503936759

Cover design by Delle Jacobs

Printed in the United States of America

CHAPTER ONE

Between Sweetwater Springs and Morgan's Crossing
Spring 1896

Maggie Baxter braced her feet against the floorboard of the rocking *vardo*. With a death grip, she clutched the smooth edge of the wooden seat of the Gypsy wagon that was her home. In spite of the chilly morning, sweat gleamed on the sides of the piebald black-and-white draught horses pulling the caravan. Urged on by the heavy hands of her husband, Oswald, they moved at a pace too fast for comfort… for safety. Dread churned in her stomach, and she fought the nausea rising in her throat.

The team is too old to be pushed this hard. Maggie had protested their speed, but Oswald's glare scared her into silence. The tree-covered hills flashed by. She looked up at the pure blue sky, clear after yesterday's rain, and prayed for their safety.

Maggie glanced at her husband, noting his clenched jaw and the tense set of his shoulders. *Dare I ask him to slow down?*

Familiar fear shivered through her, and she held her tongue, pulling the wool blanket tighter around her shoulders. The wind tugged at the red scarf she wore to contain her hair. Before she could tighten the knot at her nape, the material loosened and fluttered away. With a squeak of protest, she grabbed for the scarf but missed. Her hair whipped across her face.

Oswald noticed, narrowing his cold blue eyes. But he didn't stop to retrieve the scarf. He'd been in a foul mood since his argument yesterday with Michael Morgan, the owner of the mine where Oswald worked. It was one fight too many. The boss had fired Oswald and ordered him out of Morgan's Crossing. And, since the man owned the whole town, he had the power to enforce the eviction edict.

This morning as they packed up their camp, Maggie had tiptoed around her husband, trying to remain small and silent lest she trigger his temper, for she had to protect the child growing within her. She released one hand from the death grip on the seat to curl her arm protectively around the great arc of her belly.

A cramp made her back ache, causing cold fingers of dread to touch her spine. Inwardly, Maggie cursed, wishing she'd chosen to stay in Morgan's Crossing.

Yesterday, before they left, Mrs. Morgan had marched over to where they'd camped. Prudence Morgan was a force to be reckoned with. The wife of the mine owner had a long history of not tolerating bullies, and she wasn't the least afraid of Oswald. The woman had pulled Maggie aside, suggesting she remain in town without her husband.

I should have listened to my intuition.

Maggie had wanted desperately to agree. She'd been reluctant to leave the comfort of the female friendships she'd formed in Morgan's Crossing, as well as the security of a doctor to deliver the baby in a few weeks. But she had no way to support herself, much less a child, and was too proud to take charity. Selling her earrings—the real gold hidden under a coating of brass—would provide no more than a few months of sustenance, a year at the most.

Although whatever love she'd felt for her husband in the beginning of their marriage had withered from his drunkenness and his abuse, after she became pregnant Maggie foolishly held on to some remnants of hope for their future. He was a strong man, and during her pregnancy, Oswald had strutted around in obvious masculine pride and treated her with heavy-handed kindness. She'd thought the idea of fatherhood had changed him.

I've made a grave mistake.

Her second error was to argue with him this morning, requesting they remain at their campsite for a few more days before traveling on to Sweetwater Springs. She'd experienced contractions throughout the night like the ones she'd had off and on for the last ten days or so. The thought of more travel had been too much for her. *Thank goodness the baby's not due for a few more weeks.*

The result of her request was to make Oswald do the opposite, hurriedly breaking camp and driving far too fast. *I wish I'd told him I wanted to reach Sweetwater Springs as soon as possible. He would have insisted on camping in that spot for a week.*

The wheels hit another pothole, jolting the *vardo*, which squeaked and groaned.

Maggie winced at the sound. Oswald had neglected the green Gypsy wagon that had once been the pride of her grandparents, built when her forebears first immigrated to America. Not only was the paint faded, but the gilding on the carvings around the door and roofline had worn thin. Although the shabby exterior of their home bothered her, Maggie was far more concerned about damaging the wheels or the structure of the caravan.

Oswald gathered the reins in one hand, picked up the coiled whip that lay on the seat between them, and snapped the lash over the team's heads.

The horses picked up their pace.

A wave of damp heat flushed her body. Queasiness roiled her stomach. *I'm going to be sick.* Muscles tense, Maggie slanted a cautious glance at her husband, need warring with fear. "Oswald, can you please slow down?" She had to raise her voice to be heard over the clattering of the wagon wheels.

The corners of his mouth tightened. He shot her a dark look, his eyes feral, teeth bared in a grimace.

That expression—one of rabid insanity—had contorted his face the two times he'd almost beaten her to death. Only the intervention of the neighbors, who'd heard her screams, had saved her. Maggie shrank back into the corner, pulled a handkerchief out of her sleeve, and dabbed at her damp face. Nausea drove her to speak. "Oswald?"

Again he flicked the reins.

The swaying of the *vardo* jolted her back and forth. Illness built in her stomach like a poison. "Please. I think the baby's coming." She made the mistake of leaning toward him in supplication.

Oswald's arm snaked out. He backhanded her across the face and knocked her into the corner of the seat.

The sting of the blow proved too much. Maggie leaned over the side of the wagon, losing her meager breakfast.

✳ ✳ ✳

Banker Caleb Livingston drove his surrey along the dirt road to Morgan's Crossing for his annual meeting with Michael Morgan concerning the financial business of the mine. He always dreaded the trip—a duty he would have enjoyed if only the mining town were two hours away from Sweetwater Springs instead of a two-day journey.

He'd spent an unpleasant night in a rough hut built for wayfarers, which was nestled in the midst of hills. He'd tossed and turned on the uncomfortable, narrow bed for what seemed like hours, only to oversleep, waking well after dawn. The late morning was still chilly, and Caleb had bundled up in his wool coat and muffler, tugging his hat low over his ears and slipping on fur-lined leather gloves to keep his hands warm.

His team of matched brown horses was fresh. They took the isolated downhill grade at a fast clip, their hooves kicking up dirt to splatter the once-shiny black surrey.

Deep in thought, Caleb relaxed his attention from his driving to focus on a topic that usually bedeviled most men—*women*. "Time to find a wife," he said, reiterating a vow he'd made at the Christmas party celebrating the grand opening of his hotel. On that triumphant night, he'd keenly felt the lack of a wife by his side who would support his ambition and admire his accomplishments, who'd shine as a social hostess and help civilize the town and warm his bed.

His mouth firmed. In the past few years, he'd given his particular attention to several worthy candidates, but they'd chosen other men—ones lacking his wealth, social status, and even, if he could be so vain, his well-formed appearance.

Caleb's pride, not his heart, had been hurt, at least in the cases of Samantha Rodriguez, now Mrs. Wyatt Thompson; Lily Maxwell, now Mrs. Tyler Dunn; and Delia Bellaire, soon to be Mrs. Joshua Norton. One twinge of loss he would admit to—he'd invested more emotion in the pursuit of beautiful Elizabeth Hamilton. Everyone in Sweetwater Springs had known of Caleb's courtship and his humiliating defeat to a cowboy.

He continued down the list. His interest in Sophia Maxwell, the Songbird of Chicago, had taken place more in his imagination than in reality. Before he could declare his interest, Sophia had made it clear her role as a professional opera singer was more important than settling down in a small frontier town—no matter how grand the hotel or appealing the owner.

But really, in spite of the list, in the last few years, Caleb had been so focused on the completion and establishment of his hotel he hadn't paid serious attention to the search for a wife. After all, he did have his sister to oversee his home. And frankly, he didn't look forward to the battles that were sure to ensue when Edith was forced to relinquish her role as mistress of the household. But a man had needs—*ones I've suppressed for too long.*

Caleb's thoughts remained fixed on his ideal woman—upper-class, beautiful, elegant, educated; yet, in the privacy of their bedroom, his paragon would cast constraints to the wind and turn into a passionate lover. *Isn't that what most men wish for?*

Once I return home from Morgan's Crossing, I'll prepare for a trip to Boston to visit my family. The hotel and bank can manage without my presence long enough for me to court and wed the right woman.

The horses swept around the curve of a hill. His mind on the intimate relations he hoped to have in the near future, Caleb didn't hear the muffled drum of hoofbeats and clatter of wagon wheels until a team of piebald horses appeared as if conjured out of nowhere. They pulled some sort of outlandish green caravan that careened over the whole road.

The driver snapped a whip.

What in the—?

The loud curses of the driver echoed the ones blasting in Caleb's brain, but his jaw was too tight to utter them. He wrenched the reins to the left, forcing his team to hug the curve of the mountain, praying the man didn't steer his horses in the same direction.

The black-and-white horses swerved to the right of Caleb's surrey. The vehicles passed within inches of each other, almost close enough to scrape paint, the bulky green sides of the wagon blurring from the speed.

From the corner of his eye, Caleb saw the driver veer too wide. His gut leaped into his throat. But they'd swept around the hill, out of sight, and he didn't dare take his attention away from his team. From behind, he heard a woman's scream, followed by the sounds of a crash and then ominous silence.

Praying harder than he ever had in his life, Caleb steered the horses to a patch of ground on the side of the road and reined in. In front of him, the land steeply dropped to a wide valley. Hands shaking, he set the brake and tied off the reins. He glanced behind. The caravan was out of his line of sight.

Caleb jumped to the ground and raced back the way he'd come. He ran to the edge of the road; the Colt he wore in a holster bumped against his leg. He followed the imprint of wheels and hooves, hoping against hope not to see people, horses, and the wagon smashed at the bottom of the cliff.

When he rounded the turn, Caleb skidded to a stop. Instead of the cliff he'd expected, the land gradually slanted away from the road to the tree line, leaving an open area of about forty feet. The caravan lay canted to the left, held up only by a mighty pine. The collision had smashed the side. The horses seemed to be fine, only shaken, the harness holding them captive.

Halfway between him and the ruined wagon, a female body lay like a rag doll on her side.

Caleb's heart stuttered, and he slipped and slid on the slick new grass to reach her, grabbing a blanket that was strewn on the ground as he passed.

The woman's long, dark hair was unbound and covered her face. Her shabby, wine-colored dress was bunched above her knees, exposing limbs covered in darned black stockings.

Caleb knelt and tugged down the hem for decency's sake. Dreading what he'd see, he gently turned the woman, hoping he wasn't exacerbating her injuries, and brushed the hair off her face. She looked young, pretty, with sooty lashes and eyebrows. Her high cheekbones and wide mouth, now compressed with pain, gave her features a Slavic appearance. Brass hoop earrings hung from her ears. Her olive skin had a pasty tinge. She must have hit her head on a rock, for blood seeped from a gash in her forehead. A welt marred her cheek.

Have I killed her? Sickened, Caleb heard only the sound of his harsh breathing and the rush of blood in his ears. He stripped off his gloves and thrust them into a coat pocket. With a shaky hand, he reached out to touch her throat. The leap of her pulse under his fingertips kicked his heart into a gallop.

She's alive! He jumped to his feet, intending to run for help. Frantically, he looked around the clearing as if he could magically summon a doctor. He caught himself and shook his head at the foolishness of the fruitless search.

Caleb mentally cast about the surrounding area, trying to remember if he knew of any settlers in the region, but could think of no one. He sank back down to his knees, wondering if he dared check to see if the woman had broken any limbs. Gingerly, he touched her arm.

She stirred, her lips parting. Her eyelids rose. Big, brown eyes flecked with gold and dazed with pain stared up at him. "My baby?"

His rib cage constricted. *Please tell me I didn't kill a child!*

Her hand moved to her round stomach. A thin gold ring showed she was married.

Caleb gasped, realizing she was pregnant.

She moaned.

Fear coursed through him. *What if the baby's hurt?*

"You've hit your head," he said with a gentleness aimed at reassuring her. "Are you hurt anywhere else?"

"Everywhere." She reached to touch her forehead.

Caleb caught her hand. "You're bleeding." His voice trembled, and he forced himself to sound confident. "Head wounds are often nasty but not serious." He reached into his vest pocket and pulled out his handkerchief. "I'm going to see to your injury." Carefully he dabbed at the blood on her forehead. A lump was rising, but the cut didn't look bad, the blood slowly oozing. "I don't think you'll need stitches." He folded the cloth and left the pad in place. "If I may touch you...?" He glanced at her for permission. "I'm sorry for the familiarity, but I must see if you've broken any bones before we move you to safety." *What scant safety there is, here in the wilds.*

The woman nodded, wincing as the movement jarred her head. "Yes," she whispered.

Tentatively, he ran a hand over her shoulder and down her arm, and then leaned over to check her other side. As far as he could tell, nothing seemed broken. "Let me check your, uh, ribs."

She closed her eyes. "Go ahead."

Caleb started with her side. *Is there a way to even ascertain if the babe is unharmed?* He didn't know the least thing about pregnancy. He splayed his hand over her stomach, moving to the top and imagining the child within. *Please, baby, be alive.*

As if in response to his plea, he felt a movement under his palm. His gaze jerked to the woman's. "Is that right?" His voice sounded shaky.

The woman opened her eyes. Her hand shifted to touch his. "Very right."

The sense of relief went all the way to his bones.

"I think that's a kick." She pushed his hand lower. "The head. I don't think he liked the ride."

"I don't blame the little tyke. I didn't like it, either," Caleb murmured, surprised to feel a ghost of levity rise in him. His neck burning from the necessary intimacy, he ran his hands down her legs, relieved to feel no obvious broken bones.

Her lips turned upward, and then she grimaced. "Oswald?"

In his focus on the woman, he'd forgotten about the driver. "Your husband?"

"Yes."

"I'm sorry. I don't know. But I'll go find out." Caleb spread the blanket over the woman, wondering if he should move her first. But he needed to see to the man, whose injuries might be more severe. He lifted the handkerchief to check her cut. The blood seemed to have stopped, so he balled up the linen, bloody area inside, and stuffed the handkerchief into his pocket.

Her eyelids drifted closed.

How could I have forgotten the man? Caleb rose, barely noticing the dampness of his trousers from kneeling on the ground. He hurried to the front of the wagon.

The horses looked at him. The one on the right kept its weight off a feathered foreleg. *Probably a strain.* But he couldn't stop to check.

The caravan leaned drunkenly against the tree, the front side collapsed over the driver's seat. Caleb assessed the caravan and doubted the wagon could be moved without extra help. "Oswald," he called, straining to hear a sound. He moved closer to the seat and saw torn work pants, stocky, flaccid legs, and sensed he was too late. Caleb had to push and shove the wreckage up and back before he could see the rest of the driver.

Oswald's head was cocked at an angle that indicated a broken neck. Blood from dozens of cuts congealed on his face and hands. His sightless blue eyes stared at the sky.

Caleb stared at the body for a brief moment. From the looks of the caravan, he'd expected a swarthy Gypsy-type wearing colorful clothing. Not a pale-faced man with brown stubble on his chin that matched his hair and patched canvas trousers.

When Caleb leaned over the body to check, he could feel no pulse under his fingers. The coppery smell of blood filled his nostrils, and he wanted to be sick. He lowered the man's eyelids.

Straightening, he swallowed hard, struggled to hold down the nausea. He wiped both hands on the front of his coat. *I've killed a man.* His steps heavy, Caleb plodded back to the woman, feeling as if his whole body had turned to stone. *How do I tell his wife?*

She hadn't stirred from her spot on the ground.

Caleb's throat tightened, and he had to swallow before he could convey the news. "I'm afraid your husband is dead." He crouched by her side. "I think he was killed instantly."

She closed her eyes and turned her face away from him.

He floundered for something more to say, but he could only manage, "I'm so sorry." *Mere words that cannot possibly convey the depth of my remorse.*

"Not your fault." She turned back, groped for his hand, and squeezed.

Her palm was rough from menial labor, but the touch heartened him. "Oswald was driving too fast."

Caleb was determined not to hide the truth. "So was I."

"He was out of control."

"I wasn't paying attention."

"I tried to make him slow down, but he wouldn't." She gasped and placed a hand on her stomach. Her muscles tensed, and her eyes widened with obvious fear. "I felt a pain. A bad one. The babe's moved lower."

"No." Caleb blurted the protest without thought.

She clutched his arm. "Yes."

"You *cannot* go into labor," Caleb ordered, anxiety clenching his innards.

"The baby is coming!" She enunciated every word.

"The doctor is a long day's ride away in Sweetwater Springs, and there's no woman for miles. You'll just have to wait."

As the contraction eased, the tightness in her body relaxed, and she gave him a wan smile. "Does everyone always do what you say?"

Is that levity in her voice? At a time like this? "They comply if I know what's best, and I usually do." Caleb strove for a humorous, rather than a pompous, tone and hoped he pulled it off. "I assure you, it's best that you do not give birth out here in the wilderness." He touched her arm. "I'm afraid to move you, but I must."

"Everything hurts."

"That settles it. I'm taking you home with me to Sweetwater Springs."

CHAPTER TWO

Even through a haze of pain, Maggie could see worry in the handsome man's dark eyes and could sense how much he wanted to hand off the problem of her and the impending birth to someone else. But he couldn't, for the pains had become too strong and regular for her to even think of traveling in a moving vehicle.

He slipped his hand under her back as if to move her.

Maggie pushed aside the blanket and reached for his arm to hold him in place. "I can't."

"Madame, you *must*."

"Maggie." *If I die, I want him to know my given name.* "Magdalena Petra Baxter. But I'm called Maggie."

"Mrs. Baxter, my name is Caleb Livingston. I'm a banker and hotel owner in Sweetwater Springs." He eased away from her grip. "I have no knowledge about babies, especially delivering one. We *must* go." Carefully, he slid his hands under her body and lifted Maggie. He carried her as if she weighed no more than a child instead of the ungainly creature she'd become. Holding in a groan of pain at the pressure of her bruised hip against his body, she slipped an arm around his neck.

He gave her a smile full of charm. "Given our informal circumstances, why don't you call me Caleb? And if I may be so bold as to use your given name?"

"Of course." Maggie stretched out a shaky hand toward the *vardo*. "The horses." She couldn't leave Pete and Patty to fend for themselves.

"I'll unhitch your team and tie them to the surrey." His eyebrows pulled together. "The back of your dress is damp from lying on the ground. Why aren't you wearing a coat?"

"I no longer fit in it." She touched the blanket. "I had this wrapped around me."

"We must get you changed."

Maggie became aware of the wet cloth of her knickers. *How embarrassing.* But she knew things were about to become far more intimate and humiliating. This man, for all he protested the coming of the baby, was about to assist her child into the world—whether he liked it or not. She sensed he wouldn't abandon her in this time of need. "I have clothes in the *vardo*," was all she said, not wanting to frighten him any further with talk of the child about to arrive. He apparently needed some time to come to terms with her labor.

"*Vardo?*" he asked. "All right."

A glance at the ruined *vardo* made her heart ache. Maggie mourned the loss of her home far more than the death of her husband. *Does that make me a bad person?* She laid her head on Caleb's shoulder, feeling an odd sense of trust.

Her lower back slowly seized up, wiping out all thought as pain took over her body. She gasped through the agony.

"What's wrong?" Caleb questioned, his expression urgent. He tightened his grip. "Maggie?"

Caught up in her travail, Maggie couldn't answer until the contraction subsided. Taking a deeper breath, she prepared to break the unwelcome news. "The baby has decided not to obey your orders and is about to make an appearance." She tried to make her statement sound light and matter of fact, but her voice quivered on the last word.

His eyes widened, and he shook his head. "But—!"

If she weren't so scared, Maggie would have laughed at his panicked expression. "You can't stop the tide," she murmured one of her grandmother's expressions.

"Oh, dear Lord." His words were half a curse, half a prayer. "What are we going to do?" He glanced up the hill as if debating about carrying her to the road.

"Caleb, we need to stay *here*. I have bedding. Supplies."

His jaw firmed, and his gaze swept the area. "There's nowhere comfortable for you."

Maggie glanced around the small clearing. "Over there." She pointed. "The spot under that tree is almost flat."

Caleb's gaze followed. "Almost is correct." His tone was wry.

"We'll just have to make do," Maggie said, making sure to sound strong. "Put me down near the *vardo* door, and I can tell you where everything is. You can climb inside and get the items."

He carried her down the hill toward the caravan.

Not for the first time, Maggie felt grateful her grandfather had built a door into the back, as well as having one in front.

When they reached the caravan, Caleb lowered her to the ground, keeping a steadying arm around her waist.

Once her left foot touched the ground, pain lanced through her ankle. Maggie cringed and picked up her foot, leaning against him.

"Another contraction?"

"My ankle. I think I sprained it." *Please, God, it can't be broken. Not with the baby coming.* "Let me try again."

He cocked an eyebrow in obvious skepticism.

"No," she protested. "I can stand. I'll put my weight on the other one."

Caleb eased the pressure of his hold.

Maggie tugged the blanket around her shoulders and braced herself against the back wall of the *vardo*, embarrassed that he must have noticed the run-down state of the caravan, and then dismissed the thought. *We have more important things to concern ourselves with.* She glanced up at his face.

Caleb watched her, his brow furrowed. He relaxed his grip but didn't lift his hands. His palms stayed in gentle contact with her shoulders.

Gentle? When have I last been touched with gentleness by a man? Not since my grandfather.... Before she could remember when, a pain seized Maggie's middle like a vise. She gasped and stiffened.

"Another?"

Her whole concentration centered on enduring the wave of pain across her belly. She didn't reply until the wave ceased. "The baby's coming," she gasped out, in case he hadn't understood the first time she'd told him. "Whether you like it or not...."

Caleb shook his head but said nothing. Instead, he took off his coat, eased the blanket from her grasp, and dropped it to the ground. He wrapped the coat around her shoulders, guiding her arms inside.

"You'll have to accept that I'm about to deliver," Maggie said, her tone firm.

Admiration glinted in Caleb's brown eyes. "You should be having hysterics right now. You're a rare woman, Magdalena Petra Baxter."

"I have no choice."

He touched her chin. "You're keeping your head high, making the best of this wretched situation, instead of sniveling and feeling sorry for yourself."

I've already done that. The dark day when Maggie realized she'd married a monster would be forever imprinted in her memory. After Oswald's first beating, she'd lain on the bed in the *vardo,* too sore to move, and she wept.

Narrow-eyed, Caleb turned his attention to the caravan. The frame had bent, and he had to wrench open the door.

They peered inside. With the left side smashed, the inside was in shambles. Shards of china and glass covered the floor. Light shone through the roof and side where the caravan had crashed into the tree, ruining the faded mural of a Gypsy encampment painted on the ceiling.

Everything's destroyed! Maggie couldn't help the wail of grief that escaped. Her mother had treasured that china—a wedding present from her husband.

Caleb dropped an arm around her shoulder and gave her a supportive hug.

For a moment, Maggie leaned against him. Then she felt ashamed to have shown such selfish emotion with Oswald dead and straightened.

He lowered his arm.

How sad to mourn dishes but not a husband. Maggie strove for composure, tried to think of what she'd need for the birth. She unhooked the ladder and attempted to pull it down, but it was too warped to move.

Caleb moved her hands from the rung. "Allow me." He wrestled the ladder down.

"If you lift that—" Maggie pointed at the table, which was in the lowered position. "There's a drawer with an oiled tablecloth inside that also serves as a ground cloth. We'll need the bedding. My, uh...." Heat flushed her face, and Maggie forced herself to continue. "My nightgown is under the pillow."

Caleb climbed inside. He braced one foot on the slanted wall and the other on the floor and gingerly stepped to the center of the *vardo*. Glass crunched under his feet. He lifted the table and took out the brown oilcloth.

Careful to keep her injured foot off the ground, Maggie braced herself with one hand on the doorframe. A contraction bent her double. When it passed, she leaned inside, her other hand outstretched.

Caleb stretched to give the tablecloth to her. Then he inched toward the bed and gathered up the bedding, tucking her nightgown into the folds so as not to drop the garment on the littered floor. With his arms full, he shuffled back to the doorway.

Maggie hopped out of the way so he could climb out.

For a man with his arms full of bedding, Caleb moved with powerful grace, a contrast to stocky Oswald who'd always lumbered in and out of the caravan, often complaining about the height from the ground. He'd broken one of the rungs of the ladder and had never bothered to repair it.

Maggie dropped the blanket by her feet. Without it, she could feel the wind chilling her back. She set the tablecloth just inside the door and extended her arms to Caleb. "Let me have the bedding. You take the oilcloth."

Careful not to jostle her, Caleb transferred his bundle to her arms and picked up the tablecloth.

"Lay this on the ground, on the spot I selected for the birth," she commanded, using her chin to point to the tablecloth. She caught herself and cringed, knowing what would happen if she spoke to Oswald in that tone. Holding her breath, she studied the man for his reaction. *Is he angry?*

Caleb didn't seem to mind her taking charge. He tilted his head, listening with an intent expression, apparently waiting for her to continue.

When a blow wasn't forthcoming, Maggie allowed herself to breathe. "Fold the bedding in half and put it on top of one side of the tablecloth, and fold the other side over the bedding. Childbirth is supposed to be…ah…*untidy*, and I don't want to soil my bedding or have it become damp from the ground." She eyed his clothes and shook her head.

"What?"

"You will ruin your fine clothes."

"I have a change of clothing with me."

"Only a rich man would say such a thing." She pointed her chin toward the *vardo*. "My apron is hanging behind the door. Best fetch it."

"I'm not wearing an apron."

She placed a hand on the bulge of her stomach and tried her luck with forthrightness again. "Will you argue with a woman about to give birth?"

His gaze followed her hand. Caleb let out a sigh of mock long-suffering and shrugged. "You win." He tied on the covering.

Laughter gurgled up in her, something Maggie hadn't thought to feel at such a time.

At her chuckle, his expression lightened. "Be warned. You won't be in labor for long. Afterward, you'll lose your advantage."

His smile took her breath away, and the laughter died within her. She knew all too well what ugliness might lie behind a handsome countenance. Maggie flapped her hand in the direction of the tree where she'd chosen to make the bed. "Go on with you, then," she said, trying to sound confident like Mrs. Morgan. "We don't have time to stand here chattering."

Indeed, she'd spoken the truth. The pain came hard this time. She gasped, bent, and panted. At last, she straightened.

"Seems like your labor pains are more frequent—about five or so minutes apart."

"And stronger, too!"

He followed her direction, walking to the flat area about twenty feet from the *vardo* under the tree. He pulled out a pocketknife from his trousers and cut pine boughs, laying them thickly on the ground before snapping out the tablecloth and floating it to cover the makeshift mattress. He strode back to her to take the bedding.

Maggie leaned against the back of the *vardo*, her hand on her distended belly, feeling the baby move. *Soon, my little one.* She closed her eyes, aching everywhere from being thrown from the wagon. *A miracle my child still lives.* Weariness tried to overtake her, and she wondered how she would make it through this.

The next contraction increased in strength, forcing her nearly to her knees. She grabbed the door frame and hung on. She rubbed her belly, finding the massage oddly comforting.

"Maggie." Caleb came at a run. "Let me take you to the bed."

She shook her head, holding onto his arm instead until the discomfort faded. "Now you can."

He scooped her up and carried her to the nest of bedding, gently lowering her.

Even so, contact with the ground made her bruises throb, and Maggie lay still until the worst passed. With a sigh of relief, she allowed herself to relax, wondering if she should have him brew some willow-bark tea for her bruises, and then decided drinking the tonic might impact the childbirth. Instead, she decided to ask for raspberry leaf tea, which would help with the birthing.

Caleb knelt beside Maggie and brushed her hair back from her forehead. "We need to get you comfortable." He moved the pillow under her head.

In the past year, she had known only small comforts—a sewing circle and the gay chatter of women, a campfire on a fine clear night, spending time with her horses. But now…Maggie held back a sob. *Without a husband, I have no idea how the baby and I will survive.*

I don't think my life will be comfortable for a long time to come.

❋ ❋ ❋

Caleb hurriedly collected all four horses. He found hobbles for the piebalds in a box beneath the caravan's seat and tied his own team to the conveyance with leads long enough to permit grazing. He found no grain in the wagon, so he distributed what he'd brought for his animals among the four.

After seeing to the needs of the horses, he used one of the blankets from his bedroll and wrapped Oswald's body for burial later. He didn't know when he'd capitulated to his fate as a midwife, but he was in it now. When Caleb could no longer postpone the inevitable, he returned to Maggie.

Helping a woman who wasn't his wife change into a nightgown was the most embarrassing thing Caleb had ever done. But with her sprained ankle and overall bruising, he couldn't just leave Maggie to struggle alone.

After an awkward attempt to undress her while she remained lying down, he gave up and assisted Maggie to stand on one foot. As she leaned her back against him, keeping the weight off her bad leg, Caleb tried to keep his gaze over her head. But he had to keep glancing down to see what he was doing, giving him glimpses of her extended stomach and yellowing bruises on her arms, legs, and back, too old to be from the accident.

He wondered what had happened. *Did her husband hit her?* He knew some men did such abhorrent acts, but surely not to a pregnant wife.

Finally, the switch to a nightgown was accomplished, and he helped Maggie lie down, and then took off her worn shoes and stockings. Her ankle was swollen, and on her direction, he found a bottle of witch hazel in the caravan to pour on a rag and wrap around the injury. Afterward, he tucked the blanket around her.

Maggie smiled wanly and thanked him but then tensed, obviously in the throes of another wave of pain.

I thought I felt terror when that caravan came at me, but this is worse. As the contraction gripped Maggie's body, Caleb's nightmarish thoughts flitted to all the women he'd known who'd died in childbirth. *Far too many.*

Even as he tried to make her comfortable, he couldn't let go of the vision of Maggie dying.

When it comes down to it, childbirth is as dangerous as war, probably killing as many mothers as battles do warriors. After all, battles come rarely, but babies are born every day. He could only imagine the courage soldiers needed to perform under enemy fire. Yet, women stared down death each time they bore a child. Caleb shook his head at his morbid thoughts.

Maggie wrinkled her forehead. "What is it?"

"You cannot stay here. We need to get you to shelter, to a woman who can help you deliver."

She placed a hand on her bulky belly. "There's no choice, Caleb," she said softly. "The child will not wait."

"Maggie, I'm serious. I don't know anything about delivering babies." *What if you die? What if the baby dies?* The unspoken questions hung in the air between them.

"How about foals? Calves?" Her teasing smile didn't quite meet her eyes.

"What?"

"Have you been with your dog when she had puppies?"

"I don't have a dog," he said stiffly, not in the least amused by her attempt to distract him.

"Too bad. Everyone should have a dog." Her expression shifted to one of sorrow; old grief haunted her eyes. "I had a dog when I married Oswald. The first time he hit me, Blackie bit him." She turned her face away. "I didn't dare take in another one." Her voice trailed off.

So that explains the old bruises. Pity and outrage warred in him. He clenched his fists, suddenly not feeling as guilty about the death of Maggie's husband. In fact, Oswald was lucky to be beyond Caleb's reach, for he had a furious need to pummel the man.

She rubbed circles on her belly.

"Kittens," Caleb said to chase the shadows from her eyes. "When I was a child, we had a cat who resided in the kitchen. A tabby. But since I wasn't allowed in the servants' domain, I rarely saw the animal. Then one night, my nanny snuck me down to watch the kittens being born. Do you think being the doctor to kittens qualifies me to deliver your baby?" he deadpanned.

"Absolutely, Dr. Livingston."

He didn't comment on her fabrication.

"I know my baby and I will be fine in your capable hands."

You're so brave. Caleb almost blurted out the thought—he who always carefully chose his words. *She must be terrified, yet she's able to joke with me.* But he held in the sentiment, not knowing how to tell Maggie he admired her spirit.

She gasped, suddenly hit with what seemed like one of the strongest contractions yet.

Helpless to ease her pain, Caleb reached to hold her hand, praying the pain would end.

Maggie pushed away his hand. She curled up and grabbed her knees, holding her breath, and shifting as if trying to get comfortable. Finally, the contraction subsided, and she panted for air. Perspiration from the effort drenched her face and chest.

He pulled his handkerchief from his pocket and dabbed the unbloodied part at the sweat on her brow. "I can't imagine the pain," he murmured.

"You ever had a charley horse?" she asked, her voice still thin from exertion.

Caleb winced and nodded, remembering the times after riding for hours that he'd woken up with one in his calf. The muscle would knot, and he'd yelp from the intense throbbing.

"Well, put a big cramp inside your stomach, and you'll know what I'm going through."

I shudder to think....

Maggie closed her eyes in obvious exhaustion. "In the *vardo*, there's a small cabinet hanging on the wall, containing many square drawers," she said without opening her eyes. "I store my herbs there. Can you bring it here? There's a tea I need you to brew for me."

Caleb squeezed her hand. *Three minutes,* he told himself. *I'll be there and back before the next one.* "I'll hurry." He jumped to his feet, loped to the caravan, and climbed inside. The cabinet hung askew on a wall. He navigated the tilted floor, his boots grinding on the glass, and reached up to take down the cabinet. A tea strainer was hooked on one side.

On his way out, he grabbed a pot and picked up a tin cup from the wreckage on the floor. Once outside, Caleb hurried to join Maggie, only to see her struggling with a fierce tightening of muscles. He set down everything and knelt, waiting.

She lay back, gasping for air and not speaking.

Finally, Caleb broke the silence. "Tell me what to expect—what to do."

She exhaled a long breath. "I've never assisted in a birth, mind you. Mining camps don't have a lot of women. And when they do, the tent or cabin only has room for the most experienced woman and maybe a female relative or a close friend. But I've heard my mother's and grandmother's stories. Childbirth makes for a dramatic retelling."

The thought that Maggie might be just as ignorant about childbirth as he was appalled Caleb.

She must have seen the expression on his face, for she smiled and patted his hand. "Ever since I started to show, I've been hearing birthing stories from the women of Morgan's Crossing. Last week, Mrs. Tisdale sat me down and told me what would happen. She was quite…specific."

"That's something, at least," he muttered. "We're not completely ignorant here."

"You've forgotten the kittens."

"How can you jest at such a time?" *This woman continues to astonish me.*

"What would you have me do? Cry? Scream? Have hysterics?"

He held up a hand. "No! Jesting is just fine. Carry on."

She glanced toward the caravan. "You need to heat water—to wash your hands and to cleanse the knife for cutting the cord, to wash the baby…and me. At least the pots won't be damaged. I have cloths prepared—for cleaning and diapers. You'll find everything for the delivery and the needs of the baby in the cupboard near the bed."

He stood and then wavered, reluctant to leave her. "Yell if you need me."

"Don't worry. I'm quite capable of making myself heard."

He laughed, surprised at the emotion. "You're a feisty little thing, aren't you?"

She dropped her gaze. "I was once."

Caleb lowered himself again to one knee. He leaned over and touched his forefinger underneath her chin, tilting her head so she met his eyes. "What happened?"

"Oswald beat the feistiness out of me."

Anger and a strange wave of sorrow washed over him. "You'll never suffer that again," he said gently. "Your husband will never harm you."

"Or my baby," Maggie said with a sob. "I was so afraid he'd hit me and kill my child."

Stirred by compassion, he moved his hand to cup her cheek. "You're safe now. I promise, you'll both be safe." He sent the assurance through his voice, eyes, and touch, willing her to believe him. Willing *himself* to believe. *Please, God, make it so.*

"When this is over, I'll need to bury your husband. Will you want to pay your respects before I do?"

"No. I'm—" Before Maggie could finish, she rolled up into a ball, her eyes glazed, her focus inward until the contraction ended. Then with a gasping breath, she lay back. "As I started to say—"

Caleb wiped the perspiration from her face.

She grabbed his hand, pulling his attention toward her. "I'm not the least bit sorry Oswald is dead. Not that I'm dancing on his grave, either." She scrunched her eyebrows together. "I feel…empty."

Caleb slanted a glance at her. "Are you sure you don't want to view him? I, ah, closed his eyes, and…." He swallowed.

"Listen to me." Maggie tightened her grip, holding his gaze intently. "Any decent man would feel remorse over being involved in such an accident. But that's all this was—an accident. Oswald was furious. He'd been in a foul mood since he'd argued with Michael Morgan and was kicked out of town. This morning, he became angry with me and was driving recklessly." She placed a hand to the deepening bruise on her cheek. "He did this to me right before...."

His gaze narrowed on the injury. "He hit you?"

"I asked him to slow down." She faltered, and then forced herself to take a breath. "He knocked me so hard I almost fell off the bench. I was sick over the side."

Remorse faded, replaced with anger. "How were you thrown clear?"

"The momentum toppled me overboard. As I pitched through the air, all I could think of was *my baby.*" She gave him a faint smile. "I called upon my childhood of tumbling with my cousins, curled my arms and legs around my stomach, and twisted so I landed on my side. With a crack of splintering wood, the *vardo* smashed into a tree. A piece broke off and flew at me. I could only protect the baby or my face, not both." She felt her forehead and winced. "I bent over my belly, and the wood hit my face."

"You chose your child," Caleb murmured in admiration, but he wasn't sure she heard him, for she plunged into a cramp. He held Maggie's hand throughout, her grip hard enough to squeeze the bones together.

When she finished and recovered her breath, Maggie gazed at him in earnest. "I'm *free* of him, Caleb."

"Then I can't be sorry for the accident."

"No, never be sorry."

Caleb touched a finger gently to her bruised cheek. "Your husband was a cad to treat you so." Confused by his rapidly changing emotions, he stood. "Let me get you some water."

"That would be nice," she murmured.

He ran to the *vardo,* where he'd seen a wooden barrel fastened near the back door, hoping it contained water. Unlatching the top, he peered inside to see it was three quarters full. The long handle of a dipper was tucked into a metal loop. He wrestled the barrel from the rings that held it and lugged it back to Maggie.

Just as he reached her, he could see another spasm tighten her body. He set down the barrel, lowered himself to her side, and took her hand. When the tremor released her, Caleb picked up the dipper and ladled some water. "Drink." He held the edge to her lips, sliding his arm under her shoulders to prop her up.

She drank thirstily, finishing the ladleful.

Caleb scooped another for her, helped her drink, and laid her down again.

"I'm so tired." She closed her eyes.

"Rest then." He rose and moved to the caravan, climbed inside and gathered what he thought she might need. Once outside, with his arms full, he heard Maggie cry out. *Barely three minutes now. How soon before the babe is born?* He worried, not knowing.

Maggie was pulled into another great paroxysm, arms and shoulders curled around her belly.

He ran to her, dropping the supplies and the pot on the corner of the bedding, and gave her his hand.

She held on as if for dear life, gasping for breaths that turned into animal-sounding groans.

"Forget the charley horse," she muttered when the contraction ended. "Try stabbed-in-the-stomach-with-a-hunting-knife."

His gut tightened in sympathy. "This will be over soon, my dear Maggie." The endearment slipped out without him noticing. *Surely this ordeal can't last much longer!*

She looked at him, her gaze serious. Half turning on her side toward him, Maggie grabbed his arm with her free hand. "Promise me something, Caleb."

"Anything," he rashly vowed.

"If I die and the baby lives, you must take care of my child."

He tried to hide his instinctive alarm at the idea. "*Nothing* is going to happen to you. You will be *fine*."

"Promise?"

Seeing the desperate need for an answer in her eyes and scarcely believing how this time with Maggie was softening what some had called his steel heart, he said, "I promise, Magdalena Petra. If something happens to you, then I will raise your child as my own."

The words drifted on the breeze, carried to heaven—a solemn vow made before God.

Maggie relaxed and lay down. "My back hurts in the worst way."

"Lie on your side," he commanded. "Let me see if massaging the area will help."

She curled into a ball.

He touched the tight muscles in the small of her back. "Here?"

"Yes."

He began to knead her, softly at first, and when she didn't protest, he dug in harder.

Maggie let out a moan.

Caleb lifted his hands.

"No, don't stop. That's helping, really it is."

Relieved he could *finally* do something to aid her, Caleb massaged her muscles, feeling some of the tightness leave her posture. "Would you like more water?"

"Yes, please." She rolled onto her back.

Again he helped her drink, then lowered her shoulders.

Maggie closed her eyes and seemed to drop into sleep, only to stir a few minutes later as a contraction barreled over her. She groaned, squeezing his fingers 'til they ached. When the constriction eased, she released him and lay back, her body limp. "They are coming faster. I don't know if I have the strength to do this, Caleb."

Once again, he mopped her damp forehead with his handkerchief. "So must every woman think at some point in her travail. Yet babies are born all the time, despite their mothers' doubts. Besides, I already know what a strong woman you are, Maggie."

"No, I'm not."

"I'm not going to argue the truth."

Maggie sipped water, nodding when she was done. "The tea?"

He laid her back down. "I'll build a fire and boil water. Then you'd better tell me exactly what to expect and what to do."

She nodded, grabbing her knees, grunting with pain and the effort to endure. When it was over, she caught her breath. "Someone's filled my insides with prickly pear cactus and is wringing me out."

Caleb winced. "You certainly have a way with words."

"I'll trade places with you."

Never. "You're doing just fine." Playfully, he tapped her nose. "If men were the ones to have babies, the human population would die out within a generation."

She chuckled. "True."

Caleb rocked back on his heels, surprised by how good her husky laughter and their repartee made him feel. He wasn't a man given to bantering with women—with anyone for that matter. Out here in the wilderness, with a woman about to give birth, he wasn't the banker or the hotel owner. *I'm just a man trying to hold his guilt and terror at bay and make sure this mother and child survive.*

CHAPTER THREE

Between Maggie's contractions, Caleb rushed about the business of setting up camp. He cleared an area near the bed, dug a fire pit, and started a fire to brew her tea. He hiked through the trees to a stream at the base of the hill, filled two buckets with water, and hauled them back to the fire.

Meanwhile, she explained what supplies were needed for birthing the baby—the washtub for soaking bloody clothes, the pot for boiling water, a pile of clean rags, a flannel blanket, the string and knife for tying off and cutting the cord, diapers and soakers, and a little cloth garment for the baby to wear.

He tried to memorize her instructions, terrified there'd come a time when he'd need to know what to do, and she wouldn't be able to tell him. Once inside the caravan, Caleb rifled through Maggie's possessions, careless of making a mess. *Or maybe I should say more of a mess.* He bundled everything into a basket that hung from a hook in the ceiling near a corner.

While he worked, Maggie dozed, only to awaken a minute or two later when another wave of pain possessed her. She panted, groaned, and grunted her way through multiple pushes through each contraction.

The next hour passed in a blur. Somewhere along the line, Caleb lost his fear, so intent was he on the birth. His world narrowed to a grim need to get mother and child through this ordeal.

After a contraction, Maggie let out a breath. "I feel better if I continuously push my way through the entire thing."

"You said Mrs. Tisdale told you to trust your body, so I suppose that is what you are doing. Would you like a drink?" He lifted up her shoulders and offered her sips of the raspberry leaf tea, holding the cup to her mouth while she drank, for he could see she was totally spent. Then he laid her back down and wiped her sweaty face.

Soon the cramping came in swift waves, one on top of the other. Maggie was so inwardly focused, she didn't respond when he spoke to her, almost as if she couldn't hear him. To get her attention, Caleb had to lean close to her face when he spoke.

After one long contraction, with intense pushing, Maggie couldn't seem to get comfortable. She tried shifting her hips one way, then the other. "This isn't working." Her eyes flew open. "The baby's coming out!"

Caleb drew back the nightgown to view the part of a woman he wasn't supposed to see. Between her legs, a hairy scalp about the size of a silver dollar gradually grew larger. He inhaled the dusky smell of birthing.

At last Maggie found a position of comfort on her uninjured side, legs drawn up to her chest, hands gripping her thighs behind the knees.

Caleb remembered he was supposed to hold a cloth to support the baby underneath her female parts, but he couldn't seem to move. He felt as if he was looking at Maggie through narrowed vision, breathing too fast, and he became lightheaded. *Keep taking slow breaths. This is no time to keel over, Caleb Livingston,* he sternly told himself. He grabbed a clean cloth and pressed it under her.

The baby's head emerged, facedown.

"It's coming!"

She ignored him, taking another deep inhale, and pushed.

With her second push, as the baby's face turned toward Maggie's knee, Caleb supported the head. He took his hand and wiped the infant's nose and mouth, pulling away the fluid, flicking it to the ground.

She took another deep breath and pushed. Labor seemed to have taken over her body, compelling her to do nothing but thrust out the baby.

With the next push, the lower shoulder slipped through into Caleb's hands, and he intuitively moved the baby downward to make room. The top shoulder squeezed out next, then the rest of the body glided out. *A girl.*

A splash of clear fluid followed. The tiny body was slippery, and he held her tightly, afraid she'd slither out of his grip. He rotated the infant faceup, holding her about ten inches away from his face.

The top of her head had a slight cone shape. Her blue-tinged hands pinked. The baby's eyes were open, alert and seemingly amazed. They connected with his.

A jolt of intense feeling, of *recognition*, flowed between them. As he gazed on the scrunched features of the infant, love surged through him. He'd never felt such a feeling before, and his chest ached with the joyful pressure. Caleb wanted to curl her to his chest and keep her safe. He pressed a kiss to her forehead, inhaling a scent that surprised him with its sweetness.

"My baby?" Maggie asked.

The infant broke eye contact with Caleb and turned her face toward the sound of her mother's voice.

He blinked back moisture from his eyes and grinned. "You have a beautiful daughter."

Maggie let out a cry of joy.

Goose bumps swept over Caleb's skin, and his voice shook with emotion. "She's so little. So perfect."

A huge smile broke out over Maggie's face. She looked at him in obvious elation. "Let me have her." Completely unabashed, she pulled up her nightgown to her shoulders, and then stretched out her arms for her daughter.

Careful not to jerk on the cord, he handed over the baby.

Maggie kissed her daughter and laid the infant face down between her breasts.

Caleb grabbed up the flannel blanket warming by the fire. Moving to Maggie's side, he laid the cloth over the baby.

The baby's head turned toward her mother.

Her expression glowing with maternal love, Maggie explored the infant's face with fingertip touches. "Oh, sweet baby, you have my mother's nose." She continued to examine her daughter, unfurling miniature, delicate fingers and obviously delighting in the child's perfection.

The baby turned her head toward a breast and pushed her feet on Maggie's stomach, slowly moving sideways.

Caleb watched in astonishment as the baby inched toward the nipple.

The infant reached her goal and, lifting her head, made several attempts before she maneuvered the nipple into her mouth and latched on.

"Oh, look, dearest. You found your first milk by yourself. Clever girl." Maggie crooned. "I knew you could. You're going to make your way in the world and find what you need."

Caleb couldn't take his eyes off the baby. "That was the most amazing thing I've ever seen in my life. I never would have thought she'd be so alert, so active, so able to search and find—" he lifted his gaze to meet Maggie's "—her dinner."

"My grandmother believed that a vigorous crawl to the breast means resiliency in life. I remember my mother talking about how strong I was as a baby, how fast I latched on. But...." She glanced down at her suckling daughter. "She's a miracle."

"She is indeed. And so are you," Caleb told her with the upmost sincerity. "With what you've just gone through, you've proven your grandmother's belief."

Maggie lifted her gaze to his. "Thank you, Caleb, for being here. Helping me through this. Delivering her. You've saved our lives."

He shook his head, denying her praise. "I'm the one who's grateful to you, for I know I've had an experience that would have been denied me. Even if I have children someday, Dr. Cameron will deliver them, and I'll be pacing the parlor. I won't see the mother and child for a while afterward. I never would have known what I'd be missing by not being there the whole time."

Maggie smiled and nodded, seeming to understand, and returned to watching her baby.

Caleb had never seen anything so beautiful. *Madonna and child.* A mystical feeling of awe touched him, and he felt connected to the divine, indeed, to all of humanity—generations upon generations of fathers who watched their wives nurse their newborns. In that moment, he forgot the mother and child didn't belong to him.

Finally, Maggie finished studying the suckling baby and smiled at Caleb.

"Do you have a name for the baby?"

"We'd discussed Oswald—horrible name—for a boy, of course. For a daughter, Anna after Oswald's mother. I wanted Viktoria, with a *k*, for my mother and grandmother. It's Hungarian. But my husband wouldn't hear of it. In fact, he barely considered that we'd have a daughter. He was so sure the baby would be a boy."

"Are you going to keep the name Anna?"

Her eyes glinted. "I don't have to use it."

"Victoria is a lovely name."

She rubbed her belly and shot him a considering glance. "Maybe I'll name the baby after you, instead. Caleb is a fine name for a boy. There's no feminine version of Caleb, is there?"

"Caleba?" he teased. "Calebina? I know. Calebimity!" Her throaty chuckle was a reward far richer than money.

"You must have a middle name."

"Two actually. Charles and, if you can believe it—" he smiled "—Victor."

"Caleb Charles Victor Livingston. Quite grand."

"I believe it suits me," he said with a mock arrogant air. His gaze dropped to the baby. "Will you call her Viktoria with a *k*, then?"

"I will call her Charlotte Victoria, without a *k*, after you—your two middle names."

Before he could speak, Caleb had to swallow down a rise of emotion. "I'm honored. The name fits her well. Far better than Caleba."

She chuckled. The gold flecks in her brown eyes sparkled like stars. "I don't know what I'd have done without you, Caleb."

"Not been in this situation."

"No," she retorted. "One far worse. My pains coming…only Oswald to help deliver the baby…if he would have even stopped. The baby and I might not have survived." Her voice lowered. "And I doubt he would've even cared."

"More fool he. Your husband missed out on—" Caleb gestured to Charlotte "—the most wondrous experience a man can witness."

"I think you did more than stand as a witness."

"Not in comparison to you, Maggie. You were marvelous."

Her eyes widened. "I have another urge to push. The afterbirth, I think."

Caleb grabbed a basin he'd brought for the task and placed it between her legs. With a gush of blood, the placenta slid out. *So much blood. Is it normal, or is something wrong?* The thought made his stomach clench. *After all we've been through, I can't lose Maggie or the baby now.* He set aside the basin, planning to later take the placenta and dig a hole for it near where he'd bury Oswald. Hopefully the distance would protect them from any animals who might smell the blood.

After he used a warm cloth to clean Maggie, Caleb washed his hands and face. His body still felt shaky after the birth experience, but his heart was full. When he returned, the baby was still nursing. He sat down next to them, Indian style, content to watch.

After a while, Charlotte pulled her head up like she was ready to stop. Then she seemed to change her mind and continued to suckle for a minute. The next time the baby lifted her head, she relaxed her mouth so the nipple slipped gently away. She turned her face and nestled her cheek against her mother's soft breast.

"I suppose we should clean her up."

"Just a little." She ran a finger over Charlotte's head. "This white coating is supposed to be good for her skin."

Caleb stood, his legs aching, and shook them out before walking to the fire. Grasping a corner of a washcloth, he dunked it into the pot of water, and then raised it, holding it aloft to cool a bit. The cloth flapped in the wind until he judged the temperature to be the perfect warmth for Charlotte's delicate skin. He returned to Maggie's side.

She held out the baby for him to wash.

He crouched and dabbed at Charlotte's cheeks.

The infant scrunched her face and turned away.

"Your first bath, my love," Maggie crooned.

Feeling like a clumsy oaf, Caleb persisted, moving as gently as he could.

"She won't break, or so Mrs. Tisdale assured me. Rub her head clean."

Caleb obeyed, slicking the washcloth over Charlotte's head and causing some of the baby's downy dark hair to swirl in tufts.

Maggie guided him in applying a diaper and dressing her in the baby bunting. After being swaddled inside her blanket and full with her mother's milk, Charlotte fell into her first contented sleep.

Caleb wondered if the babe had a sufficient wardrobe. He felt an urge to rush to Sweetwater Springs and place an order for baby clothes and such. "I should attend to the cord." He used his pocketknife to fish the string and butcher knife out of the pot of boiling water and held them aloft to cool.

"Remember," she instructed. "Tie off the cord about an inch and again at four inches. Cut between."

Caleb knelt by her side and followed her instructions, tying the strings tight. The umbilical cord surprised him with how soft it felt, yet he still had to apply a certain amount of pressure to cut all the way through. He wiped off the blood, and the task was done. "There."

"Well done, Dr. Livingston," Maggie said, her eyes bright with exhilaration.

For the first time, Caleb became aware of his hunger. He'd been so focused on Maggie and Charlotte, he'd failed to heed the call of his body's needs. "I'll fix us something to eat." He went to wash up again, then moved to the campfire, opening a can of corned beef hash and one of peas. He set them at the edge of the fire to heat for dinner. From a basket he'd taken from the surrey, he brought out the last of the bread and cheese his housekeeper, Mrs. Graves, had sent along with him for the journey.

One of the horses nickered as he waited. Probably thirsty. He'd water them soon.

When the food was warm, he dished some up and brought the plate to Maggie, along with another mug of tea. "I'll hold the baby while you eat."

Maggie gave the dozing infant a kiss. "It's hard to let her go, even to you."

Caleb chuckled. "I'll be right here under your eye the whole time." He bent to take the baby.

"Support her head."

"I am." He brought the infant to his chest. Charlotte was so tiny, seemed so fragile, yet he'd already witnessed her strength. This time Caleb was the one who explored the baby, softly touching her button nose and running a finger over the petal-soft curve of her cheeks. "I think she's going to have your cheekbones," he told Maggie.

Her mouth full, she could only wrinkle her nose before she finished her bite. "Oh, I hope not."

Caleb couldn't imagine why. He shot her a puzzled look.

She rubbed her cheek. "Because they make me look different."

"You are a lovely woman, Magdalena Petra. Your looks are more out of the ordinary than most women around here—not that we don't have some attractive ladies in our town. I think that only makes you more interesting." He thought of Delia Bellaire. "Reverend Joshua's betrothed also possesses exotic beauty, so you won't be the only peacock among the chickens and swans of Sweetwater Springs. The Bellaires are to return to town today. They've been staying at a hotel in Crenshaw."

"Reverend Joshua has spoken of her. His face always lights up when he does so. I know the Morgans and some others from Morgan's Crossing plan to attend the wedding."

Caleb tried not to think of his ambivalent feelings toward the Bellaires, who hadn't been honest with him about Delia's illegitimacy and Negro blood, although the wedding was good business for his hotel....

He held the baby in front of him and focused on her, making a playful face. "Charlotte will be lucky if she's blessed with her mother's looks. Right, sweetheart? Although perhaps I shouldn't say so, I wouldn't want you to have your head turned by all my compliments."

Maggie chuckled. "Well, I guess a few are all right."

"Glad I can get away with some." Seeing she'd finished eating, he gave Charlotte one last look. "Ready to return to Mama?" he asked the baby.

Maggie set her plate and silverware on the ground and held out her hands.

Carefully, Caleb deposited Charlotte in her arms. "You two rest for a while."

"We will. But you need to eat."

He grinned at her bossy tone. "Yes, ma'am." Caleb saluted and sauntered over to the fire to dish up the corned beef hash and peas. He spooned out the food, poured some water into a cup from the pack he'd brought with him, added a slab of bread and cheese, and returned to her. But he saw she'd fallen asleep, and the baby with her. Keeping an eye on mother and child, he gobbled down the meal, aware Oswald needed a burial—as rotten a chore as he'd ever undertaken.

Only when he'd finished eating and set the bowl on his lap did Caleb realize he still wore the apron. With a wry shake of his head, he took off the garment and folded it. He sat for a bit, weary, but with a deep sense of peace.

Charlotte made a sound.

"Do you think she's hungry already?"

"We'll see." Murmuring soft endearments, Maggie unbuttoned the slit in the bodice of her nightgown and brought the baby to her breast.

Honoring the mother-baby moment, he glanced away, but the image lingered as beautiful and awe-inspiring as a medieval painting of the Madonna and the Christ-child painted by one of the masters.

"Caleb," Maggie chided. "After all we've been through, I think we can cast modesty to the winds."

With a feeling that he might be casting more than modesty to the winds, Caleb Livingston, staid banker that he was, brought his gaze back to mother and child and looked his fill.

❋ ❋ ❋

Maggie hurt all over, and yet she'd never felt happier, or more content. Lying on the bedding, which Caleb had changed, with her head and shoulders propped on pillows, Charlotte in her arms, she watched the man move around the campsite. He'd cleaned her up and soaked the soiled clothes in the washtub. He built up the fire and taken care of both teams of horses. He'd followed her directions and found the Mason jar with liniment under the bed—luckily unbroken—and rubbed the ointment on Pet's strained leg.

He unloaded the *vardo*, setting her scanty possessions in piles, and brought a bedroll from his surrey and spread it out a few feet from Maggie's. Then he'd taken Oswald's shovel and the basin with the afterbirth and disappeared.

Without Caleb saying so, she knew he'd gone to bury her husband.

For the first time, Maggie thought of Oswald with a pang of grief, not so much for missing him, but for what he was missing—their sweet baby. She remembered how he'd appeared during their courtship—handsome and strong, offering a shoulder to lean on when she was grieving the death of her grandmother, her last living relative. He'd swept her into a marriage while she'd been vulnerable and without giving her time to form an opinion of his character.

No, I did that to myself. I could have put my foot down, not let my fears of being alone sway me into thinking I was in love.

What a foolish girl I was!

The baby stirred in her arms.

Maggie glanced down at her daughter, swaddled in faded plaid flannel. She'd cut down an old shirt of Oswald's to make the small blanket. Love swelled her heart until she thought her chest couldn't contain the emotion. "But then I wouldn't have you, my darling Charlotte," she murmured to her daughter. "I'd go through everything twice over to have you." Exhausted, she laid her head down on the pillow and drifted off.

A squeaky wail startled her awake. Dusk had fallen, casting a purple-gray haze over their surroundings. The flannel cloth wrapping the baby was wet. *I need to change her.* Maggie struggled to sit up, gasping as her abused muscles protested.

"Let me." Suddenly Caleb was at her side, supporting her back.

"Charlotte needs a diaper and a soaker. We didn't put one of those on her before."

"Don't move." He ordered. "I'll take care of everything."

Maggie smiled at his tone, doubting he'd ever changed a baby. *Well, I haven't, either.* She'd had no younger siblings, only some older cousins. *But Caleb did well enough earlier when he put on Charlotte's first diaper.* She pointed to the pile. "We'll first pin one of the diapers on her. Then come the soakers—the knitted pants—over it." All the soakers she'd knitted were stacked together. "Find the tiniest pair."

He rummaged through the pile, and then held up a miniscule multicolored one for her to approve.

Maggie had knitted the soakers from leftover pieces of yarn, careful to keep the knots on the outside so they wouldn't rub against the baby's tender skin. Embarrassed, she realized the little panties conveyed the poverty she'd lived in, the shifts she'd made to economize when Oswald drank up too much of his wages. *Maybe Caleb won't notice how rag-tag they appear. He's probably never seen soakers before. For all he knows, that's how they're supposed to look.* She almost snorted at her own wishful thinking.

Caleb's brows pulled together in a frown. "We need to clean her."

"There's a bottle of oil in the basket."

Caleb glanced at the sky, and his mouth firmed. He looked down at her. "We'll be camping here tonight. I don't like it, but we don't have a choice. I don't want to move you, and that horse of yours needs to recover more. At least the sky is clear and, hopefully, will stay that way. I'll keep the fire going and stand watch."

"Is that necessary?"

"Birth and death happened here, Maggie. Both involved blood, which will attract animals. I dragged Oswald's body some distance, but I didn't want to be away from you two for long, so I only dug a shallow grave."

"I suppose you're right."

"When we return home, I'll have Oswald's remains dug up and transported to Sweetwater Springs."

Even if she'd loved Oswald and wanted him nearby, buried with all the trappings of a funeral, she wouldn't wish on anyone the job of digging up a body that was several days old. "No. I want him left here."

He looked taken aback. "Are you sure?"

The question fired her up. "I'll not pretend to be a grieving wife—tending Oswald's gravesite, leaving flowers. No," Maggie said sharply, knowing she was going against convention, and Caleb struck her as a very conventional man. "I don't want Charlotte to visit his grave, either, thinking she can talk to her father. I'd rather she not think about the man who sired her."

"That's not something a child forgets, Maggie," he said in a patient tone. "Charlotte will know she had a father. She'll ask questions. What will you tell her?"

"I don't know." Maggie looked away. "But I have plenty of years to figure it out."

Caleb sighed. "All right. I'll honor your wishes." Suddenly looking weary, he rubbed his forehead. "Truth be told, I understand your stance."

The fight went out of her. "Thank you." Maggie glanced at the fire, at the dead wood he'd dragged nearby to dry, and decided to change the subject. "Why don't you build a second fire, and we can sleep between them? You can't stay awake all night."

"I'll do whatever I need to guard you and Charlotte."

His protectiveness made a thrill shoot through her. But still, Maggie couldn't allow herself to lean on this man, whom she'd known only for a few hours—no matter what they'd gone through together or how close she felt to him. "We can take turns keeping watch. There's a rifle in the *vardo*, under the seat."

"I have one, too."

"Good. We'll both be prepared. I'll have you know I'm a crack shot."

He gave her a smile of admiration. "Why doesn't that surprise me?"

At his words, a glow spread through her. "Oswald didn't appreciate how I could out-shoot him."

Caleb threw back his head and laughed. "I don't doubt it. Any other time, I wouldn't appreciate it, either. Not that I'm much of a shot with the rifle anyway. I'm a banker, remember? I've no need or interest in hunting. But the Colt is a different matter." He patted his hip where the pistol would rest if he were still wearing his gun belt. "You can't live in a Western frontier town, be responsible for a great deal of money, and not know how to use a gun."

Maggie sensed he wasn't a man given to unrestrained laughter, and the fact that he'd done so over her ability to shoot—a topic that had infuriated Oswald—made her feel a warm connection with him.

Caleb patted her shoulder. "After your ordeal, you'll need your sleep." He raised a hand to still the protest she was about to make. "I'll build a second fire as you suggested. You can keep your rifle next to you. I'll wake you if there's a reason."

She smiled at him. "Thank you for everything."

He gazed at her with an intense look in his eyes. "Sleep, Maggie. I promise, I'll keep you both safe."

Maggie allowed herself to relax. But even as she drifted into slumber, she told herself not to become too dependent on Caleb Livingston's protection.

CHAPTER FOUR

Despite lying between two campfires, Caleb slept fitfully, a hand near his rifle. Even in his sleep, he was conscious of an instinctive need to guard the woman and child entrusted by the Almighty to his care.

During the night, Charlotte had awoken several times, letting out a hungry cry, which startled him awake. Maggie awkwardly changed Charlotte's diaper, her movements indicating the pain and stiffness of her body.

In the glow of the fire, he watched Maggie nurse the baby, conscious of the rare opportunity for an unmarried man to gaze his fill at the age-old maternal act of a woman giving sustenance from her body. He wondered if all fathers felt the same awe at the sight. Then he marveled that he felt like a father to the child.

Once in the predawn dark, they'd left the baby bundled up on the bed, while he carried Maggie to use the privy. Afterward, she snuggled with her daughter, and both dropped back to sleep.

Each time, he lingered in wakefulness, watching the flickering firelight play over her features until sheer exhaustion carried him under. But even then, nightmares disturbed his sleep—replaying the events of the day, increasing all his helplessness and guilt.

Something startled him awake. Heart thumping, Caleb grabbed his Winchester and surged to his feet, raising the rifle. With a swift glance to make sure Maggie and Charlotte slept, he surveyed his surroundings.

Gray dawn light filtered through the trees. He strained to hear any sound, but the blood beating in his ears muffled his hearing. Slowly he pivoted, not seeing or sensing any danger. For the first time, Caleb regretted not spending time learning woodsman skills.

A bird chirped in a nearby tree, breaking the stillness of the early morning. *Surely the bird would be silent if danger threatened.* He lowered the rifle, realizing his arms, shoulders, and back ached from carrying Maggie around, as well as the other unaccustomed labor he'd done the previous day.

This time Caleb took a longer look at the sleeping woman. When his gaze dropped to Charlotte, he was surprised to see the baby's eyes were open. He moved closer and crouched to gently brush the back of his finger across her cheek. He'd never felt anything so soft.

Her lips moving, Charlotte turned her face toward his finger.

Obeying a mad impulse, he slid his hands under the infant's head and bottom, scooping her from her mother's arms, making sure to bundle the blanket around her. He brought the baby to his chest, marveling at how tiny she was, and tucked his coat around her to shield her from the chill breeze.

She made a cooing noise.

Fearing the baby might wake Maggie when she needed healing sleep, Caleb carried Charlotte with him, climbing up the hill to the road, careful of his footing in the dim light. He walked toward his surrey, the wind at his back, from time-to-time glancing down at the baby to see how she fared.

Charlotte didn't seem to mind being taken away from her mother, for she stared at him with wide eyes.

When he reached the surrey, Caleb climbed into the seat and settled the baby on his lap. The air was warmer inside, for the back of the surrey blocked the breeze. "Yesterday, you didn't exist in the world, little one, except as a dream of your mother's," he told her in a low intimate tone.

Her blue eyes tracked the sound of his voice. She turned her head.

It seemed to him that Charlotte already displayed character and personality. *She's her own little person. What had I expected? Probably something more larvalike.* The thought made him laugh.

Caleb continued the conversation that didn't feel at all one-sided. "If all had gone as planned yesterday, by now, I'd be in Morgan's Crossing. I would have passed your family's wagon—barely giving your parents a nod and wondering about the outlandishness of a Gypsy caravan in the wilderness of Montana—before they traveled out of sight. Even if they'd settled in Sweetwater Springs, I might never have met your parents—that is, not to actually converse with. By your mama's account, your father wasn't a man I'd care to be around. I might have seen them in church or done business with them at the bank. But probably, they would never have had enough money to use the bank."

Caleb fell silent, marveling at all that had taken place in the last twenty-four hours. *That saying—that life can turn on a five-cent piece has just happened to me. To Maggie and Charlotte, as well.*

A tiny hand thrust out from the blanket.

Caleb started to fold the baby's arm back inside the warmth of the blanket, but Charlotte grasped his finger. He paused, marveling at the strength in her grip, and studied the tiny fingers and delicate shell fingernails. Lowering his head, he kissed her hand before tucking it back inside the blanket.

I'm transformed. Caleb wasn't sure in what way—just that he was different because of this precious child in his arms. Nor did he quite know what that meant for the future.

Charlotte's not yours. Don't become attached.

Too late. He became conscious of a sense of elation, of a wave of intense emotion washing over him, deepening his bond with this child. *Love?* Tears sheened his eyes. Could a father feel more intensely for his daughter than what Caleb felt for Charlotte? He couldn't imagine loving his own baby more. *Charlotte feels like she belongs to me.*

He gazed over the valley in front of him, framed by distant peaks. Pink and orange streaked across the blue-gray dawn sky, washed with shades of purple. Mauve clouds with jagged edges floated over the low golden light of the rising sun.

"'I will lift up mine eyes to the hills, from whence cometh my help.'" Caleb quoted the psalm, realizing with a mystical sense of gratitude that the Lord had, indeed, answered his frantic prayers for the safety of mother and child. "Thank you," he said to the heavens. He usually confined his praying to church services, but now he could understand why the ancient prophets and Jesus had traveled into the wilderness to commune with God. *There is something about the vast celestial beauty that seems to reflect the presence of the Divine.*

He glanced down at Charlotte. "If David had lived in Montana instead of Israel, he would have written, I will lift up mine eyes to the skies."

The baby moved her head to the side, and her mouth fastened on his wrist, as if searching for a nipple. "You must be getting hungry, little one."

Although reluctant to leave the peacefulness of this spot, the last thing Caleb wanted was for a hungry baby to start squalling and wake up Maggie, who'd probably be frantic when she couldn't see her child nor move to find them. She'd probably never again trust him with the baby. "We'd best be getting you back to your mama," he told Charlotte. "We have quite a day ahead of us. You're about to experience your first drive."

Caleb climbed out of the surrey and walked back the way he'd come, glad to see Maggie still sleeping.

She lay curled on her side, one hand tucked under her chin.

He hated to wake her, but with Charlotte starting to squirm, he didn't have much choice. The baby needed her mama. Best give Maggie a gentle nudge instead of being startled awake by Charlotte crying.

Caleb crouched next to her, the baby in his arms. He called her name softly to pull Maggie out of her exhausted slumber.

She blinked open sleepy eyes that took several seconds to focus. "Oh! I was having a nightmare." She tried to sit up and stopped, wincing.

He held a hand to stop her. "Just lay back. I'll give you Charlotte so you can nurse her. While you do so, I'll see to the horses and make breakfast." He grimaced. "We finished the last of the bread and cheese last night. I'll see whatever cans are in my emergency supplies."

"I have cornmeal. You can boil it for mush. Just stir it well to avoid the lumps. There's some molasses left for a sweetener."

His frown deepened.

Maggie chuckled. "Not used to cornmeal mush for breakfast, eh?" She took her daughter from him. "Good morning, sweetness." She rained gentle kisses over the baby's face, before moving to hitch up her nightgown.

Caleb turned and headed toward the horses. First he stopped to check on the injured gelding, Maggie had called Pete. When he ran his palm down the animal's leg, he could still feel some heat and swelling, but not nearly as bad as yesterday. *That liniment must be very effective.* He wondered if it would work for people. If so, Maggie could use the ointment on herself.

An image of rubbing the liniment on her body flashed in his mind, making him uncomfortable with his sexual thoughts. After last night, he'd been as intimate with her as a man could be with a woman without having physical relations. *Do I still have that role with Maggie—doctor/ midwife? Do I continue to help her in ways that are improper but necessary for her comfort?*

As he went about the business of taking care of the horses, watering them and dispensing the last of the grain, and then fixed breakfast, Caleb pondered the puzzle of his relationship with Maggie Baxter. While he doubted even the severest critics would impugn her reputation for being alone with him—not given all that had happened—he wondered if he now was responsible for her and Charlotte in the eyes of society. His heart stuttered at the thought, and he wasn't sure if the reaction was from fear or excitement.

He'd wanted a wife. *Had the accident been God's way of giving me one—and a daughter, as well?* Goose bumps shivered down his arms. Maggie certainly didn't fit the characteristics he'd wanted in a wife. *For heaven's sake, a woman who appeared to have a Gypsy heritage? How can I even consider marrying her?*

But Caleb knew he liked Maggie and admired her courage. They now shared a bond. *Is that enough for a marriage, especially considering our differences? Would I come to regret marrying her?*

With a wooden spoon, he stirred the cornmeal mush in the pot, as if shaking the thoughts out of his head. *Now's not the time to figure out my obligations to Maggie Baxter.*

Wishing he had more appetizing food than cornmeal mush and jerky, he brought a bowl over to Maggie where she sat with her back to the tree, a pillow cushioning her spine, holding the sleeping baby. He crouched at her level and held out the bowl. "Trade you food for a small girl child."

She eyed the bowl. "I think you'll have to raise the stakes."

"I'll give you a voucher, valid tomorrow. I'll even throw in dessert."

"Apple pie?" Maggie's eyes lit up. She playfully licked her lips, going along with their joking.

That flick of her tongue made Caleb notice how kissable her wide mouth was. *Don't even think such thoughts. A new widow, a new mother....* He set the bowl on the ground and took Charlotte from her. "Eat," he ordered, perhaps more sternly than necessary. "You need to keep up your strength."

She wrinkled her nose. "As you command." She picked up the bowl.

"I do." Caleb settled into a cross-legged sitting position with the baby on his lap. He extended a finger to Charlotte, who grabbed it. "I wish I had more to offer you. My housekeeper only packed enough food for the journey to Morgan's Crossing."

Maggie gave him a rueful smile. "Oswald quarreled with Michael Morgan, who fired him and ordered us to leave town. Oswald refused to allow me to shop for supplies before we left, even though Mr. Morgan had given him his final wages. "Well," she said, shrugging, "at least he didn't have time to drink them away at the saloon."

Caleb frowned. The more he heard about Oswald Baxter, the less he regretted the man's death. "That reminds me. I emptied your husband's pockets before I buried him. I have his handkerchief, watch, and money."

Her eyes shot wide in a look of horror. "I didn't even think of that. By the time I remembered, it would have been too late."

"Stop, Maggie," Caleb chided. "That didn't happen. There's no need to be so hard on yourself, especially given all you've been through." He jiggled the baby a bit, making a funny face at her. "Right, Charlotte?" he said in a fatuous tone. "You agree with me? Your mother should rest easy."

Her expression eased. "I guess you're right. I do have an active imagination."

He gestured for her to continue eating. "As much as I wish we could reach Sweetwater Springs today, neither you nor your gelding can travel that distance. But I don't want us camping in the open, either. There's a small way station about an hour from here, longer, of course, at the snail's pace we'll need to travel. But we'll be safe indoors and can sleep in peace. The extra day will give you and your horse more time to heal."

Maggie glanced at the caravan, her expression showing an obvious sense of reluctance. "My grandparents built that *vardo* when they came to America. We had more family back then. My great-uncle also built one—a more traditional *vardo*, a light blue color. The two families traveled together for many years." She paused, seeming lost in memories of the past.

"Where did your family come from?"

Maggie opened her mouth to tell him, then stopped.

He glanced at the *vardo*. "Do you think to surprise me? It's obvious there's Gypsy blood in you somewhere. I'd heard of Gypsies living in America in the East and in the South, but not in Montana."

"My mother fell in love with a *gajo*—an outsider, which is rare and forbidden. Mama quarreled with her family and ended up running away and marrying my father. Her parents were tinkers and traveled around a circuit of towns. My father died when I was seven, and Mama and I returned to her family. My great-uncle had never forgiven her for marrying a *gajo*, but Mama was an only child, so my grandparents took her back. There was a great quarrel over that decision, and the families split, each choosing separate directions. My great-uncle's family headed toward Texas, and we lost touch."

"What about your father's parents? I'm surprised they allowed you to go with your mother's family at all."

"Papa, too, was an only child. After he died, *Opa* and *Oma* insisted we live with them, so I could continue going to school—another thing that displeased my great-uncle. Gypsies are not keen on education," she said with a wry smile. "Mama and I didn't want to live with them, but she knew they could have forced the situation and taken me away. No one would have faulted my grandparents for keeping me away from the *dirty Gypsies*." Maggie's voice turned bitter.

He could see her point.

"But in the end, everyone compromised. Mama and I lived with *Opa* and *Oma*, who fussed over me. As much as I loved them and enjoyed school, when summer came, I'd wait anxiously for my other grandparents to arrive, which they usually did within a day or two. Then we'd be off traveling. I loved the freedom and seeing new places. The summers always sped by too fast."

"Sounds like an adventurous childhood. Not unlike my own between Boston and the West."

"I wouldn't trade it. Yet...."

"What?"

"I don't fit in," she confessed. "I'm neither fish nor fowl. Not completely Gypsy, yet not the same as my father's family."

Maggie's Gypsy blood should bother him. If fact, if he'd met her under other circumstances, he'd have given her short shrift. But the emotion behind her words resonated with him. Caleb *knew* what it was like to be neither fish nor fowl—too much of an uncouth Westerner to fit in with the Boston bluebloods and too aristocratic for Sweetwater Springs.

"I don't want to leave the *vardo* behind, Caleb."

The wistfulness in her tone made him resolve to find a way to save her home. *I'll send Phineas O'Reilly back for her caravan. He's a good carpenter and can maybe fix it up enough to travel. But I don't want to give her false hope.* "I'm sorry, Maggie. There's no way we can salvage it today."

She looked down and nodded, and then took a bite, her gaze on her food.

He let her be, knowing she needed to come to terms with her situation.

Maggie finished eating and set the bowl and spoon on the ground. "If you could help me...." She waved toward the clump of bushes and rocks they'd used as a privy.

"Let me tuck Charlotte in my bedroll." He rose and moved to his sleeping spot, making a nest for her. He lightly brushed the baby's cheek with his finger. "We'll be right back, little one. You behave yourself, hear?"

Caleb returned to Maggie. He stooped to lift her in his arms. After so much practice, he'd become an expert Maggie-carrier, and he liked the way she smiled and how comfortably she slipped an arm around his neck.

In the daylight, without the bulk of her pregnant belly, she seemed much smaller. *Perhaps I hadn't noticed her height because Maggie has the spirit of an Amazon.*

❋ ❋ ❋

Maggie did not speak a single word of complaint about how painful it was for her to ride on the seat of Caleb's surrey. She tried to distract her mind from the pain by telling herself it could have been worse. After all, she was wrapped in a blanket—having refused Caleb's coat—with a second one over her legs. The leather seat cushion was far more comfortable than the wooden seat of the *vardo*. The driver wasn't Oswald. Caleb had managed to stuff the surrey with as many of her belongings as the vehicle could hold, and miracle of miracles, her baby was safe in her arms.

If only one of those arms and shoulders, and, indeed, her whole right side didn't ache and throb from landing on the hard ground yesterday. Add to that the birth soreness from her back and abdomen to her thighs and the headache from where she'd hit her forehead.... She glanced down at her baby. *Yes, I have too much to be thankful for to complain to the kind man who'd saved us.*

She took a deep breath, inhaling the loamy smell of the forest. *Thank goodness Caleb was there to help me through it.* Maggie cast a glance at him, admiring his profile. Even with a few days' growth of a beard and his clothing in far more of a disheveled state than when she'd first met him, the banker was definitely a fine-looking man.

Caleb didn't notice her stare. His attention was focused on driving. He held his team to a slow walk to accommodate Pete's injury.

Maggie looked behind her to check on her horses, even though she had to shift her body because her neck was too stiff. The rest of her muscles protested the movement.

Tied to the back of the surrey, Pete shuffled along next to Patty. Only the slightest favoring of his foreleg told of his injury. *You can do it, boy,* she silently urged the gelding. *Tomorrow we'll arrive in Sweetwater Springs, and Caleb has promised you fine treatment, including apple slices and carrots.*

Feeling guilty, she turned to face the front. *When was the last time I was able to offer such a treat to my horses?* She hadn't been the only one to suffer from her decision to marry Oswald. *How could I have been so foolish—so taken in?*

Not for the first time, her thoughts lingered on their courtship. She searched for clues to Oswald's true personality. In hindsight, she could see them. He'd hidden his real self behind an almost animal magnetism. What had seemed like a wish to take care of her had really been a need to possess her, to control her every thought and move. *I held out my wrists for his shackles.*

She glanced down at Charlotte, sweetly sleeping in her arms. The horror of what her daughter's life would have been with such a father—if her baby would even have survived her birth—made her feel sick.

Never again. Maggie knew she could not afford to make such a grave mistake in choosing a husband, because she wouldn't be the only one to suffer from a poor choice. Watching harm come to her child, perhaps the other children she would bear, as well as her animals, would torture her.

Maggie shifted Charlotte deeper into the crook of her arm, so she could free a hand and touch one hooped earring. If she sold the gold, she could pay to have the *vardo* fixed. That would take care of a home for them. But she'd need to feed and clothe them, as well as provide food and shelter for the horses, so she had to find work as soon as possible.

Maybe I can take in laundry. Without Oswald's knowledge, she'd earned a little money by secretly helping Mrs. Rivera, who did the laundry for Morgan's Crossing. Sometimes the woman had more washing than she could handle, especially during the rush times when Father Fredrick, the Catholic priest, or Reverend Joshua Norton came to town to hold a Sunday service, or the times the Morgans threw a party. Their last shindig had been to celebrate the birth of their latest daughter, Darcy Angelina.

She sighed, thinking about baby Darcy's pretty clothing, some edged with lace. Although the clothes were handed down from her older sister, Mary May, they were in almost pristine condition compared with the faded garments Maggie had made for Charlotte, even if every stitch was set with love. She'd laundered those tiny pretty dresses and dreamed of her own baby wearing them.

Charlotte and baby Darcy would have grown up to be friends. With another sigh, Maggie thought of the friends she'd made in Morgan's Crossing and how much she'd miss them.

Frowning, Caleb glanced at her. A wrinkle furrowed between his brows. "Are you in pain? Do you need me to stop?"

She gave him a reassuring smile. "Just thinking."

He obviously didn't believe her, for his eyes narrowed, making his handsome features look intimidating. Despite her pain and melancholy thoughts, his attempts to pry more information made her chuckle. "Does that work with other people?"

His expression changed to puzzlement. "What?"

"That narrow-eyed, studying-you-until-you-confess-all-and-do-what-I-say look."

Caleb laughed. He seemed about to answer, then shook his head and laughed again. "Apparently not with you, Magdalena Petra."

Maggie shifted in her seat and lifted her chin. With a smile of mock condescension, she agreed. "Not with me."

Their teasing exchange lifted her spirits, and Maggie realized that if she chose to make a home in Sweetwater Springs, she could make new friends. She'd already developed a deep bond with this man, and maybe her next friend would be the sister he'd spoken of. *Or perhaps I can return to live in Morgan's Crossing.* The thought captivated her. *How wonderful to have choices!*

From under her eyelashes, again she glanced at Caleb's handsome profile. *Yet living in Sweetwater Springs also possesses definite appeal.*

CHAPTER FIVE

They plodded toward Sweetwater Springs at a snail's pace, the top of the surrey blocking the strong morning sunlight from shining into their faces. Caleb had never driven so slowly in his life. If it weren't for Maggie, whether they were riding in companionable silence or engaging in teasing conversation, he would have gone out of his mind with boredom. Between the bank, the hotel, and the civic concerns and activities he was involved in, he seldom was without mental and physical occupation.

Luckily, he found Maggie's presence both soothing and stimulating, although he wasn't sure how she'd managed to make him feel both. Maybe because in the two days he'd known her, she hadn't once complained, although she certainly had reason to. Even during her labor, her talk of charley horses and stabbing knives held no hint of a whine or self-pity. If his sister had been through a tenth of what Maggie had endured, she would have peppered him with her august opinion and a litany of complaints. He'd long since learned to close his ears to her, while nodding as if listening—something that tended to infuriate Edith when she caught on to his inattention.

Speaking of Edith, should I warn Maggie about my sister? How she can be difficult?

Maybe ease into the topic.

He glanced at her. "Have I mentioned my widowed sister Edith Grayson lives with me?"

"That must be nice," Maggie said, her tone wistful.

"It has its moments." A true statement, for there was affection between Caleb and his sister, even if he often had to delve for the feeling. "We grew up in Boston and in some areas of the West. My father was a…wanderer."

"A Gypsy like me," she said, her eyes teasing.

"Something akin to that. Black Jack was a gambler with cards and business investments that inevitably paid off, adding to the family coffers—although that often upset the townsfolk, making another move imperative." Even as he said the words, Caleb marveled that he'd just shared something so private.

Maggie listened with wide eyes, her mouth slightly parted.

"Edith married Nathaniel Grayson and settled in Boston—a life that suited her. She was happy in her marriage, in her role in society, with her son, Ben. But her husband's family wasn't pleased with his choice of wife and made trouble. They were most particular in regard to their two sons and had already picked out wives for them."

"Go on.…"

He slanted her a look of wry amusement. "Very well."

"My father's family is quite distinguished, but he was the black sheep, running away to the West when he was barely more than a boy and marrying the daughter of a schoolmaster. So even with my father's greater wealth, Edith wasn't good enough for the Graysons. Our blue blood was tainted." He said the words lightly, but old pain still stung.

Sometimes, when he was most frustrated with Edith, he tried to remember the circumstances that had changed her from the carefree girl of his youth to the *difficult* woman she was today. The change had begun in those times they'd lived in Boston, when they'd struggled with the strictures that ruled society, learning they could fit in, but only if they narrowed their behavior to accommodate the standards of polite society—something they'd both learned to do, until that way of life became second nature.

"After Nathaniel's death, the Graysons didn't soften toward Edith and Ben. In fact, they blamed her for the illness that led to his demise, implying if he hadn't married her, he wouldn't have gotten sick. Boston became too painful for my sister, and she and Ben moved out here to live with me. Unfortunately, Sweetwater Springs doesn't suit her. Nor does the town offer the type of men who'd persuade her to remarry. We don't speak of Nathaniel much. I sometimes suspect she mourns him still."

Maggie's expression softened with obvious compassion. "How horrible for her!" She shook her head and glanced down at Charlotte. "I can't imagine treating my child that way. My grandchild, either." She took a breath. "Although I do envy your sister having a happy marriage. I wish I could grieve Oswald's death instead of feel only relief."

Caleb glanced at Maggie, struck by the wisdom in her statement. He doubted Edith ever considered *gratitude* when she thought about the death of her husband. The words of Alfred Lord Tennyson came to him. *'Tis better to have loved and lost than never to have loved at all.*

The poet's words certainly apply to my sister. "Perhaps when you two become further acquainted and the time seems right, you can tell Edith so."

"Oh, I couldn't presume…."

Amused, he cocked an eyebrow at her. "Oh, I doubt that, Magdalena Petra. I doubt that very much."

"Wretch." She smacked him playfully on the leg.

With his chin, Caleb pointed to the left to a rough-built outpost. "Well, this *wretch* is about to get you and Charlotte to shelter. And just in time. I don't like the look of those clouds moving in from the east. I think we'll have rain soon."

Maggie lifted her hand to shade her eyes from the sun and gazed at the sky.

"I'm afraid the cabin is about the size of your caravan, but the horses will be comfortable. El Davis, the teamster, built a big enough stable to house his six-mule team."

"I know Mr. Davis. He seems a kind man. Quiet. Shy. Doesn't frequent the saloon."

Caleb glanced at Maggie, curious about her observation. He'd never given Davis much thought, although the man deposited his considerable savings at the bank. "I suppose you're right. He's the same in Sweetwater Springs. Not at all what you'd think of a mule-skinner."

He guided the team, driving to the left into the cleared-out place in front of the cabin. He reined in, set the brake, and tied off the reins. "Don't even try to move on your own," he ordered. "I'll come around to hand you both down."

"I'm not so foolish," Maggie chided. "I know I can't put any weight on my ankle, and I wouldn't want to risk falling with the baby."

Caleb hurried to the cabin and pushed open the door. The interior hadn't changed since he'd left yesterday morning—a cot on each wall with bare mattresses and two sawed-off ends of logs for seating near the fireplace that also could be used as firewood if a blizzard stranded a traveler and the woodpile ran out. An empty crate was nailed to the wall and held a pot and a tomato can. Two spoons sprouted from the rusty tin. With no windows, only the doorway provided light and air, except where both seeped through the places where the chinking in the walls had fallen out.

As was the custom, when he'd left the cabin, Caleb had stacked firewood and kindling neatly in the corner—replacing what he'd used. He'd had the forethought to bring the right length of wood from home, so he wouldn't have to search for logs and chop them into usable pieces. He quickly built a fire.

Satisfied that everything was in order, he backed out and walked to the surrey, rubbing a hand over each horse's head as he passed around the front. When he reached Maggie's side, he slid one arm under her knees and the other behind her back, hefting her to his chest.

She held the baby in the curl between her legs and stomach. "We must be so heavy."

"Yes," he admitted with a cheerful grin. "But how often do I have a chance to hold not one but two beauties?"

Maggie chuckled and rolled her eyes.

What has gotten into me? Caleb Livingston, a flatterer. Careful of the footing, Caleb carried her to the cabin, turning sideways so they could fit through the door. He deposited mother and child on the nearest bed.

She glanced around. "This is cozy."

"An improvement from yesterday." He moved to the door. "I'll start unloading." He walked to the surrey and began with the bedding, so Maggie could lie down if she wanted, for she should probably sleep when the baby did. He glanced at the graying sky. For that matter, with no activities to do all day, he could use a nap, too.

After everything was out of the surrey, he tended to the horses, watering and currying them, rubbing liniment on Pete's injury. He staked out both teams to graze for a while before he moved them into the stable. When Caleb was finished, he washed up in the small stream, then stood and stared at the bubbling water thinking.

He walked into the cabin to see Maggie nursing the baby. "I think you should soak your sprained ankle in the cold water. Maybe, ah…clean yourself a bit. I think we'll have an hour or so before the storm hits."

"That sounds heavenly. But what about Charlotte?"

He glanced at the baby. "I'll watch her for you."

Maggie gave him a skeptical look.

"Why Charlotte and I, we're ole friends," he drawled. "We spent the early morning together before you woke up."

"You did? I mean, I know you had her, but I thought you'd taken her up just the moment I awoke."

"Nope." Even as he spoke, Caleb marveled at how he sounded. He couldn't ever recall using a Western drawl. *Does that mean Maggie is a good influence on me or a bad one?* He knew what his Eastern relatives would believe. That thought was enough to banish the drawl for proper clipped Bostonian speech. He jerked his head toward the door. "I'll be outside. Call me when you're ready."

"I will after I change Charlotte. I'm sure you don't want to cope with a wet diaper."

Fist to chest, he struck a mock heroic pose. "Madame, I am here to attend to your every need, including those of your delightful daughter."

Maggie giggled and waved him off. "Be gone with you."

Once outside, Caleb wandered to the stream, searching for the best place for Maggie's ablutions. In front of a tangle of budding bushes, he found the perfect spot—with a flat stone on the bank where she could sit and dangle her feet in the babbling water, which formed a tiny pool surrounded by slimed green rocks. She could also bend to wet a cloth to clean her face and body.

The image made Caleb remember the sight of Maggie's bare breasts. He shook his head, looked up at the clouds building in the sky. *Best not to think those kinds of thoughts of the widowed new mother who is under my protection.*

But it's just become too darn hard not to. Caleb crouched, took a breath, and dipped his hands into the stream. He cupped his palms and brought up cold water to splash his face, hopefully cooling his thoughts, as well.

❄ ❄ ❄

That night after a supper of stewed beef and corn from cans, Maggie sat on a bed in front of the fireplace, listening to the patter of rain on the roof and the snap, crackle, and pop of burning wood. She watched Caleb rise from the other cot to bar the door and pull in the latchstring. Now the walls of the wayfarer's cabin sheltered them against the elements and any dangerous predators—human or animal. The flickering orange and yellow flames of the fire cast the only light in the darkness.

Maggie had just finished nursing Charlotte, who lay heavy-eyed in her arms. Her body was still sore, but if she didn't move, no aching muscles reminded her of the pain. Although she wasn't sleepy, a lazy feeling of lassitude crept over her. She let out a contented sigh.

At the sound, Caleb, who'd been staring into the fire, gave her a sharp glance.

"I haven't felt this safe in a long while." She looked down at her sweet daughter. "I hadn't realized the dread I lived with every day. I'd become so used to always feeling anxious or fearful."

"I hope you'll never feel that way again, Maggie…that *neither* of you will."

You are such a good man. Knowing Caleb was still sensitive about the accident and Oswald's death, she didn't utter the words. "Tell me more about your family. You didn't say anything about your nephew. How old is he now?"

"He just turned sixteen and has shot up to be almost as tall as me."

"Does he look like you, too?"

"There's a strong family resemblance among the three of us. We favor my father's family."

She looked at Caleb's handsome features, thick brown hair and dark eyes. *They must be an attractive family.*

"Ben is shaping up quite well. He got in a spot of trouble—no, I should be honest and say *a great deal* of trouble when he was younger. His mother spoiled him. I was busy and tended to pay him scant mind. And unbeknownst to either one of us, he was struggling with missing his father. Add a little bad company—" his mouth quirked in a self-depreciating smile "—along with the Livingston arrogance, and you have a recipe for disaster."

You're not arrogant. A little high-handed at times, but only for what you consider my comfort and protection. But she wouldn't admit that to him. "What happened?"

"Ben and another boy started setting fires to the school privy. That would have been bad enough, but he blamed a pair of orphan twins in a deliberate attempt to get them kicked out of town and sent to an orphanage."

She gasped at the boy's wickedness.

His expression mirrored her thoughts. "A low time for all of us. His mother...well, Edith had been inclined to baby him, and unfortunately still has that tendency. But when the evidence came to light, even she could not excuse Ben's behavior."

"What happened to the twins?"

"They were quite the troublemakers at the time, which made them easy to blame. Samantha Rodriguez, a widow who'd inherited a local ranch, adopted them, as well as an Indian boy. She'd traveled here from Argentina, bringing her son and these midget horses, about yay high." He measured the distance from the floor to his hand. "They are called Falabellas."

Maggie couldn't believe such a thing. "Horses so small?"

"Wait until you see them. The whole town is full of the little creatures, for she has bred the midgets, and the foals are snapped up before they're born. I'm on a waiting list for one from the next batch for Ben. He already has a riding horse."

Maggie wondered if a boy as bad as Ben deserved a miniature horse.

Caleb picked up a long stick and stirred the fire. Sparks flamed up the chimney, and the smell of smoke puffed into the air. "The twins' adoptive mother fought for them, as did the man she married afterward, Wyatt Thompson, as well as a few others. But they were outvoted. The twins and the Indian boy ran away and hid in some caves. Ben and his friend Arlie went after them, and they became lost in the cave system. Arlie fell and broke his leg, and the twins and those Falabellas rescued him. They turned out to be heroes, and my own flesh and blood was the villain."

"You believed *you* were the villain, too," she said in a sympathetic tone.

"I was so angry with Ben, and also with myself. Based on the boy's accusations, I'd taken a stand against the twins." His lips pressed together. "Well, you can be sure I tightened up the discipline on my nephew."

"But you said he's shaping up well."

The ironic quirk returned to his mouth. "A combination of me getting him involved with planning the Christmas party for the opening of my hotel and his interacting with another boy—the son of one of my employees. Dirt poor, the Salter family is. I threw Ben and Matthew Salter into some work together, and darned if they didn't become good friends. And somehow the plight of the Salters touched a hitherto unknown sense of compassion in Ben. That's when I found out about him missing his father. I suspect he was lonely, too, for the other children shunned him because he'd been mean to them and for what he'd done to the twins."

Maggie hadn't expected to feel sorry for the boy, but Ben's turnaround touched her. "That's quite a story."

"He and Matthew work for me after school doing errands for the customers and staff. I've started Ben on learning bookkeeping. He's quite good at it."

"Sounds just like his uncle."

"In both the good and bad ways."

"I doubt you have bad ways, Caleb. You've been the soul of kindness to me."

Caleb gave her a look of obvious exasperation and waved a hand as if brushing away her words. "Anyone would have done the same thing, Maggie." He paused. "Well, maybe not outlaws and such. But it's common human decency to stop for an accident you caused and help the survivors."

"And deliver a baby?"

"I'm no saint, Maggie," he warned. "Don't make me out to be."

"Saint Caleb," she mused in a teasing tone. "It does have a certain ring."

"Maggie," he growled.

She chuckled.

He shook his head, a rueful smile playing about his mouth.

She ran a light hand over her daughter's head. "I've been doing some thinking, and I'm sure you'll concur...."

Caleb looked askance.

"There's no need to mention when Charlotte was born, is there? The accident could have happened afterward."

"Are you concerned about your reputation if it were known I'd delivered the baby?"

There was an odd note in his tone, almost as if her suggestion bothered him. "Why, yes," Maggie said, making an attempt at lightness. "And yours. I'm sure a banker must maintain a professional image." Something about the stillness of his body made her stop talking. Best not confess her fear that he'd consider himself responsible for them, perhaps even feel compelled to offer marriage. *He's been so kind and doesn't deserve to be saddled with us. He needs a wife of his own social station.* To be sure, he hadn't suggested any such course of action. But she saw his growing attachment to Charlotte and thought such feelings might motivate him to make decisions he'd later regret.

"If that is what you'd prefer," he said, his face expressionless. "It's probably for the best."

"I think so. We don't have to lie or anything. No one would even suspect you'd delivered a baby."

"If we also don't mention spending the night here. Instead, we headed straight for town...."

Maggie thought through what Caleb was saying and realized he was right.

He held up a hand. "However, Dr. Cameron and Reverend Norton must know the truth. I can vouch for the discretion of both men."

"Very well." She glanced down at her daughter and saw the baby had fallen asleep. She rose and carried Charlotte to the bed, setting her down in the middle and tucking covers around her.

Caleb watched her.

In for a penny, in for a pound. Overcome by an impish mood, Maggie leaned forward and grasped his wrist. Taking a seat facing him, she turned over his hand.

"What are you doing?"

"Reading your palm," she said in a matter-of-fact tone, but couldn't resist giving him a teasing glance from under her lowered eyelashes. "My grandmother taught me how."

He tried to pull back.

She held on.

With an exasperated cast of his eyes toward the heavens, he subsided.

Maggie tilted his palm toward the light of the fire, so she could see the lines. "My grandmother had quite a gift." She studied his hand for a few minutes, noting the broad palm and the long fingers, the lack of calluses of the kind that had hardened Oswald's thick heavy-knuckled hands. For a brief flash, she envisioned Caleb running his hands over her body, stirring her senses. *His touch wouldn't feel rough on my skin.*

The sensual thought shocked her, and Maggie bent her head to hide a blush of heat in her cheeks. "See how your heart line ends under your middle finger?" She traced the line. "That means you take a direct, unsentimental approach to relationships." She looked up to see his reaction.

His mouth turned down as if he worked to suppress a smile of disbelief.

Skeptical man. "Your fate line is straight, indicating you have a focused life plan."

"Go on."

"This branch to your life line shows an intensity for your occupation—often to the point of working too much. And your life line, hmm…. You keep your feelings to yourself, you don't tend to be adventurous, and you feel comfortable with routine."

Caleb gazed at her for a moment. "All true. Although I think you could have discerned such things from our conversations—from some of the details of my life." He twisted his hand and captured hers, turning the palm up. With a forefinger, he traced her life line, sending goose bumps shivering over her skin. "What did your grandmother read in your palm?"

Struck by a memory, Maggie gazed at him, speechless.

"What?"

"I'd forgotten," she whispered, thinking back. "It was so long ago."

"Well?" He quirked an eyebrow. "Are you going to tell me? It's only fair."

"A long life." She splayed her fingers to open her palm and traced the line for him to see. "A short marriage." *Followed by a second marriage.* She curled up her fingers, denying the truth of her palm. *I will not marry again.* Maggie tried to shake off a sense of foreboding. "Guess my relationship with Oswald was inevitable. Good thing my short marriage wasn't to a man I loved."

"Did you ever read Oswald's palm?"

"Not before we married, more fool me, for I would have seen his temper line." She tapped a spot below where Caleb's thumb and forefinger joined. "But when things began to go bad, I did one time as he slept. He was a heavy sleeper when he was drunk. My only consolation was his short life line."

"Some consolation."

Not wanting to say more about the prediction mapped out on her palm, she tried to disengage.

He refused to release her. Instead, his eyes heavy-lidded, Caleb brought her hand to his lips, pressing a soft kiss into the center of her palm, the touch of his lips sweet yet sensual. "My reading of your palm tells me your life has changed, and you are now on the path to happiness."

Still feeling the tickling tingles from the kiss on her palm, Maggie tugged her hand free. "I hope you are as good a fortune teller as my grandmother," she said lightly to hide her reaction. "Well, it's late." She stood. "I think I will join Charlotte and get what rest she allows me."

"Pleasant dreams, Magdalena."

Remembering, Maggie shivered. "I hope so. I had nightmares last night. In one, I couldn't find Charlotte." She shuddered. "Between that and the baby waking me up...." She'd been so relieved to awaken and feel the infant in her arms. She'd even pulled back the blanket, striving in the dim firelight to see the rise and fall of her daughter's chest.

"I had nightmares, too. After the day we'd been through, how could we not?"

"You're right."

"I'll turn my back so you can get ready for bed." Caleb shifted away.

As she quickly changed from her dress to a clean nightgown, Maggie thought of her nightmares, praying they wouldn't haunt her tonight. Surely not in the safety of the cabin, with Caleb so near.

But Maggie suspected, whether she liked it or not, nightmares might continue to be part of her future.

CHAPTER SIX

The next day, they reached Sweetwater Springs in the late afternoon. The rain had stopped before dawn, but the muddy road slowed their journey.

Relieved to reach the town, Caleb could finally relax his vigilance. *We're home safe.*

Maggie and Charlotte slept. For the moment, all was at peace.

Caleb felt suspended between the horror of two days ago and the difficulties he knew he'd soon confront when he entered the house with a Gypsy woman and her baby.

Edith will not be pleased.

Not that he intended to mention the Gypsy aspect to Edith. But eventually, his sister would find out, especially if O'Reilly was able to salvage Maggie's *vardo* and bring the caravan back to town.

But even more than the thought of her displeasure was the discomfort he knew Edith might subject Maggie to. Caleb wished he could tell his sister the whole story first, somehow find a way to touch her sympathy—an emotion he knew existed, even if she seldom exhibited kind tendencies.

He transferred the reins to one hand and turned to Maggie, holding the babe close. In sleep, her features had relaxed from the drawn look she'd so often worn since he'd known her. A wave of affection for her—for them both—swept over him.

He touched Maggie's shoulder, hating to wake her. "Maggie," he said softly so as not to disturb the baby. "Wake up. We've arrived."

She stirred. Her lips parted, her heavy eyelids lifting to reveal gold-flecked brown eyes. When she saw him looking at her, she straightened, glancing down at the baby, then ran a hand over her hair. "I must look a fright."

You look beautiful. "Not at all."

She glanced down at Charlotte and shifted the baby a few inches. Then she looked around them. "Is this Sweetwater Springs?"

"My house is coming up on the right. The three-story brick one."

As Caleb drove slowly past his home, he surveyed his mansion with fresh eyes, wondering what Maggie would think of the place. He'd built the house to his own design, wanting a home that would reflect his dreams. The stained-glass windows sparkled in the sun, and the plain glass ones gleamed from regular cleaning by his housekeeper. A low brick wall topped with iron fencing circled the yard. The place showed better when the flowers and bushes were in bloom.

Maggie glanced to the house and back to him, her eyes wide. Apprehension lurked in their depths. Her mouth quivered. "Is *that* your home?"

He nodded

"I never imagined such a house.... Why, it's far grander than the Morgans'—a veritable mansion."

Caleb gave her a rueful smile. "How could you know what kind of home I have? You haven't been to Sweetwater Springs before." *And you lived in a Gypsy caravan.* "Ignore the fancy surroundings, Maggie. We've been camping out the last few days in considerable discomfort. Just think of the house as a place with food, a hot bath, and a soft bed to sleep on— one more comfortable for your aches than what you've had thus far."

Maggie's lips turned up in a partial smile that didn't reach her eyes.

Caleb drove the surrey into the driveway next to the house, leading to the stable, and reined in. As he tied up the reins and set the brake, he glanced at Maggie. "I bid you welcome," he said in a playful tone, hoping to banish her trepidation. *Good thing she didn't see my fancy hotel down the street. That might make her turn tail and run back to Morgan's Crossing.*

Jed appeared from the stable and hastened toward them, wiping his hands on a rag, which he tucked into the pocket of his overalls. "Mr. Livingston," he called. "I didn't expect you back for days."

Caleb climbed down and moved to meet his stableman. "Well, there was a mishap along the way." He glanced behind him at Maggie, and then back to Jed. "This is Mrs. Baxter and her newborn daughter. They were recently in an accident. I need you to fetch Dr. Cameron to examine her and the baby. Then once you see to the horses—Mrs. Baxter's gelding sustained an injury to his back left leg—and unload the surrey, I want you to go for Reverend Norton—the *elder* Reverend Norton." *After everything she's been through Maggie is probably in need of spiritual consolation.* "I'll have further instructions for you after the doctor has been here."

"Yes, sir." The man trotted away.

Caleb moved to Maggie's side of the surrey.

She sent an apprehensive glance toward the widows of the house. "Let me try walking. My ankle certainly has had enough rest."

"You couldn't put weight on it this morning."

"That was a long time ago. Please?"

Obviously, the last thing she wants is to be carried into my house. He reached up for Charlotte.

Her expression tight, Maggie held out the baby.

"Come here, Sweet Pea." Caleb took the infant into his arms. He held Charlotte with assurance, her head supported in the crook of his arm. With his other hand, he helped Maggie from the seat.

She landed on her good foot, brushed at the wrinkles of her dirty dress and smoothed her hair. "Oh, dear. What will your sister think of me?"

Nothing good. He didn't know which would be better, to whisk Maggie into the house and pray she'd receive a warm welcome, or give her a hint of what she might be facing. The sight of Mrs. Graves's dour face peering out the kitchen window made up his mind.

Maggie lowered her arms. One of her hands clutched a fold of her skirt.

"I must warn you that neither Mrs. Graves, who is my housekeeper, or my sister are very...*hospitable* women. Please don't let their disapproving attitude concern you. They are that way with everyone." He leaned closer, as if to tell her a secret. "They are the price I pay for a well-run home."

Maggie gave him a slight nod and held out her arms for the baby.

Caleb handed Charlotte back to her and firmly cupped Maggie's elbow to brace her, for he was convinced she wouldn't be able to walk.

Sure enough, she took one step and hopped, wincing.

Without waiting for an argument, he swung her into his arms and carried her and the baby toward the side door. He figured if they went through the kitchen, Mrs. Graves could feed them right away. He was famished, and he was sure Maggie was, too.

Before he could figure out how to turn the knob with his hands full, the door opened.

Mrs. Graves stepped out of his way, and he carried the Baxters inside.

Maggie looked around with obvious interest.

The kitchen was redolent with the smell of stew and gingerbread. His stomach grumbled. He gave a quick glance around the familiar room. Everything was in its proper place. Ruffled blue-checked curtains framed the back and side windows. A rectangular white table in the middle took up much of the space. A rocking chair sat next to the big black stove.

He knew the pie safe and icebox were stocked with food. White cabinets with gray counters lined the walls and a butler's pantry. But somehow the room seemed different. A minute passed before Caleb realized that *he* was the one who'd changed and had a new appreciation for the comforts of home.

Mrs. Graves pulled a pan of gingerbread from the oven. "Mr. Livingston, we did not expect you back for several more days." She wore an apron over a gray dress. Her hair was tightly pulled into the usual knob at the back of her head.

"There was an accident to Mrs. Baxter's vehicle. She was injured, and I returned with her." He moved toward the rocking chair.

Mrs. Graves nodded, her customary sour expression not changing to one of welcome.

Edith, wearing a rose-colored shirtwaist and skirt, sailed into the room. "I heard the horses." She stopped and gaped at him holding Maggie. "Well, I never!"

Caleb couldn't help grinning at Edith. "*Never* is right. Been feeling that way a time or two myself lately." He set Maggie into the rocker. Once he'd assured himself she was settled, he turned back to his sister. "Edith, this is Magdalena—Mrs. Oswald Baxter—and her daughter, Charlotte. Maggie, my sister, Edith—Mrs. Nathaniel Grayson."

Maggie smiled a greeting.

His sister's brows pulled together in a familiar critical look, as if assessing Maggie's crumpled and dirty attire, which hadn't been fashionable in the first place.

Edith gave a cold nod in return.

Caleb frowned a warning, hoping that would be enough to keep her quiet. He couldn't always control his sister if she insisted on venting her opinion. *Maybe if I speak fast enough first.* "Edith, Mrs. Baxter has had an exceedingly trying time. An accident, which I caused—"

"*No*, he is mistaken, Mrs. Grayson," Maggie interjected. "My husband was driving entirely too erratically. Our crash, and Oswald's death, were entirely his own fault. Mr. Livingston is *not* to blame."

"We will not argue." Caleb shot a quelling glare at his sister just in case she pestered them for more information. "I've sent for Dr. Cameron to examine Mrs. Baxter and Charlotte."

Edith's expression pinched.

"I'm sure if Dr. Cameron gives Mrs. Baxter permission, she will want a bath." He glanced at Mrs. Graves. "If you would prepare the guest room...."

Her vinegary expression conveyed her disapproval. "I will see to it."

The ring of the front doorbell stopped their conversation.

Mrs. Graves hurried away.

Through the doorway from the kitchen, he heard the sounds of the doctor talking to Mrs. Graves in his Scottish brogue. They seemed to be discussing the weather. The monotone reply of his housekeeper was in keeping with her character.

Caleb shook his head. The only reason he kept the woman on was because she was such an excellent cook, and he'd be hard-pressed to replace her.

Redheaded Angus Cameron moved into the kitchen. He was dressed in a black frock coat with sagging pockets and carried a battered leather doctor's satchel in one hand and what looked to be a scale in the other. He glanced from Maggie to Caleb, a twinkle in his eyes. "Oh, ho, what have we here?" he asked in a jovial Scottish brogue. "Yer home too soon and with such fair company besides."

In spite of his annoyance with his sister and his concern for Maggie, Caleb couldn't help but chuckle.

Only Angus Cameron could get away with such levity. The popular doctor had never displayed the pompous composure common to his colleagues. His easy manner, good humor, and pockets full of candy for the children made him popular with most of his patients. Only those of Edith's critical ilk complained of the man's lack of professional dignity.

Dr. Cameron's swift glance from Caleb to Edith took in his sister's stiff-necked huff. He nodded an acknowledgment before shifting his attention to Maggie and giving her a wink.

Caleb followed the man's gaze.

The anxious expression on Maggie's face vanished, and she responded with a wide, dimpled grin.

Jealousy stabbed Caleb. Maggie had never smiled like that at him. He hadn't known she had dimples. *Granted, she hasn't had much to smile about.* He looked at his sister. "If you will give Mrs. Baxter some privacy."

Edith's chest swelled in apparent indignation. "Entirely unseemly, Caleb. Therefore, *I* must remain, and *you* must go."

"There are some things I want to say to the doctor." Caleb shot Edith a commanding look and jerked his head to hurry her out of the kitchen.

Dr. Cameron didn't miss the by-play. But he remained silent until Edith left the room, and the door closed behind them.

Caleb looked at the scale. "What's that for?"

"To weigh the wee one." Dr. Cameron touched the hook on the bottom of the scale. "I'll wrap her in a blanket with a strong knot. I'll attach the hook in the knot. She'll be quite safe, I promise."

With a quirk of his eyebrow, he glanced from Maggie to the baby. "Whom shall I examine first?"

"My baby," Maggie said.

"Charlotte is perfectly fine, Mrs. Baxter," Caleb chided. "You, however, are *not*. Allow the doctor to see to you first." He leaned over her. "Let me take Charlotte."

She handed the infant to Caleb.

Dr. Cameron watched this transfer and crooked an eyebrow. "Uncommon turn of events," he said, his brogue thickening.

Caleb shot the doctor a warning look.

Dr. Cameron's mouth turned down in an apparent effort to suppress laughter, but he couldn't hide the gleam of amusement in his eyes. "Perhaps one of you should fill me in on what has occurred, starting with introductions."

❀ ❀ ❀

After Dr. Cameron gave permission for her to bathe, Maggie stepped into the white-tiled bathtub that was large enough for her to stretch out in—bigger even than the claw-footed tub in the bathroom of the Morgans' house. She groaned at the luxurious feel of the hot water, scented with Edith's rose soap. She'd never bathed in anything but a small, wooden half barrel—unless her family took advantage of the hot springs that riddled the area and the rivers and lakes in the summer.

The room, clad in white beadboard, awed her with its toilet, sink and mirror, and snowy cabinets; the small, white octagonal tiles covering the floor; the coiled radiator sending pleasant warmth into the room, and the rose-patterned rug lying in front of the tub. Immersing her stiff and sore body felt like the most wonderful luxury imaginable. If part of her mind didn't linger with concern on her baby, she'd have gladly soaked until the water cooled and her skin shriveled like a prune.

Maggie couldn't imagine a life where you could take a hot soak anytime you wanted. In this house, Saturday night baths in the winter wouldn't be a grit-your-teeth chore where, even though the tub was close to the stove, goose bumps popped out on the body parts facing away from the fire. More than the huge space and the fancy furnishings, this bathtub was the best part of Caleb's home.

I want a bathing room like this in my house. The longing surprised her, for to wish for such extravagance was so unlike her. *No,* she scolded. *You want the vardo fixed and livable again.* She touched her earrings, praying that they'd fetch enough to repair her home.

She allowed herself a few minutes to relax and enjoy the warmth seeping into her sore muscles before she reached for the soap. The bar was obviously unused—smooth, white, and perfectly shaped. When she brought the soap to her nose, she inhaled the heavenly scent of roses and some kind of sweet spice.

Edith smells like this.

The woman had shown Maggie how to work the toilet, sink, and bathtub, her disapproval evident from her stiff posture and stilted tone. She'd also brought one of her own nightgowns and dressing gowns for

Maggie to wear after her bath—both made of creamy pink flannel with soft lace around the neck and wrists.

Maggie picked up a thick square of terry cloth that matched the towels, with a curly *L* on the front. Although reluctant to deface the surface of the soap, she ducked the bar and the washcloth into the water and scrubbed herself from face to toes. Then she closed her eyes, slid all the way under to wet her hair, soaped the long strands, and ducked under again. She finished by rinsing with clean water from the faucet. Her hand hovered over the drain plug. *Should I leave the water for Caleb?*

Then she realized he wouldn't want to smell like flowers and spice, and the hot water was so plentiful that there was no need to share. With a shake of her head at the realization, she pulled the plug. Fascinated, she watched the water gurgle down the drain.

With her hand on each side of the tub, Maggie stood, muscles protesting the movement, although not as badly as before the soak. Even though she tried to keep her weight on her left foot, the surface was slippery, forcing her to shift for balance. A stab of pain shot through her ankle. She bit her lip to keep from crying out and took some quick breaths until the agony eased.

She twisted her long rope of hair to wring out as much water as possible before grabbing up a thick towel and drying herself. She marveled at how the tiny loops of the material easily absorbed water. When she wrapped the towel around her body, the length enveloped her from the top of her breasts to her calves.

There was no way she could just step out of the tub, so Maggie sat on the edge and shifted her legs over one at a time. Her feet rested on the rug. She paused for a minute, bracing herself to stand. As she pushed up, the rug provided a secure purchase for her feet, and she was able to keep most of her weight on her good leg. But still, the effort hurt.

Maggie hated being in pain, hated that her injured ankle made her dependent on Caleb. *How long before I can walk?* Dr. Cameron had prescribed five days of bed rest for her body to recover from her injuries and childbirth and another five of careful movement and continuing repose. The amount of time seemed endless. She resisted the idea of being beholden.

She donned Edith's flannel nightgown. The matching quilted dressing gown went on next. Satin ribbons along the bodice tied the front securely. Both garments were too long, the hems pooling on the floor.

Using the towel, Maggie rubbed her hair as dry as possible and then finger-combed out the snarls, wishing she'd brought along her brush. The thought made her heart ache. The loss of a brush was small compared with the destruction of the *vardo*, and Caleb had promised to send Jed to pack up the remainder of her possessions.

I'll have to borrow Caleb's comb again. She sighed, wishing for the wayfarer's cabin where it had seemed simple to share their scarce food and possessions. Already she missed the privacy and intimacy....

With one hand, Maggie gathered up the extra material of her garments, and with the other, she gripped the edge of the sink to brace herself. She hopped to the door and cracked it open, hoping to see Caleb and avoid Edith. *The less I have to deal with that woman, the better.*

Through the opening in the doorway, she spotted Caleb holding Charlotte. He stood in front of his sister, and she could see his face.

Edith shifted to the side, giving Maggie a clear view of her expression.

The woman possessed the same striking good looks as her brother, characterized by large, dark eyes and patrician features. Her skin was fine and pale, with only a few lines around her eyes and the corners of her mouth, now turned down in disapproval.

Edith narrowed her eyes at her brother in obvious suspicion. "Is Mrs. Baxter a *new* acquaintance? You didn't know her before?"

Caleb apparently caught her drift. Obvious anger made his eyes narrow. His icy gaze sent a chill down Maggie's spine.

"You malign Mrs. Baxter's character, Edith," Caleb said coldly. "And mine."

Maggie didn't know whether she should confront the woman, grab her baby, and leave, or step back and shut the door, pretending she hadn't heard this conversation.

Caleb gazed down at the baby. "It is impossible to explain, even to myself. Charlotte is not my daughter by blood, but my feelings for this child are familial, indeed."

With a bittersweet feeling of sadness, Maggie wished Charlotte had a father who loved her in the way this man did.

Edith fisted her hands on her hips. "What has come over you?" she snapped. "You never held Ben when he was a baby."

"That was sixteen years ago, Edith. Allow me to have acquired some life experience since then." He dropped a kiss on Charlotte's forehead. "I wish I had held Ben when he was a baby. I didn't know what I was missing."

"I think that woman—" Edith's voice trembled "—has bewitched you."

"Perhaps she has. Or her daughter is magic. Or both."

Was that amusement in his tone?

"But I'll tell you this. I saved Charlotte's life, but somehow...." Here, he paused, his voice dropping low. "Edith, somehow she has changed mine."

Edith opened her mouth, as if to scoff. She frowned and glanced at the baby.

Thinking what? Maggie wondered. It was true her baby had marked him. She had glimpsed genuine warmth when Caleb held or even *looked* at Charlotte.

Caleb gave his sister a beseeching look. "Can I call upon you to support Mrs. Baxter during her convalescence?"

"For the convalescence, certainly. But, you can't allow an unknown lower-class woman and baby to stay here for longer."

"Would it have made a difference if she were fashionably dressed, Edith? You were quite eager to accept the Bellaires."

"Yes, and look what came of that." Edith's words dripped disdain.

"This is my house." Caleb obviously strove to keep his tone reasonable. "I will do whatever I wish."

"Now you're being autocratic. Being selfish, foisting strangers upon me. You have no idea who this woman is, and what she will demand of us?"

"I do have an idea of who she is, and I think if you give her a chance, you will like her."

The woman pressed her lips together in a stubborn line.

"Have you no compassion, Edith? No Christian charity?"

"Of course I do. Did we not have Andre Bellaire and his daughter staying with us for months? I've learned not to be so trusting of strangers, taking them into your home so they can betray you."

Maggie couldn't help a sudden sharp intake of breath.

Both of them turned in her direction.

Edith's eyes narrowed in censure. "Mrs. Baxter, you are in *dishabille*. That is not appropriate before my brother."

Maggie didn't know what *dishabille* meant, but the woman's condemning up-and-down glance at the dressing gown was enough of an answer.

"Edith!" Caleb reprimanded. "Mrs. Baxter is our *guest*. She has been through a horribly painful experience. My seeing Mrs. Baxter in a dressing gown will do no harm. Especially if you don't go squawking the news all over town."

"Do not accuse me of gossip, brother," Edith snapped, matching Caleb's tone. "I have no idea of Mrs. Baxter's circumstances, and I'm giving her a hint about what is and isn't done."

"More than a hint—a harangue."

A wave of fatigue washed over Maggie, and she drooped. *Oh, for my dear vardo. I could crawl into bed with Charlotte and close out the world.* Suddenly the guest room seemed too far away to hobble to with her lame ankle.

"Hold the baby." Caleb thrust Charlotte at his sister.

Eyebrows high, Edith took the infant.

Maggie was relieved to see the woman didn't immediately drop her daughter on the floor, and she supported the baby's head. *Well, Edith should know what to do, for she's a mother.*

Caleb took swift strides to Maggie's side and scooped her into his arms. "We have the guest room ready for you, and I brought Ben's cradle down from the attic for Charlotte. Do you think she'll mind blue bedding?"

"How kind you are," Maggie murmured in a low voice so Edith couldn't hear. In the *vardo*, Charlotte would have slept with her for there wasn't room for a cradle. Suddenly tired, she wished she could lay her head on his shoulder like she had a few times before when in his arms. *We can no longer indulge in such intimacies.* The thought made her heart pang, but she refused to question why.

Caleb carried her into the bedroom, dominated by a spindle four-poster bed. A puffy blue satin cover was pulled back to expose crisp white sheets.

She looked around. Blue velvet curtains were drawn back from a window to let in light. A cradle sat next to a blue velvet wing chair. A washstand ensured she wouldn't have to use the bathing room to keep her hands and face clean. Her single dress would be lost in the big wardrobe, and the bureau was another unnecessary piece of furniture, for she had nothing to put inside. A small table held what looked like a game.

Edith entered with Charlotte.

Maggie glanced at her, expecting to see the woman frowning at being forced to carry the baby.

But as Edith bent over the cradle to lay down the child, her pinched expression softened, and a hint of a smile lingered about her mouth.

My Charlotte works her magic. Feeling better, Maggie allowed herself to recline. Plump goose down pillows cushioned her sore back and shoulders. *Ahhh.*

Without a word, Edith left the room. Her lips, once again, pressed thin.

The woman needs to hold Charlotte for several hours, so the baby's goodness can seep into her heart. Maggie shifted so more of her weight rested on her uninjured hip.

Not that I can spare my baby for so long. My darling is still too new and precious to give her to someone else for more than a few minutes.

Caleb came in and tucked the featherbed around her. "Are you comfortable?"

"Very."

"I'll be up with a tray and some ice for your ankle."

Although she was hungry, Maggie grimaced. "I'm sorry you have to wait on me."

Caleb's eyebrows drew together. "We won't go over that argument again," he said in a stern tone.

"Why not?" she asked, unable to resist teasing him. "I'll keep winning."

He shook his head. "You're a guest in my house. I *have* to let you win."

"Oh." Maggie chortled. "And what was your excuse when I wasn't a guest in your house?" Laughter bubbled within her. She couldn't remember ever having this sense of playfulness with a man. The feeling was rather intoxicating. *Am I flirting with him?* She'd never behaved in such a way before, but she'd witnessed other women flirting with handsome men.

"I think being in the midst of childbirth makes you a winner in any dispute."

"I should have thought ahead, then, and had all our future arguments at once."

"Oh, no! That was enough of a nightmare experience without you making it any worse." Caleb chuckled.

The sound swelled her heart. Caleb always seemed so serious. Making him laugh gave her an odd sense of feminine power. "A little disagreement is good for the soul," Maggie said in a smug tone.

"Says what philosopher?"

She made her smile mischievous. "The one whose name starts with M."

"Only you, Magdalena Petra. No one else dares cross me."

Maggie wrinkled her nose. "It's not good for *anyone*—especially a grown man—to always get his way." She tilted her chin as if in hauteur. "He becomes too self-important."

Caleb's smile died away.

Oh, dear. Did I just hurt his feelings?

A knock sounded on the doorframe. The stableman stuck his head into the room. "Ah, sir...."

"I'll be right back," Caleb told Maggie. He walked out the door, partially closing it behind him. "What is it, Jed?"

"I went to the parsonage like you wanted, Mr. Livingston. The elder Reverend Norton wasn't there."

"Did you leave a message for him to call on Mrs. Baxter?"

Although Maggie tried not to eavesdrop, the rumble of the men's low voices was loud enough to hear.

"Ah, no, sir. Reverend Joshua was there with his ma. Mrs. Norton kindly invited me in and asked me what I needed."

A pause followed. "I suppose Reverend Joshua will soon be paying a visit."

"I 'spect he's right on my heels."

"Tell Mrs. Graves to add tea, sandwiches, and cookies for Reverend Joshua to the tray for Mrs. Baxter. I'll send him up when he arrives."

Maggie wondered why Caleb's voice sounded resigned. *Does he not like Reverend Joshua?* She couldn't imagine how he could dislike the personable minister, who she'd known from Morgan's Crossing.

Perhaps Reverend Joshua has chided Caleb in some way, thus earning his disapproval.

Maggie had only met the elder Reverend Norton once, for the minister was too busy to leave Sweetwater Springs for Morgan's Crossing more than once or twice a year. With his son's return from a stint in Africa as a missionary, Reverend Joshua had begun a circuit to Morgan's Crossing as well as Buffalo Hollow and Honey Grove, two tiny prairie towns a few days ride away.

She still remembered Oswald's anger toward the younger minister, who'd asked to speak to him before he'd performed their wedding ceremony. After his discussion with Reverend Joshua, Oswald had erupted from the meeting hall, his face red with anger. He'd complained about the minister sticking his nose into their business. *Another warning I should have paid attention to.*

In her meeting with him, Reverend Joshua had discussed not just the joys of marriage but also the difficulties. He'd questioned the speed of their courtship and stressed the need to wait to acquire more knowledge and surety of the disposition of her future partner. She'd had the impression the young minister might have spoken from personal experience, not just from that of those he ministered to or his recent encounter with Oswald. *If only I had listened to him.*

She glanced at the cradle. *No. Charlotte is worth all the pain Oswald caused me.*

Caleb entered the bedroom, leaving the door wide open. "Earlier, I sent Jed to alert Reverend Norton to your presence here. I thought, after everything that's happened, you might be in need of, ah...*spiritual* counsel."

"Very thoughtful of you, Caleb. I think we might *both* be in need of spiritual comfort."

He grimaced.

"Do you not like Reverend Joshua?"

Caleb's smile was rueful. "I wouldn't say I dislike the man, rather...." He shrugged. "The story is not completely mine to tell, so I will say no more."

Curiosity made her want to question him further, but Maggie held her tongue. She could only think the better of him for not spreading gossip. Oswald had always enjoyed relating news of others' misfortunes in the most mean-spirited way possible. She'd often wanted to press her hands over her ears to shut out the sound of his voice. But she hadn't dared, for that would have angered him, with dire results.

I've spent our whole marriage tiptoeing around Oswald lest I set him off.

Once again, Maggie glanced at the cradle. *I have to be strong for both of us.*

The days of holding my tongue out of fear are over!

CHAPTER SEVEN

Having satisfied his ravenous appetite, Caleb retired to his study to await the clergyman, wanting to intercept the minister before he spoke with Maggie. He wasn't looking forward to telling the man what had happened, but he felt Reverend Joshua needed the information so he could best counsel her.

Caleb had taken several months to stop inwardly bristling around Joshua Norton, although he always treated the younger minister with polite reserve, which the man returned in kind. He apparently hadn't forgotten Caleb and Edith's repudiation of Delia Bellaire when they'd discovered his houseguest had Negro blood but was passing herself off as a white woman.

Delia's father, Andre, had suffered a heart attack on the train, landing the two of them in Sweetwater Springs. Caleb had invited them to stay while Andre recovered. Egged on by Edith, Caleb had initiated a mild courtship of beautiful Delia. While his heart hadn't been engaged, he'd admired the young woman and believed her wealth and education would make her a suitable match.

Instead, she and Reverend Joshua had fallen in love, which turned out to be a good thing. Caleb did not want a bride with Negro blood; whereas, the minister didn't seem at all put out by the idea of Delia's murky racial heritage. *He understood the quality of the woman beneath her skin,* his conscience pointed out.

Since the quarrel with the Bellaires, Caleb had seen the minister around Sweetwater Springs and listened to his sermons when he preached instead of his father, but the two men had only exchanged polite greetings. Otherwise, they steered clear of each other.

Their mutual avoidance was made easier by Reverend Joshua taking on the role of circuit preacher and being gone part of every month. While their new house was being built in Sweetwater Springs, the Bellaires departed on the train for the city of Crenshaw. Even when Caleb's hotel opened at Christmas, the Bellaires hadn't returned, probably not wanting to be his guests even if they were paying for the privilege. The minister made frequent visits to his betrothed.

Andre Bellaire had started building a new brick house—a mansion that rivaled Caleb's in size—for himself, his daughter, and his soon-to-be son-in-law on a back street near the Reiners'. With the completion of Anthony Gordon's office building, and later Caleb's hotel, there were plenty of skilled workers to throw at the new house, and the dwelling had gone up at almost magical speed, helped along by a milder winter than usual. Now that the house was livable, Joshua and Delia's wedding was scheduled to take place in a week, with the reception being held at the hotel.

A knock sounded at the front door. *Probably the subject of my thoughts.* He moved from his office to the front door to answer.

Sure enough, Reverend Joshua waited on the porch. The minister was dressed in a well-cut suit, something he could afford due to the fortune he'd inherited from his late wife's family.

Conscious of his dirty, rumpled attire, Caleb waved an arm to usher the man in.

Although Caleb could tell Reverend Joshua noted his disheveled appearance, he appreciated the minister had too much tact to comment, merely uttering a quiet greeting. Once inside, the minister removed his bowler and placed it on the hat rack.

Since his arrival from Africa, Reverend Joshua had put some weight on a frame that had been too thin, making his face less austere than his father's. The lines around his eyes and mouth had smoothed out. The vivid blue eyes he'd inherited from his father showed more life than previously, and he had an air of energy, which before he'd lacked. Returning home and falling in love had obviously worked wonders.

Caleb couldn't begrudge the minister his recovery.

They exchanged solemn greetings.

"Jed said you wanted to see me? That you have a lady visitor? If she's from Morgan's Crossing, then perhaps I'm acquainted with her."

Caleb let out a long breath of relief, knowing Maggie would have an easier time speaking with the minister if he weren't a stranger. "It's a rather long story. Come into my study, and I'll give you the…*details* before you go upstairs. Magdalena Baxter is her name, and she's currently in the blue guest room." No need to direct the man; he'd visited on many occasions when the Bellaires stayed here.

They entered Caleb's domain, a pleasant room with a big desk near windows bordered with stain-glass, plenty of bookshelves, and leather wing chairs bracketing a small round table in front of a fireplace.

Instead of sitting behind the desk, he led the minister to the chairs and gestured for him to take a seat. "Can I pour you a drink?" He was sure of the answer but made the polite gesture anyway. He'd never known the Nortons to imbibe.

"No, thank you."

"Very well. There's tea for you in Mrs. Baxter's room." Caleb took the other chair. At a loss for where to begin, he steepled his fingers and stared at the pattern of red, blue, and green light falling on the floor from the angle of the sun through one of the stained-glass windows. "I've had a most tumultuous few days, and before you see Mrs. Baxter, I feel the need to explain what has occurred."

A shadow of concern swept Reverend Norton's face. "I know Mrs. Baxter. Is she…well?"

"Doctor Cameron says she is, but let me tell you more. You might be aware Michael Morgan does business with my bank, and that I make an annual business trip to Morgan's Crossing. While on the journey, I was not paying close attention to my driving and allowed my speed to increase." With a forefinger, he made an *S* motion. "That hilly section after you cross the second stream."

Reverend Joshua nodded, his gaze intent.

"From the opposite direction, Oswald Baxter was driving that ungainly caravan of theirs, whipping his team to a dangerous pace."

Reverend Joshua sucked in a swift breath.

"Yes." Caleb's stomach tightened at the nightmarish memory. "They drove off the hill and crashed into a tree. Oswald Baxter was killed, and Maggie, uh, Mrs. Baxter was thrown clear, and she went into labor a few hours later."

"Jed said there was a baby. Amazing she and the child survived."

His heartbeat sped up. "I don't have to tell you of my fear that they would not make it—alone in the wilderness, not another woman for miles—with only me, who hasn't the slightest bit of knowledge of babies, much less how to deliver them."

"You must have been terrified."

Caleb let out a long slow breath and leaned his head back against the chair, unable to put his experience into words.

The two sat in silence for long moments.

Finally, Reverend Joshua shifted. "I sometimes receive what I call God-prompts—strong, ah, intuitive or *Divine* messages—nudges, actually—encouraging me to say something that seems most unusual or unlikely or even…*vulnerable.* Most of the time my response to these God-prompts is reluctance—sometimes the *utmost* reluctance, for to speak up would seem to open myself to ridicule."

Caleb lifted his head and stared at the man in puzzlement. *Whatever does that have to do with what I just told him?*

Reverend Joshua rested his gaze on him. "Over time, I've learned to heed the God-prompt. Doing so seems to accomplish the purpose."

"Stop talking in riddles," Caleb growled.

Reverend Joshua held up a placating hand. "Sometimes I'm the most obtuse when I am uncomfortable to reveal something about myself or discuss topics…*private* topics that men do not normally talk about—such as childbirth and other *intimacies* in their marriages. But I'm receiving that prompt now to speak of a time that was very painful, a story I'm reluctant to share. But perhaps you will find my experiences helpful."

Although still annoyed, Caleb settled back to listen. Hopefully the man would soon stop going in circles and get to the point.

"When we arrived in Africa, Esther, my wife, was already with child and not having an easy time of it. In spite of her zeal to bring the Gospel to the heathen, she was not adapting well to the reality of life in a Ugandan village. She wanted to preach to the natives but not live among them—holding the people at a distance and not developing friendships with the women. This philosophical difference caused a great rift between us that never healed."

Caleb found himself interested in spite of his impatience and began to see a glimmer of where the man might be going.

"When her time came, Esther refused to have a native midwife attend her. So there was only me." His voice rasped.

Caleb grunted in agreement.

"Of course, I knew nothing about birthing a child, and neither did my wife. Her labor was a hellish nightmare. Long, painful. She screamed and cried and railed at me."

Caleb could vividly imagine such a horror.

"I believe Esther might have died, and Micah with her, if several of the women, including the midwife, hadn't forced themselves into the house and pushed me out of the door. I don't know what those women did, but somehow eventually the baby arrived, and both he and my wife lived." He took a breath. "So you see, I know how frightening it is to deliver a baby when it seems the mother's life and that of the child are in your hands."

Caleb jerked to his feet, strode over to the silver tray holding bottles of water and spirits, and poured himself a glass of brandy. He took a sip, feeling the fiery liquid burn away the tightness in his throat. "At least Maggie knew what to do." In the emotion of the moment, her given name had slipped out, but he didn't correct himself. "Thankfully some of the other women in Morgan's Crossing had given her information, and she had her mother's tales. But if she hadn't known...." He shook his head and took another sip. "She was a trouper."

Reverend Joshua's gaze tracked him.

Feeling a bit more relaxed, Caleb returned to the chair. As he sat, his stiff muscles protested, reminding him of Maggie's far more serious aches and pains. "From the accident, Mrs. Baxter has a sprained ankle and is sore and bruised all over, especially on the side where she landed. Then of course, there is the toll childbirth takes on a woman's body, which I'm sure must be great, although she does not complain."

"Mrs. Baxter's spirits seem well? That is, she is attentive to the baby?"

Caleb looked askance. "Of course."

"There isn't an *of course* about it. I've ministered to some women who fell prey to low spirits after a birth. Not bonded with the child as they should. Neglected the baby. But I'm glad to hear that isn't the case here. Sounds like Mrs. Baxter sailed through with flying colors."

"Really, Reverend Joshua," Caleb snapped, resentful. "I doubt any woman would say she *sailed* through childbirth."

Reverend Joshua gave an understanding shake of his head. "You're right. I shouldn't have spoken with levity about labor, which is really a harrowing...and sometimes *fatal* experience."

Silence settled. They sat in apparent male accord—grateful that men did not have to carry and birth babies.

Caleb cleared his throat. "You missed the best part, though, by not being there in the instant your son was born."

The minister sent him a puzzled look.

"When Charlotte came out into my hands, I've never felt anything like it. Her eyes met mine in a moment of connection. If ever I was in need of proof humans have souls...." He shook his head, remembering and struggling to put his emotions into words. "She was only a minute old, but I saw the ageless soul within her. I wanted to fall to my knees in awe or weep or yell in triumph."

Apparent wistfulness showed in Reverend Joshua's eyes. "Micah and I had such a moment as you describe, when first I held him. But I don't think my wife felt that same sudden bond."

The very fact of having such a personal discussion felt beneficial in some way. Caleb ventured to comment. "Your marriage sounds as if it was..." *Horrible, isolated, sad....* He couldn't even find the right word to describe what he meant.

Reverend Joshua's lips turned up in a sad smile. "The *idea* of marriage with Esther had seemed so promising. The gradual disillusionment was...*painful.*" He gave Caleb a thoughtful look. "I don't want to frighten you away from marriage. I believe circumstances played a great part in the difficulties Esther and I experienced in the years before her death. We probably would have muddled along just fine if we'd remained in America."

"I will venture to say...a marriage with Delia Bellaire will be much different than you experienced before."

Reverend Joshua's smile widened. "I believe Delia and I will find true happiness."

Caleb gave the minister a considering glance. "I believe you will."

"It seems we are no longer at odds, you and I. I'm glad." Reverend Joshua's expression grew serious. "I appreciate you and Mrs. Grayson keeping Delia's secret."

Caleb held up his hands. "Not my business. You, as her husband-to-be, know the truth. That is a choice a man must make for himself... and his offspring."

"You said the baby's name is Charlotte?" Reverend Joshua asked in an obvious attempt to ease the discussion away from what could become a disagreement.

"Charlotte Victoria."

"Lovely. If her mother is up to it, we can christen the baby on Sunday."

Caleb ran a hand over his neck and squeezed, feeling the knots under his fingers. "I don't even know what day it is." Sudden weariness weighed him down. He twisted his head, trying to loosen the tension in his neck, before lowering his hand.

"Monday."

"The doctor said she needs bed rest for at least five days. After that, she can have limited movement but still must rest. But I imagine she'll be able to attend church. We can see how she feels on Saturday. I should take you to her." He placed his hands on the arms of the chair to push to his feet.

"Stay, Caleb." Reverend Joshua's soft tone held a note of command.

Startled by the minister's usage of his given name, Caleb subsided back into the chair.

"I think there is more to the story. You skimmed over Oswald Baxter's death."

"She asked me to leave him buried where he is." Speaking of the man reminded him of his guilt and irritated him.

"There is something to be said for unburdening your heart," Reverend Joshua stated gently.

"What do you want me to tell you?" Caleb demanded. "I killed a man out of careless inattention? Made a wife a widow, a baby fatherless? Have I guilt? Remorse? I don't in *hell* know!" He banged a fist on the arm of the chair, uncaring that he'd just cursed in front of the minister.

"Caleb, listen. Oswald Baxter was not a good man." Reverend Joshua spoke with precision, as if choosing his words carefully. "I suspected so when I counseled him and Maggie before their wedding. Indeed, I urged Maggie to postpone the ceremony. But with only suspicions, I could not be more forthright. They had not been long in the area, and his character wasn't well known at the time. And I was not very acquainted with the people of Morgan's Crossing. Today, I'd know to ask the Morgans or Mrs. Tisdale or a few others for their opinions. Later, as I heard tales of the man's abuse of his wife…well, I did feel guilt and regret for joining those two in holy matrimony."

Caleb gave him a sharp look, assessing the truthfulness of his words, and saw anguish in the minister's eyes that matched his own feelings of helplessness and guilt.

Reverend Joshua's shoulders slumped. "Am I sorry Oswald Baxter did not have a chance to repent of his evil ways? Yes, of course. But in my experience, a man who abuses his wife does not stop, so I cannot be sad that Maggie Baxter is free of her husband. I urge you to rest your conscience in this matter."

"I cannot. I feel a heaviness—" Caleb thumped on his chest "—at the loss of life."

Reverend Joshua leaned forward. "You would not be a good man if you didn't feel some remorse, Caleb. Bad men have no such conscience to trouble them. Nor would you be a good man if you didn't care about the abuse Maggie Baxter has suffered. Bad men condone abuse to those who are weaker and often indulge in such behavior, as well."

Caleb thought about the minister's points.

"Your inattention could possibly have contributed to Oswald's death, but we'll never know that for certain. What *is* certain is that you saved Maggie's life and that of her unborn child. And I believe the experience has done you good. You are a different man, Caleb Livingston. I can feel it."

The minister's brows drew together. "A person might have a profoundly life-changing experience, yet if he returns to his prior circumstances and way of life, that understanding can fade like a dream," he warned.

"I'll keep that in mind." After living through the nightmare and the miracle of Charlotte's birth, Caleb doubted his life would ever be the same.

What am I going to do about Maggie and Charlotte?

❋ ❋ ❋

When Maggie saw Reverend Joshua step through the bedroom door, tears welled up in her eyes and spilled down her cheeks. She swiped them away with her sleeve. "I don't know why I started crying, Reverend Joshua. I was fine, really I was."

He pulled a handkerchief from his pocket and handed it to her.

"You came prepared." Maggie tried to sound playful but suspected she'd failed.

"I carry several, for I often make people cry," he said, his tone light.

Maggie glanced up at him.

His smile was kind, and compassion softened his eyes.

"I suppose seeing a familiar face...."

"Of course." He walked to the cradle and peered at the sleeping baby. "God has blessed you with a beautiful daughter."

Maggie couldn't hold back another wave of tears. "I was so frightened, Reverend Joshua."

"All women are fearful when labor is upon them. But you certainly had special circumstances. Alone, without a doctor or other females. I imagine you felt terrified."

"Mr. Livingston was *wonderful,*" Maggie said, sitting up to defend Caleb if need be. "Charlotte and I owe him our *lives,*" she said, her tone fierce. "And don't believe his ridiculous claim that Oswald's death is his fault, for I will strongly oppose such a statement."

"So I see." His smile widened. "I believe Mr. Livingston has taken a reasonable stance in the matter and is not overburdened with guilt."

"He's not overburdened with guilt *anymore*." Maggie subsided and leaned against the pillows. "I certainly nagged him enough on the topic. Stubborn man."

Reverend Joshua quickly brought a hand to his mouth, covering a cough that sounded suspiciously like a choked-off laugh. When he lowered his hand, his expression was appropriately grave, but his eyes danced. "I believe Caleb Livingston has met his match in you."

He motioned to the tray of dishes on the bed next to her. "I see you've eaten. Mrs. Graves is a good cook. You'll be well fed while you're here."

Maggie waved at the game table. "She left tea and cookies. Oatmeal. Said you like them."

"I do. Would you like some tea?"

She shook her head.

Reverend Joshua walked to the table and poured himself a cup of tea. A floral fragrance filled the room. Then he put two cookies on a small plate. He carried the cup and saucer in one hand and the plate in the other and returned to Maggie's side, placing them on the nightstand in order to pull a chair over to the side of the bed. "Would you mind if I move the cradle a few feet? I'll reposition it back before I leave."

"Of course."

The minister shifted the cradle with obvious care to not wake the baby, then sat down, picked up the cup and saucer, and took a sip of tea. "Now for a more serious discussion." He set the cup and saucer back on the nightstand. "You have been through quite an ordeal, Mrs. Baxter, which must have taken an emotional toll on you."

Traitorous tears blurred her eyes again. "I'm *not* sorry Oswald is dead." A sob burst from her throat. "In fact, I'm grateful. It's so sinful of me, I know." She dabbed at her eyes.

"The commandments tell us not to kill, which you didn't, and to honor your husband, which I'm sure you did when he was alive." He dipped his head to catch her eye. "Am I correct in that?"

She nodded but couldn't meet his eyes and hid behind the handkerchief.

"Well, the commandments do not say you need to honor Oswald after his death if he wasn't a man who deserved such; therefore, I do not believe you're sinning."

Maggie lowered the handkerchief, feeling as if a load had rolled off her shoulders. "I should have listened when you told me to postpone the wedding." She glanced at the baby. "I keep telling myself Charlotte was worth all the pain of my marriage."

"Sometimes, time alone isn't enough to discern someone's true character." He let out a breath, his eyes sad." I knew my wife for several years before our marriage. Often dined at her home and was around her on many other occasions. Character may not be revealed until circumstances change. Marriage is a very imperfect science."

"Yet you're marrying again," Maggie pointed out. "When I've heard you speak of Miss Bellaire, you've sounded enthusiastic. How do you know you'll find lasting happiness?"

"Besides emotional feelings of attraction, you mean?"

"Yes."

"I guess you can say I've witnessed circumstances testing Delia, and I feel I can depend on her real character." His expression grew thoughtful, as if remembering. "We will have challenges, of course. All couples do."

"I don't plan to marry again, Reverend Joshua." Maggie crossed her arms over her chest. "I plan to devote my life to raising my daughter."

"Very admirable."

She shot him a challenging look. "You won't argue a woman's role as a helpmate? Her destiny to marry?" To Maggie's ears, her question sounded belligerent and not at all the way one should speak to a minister.

"I think there's no need for me to argue that point," Reverend Joshua said in a gentle tone. "You will find your way."

Maggie tried to puzzle his meaning. Then he leaned forward and smiled at her daughter, and she did so, as well, forgetting his cryptic statement.

Reverend Joshua touched Maggie's hand. "Let's talk about Oswald. Mr. Livingston tells me you don't want him transferred to the graveyard in Sweetwater Springs. Have you changed your mind? I could conduct a funeral, or at least a burial service. Or my father could, if you prefer."

Maggie shuddered. "No, leave Oswald be."

"What about a service?"

Maggie shook her head. "No one here knew him. If you could say a prayer for his soul…."

She let out a long, slow breath. "So sad to live the kind of life where no one mourns your death—but, in fact, is relieved by it."

Reverend Joshua stroked his chin. "I think you just gave me my topic for a sermon."

A sardonic laugh squeezed out of her. "Well, then my husband's death has done some good, after all."

CHAPTER EIGHT

After he'd quickly bathed and changed, Caleb walked to the cabinetmaker's shop located on a back street of the town. He'd commissioned wine shelves from Phineas O'Reilly before and knew the man was reliable and did fine work. The only problem was the carpenter's propensity to gossip. The last thing he wanted was his personal business spread hither and yon. Hopefully, he could swear O'Reilly to secrecy.

The front window in the false-fronted building gleamed in the late afternoon sun, showing off a display of painted statuettes—animals and figures of the Madonna carved by Pepe Sanchez, who worked at the livery. Last Christmas, Caleb had bought a crèche from the stableman to give to Edith for Christmas.

The signage above the window in crooked letters proclaimed: PHINEAS O'REILLY, COFFIN MAKER, CARPENTER, AND CABINET-MAKER. He'd always thought it ironic that the bulk of O'Reilly's income came from coffins and had counted himself blessed not to call upon the carpenter for that service.

Guilt made Caleb wince. He wasn't reconciled to the thought of Oswald Baxter lying without a coffin in an unmarked grave in the wilderness, but he needed to respect Maggie's wishes.

He toyed with the idea of commissioning a headstone for the man, so someday Charlotte would know the site of her father's grave. Although, Caleb supposed he could take her there if she ever wanted to go. The place was burned into his brain and wouldn't be hard to find, no matter how far in the future.

I'm imagining a future with the child. Will Maggie even remain in Sweetwater Springs so I can see Charlotte grow up? I'll do what I can to make that happen.

Caleb opened the door and entered the shop, inhaling the scent of sawdust and varnish. The carpenter's latest wares, a commode, a credenza, and a side table—all with decorative inlay on top—were displayed in the front room. But there was no one at the counter. Through a back door that led into the workshop, he could hear the grinding of a saw. "O'Reilly!"

The sawing stopped. A burly man ambled through the door, wiping his hands on a short canvas apron. He wore his rust-colored hair in a tail, and his bushy beard was untrimmed. "Mr. Livingston, what can I do for you? Another wine rack?"

"Not this time." Caleb hesitated. "I have a commission for you, but I need your discretion. I'm planning a surprise."

O'Reilly rubbed his palms together. "My favorite kind."

"Well, this won't be your usual gift." He forced out the story. "While on the road to Morgan's Crossing, my surrey and a caravan crossed from different directions. Both of us were driving too fast on hilly terrain, and his vehicle ran off the road. The driver was killed, but his wife and baby survived. The caravan, which is the woman's home, was wrecked—at least the left side and part of the roof. The structure might still be sound."

O'Reilly rocked back on his heels. "You want me to cobble it back together, Mr. Livingston?"

Does the man think I'm cheap? "Would I have you *cobble* something?"

O'Reilly gave him a sheepish look. "Guess not, eh."

"The wagon is a ways out, almost halfway to Morgan's Crossing—about an hour past the second wayfarer's hut. I'll send Jed with you—both to help you fix the vehicle enough to travel and to drive the caravan back early or late enough so no one sees it. Once it's here, secretly park it in that barn of yours where you keep your wood and work on it there. I want the whole thing restored until it's shiny like a new penny."

"Will cost you plenty of 'em shiny pennies."

"That I know. But I also know I can trust your expertise. It's a Gypsy wagon. Has some detailing on it. Green and gold. A painting on the interior ceiling."

"You have a time limit on this project?"

"As soon as possible."

O'Reilly tugged on his beard. "If I might make a suggestion...."

Caleb made a go-ahead motion.

"If money is no object and time is short, how about hiring Pepe Sanchez away from the livery for a bit? It's still a slow time of year for them, so Mack Taylor might not mind." He waved toward the figurines near the window. "Pepe's a right dab hand at painting things."

"Good idea." Caleb had no doubt Mack would let his stableman go along. *After all, I hold the note on that expansion he's about to undertake.* "I didn't really notice what was painted on the ceiling—the picture was faded, and with the accident and all, I had other priorities. But from what I recall, it will take an artist to restore."

O'Reilly's grin showed some missing teeth. "Pepe will like that you called him an artist."

"What else do you have in mind?"

"Instead of bringing the thing here, I suggest we take it to Gideon Walker's. It's a tad-and-a-mousetail closer to where the caravan lies now, and if he does some of the work with me, then we'll be finished in no time."

"Excellent." Caleb nodded. "Although, the Walker place isn't as close as you imply. As an eagle flies, maybe, if you could travel cross-country. But they live on a different road. You'll have to drive with the caravan toward Morgan's Crossing and then take the right-hand fork in the road and backtrack."

"We'll manage."

"At least this way, there will be less chance of the secret getting out."

O'Reilly guffawed. "At least not from Walker. Iffen you don't count his quotes and such, I don't think I've heard him speak more than a hundred words together in all the time I've known him."

Caleb thought of the man who'd been a hermit before marrying a mail-order bride. "He does make a few words go a long way." He drummed his fingers on the counter. "I'll still send Jed with you and Pepe. Once you have the wagon moved to the Walkers, he can return and fill me in on the details, as well as let me know anything you might still need to finish the job."

The carpenter tugged on his beard again, obviously thinking. "I should buy extra gold paint. That stuff's expensive, and Pepe only keeps a short supply in."

"Done. And Pepe can have any that's left over. Take boxes to pack the Baxter's belongings. Separate the husband's clothes and such so Mrs. Baxter doesn't have to see them until she's ready."

"Shore will, Mr. Livingston."

Now to face the Cobbs. Caleb walked out the door and strode to the mercantile, not even tempted to stop in at the bank or continue on to his hotel, which normally would have been his first order of business upon returning to town. Although vaguely aware such disinterest was not like him, he was too focused on a mental list of what he needed to purchase for Maggie and Charlotte to pay his unusual behavior any mind.

Lost in thought about how to explain Maggie's situation in a way that would keep gossip to a minimum, he only nodded at passersby and didn't stop to talk. When he reached the doors of the brick mercantile, the need to deal with the unpleasant proprietors brought back his attention.

While in the past he'd often sided with the Cobbs on civic issues and other matters, he'd never warmed to the couple, and he knew they could treat some of their customers abominably, especially those they considered beneath their notice. If Maggie had arrived here with Oswald and that Gypsy caravan, the Cobbs would have given her short shrift. He intended to prevent that kind of behavior if he could.

Inside, Caleb inhaled the familiar smell of pickles and baked goods. In the last year, as the town grew, the Cobbs had crammed the store with goods that might appeal to a wider variety of customers. Lately they'd talked about hiring Caleb's construction crew to add another room to the building when the men were through with the Norton-Bellaire house.

The large room was quiet, and Caleb didn't hear movement on the other side of the high aisles. He was grateful no one was in the store at this time, for he didn't want to have to explain more about Maggie and Charlotte than he had to. Nor did he want prying eyes gossiping about his purchases. Probably everyone was home getting ready for supper, and no one would disturb him.

Mr. Cobb stood behind the counter, adding figures on a ledger. His wife was nowhere in sight. Although it was still bright, the sun only starting to drop, he'd lit a lamp for extra illumination. The glow of the lamp reflected off his shiny bald pate, rimmed by a tonsure of hair. He looked up and his bulbous red nose twitched. "Ah, Mr. Livingston, you've returned. Always a pleasure to serve you."

"Good evening, Mr. Cobb. Is your wife around? I have some shopping...eh, female shopping to do."

The man cleared his throat. "Mrs. Cobb is making supper, but I'll send her right in." He disappeared through a partially opened door that led to their personal quarters.

In a few minutes, Mrs. Cobb hastened out to meet him. She was as short and round as her husband was tall and thin. The woman gave him a professional smile, which didn't come near to reaching her close-set brown eyes. She wore a dark-gray shirtwaist and skirt trimmed with red embroidery. The balloon sleeves made her arms look heavy.

Edith had also taken to wearing the fashionable puffed sleeves. Caleb thought the style ridiculous, but he had a feeling Maggie might like a dress with red embroidery. "Mrs. Cobb, I have guests staying at my house—a woman and her baby. Due to an accident, they are in need of new clothing and other necessities…well maybe more than necessities."

The shopkeeper's gaze sharpened. "I heard there was trouble. That you have a guest."

"While driving from Morgan's Crossing, Mrs. Baxter and her husband suffered an accident with their wagon. Unfortunately, Mr. Baxter was killed. But mercifully, his wife and baby daughter were spared."

"Ah," Mrs. Cobb said in a knowing tone and laying a finger to the side of her nose. "And you were on your way to Morgan's Crossing for banking matters. How lucky they are that you rescued them. Why—" she warmed to her story "—they probably would have died out there in the wilderness." With a flourish, she laid a hand on her ample chest. "You are a hero, Mr. Livingston."

Enough of the dramatics. "Just someone who was passing by, Mrs. Cobb," he said in a dismissive tone. "No need to make more of my assistance than it was."

"But they are staying with you. That's assistance, indeed. I'm sure Mr. Gordon will want to interview you for his newspaper."

Caleb was sure of that, too. He suppressed a groan. He didn't like the idea of prevaricating with Ant Gordon, who was a friend. The two had partnered in business, as well, using their joint building projects—Ant with his office building and Caleb with his hotel—to make deals on supplies and materials.

"Now…." Mrs. Cobb changed from gossiping biddy to greedy merchant. "If you could give me Mrs. Baxter's height and approximate measurements. She just had a baby, you said?"

"Only a few days old." He tried to think back to when Maggie had stood outside the caravan. Seems the top of her head had come up to his chin. "She's yay-high." He measured her height with his hand. "And about this...." With both hands, he outlined Maggie's figure. The back of his neck burned. "Money is no object, Mrs. Cobb. Please bring out what you have."

Her close-set brown eyes gleamed. "She's in mourning. I do have some items in black that should fit her, with perhaps some simple adjustments."

Mourning? Caleb frowned. He didn't want to see Maggie wearing black for Oswald, but he supposed pandering to tradition was necessary.

"I also have several white cotton shirtwaists, some with lace."

Caleb nodded in approval.

Mrs. Cobb frowned in obvious thought. "She'll need her skirts looser for a while, but she can always take them in when she has lost weight. I have several plain ones—a navy blue and a dark gray should do."

He remembered that the faded dress—probably once a burgundy hue—Maggie had worn since he'd known her had suited her coloring. But Caleb supposed he couldn't purchase anything bright for her until some respectable period of mourning had passed. "She needs a coat," he said briskly. "Hat, undergarments, night attire, shoes." He tried to think of the size of Maggie's feet and spanned the air. "About this size."

Mrs. Cobb tapped her chin. "Let me gather what I have in mind. Have Mrs. Baxter try everything on. As long as she doesn't wear anything, you can return the item for a different size."

Caleb nodded his permission. While Mrs. Cobb selected items and carried them to the counter, he perused the shelves, wondering if there was anything else that would take Maggie's fancy. Some jewelry in a case on the counter near the door that led to the living quarters caught his eye. Pearls would be a good replacement for those cheap-looking earrings she wore.

But a gentleman didn't give a lady who wasn't his wife or female relative such expensive gifts. He toyed with the idea of using them as a celebration of Charlotte's birth but knew that still wouldn't be right. And even if he offered, he suspected Maggie wouldn't accept the earrings.

His gaze fell on the boxes of chocolates, some imported from Europe. *Now that would be an appropriate purchase.* Caleb moved a gold foil box to the center of the counter. *I probably should buy some for Edith to sweeten her disposition about our guests.*

He added a second box along with some peppermint sticks for Ben before looking around for more. He wished he could buy Maggie oranges or lemons for lemonade. But at this time of year, exotic fruit wasn't obtainable.

Caleb opened the top of a square box made of thick rose-patterned paper to see handkerchiefs. He selected two plain ones and another bordered with lace. A red knitted shawl in a neat stack next drew his attention. *Maggie will like the bright color.* He glanced at Mrs. Cobb, busy removing a hat from a hook on the wall, and grimaced, pulling out a black shawl instead.

He walked over to the counter and set it next to the chocolate. He frowned at the bleak color, then spun on his heel, stalked to the pile, and grabbed the red one, as well, bringing his latest acquisition back and thumping it on top of the black one. Luckily the thickness muffled the sound, and Mrs. Cobb, who'd vanished around an aisle of shelving, didn't pop back out and demand an explanation.

Caleb suppressed a grin and searched for what else he could purchase, strolling up and down the two aisles. He noticed an ivory toiletry set, comb, bristle brush, and hand mirror and remembered how he'd had to lend Maggie his comb. He added the set to the goods on the counter.

Several shelves held children's toys, and he wandered over to see if there was anything for babies. He chose a rattle and a miniature cup, both made of silver. In the middle of the shelf a German Bisque doll with blonde hair and blue glass eyes stood in pride of place. *That doll is probably the dream of every girl in Sweetwater Springs.* He chuckled and took the doll off the shelf, holding it up to the light from the windows, so he could examine the blue silk and lace dress.

The doll was longer than Charlotte, but he couldn't resist. *She'll grow into it.* He carried the toys to the ever-growing pile on the counter.

Mrs. Cobb raised an eyebrow when she saw the doll lying on the red shawl.

He braced himself for a critical comment.

But the shopkeeper made no such remark.

She's probably too busy counting her profits.

Instead, Mrs. Cobb laid a hand on her latest deposit. "I have diapers and several pairs of soakers. You'll need a lot of those. A blanket, baby garments, and two bonnets—one plain and one lace."

Caleb stared at the mound on the counter and realized he should have brought Ben and Jed on this expedition to help him carry everything home. "I'll take some of the baby things with me, as well as a few of the necessities for Mrs. Baxter. I'll either return for the rest or send someone."

"Shall I put this on your account, Mr. Livingston?" Mrs. Cobb moved behind the counter and opened a ledger.

"Please. I'll settle up with you at the end of the month like always."

With a sly smirk, she asked, "Shall I wrap everything?"

Caleb could just imagine the sight he'd make walking down the street carrying a doll and female clothing. "Of course." He waited with impatience while Mrs. Cobb recorded everything.

When the woman finished, she began with folding the undergarments.

The sound of the door opening made him turn to see his nephew walking through the door.

"Uncle Caleb." The boy bounded over. "You're back early." His gaze fell on the overflowing counter. "You're buying all this? A doll? Women's, ah...." Ben turned away from a camisole edged with lace and threaded with rose satin ribbon to stare at Caleb, his gaze narrowing until he looked suspiciously like his mother when she was on a rampage. "What is going on?" His tone held a disrespectful edge.

"We have company at the house," Caleb said with a quelling look. "A family that suffered an accident and lost everything. I'll tell you more on the way."

The boy's critical expression vanished.

Caleb picked up the packet of women's underthings that Mrs. Cobb had wrapped in brown paper and tied with twine from the counter and shoved it at Ben's chest. "You're just in time to help me carry all this home."

Ben eyed Caleb's purchases. "I think you should have borrowed El Davis's wagon to haul that lot home."

"You'll do just fine as a pack mule, Ben." As Mrs. Cobb finished wrapping the parcels, he gave each one to his nephew. When the boy could no longer hold any more, Caleb began loading his own arms. Luckily with the clothing neatly folded, the garments didn't take up so much space, and he wouldn't need to make a second trip.

Mrs. Cobb, wearing a self-satisfied air, bustled out from behind the counter. "Let me get the door for you."

Caleb walked outside, giving a nod of thanks to the shopkeeper.

Ben followed. The boy took a long step to Caleb's side. "What's this all about, Uncle?"

He glanced at his nephew, figuring he needed to be clear about the delicacy of the situation. "One thing I've noticed since you've been working at the hotel is how you've developed discretion. The urge to feel important because you have knowledge that no one else has can be quite powerful, which is why people spread gossip."

"You mean like Mr. O'Reilly?"

"Yes, if necessary the carpenter does keep business matters close to his chest, as do the Cobbs—I will give them that. But O'Reilly isn't mean-spirited about gossip—he's more the curious type. The Cobbs seem to enjoy malicious gossip. But, *if* you ask for their discretion, they'll keep what's bought in their store close to their chests."

"So, you buying the doll and the woman's clothes needs my discretion?"

A wary note in the boy's question made Caleb hasten to explain. "Nothing improper or illegal, I assure you. There will be enough gossip as it is, and as much as possible, I'd like to keep it to a minimum."

"Understood, sir. Now are you going to tell me?"

Caleb hesitated. Since working at the hotel, Ben had contracted a case of hero worship. Only now, when he was possibly about to tarnish his nephew's image of him, did Caleb realize how much the boy's regard meant to him. He took a breath. "On the road to Morgan's Crossing, I was driving too fast." He sent the boy a wry glance. "Let that be a lesson to never let inattention overcome you when traveling through hilly countryside."

"Yes, sir."

"A wagon was approaching from the opposite direction, the driver deliberately urging his team to a reckless speed. We came around a bend, narrowly avoided crashing."

"I'll bet that was your doing."

"And perhaps a few angels riding my horses." The thought hadn't occurred to him before, but the fanciful notion seemed right, somehow. "The other driver wasn't so lucky. He went off the road. His team swerved to miss a tree, but the wagon crashed. He was killed. His wife and infant daughter survived."

Ben listened to the story with a rapt expression. "Were they hurt?"

"The mother, Mrs. Baxter, was able to protect her child. But she suffered massive bruising and a sprained ankle. She is quite lucky, though, that her injuries weren't worse."

Ben hefted the packages in his arms. "So they're the ones you bought all this for."

Caleb tipped his hat to a woman they passed. "The Baxters seemed to have few possessions anyway, and much of those were damaged. Also, in my haste for us to leave the accident site, I didn't take the time to gather more than a few necessities for them."

"What about the man?"

"I buried him."

Ben fell silent, looking ahead.

Caleb wondered what his nephew was thinking.

"How awful for you. And even though the accident sounds like it was the other man's fault, your inattention was a contributing factor that must make you feel responsible."

Caleb halted, staring at the boy—no, young man, for Ben was almost tall enough to look straight into his eyes. He hadn't expected his nephew to show so much empathy. Then he caught himself. He was thinking of the old Ben—the boy of three years ago, who'd acted with malicious intent to harm the twins. But the young man he'd been seeing since Christmas had displayed sympathetic qualities on several occasions. *I should have noticed sooner.* "You are growing up to be a good man, Ben. One I'm proud of."

Ben flushed and ducked his head.

Caleb resumed walking. "You are right. I do feel bad about what happened to the man and responsible for Mrs. Baxter and baby Charlotte. But not because she is requesting my assistance. She has shown bravery in a difficult situation, and I must confess to finding Charlotte endearing."

"So you got her the doll?"

"Yes. I'm sure both Mrs. Baxter and your mother will give me grief over that purchase."

"I don't know about Mrs. Baxter, but I do know my mother, and you're in for it, Uncle Caleb."

"Yep," he agreed. "When we get home, you'd best toss the parcels on the floor and run for it. Take refuge in your room."

"I won't stand craven," Ben said in a scornful tone.

Caleb grinned. "I was jesting. However, I should not have been disrespectful toward my sister. I know she means well."

Ben grimaced. "If Mrs. Baxter is poor, Mother won't like putting them up. It was different with the Bellaires."

"You just leave your mother to me."

"Oh, I intend to," Ben said wryly.

Caleb thought for a moment and decided the best way to deal with Edith was to not have to deal with her. "Let's go quietly through the front door to avoid Mrs. Graves in the kitchen, then silently take the stairs to Mrs. Baxter's room. If we're lucky, no one will see us."

Ben grinned. "Sneaky, Uncle Caleb."

A little spurt of guilt had him questioning if he should be colluding with the boy against his mother. *But, then again, this is for Maggie's comfort,* he tried to reassure himself.

No sense in setting Edith off and having Maggie get caught in the crossfire.

✳ ✳ ✳

"Whatever are you two about?" Edith's stentorian tones rang down the entryway. With a swish of skirts, she bustled toward them, her heels clicking on the black and white tile.

So much for a stealthy entrance. "A little shopping for Mrs. Baxter. Some necessities."

Her gaze swung from Caleb's full arms to Ben's. "How many *necessities* does one woman need?"

"I don't know, Edith," Caleb said with an edge in his tone. "Judging from your wardrobe, a whole store full."

"It's for the baby, too," Ben said, obviously trying to rescue him. "Babies need a lot."

She glanced at her son. "And how would you know what babies need, young man?"

Both of them winced.

"Geez, Ma. Babies are all over the place."

Good point, although a tactical error in your delivery.

"You know better than to call me *ma*, young man. And don't you have schoolwork to do?"

"Yes, *ma'am.*"

Caleb tilted his head toward the stairs. "Let's take these parcels up to Mrs. Baxter, Ben. Then you can get started on your homework. If you still need help with your Latin, let me know and we can work on it after supper." *That should mollify Edith.* He moved toward the stairs.

"I'll come, too." His sister followed him. "I want to see these *necessities* you've bought."

Caleb stopped so abruptly that Ben almost walked into him. "All right, Edith. If you must know, more than necessities. Perhaps I did go overboard. But as I've explained, I bear some responsibility for Mrs. Baxter and her daughter's plight. Therefore, I did not stint with my purchases." His gaze bored into hers. "Even luxuries cannot make up for a death."

She lowered her gaze.

"I do not want you making Mrs. Baxter feel uncomfortable or beholden." Caleb jiggled the parcels in his arms. "For then her pride will not allow her to accept them, and she and Charlotte are in sore need."

Edith crossed her arms over her chest. "This is ridiculous, spending this kind of money on a woman who's practically a stranger."

"Mother, Uncle Caleb is showing Christian charity," the boy said, sounding uncannily like Reverend Joshua. "No, *beyond* charity. Generosity. Why are you faulting him for that? It's his own money, after all, to do with as he pleases."

Edith huffed. "Since when do you take your uncle's side? He's barely acknowledged you for years."

Ben flushed, but he squarely met his mother's gaze. "That's untrue, Mother, especially lately."

"Enough, Ben," Caleb said firmly. "Although I appreciate your defense, there's no need to argue with your mother on my behalf."

Ben squared his shoulders and lifted his chin. "I don't agree, Uncle. Mother is being unjust."

Edith made a small sound.

When Caleb turned to her, instead of the disdain he expected, he saw her eyes held a stricken look.

Edith placed a hand to her chest. "You sounded like your father."

They looked at her in silence, both clearly unsure what to say.

She pulled a handkerchief from her sleeve and dabbed her eyes.

Ben shifted his parcels, trying to free a hand. "I'm sorry, Mother. I didn't mean to distress you."

"No, son. The thought of your father distresses me because I miss him still."

The smile she gave her son wavered, yet held more vulnerability than Caleb had seen from his sister for a long time. *She's the second person who's been vulnerable today. Maggie must be working Gypsy magic, even from upstairs.*

Edith touched Ben's shoulder. "You do him proud, son. I only wish your father could see you…that he'd been by your side all this time."

Ben leaned over and kissed his mother on the cheek. "So do I."

Caleb thought of the baby upstairs who would grow up without a father. By Maggie and Reverend Joshua's accounts, Charlotte would be better off without the man. But what if fatherhood would have changed Oswald? *Certainly experiencing Charlotte's birth, bonding to the baby, has changed me.* Maybe Oswald would have doted on his daughter and reformed as a man and a husband. Caleb had known of a case or two where this had happened.

He'd been assuaging his conscience by thinking Maggie and Charlotte would be better off without the man. *But what if I'm wrong?*

CHAPTER NINE

Ben snuck a sideways glance at his uncle. He couldn't quite put his finger on what was different about him, but something was. Uncle Caleb looked the same, formal in his black suit and gray-and-black waistcoat, but his posture had changed. He'd always held himself with a certain rigidity that Ben had taken for granted, until now, when he saw his uncle seemed.... *Relaxed* was the best word he could come up with. Also, his expression seemed lighter.

He followed his uncle up the stairs, shifting the armful of parcels he carried for better balance. His mother climbed behind him. She didn't say anything, but the feeling of her disapproval preceded her, making Ben's back tighten.

Uncle Caleb turned right and into the open door of the blue guest room. The room had remained empty since the Bellaires' abrupt departure, for a reason the adults had remained closemouthed about. Toward the end of their stay, Ben had taken to dropping by and playing chess with Andre Bellaire, who was recuperating from his heart attack.

He'd liked the older man, who didn't talk down to him and was easy to converse with, especially about business—something he'd only become interested in since working at the hotel. The man's stories about his company in New York made Ben determined to visit the city someday.

Uncle Caleb knocked on the bedroom door.

A female voice bade them come in.

Ben followed his uncle into the room and looked at the woman in the bed. He didn't know what he'd expected—someone older perhaps—not someone young and pretty, with big brown eyes, high cheekbones, and a wide mouth. Her dark hair hung in a long braid. He winced at the cuts and bruises on her face. *No wonder Uncle Caleb feels bad.*

"We come bearing gifts, Mrs. Baxter," Uncle Caleb said in a tone of hearty good cheer. "And here's my nephew Ben, whom I've conscripted into the job of pack mule."

Hearing the jovial note in the man's voice, he shot his uncle a puzzled glance. If he believed in fairies, which he didn't, Ben might have thought him a changeling—if the Fae ever took adults, that is, not just swapped babies.

The woman held an infant, and her joyful smile at his uncle made her bloom from merely pretty to exotically beautiful, even with her face marred by her injury.

Suspicions started to nag at Ben. Women did not smile at his uncle like that. Mostly, they were polite. Only those who set their caps at him acted simpering and coy, but this woman seemed open and natural in her good humor.

Still radiating displeasure, his mother silently entered the room. Her lips pressed into a thin line, and she stood next to Ben, smelling of rose scent.

One by one, Uncle Caleb set the parcels on the bed. "I bought you and Charlotte some necessities."

Mrs. Baxter's smiled faded.

Uncle Caleb held up a hand. "Don't say it, Mrs. Baxter. I am responsible that you and the baby have so few possessions at your disposal. We've argued this point before, and we won't do so again."

Ben began placing the parcels on the foot of the bed.

Mrs. Baxter glanced at his mother, a hint of mischief in her big brown eyes. "Is he always so domineering?"

Ben froze, aghast that the woman dared speak about his uncle in a playful way—to his mother, of all people. He cringed, knowing the tart response the woman was about to receive and hoped good manners would at least keep his mother within the bounds of politeness. His arms tightened around the remaining parcels.

Mother's lips quivered, then widened. She gestured to Uncle Caleb and chuckled. "You see what I have to live with? Brother or not, I never win against him."

Ben almost fell over in surprise. *Maybe fairies did exist, and they've also taken my mother.*

Uncle Caleb glanced over at Mother, his dropped jaw making him look as astonished as Ben felt. Then he slipped Ben a wink. "The ladies are conspiring against me. You'd better take my side, for we men have to stick together."

Ben couldn't resist the chance to tease back. "Oh…I don't know, Uncle Caleb. I might have to agree with Mrs. Baxter and my mother." He tried to remain stone-faced but couldn't hold back a grin.

"Betrayed by my own nephew," Uncle Caleb said in a tone of mock despair, placing a dramatic hand on his chest.

Everyone laughed.

Ben couldn't believe his uncle and mother were acting playful. Their rare by-play gave him a good feeling. *Maybe Mrs. Baxter is a fairy godmother.* He snuck another glance at her, noticing her eyes had a slight upward slant. *She looks like she could be one of the Fae.*

Uncle Caleb dropped a hand on Ben's shoulder and glanced at Mrs. Baxter. "I'd like to properly introduce Charlotte to Ben." He extended his arms. "May I hold the baby?"

Mrs. Baxter's joyful smile was back. She lifted the child and held her up.

Uncle Caleb strode to the side of the bed and took the baby, settling her into the crook of his left arm in a smooth way that spoke of practice.

They are the reason for changes in my uncle! A sudden wave of jealousy made his chest tight. He wasn't used to sharing his uncle's attention, as little as it was.

Ben recognized the emotion from the past and didn't like the way it made him feel now. *I'm not a child anymore. I'm almost a man. Uncle Caleb said he was proud of me, and my mother told me my father would be proud. I'm too old for this.* He took a deep breath, and the constriction in his chest loosened.

His uncle jiggled Charlotte, staring into the baby's face. "Hello, Sweet Pea." He tilted the infant so Ben could see her.

Charlotte looked like any other baby he'd seen. *Maybe a little smaller than most.* He leaned forward to study her, the long feathered eyelashes, little nose, and the rosebud mouth. *Maybe prettier.*

Charlotte's gaze fastened on Ben's face.

The tightness in his chest warmed and loosened. "Hiya, baby." *Maybe there is something special about her to make my uncle act so fondly.*

His uncle brought the baby back to his chest and rocked her. "I brought you a gift."

"*We* brought more than *a* gift." Ben had never dared tease his uncle before, even with the closer relationship they'd had since Christmas, but he liked doing so today. He set down the remainder of his parcels on the bed, next to his uncle's pile.

Uncle Caleb didn't look up. If anything his smile at the baby grew more fatuous. "A sweetie like you deserves plenty of presents."

Dumbfounded, Ben stared at his uncle. He glanced over at his mother to see her reaction.

Edith, too, stared at her brother in apparent shock. One hand clenched and released, rising as if to reach out to him.

Ben expected his mother's mouth to pinch and her brows to pull together, creasing her forehead. But instead her gaze looked soft and far away, and a smile played about her lips.

My world has turned upside down, and I don't know which way is up. His gaze swung back and forth between the two adults. *But I don't think I mind one single bit.*

Uncle Caleb glanced from Mother to Mrs. Baxter. "Perhaps my first gift will help to sweeten the disposition of the ladies." Shifting Charlotte into one arm, with his free hand, he searched through the parcels, squeezing a few until he came to one that seemed hard. "Ah." He unwrapped the paper to reveal two gold foil boxes.

Ben recognized the expensive chocolate imported from Europe. Uncle Caleb always gave his mother a box at Christmas or on her birthday, and she allowed Ben some pieces. He loved the chocolate, but even though his allowance was bigger than any other child's in Sweetwater Springs, he'd never bought a box of the chocolates because he preferred to have more candy for his money.

With a flourish, his uncle presented one to his mother. "Sister, dear."

With eyebrows raised, she accepted the gift. A smile played on her lips. "How thoughtful of you, brother. *Surprisingly* thoughtful."

Grateful his mother had taken the chocolate with seemingly good spirits, Ben turned to observe Mrs. Baxter, curious about her reaction. His uncle seemed to watch her with the same eagerness.

Mrs. Baxter tilted her head in puzzlement, then slit the seals of the box with her fingernails, and lifted the cover. She gazed at the squares inside for a long moment without a reaction.

The expectant look on his uncle's face changed to a narrow-eyed expression of concern. "Maggie, is something wrong?"

Ben noted Uncle Caleb's use of their guest's first name. With a surreptitious glance at his mother, he saw by the tightening of the skin around her eyes and mouth that she had, as well.

Mrs. Baxter glanced up, an anxious look in her eyes. "I don't know what this is." Her tone sounded uncertain and small, almost as if she was afraid of causing offence.

Imagine not knowing about chocolate.

Pain flashed across Uncle Caleb's face, followed by an angry tightening of his jaw.

Not knowing why the woman seemed afraid or his uncle upset, but wanting to lighten the tension, Ben leaned over as if to peer into the box, which was really too far away for him to see. He pretended to take a big sniff. "Guess Uncle Caleb could be giving you pressed turds, Mrs. Baxter." He paused a beat for dramatic effect. "You'd smell it, though."

"Benjamin Nathaniel Grayson!" exclaimed his mother.

"Rascal," Uncle Caleb cuffed Ben's shoulder, but he didn't sound upset.

Mrs. Baxter's mouth quivered and then bloomed into a wide smile. She chuckled. "Only fair, since I happen to know my daughter has given him that kind of gift before."

"Yes, but then I handed Charlotte off to you," his uncle quipped. "So you're the one ending up with her presents." He slanted a look and a slight nod of apparent approval Ben's way.

His mother huffed but more in amusement than criticism. "Really, you two." She slit the seals of her box, opened it, reached inside, and pulled out a piece, holding up the candy for Mrs. Baxter's view. "Chocolate."

"The finest chocolate you will find in Montana," his uncle interjected with a grin.

Mrs. Baxter's eyes widened. "I've eaten chocolate cake but never candy. My grandmother on my father's side had an antipathy to sugar. She believed sweets weren't good for us, and since my mother and I lived with my grandparents...." She shrugged. "At lunch, my friends would sometimes share their cookies, though. And when I had a penny, I'd secretly buy a peppermint stick from the store."

"I must warn you, Mrs. Baxter," his mother said in a stern tone. "My brother is starting you off with the best-tasting chocolate." As if shaking a finger, she waggled her piece of candy. "This comes from Europe. Caleb will spoil your palate for American chocolate."

Ben could tell his mother wasn't serious as she pretended to be.

His uncle rolled his eyes, and he gestured to Mrs. Baxter's box. "Try one."

Ben leaned over his mother's arm to look at her candy. "May I?"

She waved encouragement and held the box closer to him.

Ben took one and held up the candy. "Mrs. Baxter," he intoned. "I will prove to you the chocolate is safe to eat." With a pretend studious expression, he took a bite, chewed, and swallowed, nodding as if in consideration, then looked down his nose, his expression haughty. "Satisfactory." A glance told Ben his uncle took no offense at the mimicry.

Mrs. Baxter laughed. "If you say so." She bit off half of her piece. Her eyes widened and eyebrows lifted. She sighed, and her mouth turned up at the same time.

Ben liked the way her wide smile brightened her face and made her bruises seem to disappear. He couldn't help but grin back.

Uncle Caleb chuckled. "I believe Mrs. Baxter finds the chocolate *satisfactory*, too, Ben."

"Such a treat." Mrs. Baxter reverently closed the box and set it on the bed next to her.

Careful with Charlotte, Uncle Caleb leaned to the side to nudge Ben's shoulder with his. "Why don't you unwrap the big gift?" He wiggled an eyebrow to indicate the doll.

Ben huffed in a mock imitation of his mother. "Just don't tell anyone I'm doing this." He untied the string and tore off the brown paper, holding up the doll for Mrs. Baxter to view, expecting to see the woman's joyful smile again.

But instead, Mrs. Baxter frowned and gave a small shake of her head. "Mr. Livingston, whatever are you about?" She glared. "A few necessities I can justify accepting, but that doll is plain extravagance."

His uncle did not look at all abashed. "You're absolutely right." He made a playful face at the baby.

Charlotte cooed.

Mrs. Baxter's expression relaxed. "So you'll return the doll to the store?"

"No." Uncle Caleb looked up from the baby to grin at Mrs. Baxter. "The doll is Charlotte's. Down the road, if *she* wants me to return it to the store, I will."

Mrs. Baxter rolled her eyes. "Mr. Livingston, I don't think—"

"Save your breath, Mrs. Baxter," his mother interrupted in a wry tone. "I know from many years of arguing with my brother that engaging with him is futile."

Ben was sure he'd soon have a sore neck from whipping his head from side to side, watching as each of the adults responded in the *oddest* manner. Never in a million years would he have thought his mother would switch from disapproval to jesting with their guest—their poverty-stricken guest—and to taking her brother's side.

The troubled expression didn't leave Mrs. Baxter's face. "Mrs. Grayson, surely you do not approve?"

"I didn't until I came into this room."

That's the truth!

"And I'm not sure whether I approve or not. But my brother is right. You have suffered, and he is partly to blame. If his conscience is appeased by generosity to you...spoiling your daughter...." She shrugged. "Truth be told, seeing him with you and your baby brings back happy memories of when we were children." Her smile looked sad. "We had far more...*liveliness* then, and I enjoy seeing him that way again."

I do, too.

Mrs. Baxter gave his mother a look of disbelief. "So you are saying I should accept these gifts because doing so makes Mr. Livingston more *lively*?"

The image came to him of his uncle doing a jig, and Ben burst out laughing.

Everyone turned to stare at him.

Ben scrambled for something to say, for he didn't think the jig image would go over well with his uncle. Then he remembered the text from Sunday's sermon. "Well, Reverend Norton says that, 'It's more blessed to give than to receive.' So you're making sure he's blessed, Mrs. Baxter." He chortled at his own cleverness.

"I'm glad to provide you with amusement," Mrs. Baxter said in a dry tone. She lifted her chin. "Nevertheless, I can't accept the doll."

Uncle Caleb skirted the argument by pointing to the unopened parcels. "Better see what else is in those. Just in case you want to make our squabble bigger."

His mother harrumphed. "Oh, for heaven's sake, you two." She moved past him to the foot of the bed. "I'll open these. If there's anything *I* think needs to be returned, I'll do so myself."

Mrs. Baxter's lips pressed into a stubborn line, but she didn't object.

His mother made short shrift of untying the parcels and holding up the contents for Mrs. Baxter's perusal. That is, until she opened the package of women's undergarments. She shoved them back into the paper—as if Ben hadn't seen them displayed in the store before—and made a shooing motion in his direction. "You, men, get out of here and give us privacy."

"May I take the baby with me until you're done?" His uncle directed his most charming smile at Mrs. Baxter.

Ben had seen his uncle give ladies that look before, but not with the warmth displayed now toward their guest. His early speculation returned. *I think Uncle Caleb's sweet on her.* He glanced at his mother. In spite of the thaw in her usual glacial demeanor, he had no doubt that she wouldn't approve of Mrs. Baxter as the wife of her beloved brother.

I don't agree. In Ben's opinion, Mrs. Baxter might just be what his uncle needed, even if he hadn't yet realized that fact. *I think their courtship could use a hand.* He splayed his fingers. *My hand.*

A brilliant idea came to him inspired by a story told by Peter Rockwell, the manager of the hotel. At Christmastime, Mr. Rockwell had borrowed Mrs. Thompson's miniature horses and sleigh and had taken harpist Blythe Robbins for a romantic ride. Ben glanced out the window at the darkening sky. Barring a sudden blizzard, there wasn't enough snow on the ground for the Thompson's little sleigh. But the little buggy…. Maybe if they had several sunny days and the roads dried, Mrs. Thompson would drive to town and loan Uncle Caleb the equipage.

Old shame shattered his excitement. A weight settled on his chest, and Ben's stomach tightened in dismay. *I'll need to ask the Thompsons if I can borrow the Falabella horses and buggy—the very family who has the greatest reason to dislike me and deny my request.*

❋ ❋ ❋

When the door closed behind Ben and Caleb, Edith walked over to the nightstand and removed the glass shade and chimney from the oil lamp. Then she opened the drawer and took out the silver matchbox. She struck the match, lit the lamp, and replaced the chimney on the cut-glass base. She went over to the chest of drawers and did the same thing with the lamp there.

Maggie watched Edith's movements, trying to gauge her feelings, but the woman kept her face expressionless. *No matter what she says, I will act friendly. It's the least I can do when Caleb has been so kind as to invite us into his home.*

After she returned the matchbox to the drawer, Edith gave Maggie a strained smile. "I'm not sure which way is up."

Not certain how to take the woman who until a few minutes ago had been so unfriendly—even hostile—Maggie pointed at the ceiling.

Edith rolled her eyes again. "The ceiling is up. Yes, I know." She placed a hand on her tightly corseted stomach. "I feel most unsettled."

"I'm sorry if we are causing you discomfort," Maggie said, wishing she could get out of bed, take Charlotte, and leave.... *That I had someplace to go if I did so.* Thinking of the *vardo* made sadness pang through her.

Edith lowered her hand. "Perhaps not all discomfort is bad." She shrugged. "I'm not sure yet, which you and your daughter will prove to be."

That's fair.

"I think since we are in such close confines and will be so for a while...you should call me Edith," the woman said with the condescending air of conferring a favor.

This time, Maggie wanted to be the one to roll her eyes. But she didn't, for she thought this might be Edith's idea of an olive branch. She'd been on a first-name basis with some of the women in Morgan's Crossing, but not Mrs. Morgan or Mrs. Tisdale, the matriarchs of the town. She sensed that starched-up Edith Grayson wasn't in the habit of familiarity. "Very well...Edith."

"And if I may address you as Magdalena?"

Maggie must be too plebian a nickname for her to use. Yet.... "My grandparents always called me Magdalena."

With a *that's settled* gesture, Edith picked up another parcel and shook it. "Shall we guess?"

"After the doll and the women's undergarments, I have no *idea* what to expect."

Edith's laugh was surprisingly light. "Caleb surprised me, too. I never would have suspected he'd purchase such things. I can only hope no one else was in the mercantile at the time, or the gossip will be all over town."

"What about the shopkeeper? Won't she share the *delicious* details?" The word came out sounding as cynical as Maggie felt.

Edith's mouth tightened into a moue. "The Cobbs? Not if Caleb told them not to." As she spoke, she continued to open the parcels and hold them up for Maggie to see and admire, before refolding each item and neatly stacking everything. Edith picked up a small, nubby package and squeezed. "This is too hard to be clothing."

"A miniature corset?" Maggie joked. "Perhaps for the doll."

"This feels harder than whalebone." Edith opened the parcel and held up a small silver cup. "Pretty. Ben has one like this. Caleb will need to send the cup away to be engraved with Charlotte's name and birthdate."

"Oh, I don't think that's necessary," Maggie said hurriedly. She didn't want to draw attention to the actual day Charlotte was born.

"What's your daughter's middle name?"

"Victoria."

"Pretty. We have a lot of Victors and Victorias in our family."

I know.

"That was what Nathaniel and I had planned to call our daughter. But we never had one...." Edith's voice trailed away, and her eyes looked sad. She tried to smile but couldn't seem to make her mouth turn up. "I've mentioned Ben's father twice today."

"Is that unusual? You don't mention him often?"

"Very. Nathaniel's loss pains me still."

"You must have loved him very much."

"I did. I tried to be a good wife to him, but I don't know if I succeeded." She sighed. "Nathaniel was a loving son to his parents, but they were very...proper and refined. I didn't live up to their criteria, and they disapproved of our marriage.

Although Maggie had heard some of the details from Caleb, Edith's sad tone and downcast eyes showed how much her in-laws' judgment still hurt. "I can't imagine anyone thinking you aren't proper and refined."

Edith shrugged. "I am now. A lot of hard lessons learned."

"Then what happened?"

"Nathaniel quarreled with them, and the relationship became quite strained. We were happy together, but he always struggled with the pain of dealing with his parents. I've wondered if that led to his death—not that they killed him, but that—" She thumped her chest. "His heart wasn't as strong to fight the illness that took him from us." She pulled a handkerchief from her sleeve and dabbed at her eyes.

Maggie remembered Caleb urging her to share her feelings with his sister and realized she intuitively felt Edith needed to hear a different point of view. "I envy you," she said frankly.

Edith abruptly lowered the handkerchief. "*Envy* me?" she echoed, her expression disbelieving. She dropped into the chair. "How could you possibly envy me?" she asked in a bitter tone.

Her gaze lowered, Maggie ran a hand over the blue bed covering. "My marriage was ghastly. I was trapped with a man who beat me whenever his will was crossed in the slightest. I tiptoed around him." She made a walking motion with her fingers. "I never knew what would set him off. I feared for my life and that of my child." Her gaze met Edith's. "The accident was the best thing that ever happened to me, for I was set free. And your brother...." Emotion choked her throat, and she had to swallow before she could go on. "Your wonderful brother saved our lives." Maggie almost mentioned him delivering Charlotte, but she remembered in the nick of time to keep their secret.

Edith pressed a hand to her mouth, a stricken look in her eyes.

"I'd give *anything* to have experienced a devoted union, a caring father for my child—even if only for a few years, even if I went the rest of my life missing him—for I would have *loved* and *been cherished* in return." Maggie dropped her voice to a whisper. "I would pay the price of lifelong mourning to have had that."

Edith lowered her hand and leaned back in the chair. She closed her eyes, but a tear leaked out and rolled down her cheek.

Maggie felt awful. *My instincts were wrong. I should have kept my feelings to myself.*

After several uncomfortable minutes, Edith sniffed and opened her eyes. She didn't move from her slumped position against the back of the chair, only gazed at Maggie. "I've not uttered a word, not even to Reverend Norton, about how bitter I've felt about Nathaniel's death. Thank you for giving me a different perspective, Magdalena. I will think on your words." She blew her nose and sat up in a rigid ladylike posture. "Dear me. I'm so emotional today." She sounded more like herself.

Maggie laughed, relieved her intuition had been right, after all.

Edith leaned forward and picked up another small parcel. "We still have a few more to go. My brother must have thought today was Christmas." She unwrapped the package and held up a rattle, giving the toy a shake. "Now *this* is much more practical for Charlotte at her age than that ridiculous doll." She handed it to Maggie.

Maggie examined the silver rattle, marveling at the expensive toy— something she never could have given her daughter. "I'm sure she'll love it."

Edith stood and moved closer to the bed, stretching to reach some of the bigger packages. One by one, she unwrapped them, exposing the contents.

Maggie's favorite was the red shawl, and she immediately picked it up and draped it around her shoulders, enjoying the thick warmth.

Edith stepped back, tilting her head as she surveyed Maggie. "That is an excellent color on you. We are of a similar coloring, so vibrant hues—red, rose, as well as black or navy—will look good on you. Although—" she pursed her lips "—I don't wear red, for I consider it too bright for a woman of my age."

"Pshaw," Maggie scoffed. "Considering that gawky son of yours, you can hardly claim to be a girl. You must be in your midthirties, but you don't look it…or at least, when you *smile*, you don't look it." She straightened, pulled the shawl from around her shoulders, and held it out. "Put this on and go look at yourself in the mirror," she commanded.

With a slight grimace and shake of her head, Edith obeyed, moving to the washstand to look in the mirror.

"Smile," Maggie ordered. "Your brother says I'm bossy, and you'll know that, too."

Edith chuckled and then turned to the mirror. "Oh, my!"

Maggie couldn't help but laugh. "Is that an *'oh, my, you're right, Magdalena*?" she teased.

Edith let out a breath. "Oh, my, you're right, Magdalena," she parroted, and then laughed in evident delight.

"Then you'll buy yourself something in red?"

Edith tried to frown, but a smile broke through. "I'll think about it."

Maggie sat back against the pillows, satisfied that she'd brought a genuine smile to Edith's face. After yesterday's lack of welcome, she never would have imagined the woman would warm up to her. *Is it too much to hope we can be friends? Or at least on friendly terms?*

Probably.

Edith frowned at the clothes on the bed.

"What?"

"Of course, you should dress in black." Edith pursed her lips. "But I don't consider black a good color to wear to weddings."

"Do you think it's bad luck?"

"Silly superstition, isn't it? But Nathaniel had a whole flock of aunts and cousins who'd worn mourning for years. They descended on our wedding like a flock of crows."

I won't jinx Reverend Joshua and Delia's marriage. "I'll wear the white shirtwaist and one of the skirts. No crows for this ceremony."

Edith took off the shawl, folded it, and walked back to set it on the bed next to Maggie. She leaned forward to stare into Maggie's face. "You have gold flecks in your eyes, so perhaps gold would be another color that would suit you."

A knock on the door heralded Caleb carrying Charlotte.

At the sight of him with her daughter, Maggie's heart gave a traitorous thump. "How was she?"

"Perfect." He raised an eyebrow, taking in everything spread over the bed. "Well?"

Edith moved to him. "Not a bad selection, brother, given the limited choices at the mercantile." She held out her arms. "May I please hold Charlotte?"

He glanced at Maggie for permission. At her nod, he gave Edith the baby and moved closer to the bed. "Do you like everything? What's your favorite?"

Maggie patted the red shawl.

"I guessed that right." Caleb preened, in obvious jest. He leaned over his sister's arm as if to see if Charlotte agreed with him.

Maggie shook her head at his silliness, but warmth bubbled inside her. They felt suspiciously like a family. Even as her heart longed for that in truth, her mind told her to stop with the fanciful thoughts. *The likes of me are not for the Livingstons.*

Soon you'll be leaving. Don't get attached.

She glanced at Caleb, who was touching her daughter's cheek, and amended her self-counsel. *Don't become more attached than you already are.*

CHAPTER TEN

Dressed in his nightshirt, Caleb stood before Maggie's bedroom door, feeling the chill of the night on his legs. She'd bade him close her door before she went to sleep, not wanting Charlotte to wake anyone when the baby cried during the night. But he was uneasy with the idea of her managing the baby by herself, or trying to walk if she needed to use the toilet. So he'd waited until he thought everyone in the house must be asleep and then crept down the hall like a thief in the night to scratch at her door. When he heard no sound, he silently opened it.

Maggie had wanted the curtains left open so the faint moonlight of the half moon would illuminate the room enough for her to see the baby. The dim light only showed him her form on the bed, curled on her uninjured side.

Satisfied that she slept, Caleb returned to his bedroom, determined to rest lightly so he could come to her aid if need be. He climbed onto the bed and scooted under the covers. The sheets were cool, but he was too lazy to crawl back out and load the bed warmer with some coals from the fireplace.

He fluffed up the goose down pillows, thinking he should feel grateful for their softness and the comfort of his mattress after two nights of sleeping in the cabin and one on the ground. So, too, should he have let himself sink into the crisp linen of his bedding, still smelling of the outdoors from drying on the line, because the clean sheets and the softness of his mattress were a luxury he usually didn't appreciate.

But he found he missed Maggie's presence—the intimacy of lying only a few feet away—where he could open his eyes and see her and Charlotte in the firelight.

For all the luxury at his fingertips, Caleb wished he was back at the wayfarer's cabin with Maggie and the baby. *We were a team pulling together for Charlotte's sake.* Now he was aware of feeling alone, of Maggie also being on her own with the baby. Caleb was helpless to care for them as he felt he should.

The feeling didn't sit right with him. No, it felt downright wrong. *But there's nothing I can do about it.*

He dozed, only to startle awake at the sound of a cry. Caleb scrambled out of bed and was halfway across the room when he realized it wasn't the baby he was hearing.

"No!" Maggie's voice was thready, vibrating with fear.

A nightmare. He cursed the accident; he cursed the brute who'd abused her.

Caleb dashed from his room and down the hall to hers and went inside, quietly closing the door behind him.

She thrashed from her side to her back, one hand flinging out.

"Maggie," he said softly. "You're having a nightmare." Obeying an inner nudge, he moved to the other side of the bed and crawled next to her on top of the cover. He captured her flailing hand before she hit him, and then slid close to her body. "Maggie, wake up."

She raised her head off the pillow. "Caleb?" Her voice was thick as if she'd been screaming in her nightmare.

"Yes, it's me." He took her in his arms, sliding one hand under her shoulders and gathering her close. "Everything's all right. You're safe."

"Safe," Maggie repeated. Shivering, she burrowed her face into his chest.

"Hey, that's your bad side."

"I don't care." Her voice was muffled.

Caleb smiled at the petulance in her tone. "Here, let's shift you to your other side. I'll be right here." He put gentle pressure on her other shoulder to coax her to turn.

"Wait, I want to see my baby." She sat up and leaned over the side of the bed, peering closely into the cradle. She placed a hand on Charlotte's chest. "She's breathing."

Maggie tucked the blanket tighter around the baby and then lowered herself back to the bed. She followed his silent command, letting out a small groan of pain when she moved.

Caleb spooned her close to him.

Maggie gave a little sigh and relaxed in his arms. "We shouldn't be doing this, but it feels so good."

"Sleep, Maggie. You need your rest. I will keep guard."

Gradually, her breathing evened out.

Only when she slept deeply did Caleb extract his arm from under her, rise, and pull out a wool blanket from a drawer at the bottom of the wardrobe. He moved back to the bed, covering himself with the blanket and curling around her, breathing in her scent—Edith's soap combined with Maggie's skin, making a fragrance that was all her own. *I'll keep the gargoyles away for a bit and then leave her sweetly sleeping.*

A few hours later, the baby cried.

Caleb jolted awake, realizing he was still on top of the bed with Maggie. "I'll get her," he murmured. He pulled his arm out from under Maggie, climbed out of bed, and went around the side to take Charlotte from the cradle. When he slid his hand underneath her bottom, he felt wetness. "Her soakers are damp. Change or feed first?"

"I'll change her quickly." Maggie sat up, grabbed some of the new diapers from the nightstand, and spread one on the bed to protect the covering. She took Charlotte from him and laid her down, quickly stripping off the sodden soaker and diaper.

He extended a hand for them.

"Thank you," she said, giving him the wet ones. He dropped them in a pail on the other side of the nightstand.

A few days ago, I never would have imagined accepting a wet diaper with equanimity. Caleb had to smile at the irony. He reached for the small bottle of oil on the nightstand and handed it to her. "We'll have to replenish this in the morning."

Maggie dabbed oil on the baby's skin, pinned on the clean diaper, and tugged a new pair of soakers over the top. "There you go, precious girl. All clean." She pulled up her nightgown, tossing the bottom over one shoulder to bare her chest, and brought the baby to her breast.

Charlotte latched on and suckled greedily.

"Little piggy," Maggie said with an indulgent smile. She looked up at Caleb. "You must be tired. Go back to bed."

Caleb became aware of the cold air in the room. "I really want to climb back on the bed with you."

"It's not proper, Caleb, not when we are all safe."

"I know." Yet, he lingered.

"You need your sleep. You have work tomorrow."

Soon you'll be able to walk and not need me. The thought should make him glad, but it didn't. "I'll see Charlotte back to sleep and give you assistance to the bathroom. After that, I'll head back to my bedroom."

Once Charlotte slept, he carried Maggie to the bathroom to use the toilet. He returned her to the bed, then took her hand. "Go to sleep. If you need me, just call."

"Thank you," she murmured, squeezing his hand, her eyes already closing.

He waited until her breathing deepened and her grip loosened. For a moment, he felt bereft. Then he tucked her arm under the covers and tiptoed from the room, softly closing the door behind him.

Caleb settled under the covers in his own bed, wishing for the warmth of Maggie's presence, although a little guilty to feel grateful that he wouldn't be woken up by Charlotte's next feeding. *How do men who live in small cabins with several babies of stair-stepping age manage? They must barely sleep.*

Maybe they take naps in the barn.

Some shiftless fathers probably did just that. But most hardworking men that he knew would have plodded on about their work—for only through their labors were their families fed, clothed, and housed. *A heavy burden for an exhausted man.*

Maggie and Charlotte have certainly opened my eyes. As he pulled the covers tighter, Caleb sensed he'd still had plenty more to learn.

❋ ❋ ❋

The next morning, Maggie sat in bed, her back propped up against two pillows, Charlotte sleeping in the cradle next to her. She wore her new dressing gown and had, in spite of her stiffness, managed to raise her arms to comb her hair and braid it into a long plait.

Although her bruises had turned spectacular shades of purple, blue, and green, she felt better than yesterday. Even though Charlotte had woken her up, she'd been so oddly soothed by Caleb's presence next to her in the bed that she'd slept more deeply, feeling secure—something she'd been missing since her marriage, when she had to share a bed with a man who terrified her.

And now he sleeps for eternity in a cold, lonely grave. Maggie shuddered at her own morbidity, thinking again how Oswald had paid the price for his temper. If he hadn't fought with Michael Morgan, and then been driving so fast out of ill humor, he wouldn't have caused the accident that killed him. She made a pushing motion with her hand, as if thrusting Oswald from her thoughts. Once again, she checked on Charlotte.

Her daughter slept like a sweet angel.

Maggie leaned back against the pillows and drummed her fingers on the featherbed. The house was silent with Ben at school, Caleb at the bank or hotel, Edith out making calls, and Mrs. Graves in the kitchen.

While Maggie knew her body needed the rest, now that she'd eaten breakfast, she had nothing left to do until Charlotte woke up. She wasn't used to being idle, and boredom was quickly overcoming her.

Maybe the next time I see Edith or Mrs. Graves, I can ask for a book. The thought perked her up. She'd been a good student and loved to read—something she'd sorely missed in the last year.

Maggie had owned some books of her grandparents, as well as her schoolbooks. But after a wintertime argument with Oswald about the need for him to chop some firewood because they were almost out of fuel, he'd taken the books and tossed them into the stove before stomping out of the *vardo*.

They'd blazed so quickly, she hadn't had a chance to rescue them. With tears in her eyes, she'd watched her precious books burn, knowing she'd probably never own such treasures again. There wasn't money to spare for fripperies, and even if she pinched pennies until she'd dented the metal, Maggie had known she couldn't trust that Oswald wouldn't destroy any other books she acquired. Even more than the beatings, the burning of her books had come close to breaking her spirit. Only the discovery of her pregnancy had given her a lifeline to hold on to while she navigated the treacherous waters of her marriage and planned her escape.

Now I'm alone like I wanted but without the vardo—the critical element to our survival.

A knock on the frame of the bedroom door made her look up to see Caleb smiling at her.

"Good morning, Magdalena Petra." He was dressed in a black suit, with a gray-and-black waistcoat. In his hand he held a small vase of purple crocuses. "Look what's blooming in the backyard."

She caught her breath at how handsome he was and couldn't stutter out words of gratitude and greeting.

"May I come in?"

Maggie nodded.

Caleb strode to the bed and handed her the vase. "Since you can't go outside yet, I brought some of the outside to you."

She touched a petal still damp from the rain. "Crocuses always make me happy. Such brave flowers, blooming when others yet sleep and bringing the promise of spring after a cold winter."

He peeked into the cradle. "And how is our girl today? Look at her sleeping so peacefully. You'd never know what a lusty yell she's developed."

"Oh, I've heard louder from other babies, so I'm sure that's what's in store for me." Maggie looked askance at him. "Aren't you supposed to be working?"

"And what makes you think I'm not? I happen to be paying a call on a future patron of the bank."

Maggie laughed. "From your mouth to God's ears."

"Actually, I was heading to the hotel and thought I'd stop in and see how you and the baby were doing. I knew Edith would be gone, and I was afraid you'd have needs, and no one would be near to help."

Maggie felt her cheeks heat. She'd made do with the chamber pot under the bed, instead of using the bathroom, and Mrs. Graves had brought the basin for her to wash up with. "All is well here."

He bent over the cradle. "I was hoping she'd be awake, and we could have a conversation."

Maggie laughed, remembering how earlier she'd hopped to the window to look out at the rainy day. Charlotte had demanded attention, but Maggie had taken far longer to hop back than if she could have walked. Her daughter had gotten quite upset at her slow response. "Some of her conversations are conducted at a considerable noise level, as I'm sure you'll soon hear for yourself."

"Well, I'd best be getting on. Is there anything you need before I go?"

"How are my horses?"

"Jed informs me that they are cared for. Pete's leg shows improvement, and he should be completely back to normal in another day or two."

She let out a sigh of relief. "Good to hear."

His smile crinkled the lines around his eyes.

She bit her lip. "I'm going to have to sell my horses. Without the *vardo*, I can't afford to keep them. Do you know anyone I could approach?"

The smile fell away from his face. "I'll make enquiries."

"I'd appreciate that."

"Do you need anything else?"

"I'd love to borrow a book."

"We have plenty. Do you know what you'd like to read?" Caleb sent her a teasing, even flirtatious, grin.

Her heart fluttered, and she couldn't think to list some choices.

"Jane Austen? The Brontës? Louisa May Alcott? Lucy Maud Montgomery? Let me think of some more of Edith's favorites." He tapped his chin, obviously thinking.

An abundance of riches. "No need. Those will do nicely."

"Which ones?"

"All of them."

Caleb laughed. "I'll be right back." He turned and left the room.

She heard his footsteps recede and waited with anticipation for his return.

Only a couple of minutes passed before she heard the sound of approaching footsteps. He must only have stopped to grab one book instead of hunt for several. Maggie tried not to feel disappointed. She had to laugh at herself. *I'm already spoiled, and I've only been here less than two days.*

Caleb's armload of books surprised her. "Surely you didn't have time to select all of those."

"No." He eyed her with a cheerful grin. "But Edith has her own shelf of volumes, and I just stole the whole bunch."

Maggie bit her lip, imagining how Edith Grayson would react when she saw her books were missing.

"I'll leave her a note. My sister won't mind. She seems to have taken a liking to you."

He sounded far more optimistic than Maggie felt. She didn't want to feel beholden to the woman, but then Caleb piled the books on the bed, and she coveted them far too much to object. Her fingers itched to explore each volume and select which one to read first. "You've brought me a treasure trove," she said softly. "While Charlotte sleeps, I'm going be in the lap of luxury, living in this beautiful house, wearing my new dressing gown, and reading books. What pleasures you've given me!"

He stood in silence for a few seconds, looking down at her. "I'm glad, Maggie. After all you've been through, you deserve these small pleasures."

"These are not *small* to me." Her cheeks heated, and she had to look away.

Downstairs, they heard the sound of a knock.

Caleb cocked his head as if listening.

The faint sound of a female voice drifted up.

"My sister must have a caller," he said. "Or perhaps someone has come to make your acquaintance. Are you up to seeing her?"

Maggie cast a longing look at her books. But she'd also like to meet the woman who'd come to call. *The sooner I can make new friends and find work to support us, the better.* "I'd like to meet her."

"No need to show us up, Mrs. Graves," said the woman, her voice echoing up the stairs and along the hall. "We know the way."

"Mrs. Norton," Caleb told her.

"You go on up," said a second woman. "I want to ask Mrs. Graves for a recipe that was a particular favorite of my father's."

Caleb stiffened.

Before Maggie could question his odd reaction, she saw an older woman poke her head into the room.

"Ah, Mr. Livingston. We've come to see how Mrs. Baxter is doing."

"Better than before, Mrs. Norton." Caleb waved a hand to usher her into the bedroom. "Mrs. Baxter, may I present Mrs. Norton?"

"Hello," Maggie murmured.

Mrs. Norton was short with gray hair tightly pulled back into a bun. She had blue eyes and a sweet wrinkled face. Without acknowledging the introduction, she moved to the bed and stopped next to the cradle, peered in, made a noise of approval, and then gazed into Maggie's face. "My dear Mrs. Baxter, you have been through the most dreadful ordeal." She extended her hand. "Thank the good Lord you and your daughter are well. You're from Morgan's Crossing, I hear."

"Yes," Maggie leaned forward and took Mary Norton's hand. "I'm delighted to meet you. Mrs. Morgan spoke so highly of you."

Mrs. Norton squeezed Maggie's hand before releasing her. "You must tell me how dear Mrs. Morgan is doing, for I see her so seldom. I hope we'll have time to chat when she comes to my son's wedding."

A beautiful woman perhaps a few years younger than Maggie entered the room. She was dressed in an expertly cut shirtwaist with balloon sleeves and a skirt of spring green with a fern-leaf pattern running through it. A green satin sash showed her small waist. A flat-brimmed black straw hat with puffs of green ribbon rested on a coif of dark hair with auburn highlights. The spring color made her hazel eyes appear green. She smiled warmly at Maggie before catching sight of Caleb, and her smile fell away.

Caleb shifted, as if uncomfortable.

Maggie glanced at him. His body seemed tense. An expression of regret crossed his face before he turned impassive, which was unlike him.

Mrs. Norton gestured to the younger woman. "But first, Mrs. Baxter, let me introduce you to the young lady who will be my daughter-in-law in ten days, Miss Delia Bellaire." She clasped her hands together in almost childish delight. "You can tell I'm thrilled, can't you?" She fluttered a hand. "Come here, dearest Delia, and meet Mrs. Baxter and greet Mr. Livingston."

Delia slanted a glance at Caleb. Although her lips turned up, her expression appeared strained.

"Delia," he said reaching for her hand and bowing over it. "You are looking well. No, more than well."

He called her Delia. At Caleb's familiar use of the woman's name, jealousy stabbed Maggie.

Is he in love with her? The thought made her stomach tighten, and an odd proprietary feeling seized her. *He's mine!*

As quickly as she staked her claim, Maggie backtracked. *He's not mine to feel that way about. Yes, we've shared a special experience, but that doesn't really mean anything except we have a friendship.*

Miss Bellaire blushed. Like Maggie's, her skin was olive, but in a warmer shade.

Maggie was sure her complexion must appear sallow next to the beautiful woman's. She became conscious of the cut on her forehead, the bruises on her face. Miss Bellaire's elegance made her feel like a Gypsy waif—a thick-waisted one. *My waist will eventually return to normal,* she tried to reassure herself.

Miss Bellaire's smile became more natural-looking. "I'm happy to be home and looking forward to the wedding." She spoke with a soft Southern drawl.

Caleb patted the young woman's hand. "I'm glad you feel Sweetwater Springs is home."

Maggie cocked her head, seeming to hear double meaning in his simple statement. *Am I imagining things?*

He released Miss Bellaire's hand.

Maggie read reluctance in the movement, as if Caleb had wanted to continue touching Delia Bellaire. She wondered if he had romantic feelings for a woman who was engaged to another man.

"I believe you'll make Reverend Joshua quite happy," he said in a sincere tone.

At the sound of the minister's name, Delia smiled so brightly her whole face glowed. She obviously deeply loved Reverend Joshua.

Oh, poor Caleb. Maggie couldn't understand Miss Bellaire's choice. *Reverend Joshua is a wonderful man, but Caleb is…is….* She couldn't even find the words to describe him. *He's Caleb.*

He gave them all a charming smile. "Well, ladies, I think I'll leave you to chat." He nodded good-bye and left the room.

The three of them waited in silence until the sound of his footsteps receded.

Mrs. Norton sent a smile after Caleb. "Such a handsome man," she said with a sigh. "Although, I should remember that inner character is what is important, not outward appearance."

Delia frowned and looked away, confirming Maggie's suspicions. *Something has, indeed, happened between those two.* Curiosity consumed her as well as something else. Her chest felt tight as if she was hurt. *Caleb's romantic affairs are none of my business,* she told herself sternly.

"Let me look at your baby again." Mrs. Norton bent over the cradle. "Oh, she's awake."

"She is?" Maggie leaned to look. Sure enough Charlotte was looking at the ceiling, as if examining something.

"Do allow me to pick her up, Mrs. Baxter. I have held every baby in this town since Reverend Norton and I arrived here when we were newly married."

"Of course," Maggie agreed, although she wasn't quite sure how she felt allowing someone she'd just met to hold her precious daughter—*someone else who isn't Caleb,* she amended. Although, she recalled, Edith had held Charlotte. But as she watched the competence in Mrs. Norton's movements, and Charlotte didn't start crying, she became more relaxed.

Mrs. Norton let out a happy sigh. "They are so dear at this age. We missed seeing our grandson Micah as a baby, for he was born in Africa. But I hope he will soon be joined by a brother or sister. Reverend

Norton and I are praying for a quiverful of healthy grandchildren." She sent her soon-to-be-daughter a teasing glance. "As is your father."

A becoming flush of pink crept into Delia's cheeks, making her look even more attractive. "So Papa has said on several occasions."

Mrs. Norton rocked Charlotte. "Maggie, you've arrived at an exciting time in Sweetwater Springs, with my son's wedding to Delia approaching. Practically everyone in Sweetwater Springs will attend, which will give you a chance to meet people. Such a *grand* occasion. Why, I become flustered just thinking of it."

Maggie shifted. "I've been hearing about your wedding. A few families from Morgan's Crossing are planning to attend. There's been a flurry of dress-making going on."

Delia's smile to Maggie was warm. "I want you to be there, too, Mrs. Baxter. Surely your ankle will be better by then."

"Why, I...." Maggie's first thought was that she didn't have anything to wear, but then she remembered Caleb had bought her new clothes. "I'd love to come, Miss Bellaire." She remembered listening to the other women discuss the wedding and her wistful wish that she could attend, too. Now, she felt almost like Cinderella receiving an invitation for the ball.

"Call me Delia, please. I'm soon to change to Mrs. Norton and don't want to confuse people with two Mrs. Nortons. I intend to make it easier on everyone to distinguish between us. Otherwise, I'll end up being addressed as Mrs. Reverend Joshua."

They all laughed.

Maggie would just as soon not be called Mrs. Baxter. She'd love to leave Oswald's name behind as much as possible. "I'm Magdalena, but everyone calls me Maggie."

Mrs. Norton glanced down at Charlotte and smiled. "And you can bring this dear baby with you to the wedding."

"What if she cries?"

"We're used to crying babies."

"You must have a big church to fit everyone."

Mrs. Norton laughed. "Quite the contrary. We will have the pews packed as well as standing room in the back and on the sides. We have to do that on the Christmas Eve and Easter services, although in the winter, many don't risk a long drive. Thank goodness a wedding ceremony doesn't take much time at all, and we can use the hotel for the reception."

Delia shot Mrs. Norton an impish smile. "I believe the time has come to build a new church. One that could hold everyone."

"Oh, my, such a lovely idea." Mrs. Norton's forehead crinkled. "But we don't really need one. Such an expensive undertaking."

Delia patted Mrs. Norton's arm. "Something to think about for the future."

"A reception at the hotel...." Maggie clasped her hands together and let out a romantic sigh. "Sounds like a lovely party."

Mrs. Norton nodded. "So good of Mr. Bellaire to take care of all the arrangements."

"You mean he insisted," Delia said with a fond smile. She glanced at Maggie. "Papa is over the moon. I'm his only child. Most of my life we've been separated, me living in New Orleans with my mother and him in New York. So he delights in spoiling me. Reverend Joshua and I tried to rein him in, but we ended up allowing him his head."

"Can you believe Mr. Bellaire is having hothouse flowers brought in?" Mrs. Norton's tone marveled. "And orange blossoms for Delia's bouquet. And the hotel is catering all the food. We are not to cook a *thing*."

Maggie wondered why Caleb hadn't mentioned such a big event for his hotel. "Mr. Livingston must be doing a lot of work for your reception."

"Oh, not at all. Peter Rockwell manages the hotel. Everything is in his quite capable hands."

Maggie wondered if organizing Delia's wedding reception was too painful for Caleb. *Is he suffering in silence?* Her heart ached for him.

CHAPTER ELEVEN

As the week went on, Maggie's bruises faded, and her ankle mended enough that she could hobble to the bathroom on her own. She still had nightmares every night. Each time, Caleb would hear her cry out and climb on top of the covers, taking her in his arms, chasing away the demon named Oswald, and making her feel safe. In the morning, she'd awaken alone and missing him.

The secret of their nights followed her around during the light of day, even though neither referred to that time together. Yet it showed in the ease between them, the way the touch of his hand on her arm or back—conventional to any onlookers—conveyed a silent intimacy.

Often Maggie had to chastise herself for allowing her dependency on Caleb to grow, instead of weaning herself from him—especially if he had feelings for Delia Bellaire. Even though she warned herself that this time with him wouldn't last—that if she came to care for Caleb too much, she'd suffer when she left the Livingston residence to forge a life on her own with Charlotte, Maggie couldn't seem to make herself stop.

Every day, members of the Norton family called on her. Sometimes the elder Reverend Norton came with his wife or alone. Other times Mrs. Norton and Delia Bellaire came together, or Reverend Joshua dropped by alone or with either one.

Mrs. Cameron visited with her small son Craig, who was starting to crawl. The two of them had indulged in lovely discussions about their babies. In many ways, Mrs. Cameron reminded Maggie of Mrs. Tisdale, both women having a great deal of common sense and a practical knowledge of medical matters, especially concerning babies.

In the evenings after Ben's homework was done, everyone gathered in her bedroom. Ben started teaching Maggie how to play chess, while Edith and Caleb vied for holding Charlotte. Caleb usually won the argument, pointing out that his sister had time with the baby during the day while he was at the bank.

On Saturday morning after breakfast, Edith entered Maggie's bedroom carrying a linen-wrapped bundle tied with white satin ribbon. "I have something for Charlotte to wear tomorrow."

Tomorrow? Maggie wasn't sure what Edith meant.

"The christening."

Maggie hadn't given Charlotte's christening any thought, having fallen out of the habit of weekly church attendance. In Morgan's Crossing, the christening wouldn't have taken place until one of Reverend Joshua's monthly visits and might have been lumped in with any other event, such as a marriage or a funeral.

She shifted the baby to one arm so she could take the bundle. One-handedly, she untied the ribbon and opened the linen covering to see a lacy baptismal gown and bonnet in soft ivory. The bodice had embroidery and delicate tucks, and lace edged the sleeves, hem, and collar. The bonnet matched. "Oh, these are beautiful."

"My mother made them when Caleb was a baby. I wore them and so did Ben."

Maggie's eyes filled with tears. She tried to sniff them away and when that didn't work, she swiped the back of her hand across her eyes.

"Are those good tears or bad tears?"

"Good. You are all so kind."

"We do our duty." Edith's voice sounded stiff.

Maggie suspected the woman was holding back emotion, not really meaning to act distant. She patted the gown. "This isn't duty, Edith.

Duty was Caleb buying baby clothes for Charlotte that would have been just fine for her to wear tomorrow. Letting my daughter borrow the Livingston christening gown is generosity, indeed."

Edith smiled. "This actually isn't the *Livingston* christening gown. That one remains in Boston. The garment is many generations old and is a family heirloom. I don't know how many babies have worn it. There's so much lace adorning the material, the baby weighs twice as much. And one of my aunties watches the gown like a hawk to make sure nothing is spilled on it, and the baby is changed as soon as he or she is wet. And of course, the infant wears extra layers of diapers."

Maggie laughed. "The mother of the baby must spend all her time fretting about protecting the gown, rather than enjoying the service."

"Yes." Edith patted the gown. "And for that reason, as well as sentimentality, I used this one for Ben." Her lips turned down. "Nathaniel's parents attended, but they didn't insist on my baby using *their* gown—the one he and his brother wore." An echo of old pain lingered in her tone.

"I'm sorry they hurt you."

"Strange, really. I hadn't thought of that memory in years." Edith gave a slight shake of her head. "Enough of the past. The future is what's important. Let's concentrate on Charlotte."

"I hadn't really considered the christening." Maggie swallowed. "Would you be willing to be a godmother to Charlotte?"

Edith's eyes lit up. "I'd love to. I've come to care for her. I suppose you'd want Caleb to be her godfather."

"There's no one else more suitable." *No man loves my baby more than he does.* A wave of emotion swept over her. Maggie didn't stop to figure out what she felt or why she was experiencing it. She touched the lace on the hem of the christening gown and returned to the original subject.

"The obligation of wearing the *Livingston* christening gown sounds enormous. I think I'd refuse to allow Charlotte to wear the gown, even if we were in Boston and someone in your family condescended to offer it."

A look of discomfort crossed Edith's face, quickly suppressed.

But Maggie could tell the thought. *The highfalutin Livingstons would never have offered the sacred gown for Gypsy Maggie's baby to wear, even if they didn't know I was one.* "Does Caleb know about this?"

"I mentioned it at breakfast, and he was quite approving. Now, for tomorrow…there's more than just a service." Edith rushed the words out as if anxious to change the subject.

"What do you mean?"

"My brother has decreed that we'll invite any of our friends who attend church to come to dinner after the service. Since the list is quite large, Mrs. Graves has been cooking up a storm. And we've placed a large order with the baker, as well as at the sweet shop."

Maggie could only stare at Edith, mouth agape. She forced her jaw closed. "A party?"

"I don't know that we'd classify it as a *party*. That's a larger and more arduous affair. No, this is a small gathering—perhaps thirty people. At least you'll be spared the Cobbs. At this time of the year, they keep the store open for several hours after church, not just for one as they usually do. They know many families who haven't risked the drive during the winter are coming into town for the first time in months, and they will need to stock up."

"Whom are you inviting?"

"The Nortons, of course. Dr. and Mrs. Cameron. And Delia Bellaire, whom you already know, although you haven't met her father, Andre. Are you acquainted with the Walkers? I believe Darcy Walker is friends with Prudence Morgan. Mrs. Walker comes from quite a wealthy, distinguished family in the East. Neither she nor her husband is much for socializing, so we don't entertain them very often. But if they are in town, we will invite them."

"I've met the Walkers. They attended the party the Morgans threw for the christening of their youngest daughter."

"Ah, you probably know all of the former mail-order brides and their husbands, then."

"We've met." Maggie wouldn't count interacting with the Walkers, Flanigans, and Barretts among a group of about a hundred people for the two days the families stayed for the party as *knowing*. "I'm best acquainted with Mrs. Brungar."

"I don't believe I've met her."

"Bertha Brungar, the former Miss Bucholtz, is shy, but so kind." Maggie thought with regret of her friendship with Bertha, whose biscuits were legendary in Morgan's Crossing. When Oswald was at his most difficult—something hard to hide in the close confines of a tiny town—the woman would bring over a basket of her biscuits. Eating them seemed to soothe the savage beast within Oswald, and Maggie had always been so grateful. "She manages the boardinghouse in Morgan's Crossing, and I doubt you could pry her or her husband from their home to come to Sweetwater Springs."

"Probably just as well. There are only so many the dining room can comfortably hold. I also expect to see the Carters, Sanders, Thompsons." Edith ticked off the families on her fingers. "All ranchers. The Gordons— he runs the newspaper, and she's the teacher. Sheriff K.C. Granger. Mr. Rockwell, the manager of the hotel. Who else? Oh, yes. Caleb has taken quite a liking to the Muths—dairy farmers on the prairie. They were quite instrumental in ending the recent thieving by the Indians."

The recitation of names made Maggie's head spin. "You call that a *small* gathering?"

Edith laughed. "Well, I must say our intimate dinners have grown in the last few years as more people have moved to Sweetwater Springs. And of course, as either Caleb or I form new friendships...."

The idea of such a gathering for Charlotte's christening overwhelmed Maggie, especially she and the baby being the center of attention. She wondered if it was too late to put a halt to the planning, and then remembered that Edith had already placed an order with the baker. "I can help Mrs. Graves with the cooking. Sit at the table and chop things, for instance."

"I'll mention it to her. I'm sure Mrs. Graves would appreciate the help, although she'll never let you know it. The woman wears a perpetual frown."

Charlotte stirred and made a small sound.

Maggie glanced over to check on her. "Oh, I'm not yet used to thinking about my baby and what to do with her when I'm working."

Edith lowered a hand to touch the cradle. "I'll have Jed bring this to the kitchen, so Charlotte can be with you."

"That would be wonderful, thank you."

Edith tapped her chin. "I think I'm missing a few people."

Oh, dear Lord. "What does everyone do with their children? Do Ben's friends come, as well?"

"The children will eat in the kitchen." Edith looked around as if searching for something. "I should have brought my list. Ben will want the family of his best friend to attend, and I need to write them down. Normally, we wouldn't socialize with the Salters. The parents work at the hotel. Mrs. Salter is the laundry woman, and Mr. Salter contributes game for the kitchens. But Caleb is fond of them as well." She shook her head in apparent disbelief. "Not that they aren't nice people. Perfectly fine, salt of the Earth, and all.

Not for the first time, Maggie wondered what Caleb had told Edith about her. Surely if the woman knew of her low-class origins—her *Gypsy* origins—she would not be holding a party to celebrate Charlotte's christening. *What will happen when she finds out?*

❋ ❋ ❋

Sunday morning, Maggie, wearing her black dress, waited at the kitchen door, under strict orders from Caleb *not to stir an inch* until he brought the surrey as close to the side of the house as possible. They'd gotten ready early because she moved so slowly, careful of her injured foot, and he wanted her and the baby situated well before church started.

After some slight alterations, the new black dress fit her perfectly. Maggie reveled in the froth of chiffon around her neck and spilling over the front of the bodice and also in a straight line down the skirt. The puffed balloon sleeves gathered above her elbow, ending with ribbon cuffs at her wrists. When she moved her head, the ends of the huge bow on the side of her black hat fluttered near her cheek.

From seeing herself in the bathroom mirror, Maggie knew the dark color became her, and she'd never felt so elegant in her life. She couldn't bear to don her coat until the last minute, so she'd placed the garment on the table.

In her arms, Charlotte lay swathed in a blanket to keep her warm from the chilly spring breeze. She'd just nursed and had dry diapers, and Maggie hoped her daughter would be good throughout the service. Edith had lent her a black velvet reticule in which to carry extra diapers and another pair of soakers in case the baby had an accident. Maggie glanced at her daughter, who looked adorable with the bonnet framing her sweet face.

"Mrs. Baxter." Ben bounded across the kitchen to join her. "Uncle Caleb said for me to help you to the surrey. Mother will go with you. I'll walk with Mrs. Graves and Jed to church."

Edith followed her son. She looked striking in a midnight-blue outfit. The skirt and balloon sleeves were attached to a high-necked, cream-colored lace bodice. She carried a capelike half coat, the sleeves cut wide to fit her dress and trimmed with mink. She wore tasteful sapphires in her ears and a matching necklace. She cast an anxious glance out the window and pressed her lips together. "Oh, dear. I see clouds on the horizon. I think we've just lost half our guest list."

Thank goodness. Maggie kept her expression calm, not wanting Edith to see her relief. The woman had worked so hard to organize something special for Charlotte's christening.

Ben winked at Maggie. "More for us to eat!"

Edith shrugged. "Well, there is that. We'll have more than enough food for everyone. I won't have to rein anyone in." She tapped Ben's shoulder. "Like the son who has an appetite like a grizzly."

Ben grinned. "Grrrr."

"This time," said his mother with a fond smile and shake of her head, "you boys will be able to eat your weight in food—*after* the adults have helped themselves, of course. And we can send leftovers home with the Salters." She glanced at Maggie. "You can't believe how pitifully thin that family was before Mariah and Abel started working at the hotel. But with four growing boys...."

Edith took a step back to survey Maggie. Her gaze rested on the earrings, and her expression pinched in disapproval.

Maggie wondered if Edith would criticize her for wearing them, for she knew ladies did not flaunt hoops, especially *brass* hoops. *Too bad. A Gypsy never parts with her gold, unless she intends to spend it.*

The surrey pulled up to the door.

"Here, Magdalena." Edith held out her arms. "Let me take Charlotte."

Maggie handed the baby to Edith and put on her black coat. The shoulders were wide to accommodate her sleeves, and a big button fastened the cuffs tight around her wrists.

Edith gave a decisive nod of approval. "That coat fits you well. I'm surprised the mercantile had a fashionable one in the right size at this time of year."

"This is Montana, where we need coats *all* year around. We've been known to have snow in the summers."

"That's true."

Leaning on Ben for support, Maggie hobbled to the surrey. Although she tried to walk normally, biting her lip against the pain, she couldn't manage to disguise her limp. She paused at the step, knowing she'd have to put her full weight on her bad foot, and took a breath, preparing to boost herself up.

"Hold on!" Caleb called from the surrey. He jumped down and came around the side. "I saw you trying to hide how much you're hurting." Without waiting for a response, he swung her up onto the seat.

As much as Maggie hated being helpless and in pain, she couldn't help the thrill that went through her whenever he picked her up. She thanked him with a smile.

Once she was settled, Caleb took Charlotte from Edith and handed the baby to Maggie.

Neither woman commented on his overbearing ways. *As much as I hate to admit it, sometimes he's right.*

Edith gathered her skirts. With the assistance of her brother, she climbed in to sit next to Maggie.

Ben saluted. "See you at church, Mother, Mrs. Baxter."

Caleb walked to the other side and climbed in. He spread a blanket over their laps and then took the reins and released the brake. With a flick of his wrists, he set the team trotting.

The air was cold on her face, but Maggie was cozy between Caleb and Edith. If she'd been with Oswald, she would have been wearing her old coat, worn thin in places. Or if she still didn't fit in it, she'd be wrapped in a blanket and too ashamed to go to church.

They were still early enough that they passed only a few families walking to church on the sides of the street, leaving the middle open for vehicles and riders. As they drove by, most glanced up and waved at the occupants of the surrey.

Caleb nodded in response.

Edith lifted her gloved hand in a regal movement that was barely recognizable as a wave.

They drove by a three-story building with a polished rose-quartz façade. Just before they passed, a boy and a woman stepped out the front double doors, followed by the tallest man Maggie had ever seen.

"Oh, there are the Gordons," Edith exclaimed. "See that dark-haired man who's as tall as a tree?" Her wave to the family was more effusive than her previous, stingy ones. "Remember I told you? Anthony Gordon—he prefers to be called Ant—is the owner of the building and the newspaper business on the ground floor. Mrs. Gordon is the schoolteacher, and the boy is their nephew David."

Mrs. Gordon was a petite, pretty woman. The disparity in the couple's heights was almost comical.

The man noticed Maggie and gave her a crooked smile. *Of course, as the newspaper editor, he'd be interested in a new face in town, especially if he's heard about me already.*

"David is the son of Mr. Gordon's sister, murdered by her husband, who then kidnapped the boy and brought him west. Terribly abused he was."

Maggie gasped, thinking of Oswald. Her arms tightened around her baby. *That could have been me.*

"That's enough, Edith," Caleb commanded, taking the reins in one hand and briefly laying the other on Maggie's arm in silent reassurance.

"But David's fine now," his sister protested.

Caleb shot a concerned look at Maggie.

She gave him a nod, silently telling him she was all right, but really thinking of her lucky escape. *Why do some men cause pain to those they should most love and cherish?* Maggie supposed that was a question she'd never be able to answer.

Caleb glanced at her. "I'll halt at the church steps. You wait until I come around to help you down. I don't want you trying it on your own," he said in a firm tone.

"Now who's bossy," Maggie muttered, even if she agreed with him.

Edith choked back a laugh. "Telling him so won't change my brother one bit, Magdalena."

"Hope springs eternal," Maggie quoted from Alexander Pope.

Caleb laughed. He slowed the team to a walk and headed the horses toward the front steps of the church. The white clapboard building had a steeple with a cross and black doors and window trim.

He had to rein in the horses and wait while a family with several children strolled by. Then he nudged the horses forward until they reached the steps. He braked, tied off the reins, and jumped down, hurrying around to give a hand to Edith.

Once on the ground, his sister thanked him with a small smile and nod. She stepped out of the way.

Maggie slid to the end of the seat and handed Charlotte to him.

Caleb passed the baby to Edith. Apparently conscious of so many eyes on them, he didn't try to swing Maggie off the seat. Instead, he placed his hand under her armpits and lifted her, gently setting her down. "I wish I could carry you up the steps and into the church to spare you pain," he murmured, holding out an arm.

With one hand, Maggie grabbed up her skirts just high enough to preserve dignity. She slipped the other around his arm and started up the three steps, Edith following with Charlotte.

He let her climb at her own pace, leaning heavily on his arm. At the top, she paused to catch her breath.

Reverend Joshua came out of the church, saw them, and walked over. "Good morning, Mrs. Baxter, Mrs. Grayson."

"Good morning, Reverend Joshua," they chorused, sounding like schoolgirls.

The minister gestured toward the surrey. "Mr. Livingston, I'll help Mrs. Baxter to a pew, so you can move your vehicle."

Maggie glanced up at Caleb. Although he seemed reluctant to relinquish her, Caleb must have recognized the wisdom in the minister's suggestion, for he nodded. Maggie let go of his arm. With a backward glance to make sure Edith was nearby with the baby, she took Reverend Joshua's proffered arm. Once inside, she saw the church was only sparsely full. Those already present turned to look at her with curious expressions.

The interior was plain, with clear glass windows on each side. A white cloth-covered altar held a simple cross and a wooden bowl, which she supposed would be used for Charlotte's christening, as well as a small vase of the same purple crocuses that Caleb had brought her. Maggie wondered if those flowers came from the Livingston yard. A piano was in the left front corner, and a cylindrical stove for heat warmed the right corner, sending the smell of burning coals into the air.

Self-conscious, Maggie slowly hobbled down the aisle, trying to hold up her head and pretend she was walking normally. Leaning on Reverend Joshua's arm—although his was no less strong than Caleb's—didn't feel as comfortable, and she couldn't help wishing for a different escort.

Reverend Joshua gestured toward the front. "Since Charlotte is to be christened today, I'll seat you in the pew near my mother."

When they reached the last row, the pews open to the front of the church, Mrs. Norton rose from the left side where she'd been sitting with a Bible on her lap. She laid the Bible on the seat and held out her hand, greeting Maggie with a gentle smile that crinkled the wrinkles on her face. "Dear Mrs. Baxter. So good to see you on your feet today. An answer to our prayers."

The thought the woman had prayed for her gave Maggie a warm feeling of belonging. "I appreciate your thoughtfulness." She released Reverend Joshua's arm and took hold of the back of the pew to steady herself.

Reverend Joshua stepped back to allow Edith to move closer.

Mrs. Norton's blue eyes lit up. "And here is dear baby Charlotte."

Edith unwrapped the top of the blanket to expose the baby to view. The christening gown cascaded over Charlotte's feet.

Mrs. Norton tilted her head. "Why, doesn't she look adorable? I don't believe I've seen that christening gown before."

Edith smoothed the material. "Ben was the last one to wear this."

Mrs. Norton cast a shrewd glance from Maggie to Edith. "Perhaps I'll see the gown again."

Maggie's cheeks grew hot. *Surely, she can't mean I'll have another baby?* She couldn't imagine ever marrying again. *What if I thought my husband was a good man, but he turned out not to be?* She gave Edith an assessing glance. *Mrs. Norton must mean she hopes Edith will have a baby. She's still young enough.*

Delia bustled up. Like Edith, she looked the picture of sophisticated elegance, in emerald green instead of blue. Pale gold swags of leaves and flowers patterned the material, with the wide collar and the tight part of her sleeves in plain emerald green without the designs. At the hem, a row of small fringes under a band of grosgrain gold ribbon swished when she moved.

A dapper gentleman who could only be her father, for they shared the same hazel-colored eyes, accompanied her. He walked with a black, silver-headed cane.

Delia gave a cool nod to Edith and a sweet "good morning" to Mrs. Norton before turning to Maggie and leaning forward to press cheeks together. "So delighted to see you on your feet."

Maggie inhaled the scent of Delia's perfume along with the intimate friendliness of her greeting.

Delia straightened and placed a hand on her father's arm. "Papa, this is Mrs. Baxter, whom I've told you about, and her darling baby, Charlotte."

Maggie covertly studied the pair. Delia, with her delicate features, looked like a feminine version of her father. Her skin was more olive than Mr. Bellaire's, and her dark hair had only a hint of auburn, unlike his, which was a rich red-brown streaked with white.

The lines around Mr. Bellaire's eyes and mouth deepened when he smiled. His concerned gaze rested on her bruised face. "I hope you are recovered from your ordeal, Mrs. Baxter." His Southern drawl wasn't nearly as obvious as his daughter's. "Such a horrendous experience for you."

"I'm getting better, sir. Thank you for asking. And I appreciate Delia's kindness in calling upon a stranger so often this week. I have been most grateful for her company."

He glanced at his daughter with a doting expression. "She will make an ideal minister's wife."

Color crept into Delia's cheeks. "Papa, how can you speak so? No one is *ideal*."

Reverend Joshua leaned in. "I agree with your father, dearest."

Delia's blush deepened. "I've *enjoyed* calling upon Maggie," she protested. "I didn't visit from a sense of duty." She looked around as if trying to change the subject. "Where is Micah?"

Reverend Joshua glanced behind him to the church entrance. "I left him outside with Scotty Salter. Here he comes now."

A boy of about ten moved up the aisle, obviously restraining himself to a sedate walk. He stopped at Mr. Bellaire's side and grabbed the man's arm, his expression alight with mischief. His eyes were the same vivid blue of his father and grandfather, although his features looked more rounded. *"Grand-père."* He tugged on the older man's sleeve.

Mr. Bellaire bent down so Micah could whisper in his ear. He straightened and grinned. "Certainly."

"I'll tell 'em." Micah whirled and started to run before apparently remembering he was in church and slowed to a walk, weaving in and out of the people coming up the aisle.

Mr. Bellaire gazed after him, a smile on his face. Then he looked down at Maggie. "Nothing like a grandson to keep an old man young. I'm glad my son-in-law-to-be has provided me with one already old enough to play with. That boy is an endless source of amusement. He wants to bring his friend over to play chess with me tomorrow."

"He called you *grand-père?*" Maggie asked, curious.

"Since Micah already has two sets of grandparents, I thought it best we call upon the language of my native New Orleans for a title."

Maggie didn't know anything about New Orleans except for the city's designation on the map of the United States, which her schoolteacher had made her pupils memorize. "But New Orleans is in Louisiana."

"Yes, but the city once belonged to the French, and their influence lingers, especially in our language. We—the *Creole*—speak French and English."

"I must go to the piano," Mrs. Norton said with a sigh. "I don't think the Sanders have made it into town today. I'm afraid you'll have to make do with my poor performance, Mrs. Baxter, instead of Mrs. Sanders's divine music."

"Any music is a treat, Mrs. Norton," Maggie assured her. "I'm sure I will enjoy your playing very much, indeed."

The minister's wife thanked her and headed toward the piano. She took a seat and began to play a hymn Maggie didn't recognize.

She sat down, making sure to leave space for Mrs. Norton, and reached up for Charlotte.

Edith handed her the baby. "I'll stand until Caleb and Ben arrive so they can see where we are. This isn't our usual pew. We typically sit in the middle of the church. Mrs. Graves and Jed always prefer to find room in the back." With a widening of her eyes, she raised her chin to indicate a couple walking down the aisle. "Here are the Walkers come to town, after all." She waved for their attention.

The white-haired man held the hand of a child of about seven, her brown curls in long ringlets. The child stopped to talk to a girl her age, and he waited with her.

Her mother continued down the aisle toward them. She had brown hair drawn back from an interesting bony face and intelligent gray eyes, accentuated by the silver-sage green of her gown. The fullness of her sleeves and the wide collar of pale lace draped around her shoulders and ending in a *V* at her middle disguised the thinness of her frame. But even the well-cut tailoring couldn't hide her pregnancy.

Edith greeted the new arrival with a welcoming smile.

When Mrs. Walker saw Delia, her smile widened, and she held out a hand. "Miss Bellaire, I'm glad to see you looking so well after your long absence from Sweetwater Springs. I'm so anticipating your wedding."

"I'm most anxious for the happy day."

Careful not to jostle Charlotte, Maggie stood to greet the new-comer. Mrs. Walker's large pearl earrings of shimmering gray made her feel self-conscious about her brassy hoops.

"Mrs. Baxter, I'm delighted to see you again." Mrs. Walker leaned forward to study the baby. "She's so beautiful." She straightened and patted her stomach. "One of the few nice things about only meeting someone once or twice a year is how babies can slip into a family and be a complete surprise when you meet up again."

Delia gestured to the woman's stomach. "I'm not the only one looking forward to a future event. Mrs. Walker, I see we're to congratulate you."

Mrs. Walker's gray eyes grew misty. "We are so blessed." She slid a sideways glance at Maggie. "Neither my husband nor I expected to marry," she explained. "Finding each other, having Julia—" she gestured toward her daughter "—has made me the happiest of women. Although I'd hoped for more children, I was well contented with the one I had. Now, after so many years...." She seemed unable to go one.

Edith stepped in. "Mrs. Baxter's baby is going to be christened today. We're having a small get-together at the house afterward, and I hope you and your family will be able to attend." She slid her gaze to the Bellaires. "You two, as well." As she spoke with the father and daughter, her expression grew pinched and her tone changed from inviting to grudging.

"I don't want to impose," Mrs. Walker murmured. "Surely, you didn't expect us."

Maggie laughed. "Quite the contrary. We did. Please come. We'll need your help to eat all the food, for Edith expected to invite the whole town."

Edith smiled. With a faint shake of her head, she said, "With the weather, many families are staying home today."

Mrs. Walker glanced down the aisle at her husband. "Of course, they must stay safe. Luckily, my dear Gideon knew I needed some social activity, so we came into town."

Maggie tucked the blanket around Charlotte. "You're not concerned about the weather?"

"No, if it starts to rain, we'll stay at the hotel for as long as need be. We have the horses with us, and no other livestock to worry about. We get our milk and eggs from the Barretts, who are our nearest neighbors. You met them at the Morgans' party."

"Yes, Mrs. Barrett and I had a long chat about babies."

"That's Lina. There's nothing she likes better than children. I'm sure she'd be whisking your baby away from you right now. Unfortunately, because of their animals, the Barretts are more homebound than we are." She touched Maggie's arm. "I'd be delighted to further our acquaintance at the party."

"I would like that, too," Maggie exclaimed with gratitude.

"A social gathering is less of an ordeal when you already have acquaintances," Mrs. Walker agreed with a sage look of understanding. "When I lived in New York, I used to dislike such events. But out here, I've made such good friends, and each opportunity to gather together is a pleasure. I'm sure you will soon have similar experiences."

With a touch on Mrs. Walker's arm, Edith drew the woman's attention.

Maggie glanced back at the church, which was starting to fill. With a dip of her stomach, she saw Caleb walking up the aisle, looking handsome in a navy blue suit.

He stopped to talk to Gideon Walker.

Their conversation appeared serious, and she wondered what they discussed.

With a nod, Caleb disengaged and moved toward them. He, too, greeted Mrs. Walker warmly but only nodded at Delia and Andre.

Maggie itched with curiosity, wanting to know why Caleb and Edith seemed distant from the Bellaires. Now that she thought about it, Edith had never joined the visitors in Maggie's room when Delia was present, although she sometimes had when Mrs. Norton or Mrs. Cameron came to call.

The more she observed Caleb and Delia together, the more she suspected he had feelings for her and had suffered rejection. From the corner of her eye, she watched his face to see if his eyes gave anything away. But his impassive expression left her no sense of his feelings.

CHAPTER TWELVE

Even months after he'd learned the truth about Delia Bellaire's illegitimacy and Negro blood, Caleb didn't know how to treat her and her father. They'd lied to him—to the whole town—perhaps not so much in words, but by their actions. Now, he and Edith knew the truth. So did the Nortons and Sheriff Granger. But he and Edith could hardly cut the Bellaires' acquaintance, for the town was too small for such odd behavior to go without remark. And with Delia Bellaire about to become Mrs. Joshua Norton, Caleb had to at least show common courtesy.

At the time of the discovery, Reverend Joshua had seemed more upset about the deception than about Delia's antecedents, but he'd obviously forgiven her. Although the lie bothered Caleb, he was more annoyed that he'd begun to court a mixed-race woman. *What if I had married her?* He suppressed a shudder.

Since the discovery, Caleb focused on feeling thankful his heart wasn't engaged, that only his pride had taken the blow. The Bellaires' departure for Crenshaw had helped speed his return to his usual equanimity. With his hotel unfinished, there'd been nowhere in town they could stay—Widow Murphy's not being the kind of rooming house anyone would want to live in for more than a few days. Even with the recent expansion of the parsonage, there still wasn't enough room for father and daughter, especially with Andre convalescing from his heart attack.

I'll ease back into a friendship with them.

So, instead of paying attention to Delia, Caleb peered down at Charlotte. As usual, when he looked at her, his heart swelled with love—a reaction that still sometimes caught him off guard. "How is my goddaughter?"

Maggie chuckled. "She's not your goddaughter yet."

Caleb made a dismissive motion with his hand, and the corners of his mouth twitched. "A mere matter of minutes…well, depending on the length of the good reverend's sermon…whichever reverend gives it…maybe more than a few minutes."

The bell in the steeple began to toll.

Reverend Joshua gestured for them to take their seats and moved away to confer with his father.

With a tilt of her head at the pew, Edith glanced in question at Caleb.

He nodded in a gesture for her to make space for him next to Maggie.

She lifted an eyebrow, but obliged him and moved to the right, so he could slide in between the two women.

Ben hurried up to join them.

Reverend Joshua took a seat next to the boy, with Delia beside him, then Micah. Andre brought up the end near the aisle. All of them together were a snug fit, but no one seemed to mind their close proximity.

As Caleb sat next to Maggie, he realized that his choice to sit beside her might stir up some gossip. But hopefully when people later saw her need for help with walking, they'd dismiss their earlier speculations.

When "O for a Thousand Tongues to Sing" caused ragged voices to lift in praise, Charlotte startled awake.

Maggie rocked her.

Singing by rote, Caleb held out a finger and touched the infant's palm.

The baby grasped his finger and turned her head toward him.

The elder Reverend Norton stood, moved to face the congregation, and began the service. "In the Name of the Father, and of the Son, and of the Holy Spirit." He made the sign of the cross in the air.

Unlike his son, who wore new tailored suits, the minister wore shabby black, with a yellowing white shirt under his waistcoat. Word was the man refused to have his son purchase anything new for him except a coat, claiming not to need finer adornment.

As with the hymn, Caleb knew the order of responses by heart, saying them automatically while concentrating on playing with Charlotte by wiggling his finger, a game he'd discovered the baby seemed to enjoy, for she stayed attentive and held on all the while.

Maggie shot him a quick smile before turning to face the minister.

With the service flowing over him like a slow river, Caleb watched the baby and made plans for the next week. Although he knew Peter Rockwell was more than capable of organizing the reception, Caleb had been lax in overseeing his small empire, instead concentrating on Maggie and Charlotte as well as dealing with the bank business, particularly several foreclosures.

In regard to taking back properties, the worst part of being the only banker in a small town was interacting with his clients—seeing them around town, mingling with them at social gatherings, and worshiping with them on Sundays. A foreclosure wasn't just a commercial transaction that ultimately usually ended up profiting him. *No.* He knew the faces of the family members who'd be impacted. Consequently, Caleb was far more lenient when people fell behind than he should have been. His Boston banking relatives would severely criticize him if they knew.

I'll make sure to go to the hotel this week. He slid a sideways glance at Maggie, who was listening attentively to Reverend Norton's sermon. *As soon as she can walk freely, I'll take her for a visit.*

As he sat there between Edith and Maggie, Caleb became aware of the fragrance of rose soap wafting from both women. *I'll have to buy Maggie her own soap.* He sorted through various scents, considering which would best suit her. *Lavender? Gardenia? Jasmine? Lily of the valley? Lilac? Honeysuckle?* He discarded each one.

Patchouli? That's a possibility. While he thought the perfume he smelled on most women too overwhelming and tended to move out of their vicinity as soon as possible, he figured the soap wouldn't be as strong, and the minty fragrance from the Orient seemed to fit Maggie.

I'll buy her a bar and see if she likes it.

Reverend Norton brought the sermon to a close. With a cringe of guilt, Caleb realized he hadn't heard a word. *Not a good start for my role as a godfather. I sure hope in the future Charlotte doesn't ask me about the sermon on her baptismal day.*

Reverend Norton's warm smile softened his austere face. His vivid blue eyes glinted when he looked at Maggie and the baby. "A christening is always a joyous occasion, as a baby begins a divine journey that will last a lifetime. Today, we are blessed to have Charlotte Victoria Baxter who will formally become part of the family of Christ." His gaze moved around the congregation. "*Our* family. This precious soul survived an accident that could have taken her life and that of her mother. Unfortunately, her father passed away."

People murmured.

"Most of the time, Reverend Joshua and I never debate about which of us will have certain duties. Our responsibilities seem to naturally fall into particular areas, such as his ministry to the smaller towns outlying Sweetwater Springs. But two days ago, my son and I did have a back-and-forth discussion about who would perform this baptism."

Reverend Joshua brought his hand to his mouth, as if covering up a laugh.

Reverend Norton's eyes twinkled. "I, as your senior minister, naturally have seniority. But Reverend Joshua pointed out that he was the one who married Charlotte's parents and counseled Mrs. Baxter during her recent loss. Therefore, I have reluctantly stepped aside in this case." He held up a hand. "But I reserve the right to give her a blessing. So Charlotte Victoria will be doubly blessed."

The congregation made sounds of approval.

Reverend Joshua stood and walked to join his father. "Will the godparents come forth with the baby?"

Maggie handed Charlotte to Caleb.

He wanted to keep the infant, but knew traditionally the god-mother held the child during the ritual, so with a smile at the baby, he passed her to his sister.

Edith settled Charlotte into the crook of her arm.

Caleb held her elbow to help his sister to stand, and together, they moved toward the altar. Unlike with the rest of the service, this time he paid close attention to the words that made him a godfather. He'd heard them many times before, but had never thought of the promises in regards to himself. Now he realized the weight of the solemn vows he and Edith were making to Charlotte. Not only were they supposed to nurture and guide her spiritual welfare, but also if something happened to Maggie, they would have the duty to raise her, for there were no other relatives to do so.

The words of the ritual bound this baby to God and to them. Spiritually, they'd just become family.

Caleb looked down at Charlotte. *You're mine.*

❋ ❋ ❋

Leaning on Caleb's arm, Maggie walked down the aisle behind Edith, who carried the baby. They couldn't move more than a few inches before someone would stop and admire Charlotte or be introduced to Maggie, often making a statement of how lucky she was to be rescued by Caleb. *If only they knew how much.*

Once outside, Caleb helped her down the steps and a few feet into the yard. He looked down at her. "Will you be all right to stand here while I fetch the surrey?"

Although Maggie's ankle ached, she didn't want to admit the truth. "I'll be fine." She released his arm and made a small shooing motion. "Be off with you," she teased.

Edith gave her a sharp look. "I still can't get over you joking with my brother." She cast Caleb a playful smile of her own. "He's always too starched up to tease. Although when we were children...."

Caleb reached up and playfully pulled on his collar. "I'll speak to Mrs. Graves about using less starch when she irons my shirts."

A small man approached, a battered felt hat grasped in both hands. Although his face and hands appeared clean, his clothes looked like they could do with a good scrubbing. Under a ragged brown coat, the front of his once-white shirt sported a colorful green-plaid patch. "Mr. Livingston." The man twisted his hat. "I need to talk to you about the bathhouse."

Caleb frowned. "We have already had several such talks, Mr. Wood, to no avail."

"Please, sir." He grabbed Caleb's sleeve. "I must speak with you."

Up close, Maggie could smell alcohol on the man's breath. The reminder of Oswald's drinking made her stomach curdle.

Caleb twisted his arm out of reach. "This is not the time to talk business," he said, his voice clipped. "Now move along."

"But, I need an extension on my loan, Mr. Livingston," Mr. Wood whined.

"You've had *three* generous extensions already, Mr. Wood, as well as extensive advice about what you need to do to make the place successful." Caleb gave the man's attire a pointed up-and-down glare. "Including laying off the alcohol and availing yourself of your own facilities. Now, be off with you." His jaw clenched with obvious anger, he turned his back on the man.

A look of pain flashed in the man's eyes, and his shoulders slumped.

Maggie squeezed Caleb's arm.

He glanced down at her, one eyebrow raised.

She sent him a glance of appeal.

With his free hand, Caleb rubbed his forehead. "Oh, very well." He partly turned. "Wood, you have until the day after Reverend Joshua's wedding. If you can't make money from that event...."

"Thank you, sir." The man continued to bend his hat.

Maggie wondered why Mr. Wood sounded resigned rather than relieved. "What was that about?" she asked as Caleb escorted her away.

"A travesty of a good business is what that was about." He almost growled the words. "Ever since his wife died last year, the place has gone downhill. The man cannot stay out of the saloon and keep his place spick-and-span like a bathhouse should be. What's the use of patronizing a place if you don't emerge cleaner than when you went in?"

"Spick-and-span?" murmured Maggie who had never heard the term.

"From Plutarch, I believe, although we'd have to check with the Walkers to be sure." The angry look left his face. "Either Gideon or Darcy, if not both, are bound to know." He turned to the Walkers, who came along behind them, both holding hands with their daughter. "I need your expertise."

Mr. Walker cocked an eyebrow, his gray eyes amused, but he didn't question them.

Up close, Maggie could see he was far younger than his pale hair made him appear, perhaps in his late thirties.

"Does the phrase spick-and-span come from Plutarch?" Caleb asked Mr. Walker.

"They were all in goodly gilt armour," the man quoted, "and brave purple cassocks among them, spicke, and spanne new."

"Thomas North translation," added Mrs. Walker, when it seemed her husband wouldn't volunteer anything more.

Caleb laughed and dropped a hand on Mr. Walker's shoulder. "I knew you two wouldn't fail me."

"We can lend the book to you, if you lack it in your own library, Mr. Livingston," Mrs. Walker commented with a sly smile, although her intelligent gaze on them was friendly. "Or, you can borrow my Latin version."

Caleb lowered his arm. "Perhaps I will take you up on the Latin edition. While Mrs. Gordon has given Ben some basic Latin, he'll need to know much more for when he goes away to school. Mine is a bit rusty."

Edith inclined her head in approval. "We'd be most appreciative."

"Do let me know if you need help," Mrs. Walker said to Caleb in a tone of cool amusement.

Caleb shook his head. "I should have known you'd be an expert in that tongue, Mrs. Walker. Probably French and Spanish and Italian, as well. How about German?"

Mrs. Walker laughed. "I don't do so well with German. I'm far more fluent with the Romance languages.

Hearing them banter about foreign languages made Maggie feel ignorant. Her schooling hadn't included such study, and she doubted Romany would count. But she did know about bathhouses. There was one in Morgan's Crossing, containing a ladies' room with two bathtubs and a gentlemen's section that held four in one room and another four in a second. Before the Morgan's party, when everyone in town wanted to avail themselves of the place, she'd traded work for a bath for her and Oswald, helping the proprietor clean out the tubs between the miners' eager usage.

With a sudden burst of enthusiasm, Maggie realized this opportunity might be the answer to her prayers for employment to support herself and her daughter. *I can take over the bathhouse and run the place!*

Maggie almost blurted out the request, but she caught herself. *This isn't the right time. He's already angry about the bathhouse.* She glanced at Caleb, immersed in a language discussion with the Walkers.

I need to figure out a business proposition and present my plan when he's alone, and I think he'll be most open to hearing it.

CHAPTER THIRTEEN

The dinner to celebrate Charlotte's christening was an overwhelming experience for Maggie, and she could only feel grateful for the abbreviated guest list, which still felt like far too many people for her comfort. Although everyone was kind and friendly, she wasn't used to being the center of attention, especially in such elevated society, and she felt awkward and out of place.

If I can only get through this dinner without embarrassing Caleb and Edith.

Seventeen people, not including Maggie, sat in the dining room around a long table that was bigger than the interior of her *vardo*. Caleb presided at the head and had seated her to his right.

Just being in the dining room impressed her. Aside from the first day when Caleb had carried her upstairs to the bedroom, and today, when he'd carried her downstairs for church, she hadn't seen much of his house or been in any position to notice more than vague details on her journeys to and fro in his arms.

A snowy damask tablecloth covered the surface of the table, laden with silver place settings and cut-glass goblets. Two silver candelabras flanked a centerpiece of crocuses and greenery in a silver bowl, and saltcellars were placed between every two settings. Maggie had never seen so much silverware, and she wasn't sure why each person needed three forks of varying sizes and two knives.

The seven children ate in the kitchen, except for two babies sleeping in cradles near their parents. The Camerons had brought their cradle for Craig, and Caleb had carried Charlotte's down and set it on the floor between them.

Maggie checked on Charlotte. Her daughter still wore the christening gown and bonnet and looked like a sleeping angel. A wave of gratitude surged through her. She glanced at Caleb and saw him gaze at the baby, a tender look on his face. Her throat tightened. To avoid focusing on him, she looked away, deliberately taking note of those around the table who'd come to celebrate Charlotte's christening.

Sheriff K.C. Granger sat across the table from her. Although Maggie knew the sheriff wore men's clothes, the sight of the woman in a mannish dark suit aroused Maggie's curiosity. The sheriff's dark hair was braided in a long plait down her back, and her watchful gray eyes studied those around her.

Even in Morgan's Crossing, Maggie had heard of K.C. Granger: After saving a young girl, the sheriff had arrived in town with a dangerous criminal in custody; the competent manner with which she'd handled the recent thieving of the Indians went a long way toward easing hostilities; and anyone who bet against her in a poker game because she was a woman inevitably ended up pushing a pile of chips across the table. The sheriff was also said to donate much of her winnings to the church.

The couple she'd seen on the way to church sat next to Miss Granger. Ant Gordon towered over his petite wife Harriet on the other side of him.

To the left of schoolteacher Mrs. Gordon sat the Salters, who appeared as uncomfortable in the elevated social situation as Maggie did. She'd met Amos Salter in Morgan's Crossing when he'd worked as a miner before abruptly leaving before Christmas. Their fine apparel—Amos in a suit and Mariah in a rose silk dress—contrasted with their careworn faces and work-roughened hands.

From time to time, Mariah made quiet conversation with Peter Rockwell, who was seated next to her. The pleasant-faced man with the honey-brown eyes was Mariah's boss at the hotel.

Mary and Reverend Norton were on the other side of the Salters. The couple had become familiar and beloved to Maggie.

From her place at the foot of the table, Edith was the image of the perfect hostess, graciously guiding the conversation, which must have been heavy going, considering she was situated between the silent Salters and Gideon Walker, who seemed content to let his wife Darcy, on his left, do the talking for both of them.

Next on Maggie's side of the table came the Camerons, and then the Bellaires and Reverend Joshua who sat next to Maggie. The two men were both solicitous of her comfort, helping her to relax, although she kept a sharp eye on everyone's manners, knowing she'd need to figure out which of her many forks and knives to use.

The conversation lagged as Mrs. Graves and Jed, both wearing their Sunday best, carried in heaping platters until the center of the table disappeared under a feast of food—golden fried chicken, roast beef with all the trimmings, mashed potatoes and gravy, baked sweet potatoes, corn, green beans with pork rinds, glazed carrots, applesauce, sweet and sour pickles, and several types of rolls with butter. Tantalizing smells wafted into the air—no doubt setting stomachs to grumbling.

Jed set a pitcher of water and another of cold tea at each corner of the table. The desserts were arrayed on the sideboard—pies with decorative crusts of leaves and flowers, several towering cakes, custard, a fruit trifle, and a dish of sugarplums from the sweet shop.

The food alone was intimidating. Maggie reflected on the plain fare she'd been able to afford after Oswald had purchased his whiskey—beans, corn, flour, potatoes, eggs, and salt pork.

From where she sat, Maggie had a view of the fireplace on the other side of the room, the coal fire sending warmth around the diners. She couldn't help but compare the details of this event to her former simple life.

The mantelpiece and surrounding shelves held decorative plates and other do-dads. A painting of a couple, the woman wearing a wide dress over a hoopskirt, hung over the mantle and reminded her of happy memories from her childhood.

As a girl, Maggie had loved playing dress-up with the old-fashioned gowns, stored in a trunk in the attic of her grandparents' home. One afternoon, her grandmother had taken out a hoopskirt from a trunk and demonstrated how to wear one, strapping the contraption around her waist. Then Grandma had donned her pink silk wedding dress, draping the skirt over the hoop and leaving the back unbuttoned, for she no longer had the tiny waist of a bride.

Even with the material wrinkled in fold lines, the ruffles flat, the fit loose, to Maggie the dress had seemed a magical creation, and she imbued the gown with romantic fantasies. When Maggie grew older and was invited to attend a barn dance, Grandma had altered the pink dress to fit her, gathering the extra material from the full skirt to flow over a bustle.

Wearing the dress that night had made Maggie feel elegant, and many men at the party seemed to agree, for she'd been danced off her feet. She'd enjoyed the attention but at the time had no plans to settle down. That came later, when everyone she loved had passed on, and she was left alone.

Maggie had planned to wear that same dress for her wedding, but Oswald had insisted on buying her a white gown—his last generous act and the one that convinced her to go forward with the marriage, even after she'd begun to doubt the wisdom of her choice.

Oh, no. Maggie bit her lip, remembering her grandmother's dress was packed away in the *vardo*. She'd hidden the treasured possession in a cedar-lined storage box underneath the bed to keep Oswald from damaging it. She glanced at Caleb, who was talking with the sheriff. *I need to ask him if there's a way to obtain my dress.*

Realizing she hadn't been eating or paying attention to the conversation, Maggie took a bite of mashed potatoes, a favorite of hers. While potatoes had been a staple of their diet, she didn't often have the extra funds for butter and milk. Since coming to Caleb Livingston's, she'd eaten the food several times, and each time, she savored the way the potatoes melted in her mouth.

Ant Gordon looked down at the woman next to him. "Sheriff, can you tell us about your trip to the reservation?" he asked in a deep, gravelly voice, and then directed a crooked smile Edith's way. "I won't go so far as to take out my notebook and pencil at the table to scribble notes for my article."

His wife chuckled. "No, but he might secretly set his notebook on his knee and write *underneath* the table."

Everyone laughed before turning their attention to K.C. Granger.

The sheriff's gray eyes saddened. "As most of you know...." She glanced at Maggie. "I went with Red Charlie to check on the tribe to see how they fared through the winter." Her jaw tightened.

Everyone waited for her to continue.

"Most made it through. Barely. Still, they lost babes and a few of their elderly." She grimaced. "But not in the same amounts they would have if we hadn't driven the cattle out to them and brought along other supplies."

Ant Gordon leaned forward, his gaze intense, as if filing mental notes. "What about their attitude toward us?"

"Probably 'bout what you'd expect. A combination of grateful and angry." The sheriff picked up her goblet of tea and drank.

Maggie tilted her head in askance. "Why angry?"

Sheriff Granger set down the glass. "Well...if some foreign government and its people had driven you from your ancestral lands, forced you to live within a certain area, hunted one of your main sources of food to almost extinction, promised to take care of you, and then reneged on that promise, wouldn't you be angry?"

Maggie understood all too well the pain of promises broken when, in all trust, you leaned your life on them. "Betrayed, hurt, incredulous, resentful." She spoke from bitter experience.

The sheriff gave Maggie an approving look. "There you have it."

Mrs. Norton set down her fork. "We are lucky Mrs. Muth was acquainted with those braves. Who knows what else might have happened? God was certainly watching over us."

The sheriff cut some pieces of roast beef. "The wagonload of supplies we brought out to the reservation won't last long. We'll need to organize a group to travel there. When I mentioned help with planting food crops, they actually seemed interested."

Amos Salter cleared his throat. "I'll go." With all eyes on him, the color deepened in his ruddy skin. "I know the despair and helplessness of seeing your family starving before your eyes...." He dipped his chin in Caleb's direction, his blue eyes bleak. "Then through the goodness of God, to have a helping hand extended...."

Moved by the simple passion and gratitude in the man's tone, Maggie glanced at Caleb, wondering why Mr. Salter aimed his words at the banker, and saw Caleb looking uncomfortable—in a good way. She'd had enough familiarity with him to know, and she wondered what he'd done to help the Salters.

He's such a generous man.

Mariah Salter patted her husband's arm with a gentle hand. Tears glistened in her brown eyes, but she gazed at Amos with a luminous expression of love and pride that made her haggard face almost appear beautiful.

Envy stabbed through Maggie. She'd never looked at Oswald that way—had never even considered the importance of picking a man who would make her proud to be his wife.

Mariah squeezed her husband's arm. "This time, I won't worry when you're gone to the Indian camp like when you were in the mine. Well, not worry as much, for you will be in good company." She leaned forward to direct a shy smile the sheriff's way.

Amos looked from Mr. Rockwell to Caleb. "I suppose I should check to see if I can be spared."

Mr. Rockwell sent the man an approving smile. "We'll miss what you bring in from your hunts, but we can go a few weeks without serving game."

Caleb nodded in agreement.

Reverend Joshua cocked his wrist and flicked two fingers in a volunteering motion. "I'm not much of a gardener. But I can wield a shovel."

His father shot him a look of pride. "And the Bible."

"But *not* at the same time," Reverend Joshua quipped.

Everyone laughed.

"I'll be a newlywed, though...." The young minister glanced at Delia. "I have to learn to start thinking like a married man and consult my wife about such decisions." He glanced at Delia.

His betrothed lifted her chin. "I'm proud of you for offering. In fact, if you'll allow womenfolk along...." She sent a questioning look toward the sheriff. "Other women, that is. I'd like to go, too."

In silence, everyone waited for Reverend Joshua's answer. "Forgive me, my dear. I was so taken aback by your offer, so *moved* by your willingness to help the native people that I needed a moment to gather the words of gratitude." He quirked an eyebrow at K.C. Granger. "However, I will defer the decision to the sheriff's greater knowledge of the situation."

As if tapping a pencil, Ant Gordon drummed on the edge of the table with a long finger. "I think I should come along."

Caleb blinked in apparent surprise, and then his eyes narrowed, and he frowned. Watching him, Maggie wondered at his reaction.

Mr. Gordon's right eyebrow peaked in an upside down *V* that matched his wry smile. "Like our good reverend, here, my gardening knowledge is minimal. Thank goodness when Abe McGuire sold me his place, he left behind a well-stocked garden and cultivated land that our hired man can handle." He glanced at his wife. "But, for the sake of starving natives, we can put my—" he slapped a hand that seemed as big as a dinner plate behind his shoulder "—*back* to use. And I'd also like to write an article, both for our newspaper and to submit to my former editor in New York for a larger audience. Maybe stir some public sympathy, which would in turn put pressure on the politicians."

Doctor Cameron let out a loud sigh. "I'd be a goin' with you, for I'm sure there is need for my services," he said, his Scottish burr strong. "But that would mean a leavin' the people here without a doctor." He huffed in apparent exasperation. "If only that young brother of mine would hurry himself to get out here. I've been expecting him for over a year. But he wanted some extra experience first. In the slums of London, of all places."

Sheriff Granger looked at the doctor. "There is need, certainly. But if something happened while you were gone...." She shook her head. "This is one of those times when you wish there were two of you."

Mrs. Cameron's glance at her husband was loving. "Or more. I need one to stay home with me and the baby."

Dr. Cameron winked at his wife. "One more to deal with the needs of my medical practice and one to travel to the reservation, while I stay home with my family." He spoke the last in a thickened brogue that had everyone laughing.

Maggie snuck a glance at Caleb under lowered eyelashes to see him looking thoughtful.

His lips firmed, and then he said, "We can cover Amos's wages." He glanced at Peter Rockwell and raised an eyebrow. "Or what you estimate you would have paid him for the game he hunted. Average the last couple of months and come up with a weekly sum."

Mr. Rockwell nodded.

Delia leaned forward and bestowed a beaming smile on Caleb. "That's *wonderful.*"

Caleb looked surprised by Delia's reaction, and then he held the woman's gaze. The corners of his mouth turned up.

What do they mean by their covert exchange? Maggie wondered, unaccountably jealous. She didn't like the idea that Caleb might share a secret with Delia.

The conversation flowed on, but Maggie stopped listening. Her stomach tight, she toyed with her food, having lost her appetite. She was not at all pleased with herself for allowing her emotions to interfere with her dinner.

* * *

With a growing sense of guilt, Caleb listened to the conversation about the Indians' affairs, feeling torn between whether or not he should volunteer. *A ridiculous impulse, really.* He had no desire to haul off to the reservation and dig in the dirt, even if he knew a thing about planting or raising livestock, which he didn't—beyond horses, that is.

He watched the faces of his guests. They were all attentive and obviously absorbed in the romantic notion of taming and saving the savages.

Maggie tracked the conversation, her eyes wide with obvious concern.

A growing sense of pressure made him consider the outlandish idea of participating in the plan. And because the impulse was so unlike him, he had to mentally take stock of his thoughts and feelings, although he was fairly certain the woman at his right and the baby in the cradle between them were responsible for the softening of his heart. *No, not heart, his outlook on life.*

Before meeting Maggie and going through their trials of survival together, Caleb doubted he would have experience any such concern about the situation. The thought of traveling to the reservation wouldn't even have occurred to him. He certainly hadn't felt any stabs of conscience at the time of the first expedition to the reservation to help the Indians, which took place last autumn.

Caleb wasn't sure if he was happy about the change in him, and, after a few minutes of thought, he decided he wasn't. *Too uncomfortable.* Life was cruel. As his father, Black Jack Livingston, used to say, *It doesn't pay to be soft.* But still he had to do something to alleviate the odd sense of obligation and in so doing, maybe please Maggie, as well.

I can pay others. That's a reasonable compromise.

Relieved to have wrestled his conscience into some sort of order, Caleb took a sip of his water, wondering if it was too early to serve wine. He set down the glass hard enough to make a thud.

Curious eyes glanced his way.

"I'll donate supplies and cover the wages of several men who'd like to go but don't want to lose out on their regular pay." To his own ears, his words sounded stiff.

Mrs. Norton clasped her hands together. "Dear Mr. Livingston. So generous."

Instead of assuaging his guilt, the emotion only deepened.

Maggie glanced over. She had no smile for him, only a look of penetrating contemplation.

Can she read my mind, see my ambivalence?

Reverend Norton nodded, as if giving Caleb a benediction. "Like before, we can ask the ranchers to contribute cattle and the farmers food and livestock."

Another idea came to him. "We might even talk to Michael Morgan when he's here for the wedding to see if any of his miners or other townsfolk would want to go."

"Excellent." Delia leaned forward to gaze at him. Her eyes sparkled. "I've *never* experienced anything like the way this community comes together to help in times of need." She tilted her head toward her father. "Have you, Papa?"

Andre rubbed his chin. "Not in New York or New Orleans."

Caleb smiled at her, surprised that he and Delia seemed to have returned to their former amicable relationship. *I guess I've forgiven her.* He glanced at Andre Bellaire. *Both of them.* The thought made him feel lighter.

He turned to Maggie, expecting, no *anticipating,* similar approval on her face.

But instead, she appeared solemn, and a small frown pulled down her lips. She glanced at her plate, picked up her fork, and pushed around the uneaten food. She hadn't eaten much, which was unusual for a woman with a hearty appetite.

His spirits took a downturn.

What is concerning her? And what must I do to make her smile again?

For in truth, Caleb cared more for her happiness and the baby's than for the plight of savages distant from him and capable of murdering them all.

CHAPTER FOURTEEN

After dessert, Edith offered to play the piano in the parlor while their guests drank coffee or tea.

With exclamations of pleasure, everyone trailed their hostess from the room.

Feeling heavy-hearted, Maggie remained seated at the table. Her shoulders drooped, and she couldn't muster the energy to stand. *If only I could magically float instead of limp into the parlor.*

Caleb returned to the dining room. "I'll take Charlotte for you."

Maggie tried to hide her flagging spirits. Apparently, she hadn't succeeded.

Caleb swooped in on her. "You need to rest."

"But the company," she protested.

"I'll take you upstairs, and anyone who wants to visit you can go to your bedroom. I'll bring up Charlotte in the cradle."

"I can walk," Maggie insisted, feeling obstinate. "Besides, what will people think?"

"No one is around to see. They are all in the parlor, eyes and ears on Edith." Caleb won the argument by picking up Maggie and carrying her upstairs.

Being in his arms, inhaling his familiar scent, felt so right, which in turn made her weepy. Feeling discombobulated by the emotion, Maggie held back tears so he couldn't see them.

Caleb strode into the room and laid her on the bed on top of the coverlet. He took the extra pillow from the other side of the bed and used both to prop her upright. "Don't move," he ordered, leaving the bedroom.

Free of Caleb's presence, Maggie hurriedly pulled her lace handkerchief from her sleeve, blotted her eyes, and blew her nose before stuffing the square of linen inside her cuff. By the time he returned with her daughter in the cradle, Maggie had erased all evidence, or so she hoped.

He set down the cradle, handed her the baby, and stopped to stare into her face.

Maggie avoided his gaze by cooing at Charlotte and leaning forward to kiss her forehead and inhale her baby smell.

"Magdalena," he said, drawing out all four syllables. "Is everything all right?"

She flashed him a false smile. "My ankle was paining me, but now that I'm off my feet, I'll be fine."

He frowned. "Why are you so stubborn? You could have told me, and I would have brought you up earlier. You could have been resting all this time."

"Don't fuss so, Caleb."

His eyebrows drew together.

"If you could be so kind and bring a glass of warm milk." She put a plaintive note into her tone.

He gave her a shake of his head, his frustration apparent. "What am I going to do with you?" He stalked from the room.

She stared after him. *I don't know.*

Caleb soon returned with the milk, which he deposited on the table next to the bed. "Is there anything else you need?"

She forced her lips to turn up. "I'm fine."

He didn't look convinced. He crossed his arms over his chest and waited.

"Caleb, you have a houseful of guests. Go be a host." She waved a hand toward the door.

Quick as a whip, he caught her wrist. "That's the second time today you've done that, bossy lady."

This time her smile was natural. "I may be bossy, but you don't follow orders well."

He chuckled. "You noticed that, did you? We're quite a pair, then." Keeping his gaze on hers, he bent to kiss the back of her hand.

Although Maggie tried to hide her reaction, the touch of his lips made her shiver. Something in his eyes said her attempts at concealment hadn't succeeded.

"I'll check on you soon." He lowered her hand to the bed and left the room.

"That man!" Maggie whispered to Charlotte, scooping the baby into her arms. "Caleb Livingston takes pride in tumbling me about." She warmed to her theme. "I'm a tumbleweed rolling in the wind around that man."

Charlotte gazed at her face as if fascinated.

Maggie gently touched the baby's nose. "Yes, your godfather. That's who I'm talking about."

A soft knock sounded at the open door.

"Come in," she called.

Delia Bellaire stuck her head in and smiled. "I see you two are settled."

Delia was the last person Maggie wanted to talk to, but she managed a friendly smile.

"May I keep you company?" The woman's eyes looked concerned.

Maggie couldn't turn her away. "Please." She gestured to the wingchair.

"I couldn't help but notice you were quiet tonight." Delia took a seat. "Subdued, actually."

How could she tell? I thought I was acting normally.

"Perhaps a bit…tired."

Delia gave her a speculative glance. "Is that all?"

I can hardly tell her I'm bothered Caleb might be in love with her.

"You've been through quite an ordeal," Delia said, as if feeling her way. She smoothed a wrinkle from the coverlet. "I'm sure your recovery will have setbacks, both physical and…emotional."

Not knowing how to answer, Maggie dropped her gaze to Charlotte and ran a finger down the baby's arm. Although the other woman spoke the truth about the switchbacks of the last week.… *How can I ask her what I really want to know?*

"Please, won't you tell me what's wrong?"

The baby turned her face to the sound of Delia's voice.

Maggie couldn't resist the appeal in that coaxing Southern voice. Before she could rein herself in, the question burst from her. "Why do Caleb and Edith avoid you and your father?"

Delia let out a sharp breath and sat back, her smile wiped away. Her hazel eyes looked stricken.

"I'm not imagining their distance," Maggie said in a staunch tone. "I've seen their behavior on several occasions now."

Delia couldn't meet her gaze. "No, you are not imagining it," she said in a low voice.

"It's because Caleb is in love with you, isn't it?" To Maggie's horror, her voice shook. "He's hurt because you chose Reverend Joshua."

Delia's hand flew to cover her mouth, and her eyes grew wide.

"Edith is probably hurt and disappointed, too." Maggie warmed to the notion. "Caleb must struggle, knowing you are back in town. Every time he sees you, he feels his loss. Underneath that proper banker's exterior, he's nursing a broken heart. He can't bear to speak to you or your father."

A peel of laughter stopped Maggie from further embellishing her story. She narrowed her eyes at Delia. "I do not think this is a case for levity," she said in an affronted tone. "We are talking about *serious* matters of the heart."

Still chuckling, Delia held up a hand. "My dear Maggie, the situation is not at *all* what you think."

"It's not?" Taken aback, she stared at Delia, but the woman's cheerfulness convinced her. "Then what is the problem?"

Delia looked away. "I cannot tell you. My father and I...Edith and Caleb...we had a serious difference of opinion. Shall we leave it at that?"

Maggie wasn't convinced, but she wouldn't stoop to begging for the story. Trying to hide her hurt, she lifted her chin. "I can see that you feel the matter requires discretion."

Delia's brow crinkled. "You think I don't trust you?"

"Do you?"

"I have a secret I cannot share." Delia played with her fingers. "I'm sorry. I don't mean to hurt you. It is not mine alone."

Like the burst of a soap bubble, Maggie's emotion deflated. She knew the feeling of having something to hide. She glanced down at her baby. *Someone to protect.* She stayed silent for a while, thinking. Finally, she lifted her head and looked directly into Delia's eyes. "I understand, for I have a secret, too."

Impulsively, Delia leaned over and touched the edge of Maggie's gown. "I am to be a minister's wife. All three of the Nortons have had conversations with me about my future obligations. In various ways, each of them has talked about the sacred trust we have in our roles, and of the need to hold people's secrets, to not condemn, yet to guide.... For if we do not do so, those who are most troubled will not feel safe in coming to one of us for counsel."

Maggie supposed Delia was right. "I never thought of that."

"Reverend Joshua...." Delia's voice faltered. "He is most concerned...due to his previous circumstances.... He told me that I too am called by God to nurture and guide his people, even if I'm not formally invested with the title of minister. For many people, he says, especially younger women, will seek me out for counsel, instead going to him or his parents."

Maggie gave a slow nod, absorbing what Delia had said. "I can see the necessity."

Delia fiddled with her gold heart pendant. "I mean, I was never one for gossip. A friend or a servant could safely confide in me. But I didn't realize the larger implications…the importance of my place at Reverend Joshua's side…until I accepted his proposal." A smile played about her mouth, and her beautiful hazel eyes sparkled. "Well, actually Micah and Reverend Joshua's proposal."

"That sounds like quite a story."

Delia lost her smile. "The story is wound around the secret I cannot share."

Thinking about what Delia said about the sacred nature of keeping secrets made Maggie take a leap of faith. "How about this? We'll trade." She wiggled her arm out from under her daughter and extended a hand. "I'll tell you my secret, and you tell me yours. It would be nice to have someone beside Caleb to talk with."

Delia's air of solemnity vanished. "Oh, I'd love to have a friend with whom I could share." She grasped Maggie's hand. "As much as I love my dear future husband and feel I can confide in him, and in his mother, as well, it's not the same as talking to a woman my age."

"Better go shut the door."

Delia squeezed Maggie's hand and released her. She jumped to her feet and rushed to close the door, her motions more like a girl instead of a woman who was about to become a minister's wife. She returned to settle in the chair and leaned forward, waiting.

"Very well." Maggie took a deep breath and let the words spill out, starting with her marriage to Oswald.

Her new friend listened with her hands clasped in front of her. Her expression changed from curious, to horrified, to fascinated.

Then Maggie finally wore down.

Delia's hand flew to her chest, and she collapsed back against the chair. "I've never heard of anything so frightening!" She patted her chest. "And Caleb delivered Charlotte! I can hardly believe he'd do such a—"

"He didn't have any choice. Charlotte was coming will he or nil he."

"I can see why you and Caleb would feel the need to protect your reputation and your concern for Charlotte. I don't think people would judge you, but you might as well not put them to the test."

"Caleb told Reverend Joshua."

"Why, that betrothed of mine! He never said a word." Delia exhaled an annoyed breath. "I know he can't. I just didn't know he was so good at secrets."

"Other people's secrets," Maggie hastened to remind her. "Not his own."

"You're right. There's a difference." Delia glanced at the door. "I'll give you the short version of my secret, and we can discuss it more another time. My father will be wondering where I am."

Charlotte fretted, stretched out an arm, and arched her back, a move Maggie recognized meant her daughter would soon demand to be fed. She nodded at the baby. "Another reason to make things quick."

"I'm not really Delia Bellaire. I'm Delia Fortier." She rushed out the words, and then, wide-eyed, paused for dramatic effect.

"How can that be?" Maggie asked, puzzled by her new friend's meaning. "You look like your father." Then she realized what Delia meant. Her parents had not been wed. "Oh."

"And that's not the worst. My mother was a quadroon Negress, which makes me an octoroon." This time when Delia hesitated, her body tensed as if waiting for Maggie's condemnation.

"I don't know what that means."

"It means I'm one-eighth Negro."

Maggie studied her friend, searching for any sign of her racial heritage. Careful to not disturb Charlotte, she sat up to lean closer to Delia and thrust her arm alongside the other woman's so the sides of their hands touched. "Look, we match. I'm half Gypsy."

Delia's eyes widened. "I didn't know Gypsies were in America. In the stories I've heard, they wandered around Europe."

"Oh, there are definitely tribes here, too. Most are in the south. You might have run into some and didn't know it." She touched her earring. "They smuggle gold."

Delia studied the earrings. "I never would have known those are gold. You're so clever."

Maggie sat back. "Hurry and tell me the rest."

"My mother had financial problems—some bad business dealings. She was going to sell me to a powerful man to become his mistress."

Maggie gasped. She shook her head as if shaking some knowledge into her brain. "I thought the war abolished slavery."

"There are all kinds of slavery," Delia said in a dark tone. "Legally, Marcel Dupuy wouldn't have owned me, but to all intents and purposes, I would have been his slave."

"What did you do?"

"I fled to my father's house. He hadn't known of my existence. To protect me, we left New Orleans, passing me off as his legitimate white daughter. On the train outside of Sweetwater Springs, Papa had a heart attack and almost died. Reverend Joshua and Micah were also passengers and came to our assistance, so we ended up here. Caleb and Edith took us in because the parsonage was too small to house us. Indeed, we are much indebted to them."

"Are you *sure* Caleb didn't fall in love with you?"

"A woman knows when a man loves her," Delia said with calm conviction. "I believe Caleb toyed with the *idea* of courting me. But he never had serious intentions. I can assure you his heart was *not* engaged."

Relieved, Maggie let out a long sigh. "But what *happened?*"

"I made the mistake of writing to my mother and telling her where I was. She sold the information to Marcel, who traveled here to kidnap me."

Maggie's mouth dropped. "And here you said you never heard of anything so frightening as my troubles," she scoffed. "Your experience was scary, too."

"But it was over quickly, and obviously Marcel didn't succeed in abducting me. But he revealed the truth of my heritage to Caleb and Reverend Joshua." She frowned. "Caleb and Edith were so upset—both about the lie and about the Negro blood. The fact that the blue-blooded Livingston line might have been *tainted*.... They asked Papa and me to leave."

Maggie's heart sank. Caleb had been so benevolent to her and Charlotte. She couldn't imagine the man she'd come to know being so unforgiving with Delia and her father. *Perhaps I don't know him well, after all. Maybe, like Oswald, he hides a darker side.*

"We were able to keep the secret. The Nortons know, of course... and Sheriff Granger, who arrested Marcel and ran him out of town with stern threats of imprisonment if he ever returned. But that's all."

Knocking sounded at the door.

"Our time of privacy is over." Delia rose to open the door.

"Is it safe to come inside?" Andre asked.

"Papa, Maggie and I were chatting." Delia stepped back so he could lean into the room.

Andre smiled at Maggie. "Good to see you resting. And I must do the same." He glanced at his daughter. "I came to tell you that I am returning to the hotel for a nap. I believe Reverend Joshua wants to take you for a drive in that new surrey of his."

"Oh, yes." Delia whirled and moved to the bed, her face alight. Bending over to kiss Maggie's cheek, she whispered, "I'm glad we're friends."

Her heart feeling heavy, Maggie could only nod. The Bellaires left the room, and she sank against the cushions and let her head fall back. Although relieved Caleb wasn't pining for Delia, the reason for the estrangement bothered her—both because the Bellaires were good people, but mostly because of the implication of tainted blood. *In his eyes, my blood must be tainted, too.* Not that Caleb had ever given an indication he felt that way.

But he feels responsible for me. She looked down at her daughter and began to unbutton her bodice to feed the baby. "For us."

Once again, Maggie thought of the bathhouse and realized she needed to do some serious planning for the future.

❋ ❋ ❋

The next day during school recess, his stomach sick with dread, Ben cornered Daniel Rodriquez Thompson at the side of the school as he returned from using the outhouse. He wanted to talk to the boy about borrowing his mother's buggy and team of miniature horses.

Daniel's Argentine heritage showed in his dark hair and olive skin. But he had his mother's blue eyes, which widened at the sight of Ben advancing on him. He raised his slanted eyebrows in obvious distress and took a step back. "Leave me be, Ben Grayson." He fidgeted, appearing uncertain about whether to run or stay.

They weren't alone for long. Daniel's adopted brothers saw them together and came at a run. They surrounded the younger boy, ready to protect him.

Hunter Thompson stepped in front of Daniel. The Blackfoot boy was about the same age as Ben, and he wore his hair in a long tail. The Indian wasn't one for talking, but he had a calm, confident way about him that spoke more loudly than words. In this case, the clear message was, *you will not harm my brother!*

Jack and Tim Cassidy Thompson flanked Hunter, their hands fisted. Both looked identical, except for the location of their freckles. Most of the time Ben couldn't tell them apart, probably because shame kept him from ever looking at their faces, and he interacted with them as seldom as possible. The twins had recently undergone a growth spurt, sprouting lanky arms and legs.

Today, Jack wore a blue shirt, or at least Ben thought the twin was Jack and not Tim, because the boy had sat in Jack's seat in the school-house. But the twins had been known to swap places just to play jokes on everyone, including Mrs. Gordon.

Ben held up his hands, palms outward. "I'm not here to hurt Daniel. I just wanted to talk."

Jack leaned forward, his chin at a belligerent angle. "We know your kind of talk, Ben Grayson. Cruel talk. Now leave Daniel alone."

Ben held up a placating hand. "I give you my word."

Jack sneered. "And we know how good that is."

Daniel stopped his fidgeting, shoved between his brothers, and looked Ben directly in the eyes. "You never said you were sorry."

Daniel's right. The nausea in Ben's stomach churned. He knew he'd *felt* sorry but had been too ashamed to make a formal apology. *The time has come.* He forced the words out. "I was wrong not to apologize for something I shouldn't even have done in the first place."

Tim, wearing a green shirt today, stepped forward. "Then why did you?" His green eyes held old anguish. He was the quieter twin, the one most likely to follow his brother, not lead.

For quiet Tim to speak up before Jack told of powerful feelings inside the boy that Ben felt hopeless to fix. "I don't know." He raised his hands and let them fall back.

The four Thompsons waited, skeptical expressions on their faces.

Ben peeled back an old wound and peered into himself, think-ing of that dark time. "My father died, which is why my mother and I moved to Sweetwater Springs. Instead of being with my friends in

Boston, I was here in the middle of nowhere. I remember being angry at *everyone*."

"Sure were," Daniel muttered.

Ben nodded in agreement. "But now that I think back, I realize...."
He sighed and ran a hand over his face. "Crazy as it sounds, I hoped that I would be caught." The truth tumbled out. "Then we'd return home."
He shrugged. "I can't quite explain it. Being here so far away from everything I knew, I could pretend my father was still alive in Boston, and Mother and I could go back home to him and our *real* life."

Silence settled between them as the four pondered what Ben had revealed.

Daniel was the first to lose his skeptical expression. "My father died, and I missed him lots. I kept waiting for him to come back."

Jack scuffed the dirt with his boot. "Our pa died, too. But we didn't mind. He were a mean ol' bastard."

Hunter elbowed him. "Language," he commanded.

Jack glanced around. "There's no one to hear but us." He shrugged.
"Us uns were glad to be rid of him." His speech reverting to an earlier time before they were adopted, indicated the boy was more distressed then he showed.

Tim sidled a glance at his twin. "But we missed our ma like you missed your pa." He shot a quick look at Ben. "Far worse."

As he remembered the skinny, shabby boys the twins had been, Ben's shame deepened. He knew what Tim meant. The twins' situation had been desperate, far worse than Ben's, for he had his mother and his uncle to care for him and a nice home to live in. They'd had no one and nothing. *How could I have tormented them so?*

All of them turned to Hunter, who shook his head. "Lost 'em," was all the Indian boy said in a gruff voice.

Ben didn't know Hunter's story. Nor, as far as he'd heard, did anyone else, although perhaps the Indian boy had told his adopted parents what happened to his family. But Ben supposed, given the recent news about how the Indians were starving and how vulnerable they were to the white man's illnesses, he could see losing a whole family. *Something I cannot even imagine.* His mind shuddered away from the thought of Uncle Caleb and his mother dying and leaving him orphaned.

They all stared at the ground. Five boys who shared the experience of being fatherless.

Ben straightened his shoulders and looked Tim in the eyes, and then at Jack—for the twins were the ones he'd wronged the most. "I'm very sorry for what I did—setting the fires and falsely accusing you. Almost getting you two thrown out of town."

Jack glared. "You've acted like an arrogant jerk ever since."

"Yes," Ben agreed. "A *mean* arrogant jerk." He made eye contact with Daniel and Hunter.

Daniel held up a finger to insert a point. "Not since Christmas, when you became friends with Matthew Salter. You've been kinda nice since then."

"Thanks." Ben dared a little smile, surprised he felt better—that the burden of shame he carried had lightened, even if it hadn't entirely gone away. "I've been trying to be *kinda nice*, so I'm glad it shows." He took a breath to finish what he'd started. "I don't ask for forgiveness—can't see that happening. But I've been sorry in here—" he touched his heart "—for a long time."

Christine Thompson, age eleven, came flying over. Her blonde braids bounced on her shoulders, and her blue dress fluttered behind her. "If you're being mean to my brothers, Ben Grayson, then I'm going to tell Mrs. Gordon and my father. He'll whip your fanny."

Jack tugged on her braid, apparently to stop her.

"Ow, Jack!" She swatted him.

Hunter reached over and released Jack's grip on Christine's braid. "Hold your horses, warrior girl. Ben Grayson means your brothers no harm."

She shot Ben a sideways glance, every bit as skeptical as her brothers had been.

Ben looked at her, speculating. At the time he and Arlie had set the fire and accused the twins, the Thompsons hadn't yet become a family. But Christine had already become attached to the boys and Mrs. Rodriguez and had been very distressed when all the boys ran away. "I've just apologized to your brothers for all that happened back when I first moved here. I want to tell you I'm sorry, too."

"About time." She plopped her hands on her waist. "Well." She sniffed, sounding like Mrs. Toffels, the Thompsons' housekeeper. "I suppose that's acceptable."

The boys burst out laughing. "You tell him, sis," said Daniel.

Christine preened.

With the worst part out of the way, Ben needed to focus on his goal. "We'd better get down to business before Mrs. Gordon rings the bell."

Daniel bounced on his toes. "Yah, what did you want with us, anyway?"

"I want to borrow your mother's little horses and the buggy."

"Why?" Daniel crossed his arms over his chest.

"Not for me, for my uncle. I want him to court Mrs. Baxter."

Daniel's slanty eyebrows pulled together. "Who's Mrs. Baxter?"

"She's a widow with a baby who's staying with us. Her husband was killed in an accident. I think she and my uncle are sweet on each other."

Christine's blue eyes were alight with interest. "Did you see them kissin'?"

Daniel scrunched his face. "Eew."

Ben shook his head. "Got to get them to that point first. Those Falabellas are magical or something. And, frankly, my uncle needs all the help he can get."

That brought a laugh from the Thompsons and lessened the tension between them.

Christine tilted her head in apparent thought. "I think that's a good idea."

Ben started to feel hopeful.

Daniel pursed his lips. "Your uncle's pretty big, though. Mama and Pa only go for short rides in the small buggy when the ground is dry and flat. No mud. No grass."

Ben turned to look at the street, and his spirits sank. Sunny days punctuated the rainy spring weather and started to dry the land. But soon rain or even snow swept in and created mud. "We might have to wait awhile 'til the road is right. *I hope that happens in time.* "When you ask your mother, tell her I'm wishful that the Falabellas will play cupid, but please do not say anything to Uncle Caleb. I don't think he's figured out how he feels about Mrs. Baxter. He's usually pretty sharp but not this time."

Daniel gave a decisive nod. "I'll ask Mama. I think she'll say yes. She likes when the Falabellas do their—"

"Midget magic," his siblings chorused.

Ben looked at them, puzzled.

"Pa says that to tease Mama," Christine explained. "Makes her angry. Well, not really angry, but she pretends to be. She doesn't like when he calls the Falabellas *midgets.*"

"She doesn't like *anyone* calling them midgets," Daniel said with a sage nod. "Gets her dander up."

Ben made a mental note to be careful. With a new surge of shame, he realized he'd used the term in derision before when he was still trying to cause trouble. Ben thought of the lesson he'd just learned. *Or maybe, I should just come clean.* He lowered his hands. "I've called them midgets before."

Daniel tipped his head and sent Ben an impish smile. "We know."

CHAPTER FIFTEEN

A week later, Caleb started for home early from the bank. Now that Maggie's ankle had healed, he wanted to take her to see the hotel. The day was bright with a moderate temperature, perfect for a stroll. The blue expanse of sky was clear of clouds. The sun had shone for three days, and except for a few lingering puddles, the mud had hardened to the right consistency. The ground was firm enough that one's feet didn't sink and soft enough to squish the ridges caused by wheel tracks, which when dried to clay could cause a walker to trip or teeter and turn an ankle.

Lately, he hadn't seen much of Maggie. When he was home, she spent a lot of time in the kitchen, helping Mrs. Graves. She seemed to have stopped having nightmares, or if she did, she didn't cry out and wake him. And with her new mobility, he had no excuse to remain with her at night to carry her to the bathroom or help her tend Charlotte. Caleb found he missed the intimacy of those special nights.

In the evenings, they no longer congregated in her bedroom, and the chess game had been moved downstairs. After supper, the group adjourned to the parlor, where he read the paper while Ben and Maggie played chess. Wonder of wonders, Maggie had coaxed Edith into playing the piano. Not long after his sister and nephew had moved here, she'd lost interest in her music. Even when he had downright asked her to play, she'd refused. But the power of Maggie's Gypsy magic proved to be too much for Edith's stubborn nature to withstand.

At first, his sister had played woodenly, as if by rote. But soon, he noticed the music starting to flow, and, once again, Edith played with a small smile on her face.

Caleb grinned at the memory and prepared to turn into the walkway of his home. The lilac bushes had burst into bloom, sending their sweet fragrance wafting his way. He stopped and studied them, an idea forming. *Maggie hasn't seen the backyard yet—my romantic backyard.*

He heard the sound of hoofbeats behind him and turned to see Samantha Thompson driving her small buggy pulled by two miniature horses. On her head was a man's brown cowboy hat, and auburn tendrils escaped her low bun and blew around her face. She wore a sheepskin coat and a pale blue scarf was wrapped around her neck, drawing attention to her cornflower blue eyes. She carried a bundle strapped to her front with what looked like a bedsheet.

He wondered if she'd be willing to wait a few minutes so he could go fetch Maggie to see the Falabellas.

Mrs. Thompson reined in next to him. "Good afternoon, Mr. Livingston. I hear you're in need of my horses. Magical need." Her eyes sparkled with mischief. She'd put on a little weight since the birth of her daughter in January, which became her.

Although not quite sure what she meant, Caleb wasn't about to pass up the opportunity. He bestowed his most charming smile on her. "You must have read my mind, Mrs. Thompson. I have a guest staying with me whom I've told about your little horses. She didn't believe me, so I'm challenged to produce them to prove I'm telling the truth."

Mrs. Thompson laughed. "I can do you one better. Why don't you take your guest for a drive to that fancy hotel of yours and back?"

"There you go, reading my mind again. Mrs. Baxter hasn't yet seen the hotel, and I was just planning on taking her for a stroll to see the place."

"My little Pattycake, here—" she patted the bundle on her chest that turned out to be her baby "—and I are calling on Mrs. Graves."

Caleb cocked an eyebrow. "No one visits Mrs. Graves if they can possibly help it."

A smile played about her lips. "Yes, but I intend to coax that pickle recipe out of her."

He chuckled. "Best of luck. My housekeeper doesn't easily give up her recipes. Miss Bellaire tried a few days ago to no avail."

"Mrs. Graves reticence is well known." With a maternal smile, she glanced down at her daughter before looking up. "But my Patricia has all our cowboys falling over to do her homage. I was hoping your house-keeper might also be susceptible."

Inwardly amused, he gave a mock mournful shake of his head. "I'm afraid you and Patricia are doomed to failure. Mrs. Graves has not even bent to smile at Mrs. Baxter's Charlotte, who is quite as much a charmer as your daughter."

The mischief was back in Mrs. Thomson's eyes. "I cannot accept defeat without trying."

"Far be it from me to stop you, especially if that means I can take my skeptical guest for a drive." He tipped his head toward the house. "Do you want to first come inside? Or should I bring out Mrs. Baxter?"

"I'd better go in and meet your guest. If you do take Mrs. Baxter for a ride, she can leave her baby with me. You two will be crowded enough as it is." Mrs. Thompson tied off the reins.

Caleb went around the buggy to help her out.

First, she handed him a leather satchel, which he suspected held dia-pers and other baby essentials. Previous to Charlotte, he wouldn't have noticed nor thought of such a necessity, for he never knew how much baby paraphernalia was required to take a little one out of the house.

He extended a hand, which Mrs. Thompson accepted in order to leverage herself out of the buggy without disturbing her baby.

He peered at her sleeping daughter, whom he couldn't remember seeing before. *Have the Thompsons been to church since Samantha deliv-ered, or have I just never noticed babies before?*

Patricia lay with her face turned toward Caleb. She wore a pink knitted bonnet and was wrapped in a matching blanket. The baby was noticeably bigger than Charlotte, with her mother's auburn brows and lashes. Probably the same hair color, too. Having a recollection of a very pregnant Samantha Thompson at the Christmas party, he thought the baby was about four or five months old.

He was surprised to see that even without the color differences, he would have been able to tell Patricia and Charlotte apart, no matter if both girls were the same size. *And here I thought all tiny babies looked alike.*

Carrying the satchel, Caleb opened the wrought-iron gate and ushered Mrs. Thompson up the brick walkway leading toward the front entrance. Once on the porch, he opened the front door for her. "I suspect Mrs. Baxter is helping Mrs. Graves." He waved to the hall on the left that led to the kitchen. "Would you like to leave your coat and all here?" He reached over to tap a hook on the hall tree.

Mrs. Thompson took off her hat and unwound the scarf from around her neck. She gave both to Caleb, before gently pulling off her daughter's hat and handing it over.

He set down the satchel, hung up her hat and scarf, and then extended his arms for the baby. "I can hold your daughter for you. I've become quite proficient." He sent her a self-depreciating grin. "I've had quite a bit of practice lately."

Again, Mrs. Thompson gave him a speculative glance that he couldn't read. "Best not. I don't want to wake her. If you could just help me…? The next part is tricky, at least if I want Patricia to stay asleep. I'll unbutton my coat. If you can slide it off…?"

The task involved more than the usual polite slipping a coat or shawl from around a lady's shoulders. He had to stand close and assist the woman in wiggling out of the coat. After helping Maggie give birth, this situation didn't faze him, although before that event, he would have felt self-conscious touching Mrs. Thompson's shoulders and arms. Still, he was glad her husband wasn't around to observe the intimacies.

Success at last. He took the coat and hung the garment on the hall tree. *And just in time.*

The sound of hurried footsteps coming down the hall told him quicksilver Maggie approached. Once the woman could move on her own steam, she surprised him by never walking at a slow pace. Today, she was wearing a plain white shirtwaist with the navy skirt and carrying Charlotte. Her hair was pulled back in a braided bun.

She stopped abruptly, eying Samantha Thompson with interest. "Oh, I didn't hear the door."

"We came in together," Caleb explained. "Mrs. Thompson, meet our guest, Mrs. Baxter. Mrs. Baxter, this is Samantha Thompson. She's the owner of the miniature horses I told you about. Remember how you didn't believe me?"

"I was in the middle of giving—" Maggie broke off the sentence, obviously recalling their secret about Charlotte's birth. She deliberately turned her shoulder to him, playfully slighting him. "I'm delighted to meet you, Mrs. Thompson." She eyed the sling. "That's an interesting contraption you're using."

"I need both hands for driving, so I rigged it up. So far, it's been working well. Helps to have my hands free." Mrs. Thompson waved her hands, and then leaned over to see Charlotte's face. "So pretty." She smoothed a hand over her daughter's head. "We'll have to admire each other's babies."

Maggie scrunched a face. "You'll have to admire Charlotte in a few minutes after I've changed her. She's a bit smelly at the moment."

Caleb became aware of the odor and was glad he no longer was helping Maggie change the baby. *Stinky diapers are best left to the mother.*

Samantha smiled in understanding and patted her daughter. "If you don't mind, I'll come along. I'm sure this one needs a new diaper soon, as well. We had a long drive in from the ranch. I had to bring Patricia, because the whole trip would be too long to be away from her. I didn't want to risk a hungry baby with me not there to feed her."

"You drove to town by yourself?" Maggie looked at her in astonishment as she jiggled Charlotte. "Your husband doesn't mind?"

Samantha gave her a catlike smile. "My husband doesn't *know*. My dear Wyatt does tend to be overbearing at times. He has this protective streak and often thinks he knows what's best," she said blithely. "I've found the best way to handle him is to go about my business and tell him afterward."

Maggie stilled, apparently taking in what Samantha said and comparing the Thompson's marriage to hers and Oswald's.

While Caleb approved of a woman feeling free to go about her business—women's business—he thought Samantha went too far.

A smile slowly bloomed across Maggie's face. "Mrs. Thompson, you've given me some food for thought."

Caleb inwardly groaned.

Mrs. Thompson laughed. "If that's the case, then you'll need to call me Samantha. If I'm going to be putting ideas into your head, we shouldn't be so formal." She shot Caleb an impish glance from under lowered lashes. "Isn't that right, *Mr. Livingston?*"

He held up his free hand in an *I surrender* gesture. "All right, Mrs. Thompson. You've made your point. But I stand by what I said at the time when we first met. Ranching is hard work for a woman. Running your spread by yourself would have been too much."

Maggie glanced between the two of them, her brow furrowed.

Mrs. Thompson looked at her. "When I first moved here, I applied for a loan to fix up the run-down ranch I'd inherited."

"Ahhh. I can guess what happened." Maggie narrowed her eyes at him. "Shame on you, Caleb. I can obviously see Samantha is *quite* capable."

"Yes, and very determined," Caleb said, sotto voce. "She's also married to one of the biggest ranchers around."

Samantha frowned and held up a finger. "I was starting to turn *my* ranch around *before* I married Wyatt."

Charlotte squirmed and started to cry.

Perfect timing, Charlotte. Caleb could tell neither woman appreciated the stance he'd taken on Samantha's ranch. *I stand by my decision.*

Hopefully, the babies will be enough of a distraction so their mothers wouldn't continue the topic of the evil banker. An upset Maggie will not bode well for my afternoon plans.

❋ ❋ ❋

Her red shawl wrapped around her shoulders, black hat already planted on her head, Maggie hurried down the staircase, still slightly bewildered as to how she'd just been talked into handing over her baby to a stranger. *But Samantha doesn't feel like a stranger.*

Maggie liked Samantha's combination of intelligence, warmth, and humor and was incensed by her new friend's recounting of how Caleb had denied her a loan just because she was a woman. She wondered if he was opposed to females owning any type of business. *Surely not,* she thought with a sudden feeling of anxiety. *That will not bode well for my plans about the bathhouse.*

Then she remembered: A few days ago, Caleb had brought home some candy from Sugarplum Dreams. When they'd eaten the marzipan treats, he'd praised the business acumen of the proprietor, Julia Ritter.

Once more, Maggie thought of the woman she'd left upstairs with the babies. She was awed by Samantha's strength with her husband—an *overbearing* husband. Samantha had said her opposition to her husband's dictates had sometimes resulted in fireworks between them, but the way her eyes sparkled hinted of passionate reconciliations. Maggie decided the Thompsons' relationship required more thinking.

At another time. Now Caleb's taking me for a ride in a miniature buggy.

She reached the large half landing and made the turn to take the lower stairs, grateful to move without pain.

The man himself stood at the foot of the stairs, one hand on the round newel post. He looked up.

His smile wrapped charming cords around her heart, making it difficult to breathe. *Nonsense*, Maggie told herself. *It's just this tight corset.* Still unable to catch her breath, she slowed her steps.

Caleb extended a hand to help her down the rest of the way.

His admiring look made warmth swirl in her belly.

"I was right about how good that red shawl would look on you. I'm glad you chose to wear it rather than the black."

"Well, if *you* approve, then it must be all right."

He ignored her joshing sarcasm. "Have I become the arbiter of fashion?" he asked in a tone of amusement, a smile glinting in his eyes. "I'll wager Samantha Thompson gave her approval, else you'd have come down here wearing the black."

Maggie wrinkled her nose at his astuteness but said nothing, allowing him to lead her from the house.

Outside, Caleb tucked her hand through his arm and escorted her down the brick walkway.

She could see the Falabella horses hitched to the buggy. "Oh, my." Maggie didn't dare look at Caleb, not wanting to see him gloat about correctly predicting her reaction to the miniature horses. Instead, she let go of his arm when he opened the gate then hurried through and over to the small horses—one gray, and the other brown with a black mane. "You little darlings!"

Caleb followed behind. "Chico is the brown stallion, and Mariposa is the gray mare."

Maggie stroked the head of the brown one, wishing she had a carrot.

Caleb extended a hand, cupping two halves of a carrot.

She looked up at him, astonished. "How did you know I wanted to give them a treat?"

He shrugged, but a smile played about his mouth. "With the Falabellas, it's an inevitable impulse. Few people can resist falling in love and wanting to spoil them."

Dividing the pieces into each hand, Maggie fed the two horses at the same time, and then petted and stroked them while they chomped away.

Caleb touched her arm. "Come, we are only borrowing them, so we cannot be long."

"You're right." Maggie allowed him to lead her to the passenger side and help her climb into the miniature conveyance. She smoothed her skirt and adjusted her shawl.

When he went around to the driver's side and climbed in to join her, the buggy gave a dip.

She cast him a look of alarm. "Are we going to be too heavy?"

"No. We're only going down the street to the hotel and back. The road is flat and dry."

Maggie settled back. The confines of the seat meant they nestled leg-to-leg and shoulder-to-shoulder in pleasurable closeness.

Caleb wasn't wearing gloves, and she admired the strength of his hands as he held the reins and directed the Falabellas.

For a few minutes, she watched the miniature team and marveled that such small creatures could pull them. *This is like being in a fairy tale—magical horses, a handsome prince—and I'm Magdalena, the Gypsy princess.*

The few people on the street stopped and gaped as they went by.

In her role as Gypsy princess, Maggie gave them a regal wave, similar to Edith's but with more friendliness.

"Don't mind them," Caleb said. "They're trying to figure out why we're driving the Thompson's buggy."

She suppressed a laugh. "I suppose we'll be the topic people discuss around the supper table tonight."

"Could be worse," he said, raising an eyebrow, reminding her of what they'd been through and how much greater the gossip could be.

I can't believe how much my life has changed. In some respects, I'm living a version of the Cinderella story.

Maggie could see the towering four-story hotel down the street, but as they drew closer, she was amazed by the size. The place was bigger than any building she'd ever seen. Like the office housing the newspaper, the outside gleamed with pinky-brown Sioux quartz polished to a sheen. Through archways, she could see a porch leading to the entrance.

The dirt street gave way to rough stone pavers made of the same quartz and looking clean, as if regularly swept. Lampposts lined the roadway. Caleb pulled to a stop in front of the hotel.

A young man wearing a blue uniform raced out the door and down the steps toward them.

Caleb set the brake. "My bellmen love the chance to take care of the Falabellas."

The bellman hurried to Maggie's side and helped her out. "Welcome to The Livingston, ma'am."

"Thank you," Maggie murmured, amused by the name of the hotel. *What if he was Caleb Snocklebury? Would this be The Snocklebury?* She suppressed a giggle.

Once Maggie was standing, the bellman raced around the other side to take the reins from Caleb.

"Water them, please. But we won't be long."

The young man touched his cap. "I'll take good care of them, sir."

Maggie walked around the back of the buggy and took the arm Caleb held out, grateful for her new clothes. She wouldn't have dared come near the elegant building in her old garb. With her free hand, she twitched her skirt into place. The wide waistband gave the illusion she actually possessed a waist—for even with wearing a corset tied much tighter than she was used to, she was still far too large for fashion. *Soon I'll look better.*

A second bellman held open one of the double doors for them, and they walked inside.

Maggie's first impression was of refined spaciousness. The hotel lobby was enormous, made of gleaming dark wood. Blue-patterned carpet was laid over polished wood floors. Blue velvet and tapestry wing chairs surrounded marble-topped round tables. In one corner stood the largest black piano she'd ever seen. Grand windows along the front let in light, and crystal chandeliers with thin glass bulbs hung from the ceiling, illuminating the room further. Maggie had never seen electric lights before, and she wondered what they would look like at night.

Mr. Rockwell, whom she'd met at the dinner party, stood near the base of the staircase. When he saw them, he strode over, wearing an ear-to-ear grin and radiating an air of excitement. His close-cut tawny curls looked disheveled, as if he'd run a hand through them. He flashed a smile of welcome at Maggie.

His animated demeanor astonished her, because she'd formed the impression of Mr. Rockwell as a rather solemn man.

The manager stopped in front of them and brought his hands together in a silent clasp, giving them a little shake as if in victory. His honey-brown eyes gleamed. "We have the most wonderful surprise for Reverend Joshua and Miss Bellaire's wedding."

"We do, do we?" A sardonic note imbued Caleb's tone. "Well, don't keep us in suspense, Peter. What astonishments lie in store to delight us?"

"Darlings!" a melodious voice called out from across the lobby.

With a half turn, and sweeping his arm in a commanding gesture, Mr. Rockwall indicated the staircase. "Tah dah!"

A dark-haired woman in a mauve gown, with the most enormous balloon sleeves Maggie had ever seen, stood at the railing of the upper landing, leaning forward slightly, arms outstretched in a dramatic greeting. Even from across the lobby Maggie could see her magnificent appearance. The woman brought both hands to her mouth and blew enthusiastic kisses, as if she were on a stage, acknowledging her audience.

Mr. Rockwell lowered his arm. "I bring you...*the Songbird of Chicago!*"

The woman turned from the rail and glided down the steps, the epitome of grace.

Caleb took Maggie's elbow and guided her across the room, moving in an unerring beeline toward the foot of the staircase.

Maggie had heard of the Songbird of Chicago. On Christmas Eve, the Morgans had attended the grand opening party for the hotel, where Sophia Maxwell performed. They'd returned with raving accounts of her beautiful voice.

Maggie glanced up at Caleb and was daunted by the dazzled look on his face, one she had never seen before. He sported a smile almost as big as Mr. Rockwell's. Apprehension tightened her stomach.

"Sophia," he murmured, bending to kiss her cheek. "What a wonderful surprise."

"Caleb, darling." Sophia Maxwell wore a mauve satin afternoon dress patterned with sprays of gold leaves, over a blouse of gold lace. She extended both hands, oozing sensuality and perfume. She had pale, smooth skin, and when she smiled, her teeth were like pearls. Her long-lashed violet-colored eyes sparkled up at him.

The woman had a generous bosom, with such a tiny corseted waist that Maggie wondered how she could breathe, much less move. *Rumor hasn't lied.* She'd never seen a more beautiful creature, and in Sophia Maxwell's vivid presence, Maggie felt reduced to a drab frump. A sudden impulse to scratch out those jewel-bright eyes made her curl her fingers, digging her nails into her palms.

Caleb bent and dropped a kiss on each of Sophia's dainty, smooth hands, and then leaned forward to kiss her proffered cheek.

Maggie bit back a gasp at the familiarity, which made a mockery of the intimacy she and Caleb had shared. She'd never seen him kiss the hand of any woman in Sweetwater Springs. *I believed I was special to him.* Hurt ached in her heart.

Sophia beamed up at Caleb and fluttered her long eyelashes in a way that seemed as natural to her as breathing. "How simply *divine* to see you again and stay at your lovely hotel, which is the epitome of comfort."

"Are you in need of comfort, dear Sophia?" Caleb asked, amusement in his tone. He released her hands.

"Oh, darling, we've had the most grueling run. Sold out every night," she purred with obvious satisfaction. "Blythe and I weren't sure we could get away."

"Blythe's here, too?" Caleb laughed and grinned at Mr. Rockwell. "Now I know the *real* reason for that burst of enthusiasm with which you greeted us."

Color rose in Mr. Rockwell's cheeks. "Not, not just Blythe," he stuttered out. "The wedding...."

Maggie took pity on him. Since Caleb appeared to have forgotten her, she held out a hand to Sophia. "I'm Mrs. Baxter," she said in her most amiable tone. *Two can play this game.* "My friends saw you perform at Christmas, Miss Maxwell, and they were *most* enchanted."

"Call me Sophia. I simply hate to be formal among friends. And we will be friends, I think." She directed a quizzical glance between Caleb and Maggie. "Oh, yes, indeed."

I doubt that very much.

Caleb leaned closer. "Where's Blythe?"

Sophia held up a finger in a listening motion.

In the silence, Maggie heard the faint strains of angelic-sounding music. *That must be a harp.* She wished they could move closer.

"Ah," Caleb said with a nod. "Are you two here for long?"

"My manager was doing the most tedious negotiations for my next role." A smile played about Sophia's lips. "But he finally arranged things to my satisfaction."

Caleb cocked an eyebrow. "And?"

"A week. Then, darling, I must return to rehearse for the role of Brünnhilda the Valkyrie. Nothing like a little Wagner to get the heart thumping." With a graceful flutter of both hands, she framed her head, and then smoothed her hands down her front. "Imagine me in blonde braids and a breastplate." She struck a pose, arm in the air. "And a sword."

Caleb threw back his head and laughed. "I might have to make a special trip to Chicago just to see you in that role."

"You do that, darling Caleb. And see if you can pry my sweet sister and her dear husband away from that ranch of theirs and bring them along. It's time they introduced my niece to some culture."

Caleb chuckled and glanced at Maggie. "Sophia's sister Lily married Tyler Dunn. Otherwise, we'd never get the likes of the Songbird of Chicago to our town. Her niece is about Charlotte's age. I seem to recall hearing word of her birth right before I left for Morgan's Crossing."

Sophia looked at Maggie with interest. "Ah, you have a newborn baby, too."

"Yes, my daughter is twelve days old," she said with pride.

"Oh, I envy you." Sophia clasped her hands together.

Maggie couldn't imagine why. *Any woman could have a baby. Not that I'd trade Charlotte for anything!* But Sophia seemed sincere, and she found herself drawn to the woman in spite of her envy.

"I can't *wait* to meet my niece. They named her Adeline after Tyler's mother. And Sophia—" one dainty hand drifted to her breast "—after me. I think I bought out all the baby things in every shop in Chicago. Why, that child already has her own trunk."

A bubble of laughter escaped Maggie, and she glanced up at Caleb. "But does she have a doll that's *twice* as big as she is?"

In perfect accord, Caleb's gaze met Maggie's. "I doubt it."

"I did give in and bought Adeline a doll," Sophia said, framing the shape with her hands.

I guess Charlotte wins. Maggie couldn't help a secret smile but kept the thought to herself.

The music stopped, and a few minutes later, the harpist joined them. Blythe was the opposite of her friend Sophia as could be. She was a slight woman with delicate features and pale skin. She wore her white-blonde hair loose down her back. Her misty gown flowed to her feet without a waistline or bustle. The color matched her eyes. Her smile at Caleb and Maggie appeared shy, almost childlike.

Peter looked at Blythe with his heart in his eyes.

Blythe returned his gaze. A loving expression changed her shy mien into one of womanly confidence.

Envy stabbed Maggie.

Peter took his betrothed's hand and drew her forward. "Darling, I want you to meet Mr. Livingston's guest." He performed the introductions.

With lowered eyes, Blythe touched Maggie's fingers with her free hand. She looked up with a small smile before retreating to Peter's side and, once again, exchanging a secret communication with her betrothed.

"We have news." Peter swung their hands. "We've set a wedding date of June fourteen."

"Wonderful." Caleb clapped a hand on Peter's shoulder. "Provided you take your honeymoon at the hotel."

Silence followed, and eyes wide, everyone stared at him.

Caleb laughed. "I'm joking. Between Isaac and me, the place will be covered."

The tension broke, and Peter chuckled. "You'll have quite a full house. Our relatives will be traveling out here for the week."

As they talked logistics about the hotel, Maggie's thoughts drifted to the idea of falling in love.

Most of her friends in Morgan's Crossing were happily married, but they were also well settled into matrimony. No weddings had occurred in the mining town since her and Oswald's. But since coming to Sweetwater Springs, she felt surrounded by couples smelling of orange blossoms—the wedding bouquet flower popularized by Queen Victoria. *First Delia and Reverend Joshua, now Blythe and Peter.*

In the midst of the happy congratulations, she glanced at Sophia to see a flash of what seemed like longing mirrored in the opera star's eyes. *I must be mistaken. Sophia Maxwell is beautiful, charming, wealthy, and famous. She couldn't possibly feel the same way I do.*

Maggie let out a sad breath, conscious of the irony of her situation. *Being surrounded by love only makes me aware of my own lack.*

CHAPTER SIXTEEN

On the drive home, feeling energized by meeting Sophia Maxwell, Caleb planned how he could persuade the two performers to hold a concert at the hotel later in the week. While many far-flung families might not be able to return to town so soon after the Norton wedding, he thought enough would be interested to pack the hotel's lobby.

Maggie leaned forward, looking from side-to-side, her eyes wide, her lips turned up with the hint of a smile. The drive had blown color into her cheeks, and she had a fresh loveliness—almost an innocence despite having been married—that made Sophia's beauty seem almost overblown.

Her zest for life and her appreciation for what he did for her—even when she was stubborn about accepting what he offered—was so different from the often blasé attitudes of many people in upper-class Boston, including in his own family. *Especially my own family.*

"Where are the sweet springs the town is named for?"

He grinned at her. "A commonly asked question. They are small and dot the town—both hot springs and cold ones. For example, there's a hot spring under the hotel that provides all the heated water I need for the building. Saves me quite a bit on fuel costs. I'll show you another spring when we get home."

All too soon, they reached his house. Caleb pulled into the drive and guided the Falabellas past the kitchen door and closer to the stables, near the entrance to the backyard. He pulled up and set the brake. "Now, for what I want to show you."

With an uncertain look, Maggie glanced back at the house.

He understood her need to go to her baby but wanted a bit more time with her. "Come with me for a few minutes. Then we'll go inside, and you can retrieve Charlotte."

Jed in his customary overalls came out of the stables, carrying a pitchfork. He saw them, propped the pitchfork against the side of the stable, and raised a hand in greeting. He ambled over, calling the Falabellas by name, giving their heads a quick rub and promising each a treat.

Caleb handed Jed the reins and tasked him with taking care of the tiny horses. He climbed out and walked around to help Maggie clamber from the small buggy. He didn't release her hand, but tucked her fingers around his arm, enjoying the feel of strolling together without worrying about her ankle.

A high brick wall covered with ivy, leaves unfurling, surrounded the yard. He guided her toward a gate sheltered beneath an arbor, leading into his landscaped backyard, which was as big as a small park and just as beautiful, containing a gazebo, a pond, a wishing well, and wisteria-covered arbors, all bisected by brick walkways.

He watched the wonder bloom on Maggie's face and turned to study his yard, as if seeing the place through her eyes—the red brick of the walkways, the spring green of the velvety grass, the swaths of crimson tulips and sunny daffodils, the lavender of the scented lilacs, the darker green of the low boxwood hedges, the rose garden that would later show a profusion of pink, red, and white flowers.

Caleb waved toward a fountain in the middle of the yard where a mermaid poured water from a jug. "There is one of our famous springs. I took advantage of the position and replaced a former springhouse with the fountain. With the icebox in the kitchen, we have no need for a springhouse. The spring flows into two channels that water the perimeter plants, fills a masonry tub and horse troughs in the stables, and runs into the meadow beyond the stable."

Maggie released his arm and slowly circled, taking in the view of the whole yard. "This is so lovely now. I can only imagine how beautiful everything must look when the flowers are all blooming. You must spend a lot of time out here."

Caleb thought for a moment and realized he rarely set foot in the backyard. Nor did he use the glassed-in solarium, even though the room was heated for use all year around. "Actually, I don't, especially not the last few years while the hotel was being built. Work kept me too busy, even when I was home."

"That's such a shame," she said with a shake of her head.

"You're absolutely right. Now that the hotel is open, I have less to do with the business, for Peter runs everything so efficiently. So there's no reason I can't start enjoying this space and take advantage of nice weather."

"You should."

Especially if I have the company of a fine woman like Maggie. Without thinking, Caleb reached out and stroked her cheek with the back of his hand.

Maggie's lips parted in a sigh.

His gaze lingered on her mouth, wide and sweet. A sudden hunger to kiss her made him draw Maggie close. He pressed his mouth against hers, softly, a gentle caress, not a searing kiss, for he didn't want to frighten her away.

Her hand on his arm tightened.

Caleb ran his tongue smoothly over her lips until she opened to him, making a small sound. He wanted to plunge his tongue into her mouth and deepen the kiss, to pull her against him and slide his hands over her curves, but he knew that brute of a husband had hurt her. This was only supposed to be a light flirtation, so he held back and waited for her to lead.

Maggie pulled back a few inches. Her eyes fluttered open, dark and luminous, the gold flecks sparkling in the sun. She swallowed and moistened her lips. She studied his face. Her generous mouth trembled, and then her lips turned up. "Why did you kiss me?"

"Because *I* enjoyed *your* enjoyment in our drive today. I know how seldom pleasures come your way, and I was glad to give you the experience. Because I lack appreciation of my blessings...." *Because you are mine.*

Caleb didn't *want* to delve deeper inside himself to find his true feelings, so he resorted to some light banter. He touched the tip of her nose with one finger. "This is the month of May. A man is supposed to steal kisses in May."

❋ ❋ ❋

Maggie's marriage had taught her well how to conceal her real feelings. Now, she tried to draw the familiar cloak of stoicism around her—to hide her response to what Caleb blithely called *stolen kisses*, which to her had felt like so much more. Somehow, she had to suppress the bubbling awareness of her physical response—that pure blissful moment in his arms, the tingles in her body, the sensations he'd created with his mouth and tongue and hands. *I didn't know kissing could feel like this.*

Caleb held out an arm and lifted his chin toward the house. "Let's go see how Charlotte is faring with Samantha."

Nodding, she took his arm. Maggie's body was still edgy, aching for more of Caleb's touch. She couldn't yet speak.

He escorted her up the walkway toward the house, from time to time glancing downward, apparently to see if she was all right.

Maggie had as much as she could do to manage a gliding stride next to him that indicated everything was normal.

They entered the side door of the glass-paneled solarium, filled with wicker furniture and potted plants. White wooden lattice panels in a filigree pattern ran along the top of the glass. A bronze-and-glass chandelier hung from the middle of a peaked glass roof.

Normally, Maggie would have stopped to stare at such a beautiful room. Instead, she moved with him across the brick floor to the inner door of the house.

Hearing female voices from the parlor, she let go of his arm and came into the room. Edith and Samantha sat on the settee, a tray on the butler's table in front of them laden with a plate of cookies and one of small sandwiches. The delicate aroma of China tea wafted into the air.

Even after two weeks of living here, drinking tea was still a luxury for Maggie. But now she focused on Charlotte in Edith's arms and moved toward her, assessing the baby's well-being.

Charlotte seemed fine. Her eyes were wide, arms waving.

Baby Patricia sat on Samantha's lap, gnawing a crust. Both looked at Maggie and smiled. Without being bundled up in their outdoor garments, the resemblance between mother and daughter was astonishing—especially the red hair and sky-blue eyes.

Edith welcomed them before looking down at Charlotte. "And here's your mama, sweet girl." She lifted the baby to Maggie.

"Thank you both for taking care of her." Maggie took her daughter into her arms, feeling as if her tilted world had just righted. She dropped a kiss on the downy head and inhaled Charlotte's baby smell before turning to Samantha. "Your Falabellas are delightful. We've had the most marvelous outing. I can't thank you enough." Determined to pretend nothing had just happened between them, she cast a grateful glance at Caleb. "Thank you both."

Samantha gave Maggie a knowing smile. "Yes, my little ones are delightful. Almost magical at times, I think."

Caleb placed a hand on Maggie's back, guiding her toward a blue wingchair. "Let me bring you some tea." He walked to his sister and watched her pick up the teapot and fill a cup.

"Would you like sandwiches or cookies?" Edith asked Maggie.

She shook her head. "I'm fine, thank you. I enjoyed some of Mrs. Graves's soup a while ago."

Edith handed the cup and saucer to her brother, who set it down on a small table beside Maggie.

Caleb accepted a cup for himself and took a seat across from her in the other blue wingchair. "We learned some interesting news." He glanced at Maggie, eyebrows pulling together. "Although, I'm not sure if it's supposed to be a surprise."

Maggie thought of Sophia's dramatic entrance—one that any person in the lobby would notice. "I think not."

Caleb took a sip of tea, apparently prolonging the suspense. "Sophia Maxwell and Blythe Robbins are visiting for a week and are to perform at the wedding."

Maggie watched Caleb's face light up as he spoke. Once again, she wondered about his feelings for the Songbird of Chicago. *Was that the reason he kissed me? Was he thinking of her?*

"The other news is, Peter and Blythe have set a wedding date for June."

Both women exclaimed in pleasure.

"Well—" Samantha leaned over and picked up a tiny coat "—I'd best be going before my husband sends the cavalry out after me." She slid Patricia's arm into the sleeve.

Caleb rose. "I'll ask Jed to bring the Falabellas around."

Edith stood and picked up the plate of cookies. "I'll have Mrs. Graves pack these so you can take them with you for the children."

"You're very kind," Samantha murmured.

By unspoken agreement, they waited until the sound of both pairs of footsteps died away.

Samantha leaned close. "I declare, Maggie Baxter, you must be a witch. I was *shocked* when my children came home the other day and told me Ben Grayson had actually apologized to Daniel and the others for how he'd treated them." Tears welled in her eyes, and she smoothed her daughter's hair. "Daniel was bouncing with joy. Well," she amended, "Daniel is always bouncing. But that conversation was obviously healing for his spirits."

"Caleb told me the story about what Ben did to your sons," Maggie murmured.

"So I hastened here to meet you, for I couldn't imagine what else caused Ben to make the peace overture. The recipe from Mrs. Graves was only an excuse for me to call."

The women exchanged knowing glances about the grumpy housekeeper.

"Then I see that you've bespelled those two, as well." Samantha waved a hand toward the door. "I've never seen them act so pleasant—in a genuine way."

"Whatever do you mean?"

"To be frank, they aren't the warmest people. Yet, to my surprise, I've actually enjoyed my visit today. I've never seen Edith be so hospitable, nor Caleb so…so…." Samantha shook her head. "I can't even find the right word. He's usually so *bankerish*."

Maggie laughed. "That's all Charlotte's doing. She's captivated everyone."

Samantha laughed. "Well, I can understand that. My Pattycakes has won the heart of everyone on the ranch, even the most curmudgeonly cowboys. And her sister and brothers adore her. The way this baby is carried around, she might never learn to walk. She'll go straight from humans to a pony."

Maggie chuckled but couldn't help a pang that Charlotte wouldn't have a similar experience with a big family's love.

But I will love her so deeply and fiercely she will never know the lack.

Even as she thought the words, Maggie knew their untruth. She'd been loved, yet she had still wished for a bigger family, especially after her father died, followed by his parents and her mother, and finally her grandmother. *If I had sisters and brothers, my daughter and I wouldn't be alone.* "You are so blessed to have a large family."

"And so I tell myself every day. And I give thanks to the Lord for my good fortune." Samantha pulled the knit cap over the baby's head. "But…a family is not just people who are bound by blood or marriage, although that is the most common. Families can also be made. I have three adopted sons and a stepdaughter whom I love as dearly as the two I gave birth to. And the children love one another and squabble and play together just the same as any siblings."

Yet to create such a family also takes money. Maggie knew she'd struggle to provide for the one chick she had and had no financial means to adopt more.

Samantha glanced at the door and back toward Maggie, lowering her voice. "I will say, I think the softening in *this* family is from more than just Charlotte's influence. *Both* of you have played a part of the mellowing of Caleb, Edith, and Ben." With a final mischievous glance at Maggie, she finished dressing her daughter and stood. "I'll see you at the wedding. I'd say we'll probably have a chance to talk then, but I'm sure the event will be a madhouse, and we'll be lucky to have even a few words."

Caleb returned, carrying Samantha's outerwear and satchel, the scarf, and knotted baby sling draped over one arm. "The buggy awaits." He set the satchel on the floor and offered Samantha the coat. "Shall we trade?"

Samantha gave Maggie a sidelong glance that clearly said, *see, I told you he's changed.* She handed over her daughter and accepted the coat in exchange.

Maggie rocked Charlotte, suppressing a chuckle at Samantha's reaction to Caleb's assistance with Patricia. But she also had difficulty in seeing Caleb as any way but warm, generous, and good with baby girls.

As if to prove her point, the man deftly took Patricia into his arms. The baby stared at him, her eyes wide. Then her face puckered.

"Oh, no you don't," Caleb teased, bouncing her and speaking in a gentle voice. "My reputation is at stake."

The baby's eyes widened, and her face cleared, but she didn't go so far as to break into a smile. She turned her head toward her mother and held out a hand.

Samantha, already in her coat and knitted hat, lifted the scarf and baby carrier from around Caleb's arm. She wrapped the scarf around her neck, looped the knotted sheet over her head and one shoulder, and pulled mittens from her coat pocket, tugging them onto her hands. "I'll take her back, if you'll haul my satchel outside."

Caleb made the exchange.

Samantha leaned over and gave Maggie a kiss on the cheek. "You two stay here, where it's warm," she ordered. "I'll see you soon."

"Good-bye." Impulsively, Maggie laid a hand on Samantha's arm. "Thank you again for everything."

With a smile, the woman left.

Maggie sank back into her chair, envying Samantha her happy marriage and her big family. She kissed the top of Charlotte's head, suddenly feeling tired. She shifted and her hip panged, indicating she'd probably done too much today. She leaned her head back, replaying Caleb's kiss. *So soft, and yet...there was male need there, too.* She tried to yank away her thoughts. *No sense in wishing the kiss meant as much to him as it did to me,* she lamented. *That way only leads to hurt.*

Edith entered the room, followed by Caleb. A smile played about her lips. "Maggie, we have something to show you. A surprise. Let's go up to your bedroom."

"Here, let me." Caleb reached for her daughter. "I haven't had my time with her yet."

Maggie placed Charlotte in his arms.

With a fatuous smile, Caleb bent over the baby. "Hello, my sweet."

Charlotte shook her arms and kicked her legs, obviously happy to see him.

Maggie's heart turned over.

"Come along, you two," Edith ordered. "I want Maggie to see her surprise before the light starts to fade."

Maggie obediently followed the other woman out of the parlor and up the stairs. She paused at the half landing, leaning over the rail to look down at Caleb and her daughter.

As Caleb walked with the baby, he appeared to be having a low-voiced conversation with her.

Charlotte looked fully engrossed in gazing at his face.

With a smile, Maggie shook her head and picked up her skirts. But she couldn't help a stab of worry at how the baby had become attached to Caleb. *Surely Charlotte's too young to miss him when we leave.*

She continued upstairs and into the bedroom to see two dresses spread over the bed—one a grape purple so dark it was almost black, and the other a lovely red. She gasped and immediately coveted both of them.

Caleb came in behind her. He shifted Charlotte to one arm and touched the purple dress. "They are for you, Maggie. What do you think?"

The dark purple gown had a black velvet collar, cuffs, and a *V* belt with black lace over the bodice and around the hem. Three tiers of frills cascaded from the shoulders, a much softer look than balloon sleeves. "I couldn't accept such a generous gift."

He fiddled with the cuff of the sleeve and barreled on, as if she hadn't objected. "I know the color is not deep mourning, and if this were Boston, of course, you'd wear black—if you attended the wedding at all. But here we aren't so strict."

I'd wear yellow in celebration if I didn't care what people thought. But I do have Charlotte to consider.

"Some of us adhere to proper ways," Edith said in frigid tones, her facial expression tight, back and shoulders straight.

Oh, dear, Edith is in need of Charlotte's magic again. Maybe I should have Caleb give the baby back to her.

"Yes, sister," Caleb said in a placating tone. "I know when Nathaniel died you wore black for longer than a year. But you did start wearing colors when you and Ben moved out here."

His comment apparently mollified Edith, for her whole body softened. She sent an apologetic glance in Maggie's direction. "I know your marriage was different than mine with my dearest Nathaniel, and I agree with my brother's assessment of the situation."

A lump formed in Maggie's throat. As each day had passed since Oswald's death, and she'd been treated with consideration and care by the people of Sweetwater Springs—especially these two—she'd realized more and more how much her husband had mistreated her.

Caleb brushed a hand over the skirt of the red dress. "This one is for later, after a few months go by. When I saw the fashion plate, I knew the color would suit you, and I ordered it."

The crimson hue attracted her. The sleeves were full at the shoulders, but they didn't have fat puffs. The high-necked red bodice had an overdress of wide lapels with broad black lace. The cuffs and collar were trimmed in black braid. A line of wide black braid ran from each hip to the hem. A second row dripped with black lacy fringe that made a *V* from the knees to meet in the middle near the hem. In between, a fan shape of black appliqués ended in a point at the bottom of the *V*.

Caleb gave her a look of boyish expectation as different from a blasé expression as could be. "Will you try on this one, Maggie? Just so we can see you in it?"

She could no more resist that appeal than she could ignore one of Charlotte's needs. She glanced at Edith, silently asking the other woman's opinion. After all, she'd been the one who'd seemed to disapprove of the presents he'd purchased on the day they'd arrived.

Edith smiled and made a little shooing motion at her brother. "Out with you. I'll play ladies maid for Maggie."

Caleb didn't move, only watched Maggie, his dark eyes hooded, as if brooding.

Her throat tight, she could only nod, and then quickly she looked away.

He rubbed a hand on Charlotte's back and left.

Once the door closed behind him and the baby, Edith gestured for her to remove her clothing.

Maggie did as commanded, feeling self-conscious about standing in front of the other woman in only her undergarments.

"Let me tie your corset strings tighter." Edith reached for Maggie's waist but paused halfway, awaiting permission.

"Go ahead."

Edith unlaced the ties. "Breathe in; then breathe out." She waited for Maggie's exhale and yanked on the strings.

The whalebones of the stays cut into her sides.

"Your waist has gone down a bit," Edith observed. "And the rest of you is filling out nicely."

"Mrs. Graves's good cooking," she said lightly. *Abundant food will do that.* Too often, Maggie had stinted on her portions, because there wasn't enough for her and Oswald to both eat well.

Once pregnant, though, she hadn't been quite as generous, knowing her body needed nourishment for the baby growing within her. Still, she'd worried that she hadn't eaten enough, that the baby would suffer for the lack of food during the pregnancy, and afterward when she nursed. The lavish meals Maggie had partaken of while she'd been living as a member of Caleb's household had been a godsend. She'd felt tremendous relief that Charlotte benefited in these first vulnerable weeks and refused to worry about how she would provide sustenance for her daughter in the future.

Worry after the wedding. The few times she'd hinted to Caleb about needing to move out, he'd changed the subject or had told her she first needed to heal or be stronger. Maggie had given herself a cut-off date for remaining at the Livingston mansion.

I'm healed. I'm strong. Somehow, the thought didn't bring the relief it should have.

Edith helped her slip on the red dress and work the fastenings.

Maggie felt like a mannequin, or maybe a little girl playing dress-up. *No, playing dress-up was fun. This is awkward. If I refuse the gorgeous dresses as my pride wants to do, I will hurt Caleb, as well as possibly insulting Edith.* She couldn't do that to the two people who'd already done so much for her.

Edith stepped back. "Oh, my. I never would have believed the transformation if I hadn't seen it for myself." She turned Maggie around so she could stand in front of a full-length looking glass.

Maggie stared in disbelief at the sophisticated stranger in the mirror who hadn't been there earlier.

"Well?" Edith prompted. "What do you think?"

Is that really me?

Edith whirled and hurried to the door, flinging it open. "You can come in now."

Caleb carried Charlotte inside.

Slowly, Maggie turned to face him, feeling self-conscious.

The appreciative look in his eyes filled her with feminine power, and she lifted her chin and straightened her shoulders.

"You look stunning." He held up Charlotte. "Look, my sweet, see how lovely your mama is."

Maggie blushed and looked away, catching sight of herself in the mirror—the sophisticated stranger—as grand a lady as Edith Grayson or Prudence Morgan. A wave of despair washed over her. *This isn't me. This is only Gypsy Maggie clothed in fine feathers.* A wide social gulf still lay between them.

Wearing a gown like this made it all too easy for Maggie to hope, which she knew would only lead to hurt.

I need to move out soon!

CHAPTER SEVENTEEN

After a sudden snowstorm made uncertainty about the wedding buzz through the town, the weather cleared. Four sunny days ensured people came into Sweetwater Springs from near and far to attend the wedding of the son of their beloved minister and his wife. The day before the ceremony, guests descended on the hotel and Mrs. Murphy's boarding house or stayed with friends.

Mack Taylor opened the livery to those folk who'd traveled a long ways and were too poor to pay for a room but who were willing to sleep in the hay, bundled next to each other in their blankets like kernels on a corncob.

In the early morning hours, a crowd of workers hired by Andre Bellaire, as well as volunteers, transformed the church into a bower of white roses and greenery and made an archway of the same outside the church door. A large arrangement of flowers bloomed on the altar, now covered with a gold cloth, and swags of flowers and greenery lined the windows and the aisle side of the pews.

As a surprise wedding gift for his son-in-law, Andre had commissioned a stained-glass window for the church. The day before, Reverend Joshua had been sent on a pastoral errand out of town for several hours, ensuring the secrecy of the installation. Because the window was on the front of the church facing away from the street, word was the younger minister hadn't yet spotted the new addition.

Set behind the altar, the large window took the shape of a pointed arch, and the background of pale glass looked mauve in some light, pink at other times of the day, and showed gold as the sun set. A simple cross in bluish-purple glass in the center drew the eye. One line of gold and orange and a second of blue and green bordered the sides of the work of art. The bottom showed two panels, each containing mystical symbols, flanking a middle one that contained a wreath of olive leaves circling the date of 1896.

The wedding was scheduled for two o'clock, but those who hadn't spent the night drove or walked into town hours early, clustering under the oak tree beside the school. Trestle tables covered with white cloths and vases of flowers were set up for a community meal, with food provided by Andre and catered by the hotel kitchen. In addition, all the housewives for miles around had contributed their specialties. The area quickly took on the air of a festival as friends congregated, people ate and talked, and children played the sedate games authorized by their elders, who'd commanded their offspring to remain looking as spiffed up as possible.

The bride was sequestered in the parsonage with Mrs. Norton, and Reverend Joshua mingled with the townsfolk. Micah remained at his side instead of playing with the other children. Obviously the boy's father wasn't taking a chance on his mischievous son getting dirty before the ceremony.

At Caleb's insistence, Maggie left her sleeping baby with him while she went to keep Delia company, although she made him promise to come get her if Charlotte became fussy.

Maggie hurried to the parsonage, careful to hold the skirt of her purple gown off the ground. She loved the sound of the taffeta rustling with each step, making her feel sophisticated, and she moved among the throngs—more people than she'd ever seen together—with her head held high and her shoulders back.

As she passed, Maggie exchanged greetings with acquaintances, surprised by how many people she recognized. After the crowd, the quiet area around the small parsonage was a relief. She knocked on the door. "Delia, it's Maggie," she called.

Mrs. Norton opened the door, peering out to make sure Maggie was alone. She wore a navy-blue shirtwaist and skirt, with full, long sleeves, a high collar and cuffs of ivory lace, and ivory appliqués along the hem.

"Why, Mrs. Norton, how lovely you look," Maggie said, stepping inside at Mary Norton's gesture.

Pink flooded the woman's wrinkled cheeks. "My son and Delia insisted I have a new gown." She gave an anxious flutter with her hands. "Even though I didn't really need one, because Joshua outfitted me quite extravagantly when he returned from Africa."

Maggie grasped the woman's hands. "Dear Mrs. Norton, from what I know of you *and* from what I've heard, you are as close to a saint as a Christian woman can be. I have no doubt you deserve to look your finest."

"Oh, no, dear, I'm not a saint," Mrs. Norton protested as she ushered Maggie into the parlor.

Taking a leaf from Caleb's book, Maggie ignored her protests. "Life is not all about denial and charity. Reverend Joshua wouldn't encourage you to have a new dress if he didn't feel it was right. And with a husband for a minister…why, Reverend Norton would put his foot down, too. So, having the approval of both men of the cloth, I think you should enjoy the feminine feeling of a pretty new dress." She spoke from recent experience.

Mrs. Norton squeezed Maggie's hands. "Well, if you think so, Mrs. Baxter—"

"And so Reverend Joshua and I have been telling her," Delia called from inside the parlor.

Mrs. Norton stepped aside so Maggie could see the bride standing in front of a full-length mirror that must have been moved from a bedroom for Delia's use. The parlor's gold wallpaper reflected sunlight from the windows to shimmer over the bride. The scent of roses and orange blossoms from the enormous bouquet resting on the sofa permeated the air.

Delia placed her hands on her hips. "But does Mother Norton listen to us?" she asked in a playful haranguing tone. "Or to her husband or my father? *No.* Then you come along and tell her the same thing about her new dress, and she decides to listen."

"Oh, no, dearest." Mrs. Norton touched Delia's cheek. "I *have* been listening. But you all are my family. Mrs. Baxter is an impartial member of our congregation."

Maggie shook her head. "I'm sorry to report that you have *no* impartial members of your congregation," she said, deadpan.

"No?" Mrs. Norton gave her a puzzled look.

Maggie couldn't help but chuckle before leaning in to hug the woman. "No one is impartial because everyone adores you."

"Oh, Mrs. Baxter, you flatter me." Pink flushed her wrinkled cheeks. "Now, I really must go out and see that everything is in order in the church. I'll return before the ceremony." She slipped from the room.

Maggie turned her attention to her friend.

Delia was an exotic vision. At first glance, her wedding gown looked deceptively simple, which was probably appropriate for a minister's wife. The unembellished body of the dress was made of cream satin brocade, with a high, square neck edged with small scoops of lace. The sleeves were plain satin, made spectacular by their puffed shape, and then along her forearms the satin fit tightly. The fabric belled out at her wrists, where froths of lace fell to midway down Delia's hands. A brocade train several feet in length trailed behind the gown.

"You look so beautiful!" Maggie rushed over and gave Delia a hug, careful not to crease the material or muss her hair. "Like a princess. I love your dress."

Delia leaned over to whisper, "A copy of Worth's, although the balloon sleeves are smaller because Joshua doesn't approve of—" she deepened her voice "—those ridiculous shapes that make a woman look like she's carrying a bag of flour on each shoulder. And they are a waste of material at that."

The two laughed together.

"I have to agree with him," Maggie admitted. "I was quite startled the first time I saw Mrs. Morgan's new dress for her daughter's christening party. Then Mrs. Walker and Mrs. Sullivan showed up in balloon sleeves, as well, although theirs weren't as big as Mrs. Morgan's. And hers weren't as broad as those of Miss Maxwell." She shook her head, indicating disbelief. "I saw her at Caleb's—Mr. Livingston's—hotel the other day. She is stunning, really. But in a good wind, our Songbird might inadvertently fly away."

"I look forward to hearing Miss Maxwell sing." Delia raised her hands to touch a lovely tiara of pearls that matched her necklace and earrings, and the long froth of lace fell back over her wrists. "I've already discovered that as beautiful as this looks, this lace is *most* impractical. The edges keep getting in my way. I don't know why I didn't think to have the dressmaker alter the length. I don't dare eat anything later, for the lace will trail in my food."

"I have pins in my reticule. We can rescue your lace so you can eat, and then unpin everything when you're finished."

"How sensible you are, Maggie! A splendid idea."

"We can't have you fainting away from hunger," Maggie teased. "Plus, you'll need to fortify yourself for the night to come."

Dusky rose flooded Delia's olive skin. She touched the frills at Maggie's shoulders. "I'm not the only one who looks elegant," she said, obviously changing the subject.

"Quite a shock to see myself in the looking glass this morning." Maggie smoothed the skirt. "I never even imagined wearing such a gown."

A knock sounded on the door.

"Come in," Delia called.

Sheriff Granger stepped into the parlor, hat in hand. She wore the same suit as on the previous Sunday, but her braid was wrapped in a high crown that would fit under the hat. She held a telegram in her hands. Her cool gray eyes warmed as she surveyed the two women. "I ran into Mrs. Norton outside, and she told me to come on in."

Maggie couldn't help wondering what the sheriff thought of their dresses. *Does she ever wear them or wish she could?* Feeling the tightness of her corset, Maggie wondered about the tradeoff of fashion for comfort. As much as she loved her dress and how pretty and feminine she felt in it, she could do without the corset tied as tight as possible to give her thick waist the illusion of slenderness. But her mind couldn't stretch to wearing trousers, comfortable as they might be.

She held a telegram aloft. The genuine joy in the sheriff's smile made her look attractive.

Maggie hadn't seen that smile before, and she wondered how many people had witnessed a happy expression on the woman's face.

Sheriff Granger waved the paper. "If I could have a private moment." She looked from Delia to Maggie and back. "I've a wedding present from me to you and Reverend Joshua that I think will give you peace of mind from a certain...."

Delia's eyes widened. "I've told Maggie *everything*. You may speak freely in front of her."

"Well, then." The sheriff handed over the telegram and motioned for Delia to go ahead and read.

Delia glanced down, scanned the message, and sucked in a sharp breath, her eyes filling. "How did you know I was worried?"

Worried about what? Maggie wondered. "Is everything all right?"

Delia waved the telegram in front of her like a fan. "Sheriff Granger brought word that Marcel Dupuy is in New Orleans, and I don't have to worry about him showing up today. I've had nightmares of him striding up the aisle to denounce me in the middle of the ceremony."

Maggie gave the sheriff an admiring glance. "However did you find out about that horrible man?"

"My father, Big John Granger, was a lawman for many years. He attended West Point before the war. He was...." Her voice thickened. "A man of great conviviality and heart. A man of integrity."

Maggie's throat tightened in sympathy, knowing the bittersweet pain of missing a beloved father.

"Big John formed many friendships that even the war couldn't destroy, although he and many of his classmates fought on opposite sides. Then, too, during the war, he had his own command. Afterward, he stayed in touch with *everyone*. I have a thick ledger with the names and addresses of men and some women all over the country, as well as a big box of his correspondence. After I shipped Dupuy out of town, it wasn't hard to find someone in New Orleans who'd keep an eye on the scoundrel. My contact dropped by yesterday to check that Dupuy was sitting tight and wouldn't be causing trouble for us."

Delia's tears spilled over. She extended a hand.

With an uncomfortable expression, the sheriff clasped hers.

"Thank you from the bottom of my heart." Delia squeezed Sheriff Granger's hand. "And I know my dear Reverend Joshua will feel the same. We are blessed to have you here in Sweetwater Springs to keep the law and protect us."

The sheriff pulled away. "Just doin' my job, Miss Bellaire," she drawled.

Maggie shook her head. "I've lived in several towns, Sheriff. Traveled through many others in a Gypsy caravan, which tends to bring the law sniffing around to make sure we weren't making off with anyone's chickens," she said tartly. "So I'm familiar with what passes for authority. I agree with Delia."

A faint flush made the sheriff lift her hat and lower it over her braided bun, pulling down the brim to shade her face. "I'd be checking out a Gypsy caravan, too, Mrs. Baxter. And keeping my eye on the inhabitants," she commented in a matter-of-fact voice.

Maggie wanted to say a sharp retort in defense of her mother's people, but she was also her father's daughter and knew the sheriff was right to be vigilant. "Keeping an eye out is one thing," she said stiffly. "Running us out of town when we haven't done anything wrong is another."

The sheriff nodded. Her gaze swung to Delia. "No frettin' now. At least not about unsavory types. I'll keep watch."

"We are in good hands," Delia said in a sincere tone. "And from now on, Sheriff Granger, Reverend Norton and I will keep you in our prayers every day."

"Thank you, ma'am. There might come a time when I'll need them." She turned on her heel and left the room, her boot heels clicking down the hallway.

Delia heaved a sigh that seemed to come from her very depths. "In only a year, *everything* has changed for me, Maggie. Sometimes I have a difficult time believing how much. I've been afraid the bubble would burst, and my marriage would never take place. But now, I can relax and enjoy this day."

"I know what you mean by your life changing," Maggie said in a wry tone. "Like slipping on ice and not knowing how you're going to land, but you know it will be hard and will hurt."

Delia raised her eyebrows. "I think *someone* caught you before you hit the ground," she pointed out. "You might remember him—tall, handsome, dark hair and eyes, banker, hotel owner? A man whom I've seen smile more in the last few weeks than in all the months I've known him put together. Not to mention carrying a baby around just like a doting father. Anyone like that come to mind?"

Oh, yes. Maggie knew she was falling hard, and the ground was rushing up to meet her.

❋ ❋ ❋

The church was packed as full as could be, with only the aisle and an area around the altar free of people. Latecomers crowded outside the open windows to see inside. A breeze wafted the scent of roses from the window arrangements and combined with the pleasant smells of perfume, soap, and horse. The sunlight shining through the new stained-glass window cast a soft pink light over the front area and elicited gasps and excited comments from almost everyone entering the building.

In a middle pew, Caleb was crammed shoulder to shoulder with Edith and Maggie—not that he minded being so close to Maggie—he just would have preferred some space. *Maybe I should have offered to remain outside or stand in the back.*

The sounds of rustling movement, throat clearing, and low-voiced conversations stilled when Elizabeth Sanders, dressed in a teal-and-lace gown of the latest fashion and with a matching hat on her expertly coiffed blonde head, moved up the aisle. The color enhanced her sophisticated blue-eyed beauty, yet Caleb felt not even a tinge of attraction for the woman he'd once courted.

Sophia Maxwell, resplendent in lavender and wearing amethyst-and-diamond jewelry, accompanied Elizabeth to the piano, where she pointed to something on the sheet music. Even distracted by her discussion with the pianist, the opera singer exuded charisma.

As if he were studying a masterpiece painting, Caleb admired the lovely Songbird of Chicago. He looked forward to hearing her magnificent voice raised in song, but the opera singer no longer dazzled him as she once had.

Blythe Robbins, clad in a medieval-type gown of flowing silvery blue, her white-blonde hair loose down her back, trailed them by a few yards. A dapper young man with a violin tucked under his arm and an older woman in gray and black who carried a flute followed behind Blythe. Once at the front, Blythe moved to sit in front of her harp, arranging her skirts to accommodate her instrument.

Reverend Norton escorted his wife to a reserved seat in the front pew. Both wore new clothes and joyful expressions.

The minister stepped in front of the altar, picked up his prayer book, and turned to face the congregation. His white-bearded countenance shone. His vivid blue gaze swept the room, seeming to make eye contact with each person, clearly welcoming all those of his flock. Not a person present, from both the town and the surrounding countryside, had failed to be touched by his ministry—through Sunday service, weddings, births, deaths, sick calls, distribution of needed clothing and supplies, counsel for the heavy-hearted, or pastoral visits to check on the isolated folk who rarely came to town.

Reverend Norton must be ecstatic to have almost everyone he serves gathered for this marriage.

The groom, his son Micah by his side, strode up the aisle. Both were clad in fashionable dark blue suits. Micah sat down next to his grandmother, and Reverend Joshua took a place beside his father. The two of them exchanged a few low-voiced and obviously sentimental words.

Caleb couldn't count how many weddings he'd witnessed, both in the West and in Boston. Like most men, he attended the ceremonies out of obligation, rather than considering them the special occasions that women seemed to feel they were. In the last years, a few weddings— such as Elizabeth Hamilton's to Nick Sanders—had been a downright annoyance, which he would have preferred to skip.

So he didn't expect Delia and Reverend Joshua's ceremony— although the fanciest ever held in Sweetwater Springs—to be much different.

But it was.

The moment Blythe plucked the harp strings, sending the first strains of "O Perfect Love" resonating through the church, a wave of emotion flooded Caleb, the force strong enough to shake him to his soul. The piano joined the harp, and his heart beat to the musical notes. The twining of the violin and flute sent goose bumps washing over his arms.

What is this? Caleb took careful inhales and exhales to regain his equilibrium but to no avail, for Sophia's magnificent voice rose above the music, and the tide of heightened sensation continued. "O perfect love, all human thought transcending...."

Throughout the ceremony, Caleb struggled to hold his emotions at bay. But, for once, logic failed to order his thoughts or calm the thumping of his heart. Striving to find a sense of balance, he listed all that was different about this wedding from any other he'd attended, imagining himself ticking the points off on his fingers.

Tick one: The force of his feelings must stem from knowing Delia and Reverend Joshua better than he did anyone else in Sweetwater Springs outside his family and Peter Rockwell. After all, he'd been a witness to the courtship that had taken place in his own home during Andre Bellaire's convalescence. He'd quarreled with them and lately made up. They knew his and Maggie's secrets, and he knew theirs. Caleb had shared with Reverend Joshua as he'd done with no other man.

Tick two: Surely his emotions intensified from seeing the happy tears flowing down Andre Bellaire's face as he escorted his daughter up the aisle. Certainly there were enough teary sniffs sounding throughout the church, and handkerchiefs coming out of sleeves, pockets, and reticules to lend credence to this point.

Tick three: The bride's glowing beauty stalled the breath in his chest. Delia was a vision in shimmering cream. Many gasped at the sight of her.

Tick four: As he watched the approach of his bride, the love on Reverend Joshua's face made Caleb's chest tighten. He looked away, unable to bear the sight of so much vulnerability.

Tick five: The tremor in Reverend Norton's voice as he spoke the words *"Dearly Beloved"* sent a shiver through Caleb, and he clenched his fists to still the tremor.

Tick six: The love and goodwill emanating from the congregation was so heavy it prickled the hairs on the back of his neck.

Tick seven: He knew both Joshua and Delia had already suffered, so the couple had a greater knowledge when vowing "for better or for worse" than most couples who cleaved to each other in matrimony.

Charlotte made a sound, and Caleb glanced down at the mother and child who'd become so dear to him.

Maggie looked up at him. Tears brightened the gold flecks in her eyes. Her lips quivered into a smile, and she moved her hand to brush his in a brief acknowledgment of their shared emotion.

The warmth from her touch lingered on his skin and broke the logical bonds he'd been forging to shackle his feelings. As he gazed into her eyes, his throat closed and his heart squeezed. In that moment, Caleb realized *Maggie* was the reason for the greatness of his emotion.

I love her.

CHAPTER EIGHTEEN

After the ceremony, when Reverend Norton had pronounced his son and daughter-in-law man and wife, Blythe began to play the harp. To the heavenly strains, the couple moved down the aisle, an excited spring in their steps. The new Reverend and Mrs. Joshua Norton both wore glowing smiles.

The newlyweds passed from the church, and then the elder Nortons walked down the aisle, followed by Andre and Micah. The rest of the congregation stood to leave.

Ben and Edith hastened out of the pew, and the people sitting on Maggie's other side left via the outer aisle.

In no hurry to move from where she sat, Maggie shifted her sleeping daughter, who'd grown heavy, to give her arm some rest. She also needed time to allow the powerful emotions she'd experienced during the wedding—especially the moment of intense eye contact with Caleb—to subside.

Caleb, who seemed absorbed in watching Sophia Maxwell, must have caught Maggie's movement, for he looked at her and smiled. "I've never heard Mendelssohn's "Wedding March" played with only a harp. Blythe is immensely talented."

"She is. *Such* beautiful music. And Miss Maxwell was glorious." Maggie dropped the singer's name in a prod to test Caleb's reaction.

"Indeed, we are quite spoiled to have them both here. Did I mention how I want to ask Sophia and Blythe to put on a concert at the hotel?"

Maggie gave him a perfunctory smile, and then chided herself for her childish reaction. *Caleb's friendships—who he loves—are none of my business.* The scolding didn't help her feel better.

Caleb cupped Maggie's elbow and assisted her to stand. When the crowd eased, he guided her out of the pew, down the aisle, and out of the church. "Why don't you let me carry Charlotte? We'll need to walk to the hotel, and with all these people, it will be slow going."

"My arms could use the rest," she admitted.

Caleb appropriated Charlotte, shifting her into one arm, with her head supported by the crook of his elbow. He held out his other arm to Maggie. "Have I told you yet, Magdalena Petra, how beautiful you look today?" He gazed at her in apparent admiration.

Maggie lowered her eyes, wishing she could believe him. She looked up at him through her lashes and slipped her hand around his arm. "I am a wren to the peacocks." She lifted her chin to indicate Sophia and Elizabeth exiting the church, together in animated conversation. "And Delia...." She shook her head. "Exquisite."

"You are most definitely not a *wren*." Caleb scowled. "What you don't understand is how beauty is not about comparisons. Your attractiveness is not Delia's or Sophia's or Elizabeth's. You are all unique. You are *Magdalena Petra*, your very own special self."

Her cheeks heated. *No matter how special I am, I'm still Gypsy Maggie.* Sadness made her look away, glancing down the street to see people flooding toward the hotel. The sound of happy conversations rose into the air. Already, a receiving line stretched into the street.

Caleb followed her gaze and smiled. "Seeing all these people entering my hotel does my heart glad. I probably don't have to tell you that I've been severely criticized for building such a *monstrosity* in Sweetwater Springs."

Immediately incensed, Maggie sprang to his defense. "Your hotel is *not* a monstrosity. It's *grand*—quite the most magnificent building I've ever seen."

His smile broadened. "I appreciate your partisanship, even though it's unnecessary. I meant I was criticized for the *monstrous* financial investment I made in such a large establishment. I took quite a risk."

"Why did you do so?"

"Is it foolish of me to want to make my mark on this town in a way that will last for generations?"

"Even if your fancy hotel is foolish, and I don't think it is...." Maggie said, slowly, thinking about his question. "If you have the money, then what does it matter to anyone else what you do with it? You're not tossing money off a cliff. You are providing a service for the community—giving employment, accommodations for guests and dining, a place to hold special events—and hopefully, you're making money, or at least breaking even."

"Since Christmas, we've been breaking even—ahead some weeks, behind some others. I'll be satisfied with that for now. Hopefully, as the hotel becomes more established, I'll earn back my investment."

They reached the line and stood behind a family she hadn't met—a couple with three children, a boy around six or seven and two toddlers. The big, blond man looked like a farmer. He held his son, who looked about two or so years old.

The boy squirmed to get down. But when he saw Maggie watching him, he stilled, staring at her with inquisitive brown eyes.

She scrunched a face and wiggled her nose at him.

His mouth opened into a wide grin that showed his teeth.

Encouraged, she made another silly face.

The boy let out an infectious belly laugh.

Maggie couldn't help but chuckle in return.

The mother turned to see what had caught her son's attention. She was tall like her husband, with dark hair and tanned skin. She wore a simple gold dress that matched the unusual color of her eyes and a straw hat with flowers on the brim. In her arms was a tow-headed baby girl with blue eyes who looked about a year or so old. The woman saw Caleb and smiled. "Mr. Livingston."

The warmth in the woman's tone surprised Maggie. In the weeks she'd been around Caleb, she'd observed that people tended to address him in a reserved, respectful manner. Until now, she'd never heard anyone greet him with genuine friendliness.

"Mrs. Muth." Caleb smiled and nodded. "I don't believe I've seen you since autumn."

"No, I remained home during the winter, although my husband braved the elements to deliver milk and take our son—" she dipped her chin to the older boy "—to school."

The line moved, and they all stepped forward a few paces.

Mr. Muth turned to join the conversation, nodding at Caleb. He had pale eyebrows over blue eyes, ruddy skin, a wide nose and mouth, and a close-cut tawny beard. His smile was more reserved than his wife's. He ran a curious gaze over Maggie's face, but Charlotte drew his attention. He raised his eyebrows in puzzlement, seemed about to ask something, and then shook his head.

"No, she's not my daughter." Caleb rocked the baby. "This is Mrs. Baxter, and Charlotte belongs to her. Although I do try to claim a percentage of the babe whenever I can."

"Spoken like a banker. Or a potential father." Mr. Muth glanced at Maggie. "I'm Erik and this is my wife Antonia, who is holding Camilla. Our eldest is Henri."

The boy in his arms pointed to the ground. "Down," he demanded.

His father rubbed the toddler's head, making the boy's brown hair stand on end. "And this one is Jacques. I'm trying to keep him corralled and clean until we get inside."

"Down," Jacques insisted in a more strident tone.

His mother laughed. "We might as well give up. At least he sat through the wedding, and the street is paved, so he won't get too dirty." She tapped her older son's shoulder to get his attention. "Henri, keep an eye on Jacques, please."

The boy had his mother's gold eyes. "Yes, *Maman*."

"Jacques should be all right," Caleb offered. "I had my employees clean the street pavers during the wedding. I can't vouch for a few hours from now, though."

Mr. Muth set down Jacques.

The small boy took off at a run, his brother after him.

Mrs. Muth shook her head. "Jacques never walks when he can run." Her daughter squirmed. "And Camilla is always after her brothers." She held the girl tighter and said something quietly to her in what sounded like French.

Mr. Muth reached out his arms. "Let me take her."

Without the baby in her arms, Maggie could see Mrs. Muth was in the early stages of pregnancy. *She will certainly have her hands full with three children so close in age.*

As they talked, the line kept moving, and soon they walked into the hotel.

Mrs. Muth's eyes grew big, and she slowly pivoted to take everything in. "Well, I be never seein' the like," she marveled. Then she brought herself up, shot her husband a guilty glance, and repeated. "I've never seen anything so big and so fancy!" She annunciated each word.

Mr. Muth grinned at her, as if they shared a secret, and their glances held.

Maggie could see the obvious love between the two, and she looked away. *Seems as if all the couples around me in this town are happily married.* The thought made her bitter for what she'd missed with Oswald, and she glanced at Caleb, sad for what she wished for with him but knew was out of her reach. Trying to push away her melancholy thoughts, she studied the interior of the hotel. The lobby, which had seemed so large during her last visit, now was stuffed with people. *And more to come....*

On Maggie's first visit, she'd centered her attention on Sophia Maxwell, so she'd missed many of the details beyond noting how grand Caleb's hotel was. Now she looked around, seeing the high, coffered ceilings and the interior second-floor balcony that ran along the back of the lobby. Several people had already climbed there to hang over the railing, which was bedecked with swags of white roses and greenery.

Maggie could understand the other woman's awe, for she felt the same provincial feeling, as if she didn't belong. The elegance of her surrounds made her resolve to firmly squash dreams of Caleb Livingston that tormented her, no matter how practical she tried to be about their relationship. "I quite agree, Mrs. Muth."

"Call me Antonia, please." She patted her husband's arm. "And this is my husband, Erik." She gave Maggie a look of apparent uncertainty. "If you don't mind, that is."

"I'd love to." Maggie sensed the woman came from humble origins, the slip with her speech showing a lack of education. "Antonia is a beautiful name. I'm Magdalena, but everyone calls me Maggie." Even Edith had given in and now used her nickname.

Charlotte stirred.

Caleb rocked the babe. "The Muths have a dairy farm on the prairie," he informed her. "How many cows are you up to now, Muth?"

The man smiled in quiet pride. "Ten. It's as much as I can do to milk them in the mornings and still have Henri to school on time." He glanced toward the mercantile. "I supply the milk for the store in town, and some—" he lifted his chin at Caleb "—like Mr. Livingston here, I deliver to directly."

"I should thank you, then," Maggie said with a smile. "Having fresh milk every day has been quite a treat. And Mrs. Graves makes such sweet butter from your milk."

The tips of the man's ears reddened, and he grinned. "Why thank you, Mrs., uh, Maggie. That's about as fine a compliment as you can give me. The only thing I'm prouder of than my herd is my family." He exchanged a tender glance with his wife.

The receiving line moved, and the Muths took several steps forward, passing under a flowered arch made of white roses and greenery, just inside of the double doors.

Caleb leaned close. "This is a second marriage for both. Their spouses died suddenly, and they had to wed quickly for the sake of the children. The boys are hers, and Camilla is Erik's."

Maggie wanted to know more. *Did the two mourn their loved ones, or was their situation like mine?* She made a note to speak more with Antonia later. "They have a love match now," was all she said, and she and Caleb walked into the hotel, closing up the space in the line.

In front of the Muths stood an elderly couple, beside a strapping man who must be their son, for he looked like a younger image of his father, only bigger. He had the same kind of dark good looks as Caleb, but where the banker was refined and polished, this man looked rough-hewn—an outdoorsman—with a head of ebony curls and an air of coiled energy. From the laugh lines around his eyes, he looked like he enjoyed life.

The elderly woman stepped forward and took Delia's hand. "Blessings on you both."

Maggie couldn't help overhearing.

The old woman glanced from Delia to Reverend Joshua. "I'm Nina Kelley, my husband is Leith, and my son is Kael. We haven't met you yet, living far in the woods as we do and not gettin' into town much but a couple of Sundays a year. On the Lord's day, we have our own services under God's cathedral." She gestured to the ceiling. The woman was tall and spare, her dress plain and outdated by a decade, but the look she cast at her husband was rich with love. "I wish for you as long and happy a marriage as Leith and I have had." She stepped aside so her husband could take her place and gave Reverend Norton her hand.

The old man moved with a limp. "Forty years, Nina and I've had, and I'll tell ya our secret."

Maggie inhaled the scent of roses from the archway. *Another happy couple.* She leaned forward a bit, wanting to be sure she heard what Leith Kelly had to say. She noticed Caleb and the Muths paid attention, as well.

Reverend Joshua smiled. "I can always use marriage advice, both for myself—" he looked down at Delia and smiled into her eyes before turning back to the elderly couple "—and for my parishioners."

"Singing," the man said in a proud tone.

"Singing?" Reverend Joshua looked puzzled.

"Yep. When yar sweetheart gits angry with ya—" he winked at his wife "—just sing her a funny song and make her laugh. And when she needs a little wooing—and believe ya me, Reverend Joshua, women need wooing all their lives long—ya go on and sing her a love ballad."

His wife nudged him with her shoulder. "You old coot," she said with affection in her tone. "The Reverend doesn't need any such advice from the likes of us."

Maggie covered her mouth to hold in her laugh. She glanced up at Caleb and saw a corresponding twinkle in his eyes.

Reverend Joshua chuckled. "I'll be sure to pay you a visit so you can teach me some of your songs. Sounds like they might come in handy."

"Ya do that, young fella. Ya and yar bride are both welcome."

"I'd love to come, too," Delia said in her soft Southern drawl.

Kael Kelley had been following his parents' conversation. Then he seemed to be distracted by something or someone outside of Maggie's view. A dazed expression crossed his face, followed by a frown.

She leaned forward to see Sophia Maxwell holding court in a circle of male admirers. *Kael Kelley is not immune to the Songbird's charms, either.*

❋　❋　❋

Like Maggie, Sophia wore purple—although hers was low-cut mauve satin with darker purple in a three-layered ruffle across the bottom. A wide sash of velvet trimmed her waist and tied with a fat fringed bow. Velvet banded the enormous balloon sleeves that ended in white lace ruffles above her elbow. She wore long gloves of white satin and carried a lacy fan. A broad choker of purple satin, wrapped around her neck, was adorned with two large mauve flowers, one under each ear. Amethyst and diamond earrings sparkled on her ears, and in a bracelet on each wrist. On any other woman, such a get-up would have looked ridiculous, but Sophia carried it off with aplomb.

Maggie noticed the singer's waist wasn't as tiny today. *She's probably worn her corset looser to give herself breath enough to sing.* She glanced at Caleb to see if he was watching the opera singer, but instead, found him gazing down at Charlotte with a fond smile. Her heart crimped.

The Muths moved forward to congratulate the Nortons, and then their turn arrived.

Maggie took Delia's hand and leaned to kiss her friend's cheek. "I *know* without a doubt that the two of you will be happy together. May God bring you many blessings."

The sparkle in Delia's hazel eyes made them look jewel bright. "Thank you, dearest Maggie. Your friendship has been a blessing, indeed, and I look forward to that deepening."

Maggie moved on to Reverend Joshua and extended her best wishes.

Reverend Joshua gave her a serious look. "I know life has been hard for you these last few years. You will have my prayers for your happiness."

Feeling moved by his words, Maggie pressed his hand. "This is *your* day," she playfully scolded. "You aren't supposed to be thinking of me."

"What better time than when we are face-to-face, and I am filled with love and gratitude. How much poorer would I be if I could not extent those feelings to others?"

Her throat tightened, and she could only nod and press his hand before moving on to greet his parents and Andre Bellaire.

In the same way as Reverend Joshua had expressed, Maggie's heart was filled with gratitude for the kindness and love she'd received since moving to Sweetwater Springs. She took several steps away to bring her emotions under control before turning to look at Caleb holding her daughter. *The comfort of loving friendship will have to be enough.*

❋ ❋ ❋

After greeting everyone in the wedding party and receiving knowing looks from others around him about Charlotte cuddled in his arms, Caleb searched for Maggie and found her standing about ten feet away. He saw Michael and Prudence Morgan heading her way and moved to meet them, knowing he owed an apology for not showing up when he'd promised to be in Morgan's Crossing.

Knowing the formidable Mrs. Morgan, Caleb also wanted to be at hand in case Maggie stood in need of his protection. He moved quickly to flank the trio.

Charlotte awoke and wiggled, sending a sleepy glance his way.

Caleb stopped within earshot just to the side of the three of them.

Mrs. Morgan greeted Maggie with a hug. She was a plain woman, who carried herself with an air of assurance. Her previously thin body and bony face had filled out from bearing four children. Her pale blue eyes were her only interesting feature, changing color depending on what she wore. Today, they'd darkened to match the periwinkle color of her dress.

Mrs. Morgan peered into Maggie's face. "You poor thing! I heard what happened. Oh, dear me. How very dreadful. I heard you were horribly cut and bruised. But you seemed to have healed well."

Maggie lifted the bangs from her forehead to expose the cut. "Better than before."

"I've always thought you had a strong streak of resiliency."

Maggie pulled up her lips in a wry smile. "I had to in order to survive Oswald."

"Exactly." Mrs. Morgan nodded.

Michael Morgan, a canny business man with graying dark hair and handsome features, frowned at Oswald's name. "We will, however, express condolences for your loss. Oswald was a hard worker and a good miner...." He obviously searched for something else positive to say. "I'm sorry," he said with genuine sympathy. "That day we argued over his mistreatment of you, and he lost his temper and tried to attack me, only to have some of the miners grab him."

Maggie shook her head. "You had to fire Oswald. I'm surprised you allowed him to work in the mine for as long as you did."

He smiled at his wife. "I wouldn't have. But as you know, my wife lacks tolerance for bullies, one of her most appealing qualities. While we know from experience with a few other couples that we can't stop husbands from abusing their wives, we do what we can to protect the women. Mrs. Morgan wanted to keep you in Morgan's Crossing under her eye. Her wishes prevailed until I could no longer condone Oswald's behavior."

"Thank you both. I am well, and so is Charlotte, and that is due to Mr. Livingston."

Mrs. Morgan glanced at Maggie's empty arms. "But where is your baby?"

"Mr. Livingston has appropriated her." Maggie turned to glance around, obviously looking for him.

Time for my entrance. Caleb strolled up. "Are you looking for us?"

Seeing him carrying Charlotte made Prudence Morgan raise an eyebrow. She leaned over to view the baby. "Oh, she's delightful." She straightened. "Now, tell me, Maggie.... Do you want to come back to Morgan's Crossing with us when we leave?"

Maggie inhaled a sharp breath.

Caleb's stomach tightened. *Absolutely not!* He held in the words. This wasn't the place to talk to Maggie about the future he envisioned for them.

Mrs. Morgan tapped her chin. "You could work with Mrs. Rivera at the bathhouse. Then, too, with all our miners, there are plenty of opportunities to remarry."

"Oh, I couldn't possibly—"

Caleb stiffened in protest.

"Of course, it's too early to imagine yourself married again. But you do have to keep your future in mind. Your daughter should have a father. A *good* father." She glanced up at her husband with a loving smile that softened her face and made her look almost pretty. "I can't tell you the comfort and the...*joy* of watching your dear husband with his children." She turned back to Maggie. "I wish that for you, my dear."

So do I.

Prudence eyed Caleb, and a speculative expression crossed her face.

Caleb could see the matchmaking wheels turning in the matron's mind. *Good to know the woman is on my side.*

Mrs. Morgan patted Maggie's arm. "You can think about it. We're staying at the hotel tonight, and tomorrow, we're traveling on the train to Crenshaw. We'll be staying in the city for a few days. Shopping for the family—" she made a *moue* "—the whole of Morgan's Crossing really, for we have a long list for the store. We've brought along the children's nanny. Mr. Morgan and I hope to have some time to ourselves, as well—see a show, dine out.... You can give us an answer when we return."

"Thank you," Maggie murmured.

Caleb waited, hoping she'd turn the woman down flat.

But Maggie said nothing more.

Her silence worried him. *Very well, I'll have to act.* Caleb started to make plans. He would have preferred to wait and give Maggie an extended courtship, but Mrs. Morgan had just forced his hand. *By the time the Morgans return from their shopping expedition, Maggie's future with me will be settled.*

CHAPTER NINETEEN

After breakfast the following morning, Maggie sought out Caleb before he left for the bank. Everyone had slept late because the festivities—dinner, Sophia and Blythe's performance, chatting with friends—had lasted well into the night. She found him in his study, sitting at his desk, pen in hand, and frowning at a ledger and some papers.

Her pulse quickening, she paused in the doorway, taking a minute to soak in the sight of him. Once she left the house, such opportunities would be few and far between. *If they ever come at all.* The thought made her heart ache.

Even looking tired, with lines furling his brow, he was handsome enough to make any maiden swoon. *And I'm not immune to his masculine charm.*

Caleb looked up, and his frown cleared. "No Charlotte?" He jabbed the pen back into the inkwell.

"Yesterday must have worn her out. She's still asleep."

"I think yesterday wore us all out."

"In a good way, of course." Maggie looked at his papers. "Do you have a few minutes, or am I disturbing you?"

He sighed and tapped the ledger. "I'm working on the foreclosure of Wood's bathhouse. Sad, really, because it used to be a going concern."

Relieved he'd brought up the very topic she wanted to discuss, she asked, "How do you know he won't pay you?"

"I woke up early. Since I couldn't sleep, I figured I'd go check on the place. I found the door wide open, Wood passed out on the floor, reeking of whiskey. When Hardy's Saloon opened up after the reception, the man probably spent all his profits." He lifted his hand in a helpless gesture. "So I'm forced to take the next steps."

Although relieved the bathhouse was available, Maggie couldn't help feeling sorry for Mr. Wood, and even more concerned about Caleb, for she could see the situation was taking a toll on him.

He tapped the papers. "I need to finish these up and then deliver them. But there's no hurry." Caleb stood, glancing out the window that looked onto the front yard and the street. "We have another beautiful spring day," he said in a determinedly cheerful tone. "But who knows how long this streak of sunshine will last. Let's go outside, into the backyard, and you can tell me what's on your mind." He came around from behind the desk.

She placed a hand on his arm. "This must be an awful situation for you."

"Perhaps I'm not mercenary enough," he said with a wry smile. "Many of my colleagues would be rubbing their hands with glee at acquiring another business dirt cheap."

"You are making light of the situation, Caleb—" Maggie squeezed his arm "—but I can see how much this bothers you."

He let out a sigh and placed a hand over hers. "If this were just a case of plain old drunkenness or laziness…I wouldn't feel so bad. But the root of the man's problem is grief. Wood and his wife had one of those enviable marriages—obviously loving and supportive. They doted on each other, although they never had children.…"

"That's probably why he's taken his wife's death so hard. He's alone."

"Does Mr. Wood have other family members he can go to?"

"He has a brother living in Crenshaw." Caleb's somber expression brightened. "I can pay for his train ticket to travel there."

"Maybe leaving this town will be good for Mr. Wood—being away from the constant reminders."

Caleb looked down at her, tenderness in his eyes and cupped her cheek. "Thank you, Maggie. Your comfort means more than you know."

"You're always so busy running things, and you've certainly given me comfort and support many times."

He brought her fingers to his lips before tucking her hand around his arm and guiding her out of the room. He stopped and released her for a moment to lift her red shawl off a hook and returned to drape it around her shoulders. He took her hand, and from there, they moved down the hall, through the solarium, and into the yard.

Maggie knew she should pull away, but she treasured this moment, knowing this occasion might be the last time they touched with affection. She knew he wouldn't be pleased with her business proposal.

Dew still lay on the grass, and the air was chill. Maggie was grateful for the warmth of her shawl. She tilted her head in the direction of the gazebo. "Let's go sit."

They strolled down the walkway and reached the white structure. *This is it.* "There's something I'd like to discuss with you."

"Sounds ominous."

Maggie gave him a quick smile of reassurance and stepped into the gazebo, pulling him in after her. "Not at all. Exciting, I think."

"I'm all for exciting, Magdalena Petra," Caleb said in a low voice, drawing her into his arms.

Pressed against him, she felt her heartbeat flutter like a bird's.

"How's this for exciting?" He lowered his head and kissed her.

The touch of his lips on hers felt soft, coaxing, not at all like the brutal assault of Oswald's mouth. His kiss asked permission, instead of demanding.

Maggie started to relax into him, sliding her hand up his chest to his shoulder, before remembering her purpose and reluctantly pulling away.

He grabbed her hands before she could retreat.

She spoke over the sound of her pounding heart. "I've been thinking about what I need to do next." She took a fortifying breath. "I'd like to run the bathhouse. I could take it over, clean it up, keep it spick-and-span. I know I could make the business successful, Caleb."

Still holding her hand, he stared at her with a dumbfounded look on his face. "What are you saying, Maggie? You want to leave me? I had a very different plan in mind for the future."

She was sure he did, knew he wanted to generously support them, perhaps for years. *I can't allow myself to be so beholden. Caleb has done enough—more than enough.* "I need to make my own way." She put every ounce of her determination into her tone.

"I bring you out here for some kisses and flirtation, and you want to talk to me about running the *bathhouse*—a place patronized by *naked men*? Absolutely *not*!"

Surprised by his tone, she pulled back her hands. "Caleb, the bathhouse in Morgan's Crossing is run by a *woman*."

"A crone missing half her teeth." He paced several steps away.

"Oh, for heaven's sake. Don't be so nasty."

He swung around. "I'm not being nasty toward the woman. I barely know her. I'm pointing out that she won't have advances directed at her the way you—" he flung out his arm in a gesture toward her "—a young and beautiful woman, would. In many towns, the bathhouse is also the whorehouse. And you'd be prime bait for men who don't know better."

Although learning how her working at the bathhouse could be misconstrued sent a shiver of apprehension through her, Maggie stubbornly raised her chin. "I can take care of myself."

He shook his head. "Not in situations like this one."

"This is Sweetwater Springs. The men will know different."

"Don't be naïve. You are putting yourself at risk."

"Caleb—"

"You could even be *defiled*, Maggie."

The ugly word hung in the air between them, making her chest tight and her stomach clench. But she couldn't let fear stop her from earning a living and providing for her daughter. "I'll have my rifle."

"A rifle is no good at a close range, although the sight might prove a deterrent. Will you carry it everywhere? Can you tote a gun and a baby at the same time?" Caleb let out a breath of obvious frustration and ran his fingers through his hair. "Now that the hotel is open, with bathrooms on every floor, there's not really the need for a bathhouse anymore."

"I don't agree. People riding in from farms and ranches might not plan to stay at the hotel. Or perhaps they can't afford to. Those are the customers who will use the bathhouse. I don't need to make much. I know how to get by on very little."

"I said *no*, Maggie, and I mean it."

"Very well, then." She crossed her arms. "How much to *purchase* the business? Name your price."

He rolled his eyes. "You don't have any money."

"Name your price." She annunciated each word.

"Fine. That run-down shack. Tiny lot. I'd let it go for twenty-five dollars. And I know for a fact you don't have twenty-five cents."

The taunt stung. Maggie uncrossed her arms, reached up, and undid an earring, then the second. She extended them toward him.

Caleb didn't move.

She grabbed his hand and slapped the earrings into his palm.

"Maggie, these aren't worth a quarter, not even a nickel, much less twenty-five dollars," he said in obvious exasperation.

"Underneath the brass coating, they are solid gold," she said coldly.

He shot her an incredulous look.

"Gypsies hide their wealth in their jewelry. Without the protection of a tribe, my grandparents went a step further to disguise their gold. These are my last pieces. So tell me, will the earrings cover the price of your bathhouse?"

He hefted the earrings. "Without a scale, I can't be sure. But I imagine so, with a bit left over."

"Then I'll buy the place."

"And if you do…even if things work out, what about Charlotte? In a few years, will you want her around naked men?"

"Once the business is successful, I can sell it."

"I won't sell it to you, Maggie. Don't be so stubborn."

She fisted her hands on her hips. "Don't tell me what to do or how to be. If you won't sell to me, then I'll find someone else who will buy it for me."

"Very well. I'll consider it," Caleb said in clipped tones. He thrust the earrings at her and turned, taking long strides down the brick path as if he couldn't get away from her fast enough.

Maggie stared after him in despair, her insides churning, hating that she'd angered him and knowing she'd hurt his feelings. Caleb was a handsome, wealthy man who, even when confronted with delivering the baby of a stranger, the body of a dead man nearby, hadn't lost his polished self-confidence. It was easy to forget he had feelings, too.

Caleb's opinions aside, I still need to earn a living.

❋ ❋ ❋

Maggie's request for the bathhouse slammed Caleb's heart into his chest. The pain wrapped around his rib cage, the binding making it difficult to breathe. He'd listened to the rest of her offer in shock and disbelief. He couldn't believe she was rejecting him for the uncertainty of trying to manage a dirty run-down bathhouse.

Now, a sense of mingled rage and despair propelled him toward the house, for if he stayed Caleb knew he might say something he'd regret. Reaching the door to the conservatory, he flung it open and entered, stopping to take a breath of the warm plant-scented air.

He glanced out the window at her. Even at this distance, with Maggie framed by the gazebo, he could see she'd remained rooted in place, staring after him.

She caught him looking and, with a flounce, turned away.

His gaze followed the sway of her bottom.

The surge of passion from kissing her, which he'd intended as light-hearted, had almost knocked him out of his boots. Caleb knew he loved her; indeed, he'd believed they'd forged a deep connection. *What a fool I was to let our kisses addle my brain so I couldn't better persuade her.*

Now that he was away from Maggie, he could begin thinking about what to do. An answer came to him, and he almost smacked his forehead. *Instead of arguing with her, I should have just offered to escort her to the bathhouse. Once Maggie saw the decrepit place for herself, she'd be bound to agree that not only was the bathhouse not worth fixing, it was no place for a woman without a husband to protect her.*

Caleb stalked toward his study, making a mental list. First, finish the foreclosure paperwork. Second, he'd go to the bathhouse and serve the papers to Mr. Wood, throwing a bucket of cold water over the body if need be to rouse him from his drunken stupor. Then, he'd supervise the man's packing in order to see he left the place with only his possessions and didn't cause any more damage. Finally, he'd escort Wood to the train station and buy him a ticket to Crenshaw, leaving him in the stationmaster's hands.

Having a plan eased the tension in his chest. He was able to take a deep breath.

I'll take Maggie to the bathhouse after I get rid of Wood. Once she sees what the place is really like, she'll put this ridiculous notion out of her mind.

CHAPTER TWENTY

That afternoon, Caleb softly knocked on the open door of Maggie's bedroom, conscious of feeling both hopeful and anxious. After a more in-depth look around the dilapidated bathhouse, his spirits had risen with the amount of problems he found with the place. If she were disgusted with the condition of the place, then maybe she'd be more amenable to a marriage proposal.

Now, he felt fairly confident Maggie would see reason, and he'd do everything possible to influence her decision. Yet, at the same time, he knew her stubbornness and feared she'd dig in her heels.

"Come in," she called in a low voice.

He poked his head into the room to see her in the rocking chair, Charlotte sleeping at her breast.

"She fell asleep a few minutes ago." Careful not to disturb the baby, Maggie stood and carried Charlotte around to the other side of the bed. She turned her back to Caleb and laid the baby in the cradle, pulling her shirtwaist into place and doing up the buttons before facing him.

He stepped into the hall so as not to wake the baby.

Maggie followed him.

"Wood is on the train, and I've come to take you to see the bathhouse. It's in bad shape, and you should know what you're getting into before you decide to purchase the place. Remember, Maggie, you always have me to fall back on. I delight in caring for you and Charlotte." He didn't mention his belief that she'd change her mind. He figured doing so would definitely kick her into contrary action.

Her smile was warm. "I know you do."

"Edith will watch Charlotte while we're gone. In fact, she told us to take our time, for she wanted the baby to herself for a while after she wakes up."

Maggie's eyes sparkled. "You are so thoughtful to arrange everything." She placed a hand on his arm. "I'm so glad you're not angry with me anymore. Give me five minutes, and I'll be ready."

"I'll meet you at the front door. We might as well walk over there." Caleb wanted Maggie to have the full impact of working and living close to the saloon, which she wouldn't get if they quickly drove there in the surrey. "I'm going to swipe a cookie from the kitchen. Do you want one?"

"No, thank you, I just had two. Mrs. Graves baked sugar cookies today."

Their normal conversation was at odds with the tension in his stomach, and he wondered if she felt the same way. He wandered downstairs, stopping in the kitchen. He probably should eat but didn't think his stomach would accept a meal. He needed this bathhouse situation settled first. A cookie would tide him over.

Mrs. Graves stood at the stove, cutting potatoes into a pot.

The smell of cinnamon baking in the oven wafted his way. *Bread pudding, perhaps?*

His housekeeper nodded in acknowledgment of his presence but as usual, didn't make him welcome.

Caleb took a sugar cookie from the jar and waved it in thanks. He didn't bother with a plate, instead eating the cookie on the way to the door. *Might as well be paper from all the enjoyment I'm taking from it.*

Maggie hurried to join him. She'd put on her earrings and carried a burlap satchel that he recognized as belonging to Mrs. Graves.

Why does she have that? He was about to ask, and then frowned, seeing she wore her old dress—clean and pressed, but still shabby. He realized she probably didn't want to worry about getting her new clothes dirty. He gave her the black shawl.

She draped it around her shoulders and stepped in front of the closed door, waiting for him to open it for her.

Caleb smiled at Maggie's back, recognizing she'd formed a new habit. When she'd first started walking, she'd gone through doors without the pause for appropriate gentlemanly behavior. Obviously, Oswald had never acted the gallant, as a man should with a lady. He liked that he'd helped her learn how she deserved to be treated.

He held open the door and waited for her to step through. Once outside, Caleb held out his elbow and was relieved when Maggie took his arm. They began to walk in the direction of Hardy's saloon.

"Tell me," Maggie said. "How did things go with Mr. Wood?"

"About what I expected. He was still passed out when I returned with the paperwork. Before I went, though, I swung by the sheriff's to pick her up. I thought having her along would be a deterrent."

Maggie frowned. "But if he's not breaking the law…?"

"Sheriff Granger said the same thing—that she'd stand by and look stern but would not interfere unless he tried to fight me or break something."

"And did he?"

"I think Wood was too hungover and blurry-eyed, wincing when he moved, shading his eyes from the light. He seemed more inclined to go back to sleep than to protest. I told him he could sleep on the train."

"Did the sheriff have to do anything?"

"At one point, she told Wood to take the ticket. Said it was a generous offer and more than he had a right to expect or deserved. Told him that now he had a chance to start a new life, and she hoped he'd leave, because she was tired of locking him up to sleep off a bender."

"So he's gone?"

"Kit and caboodle. I dumped the contents of all the drawers into an old trunk of his. Took down what was on the shelves or hanging on the walls. Luckily, I'd driven, so I put the trunk in the surrey and the three of us went to the train station, where I bought him a ticket. The stationmaster promised he'd make sure Wood got aboard and didn't sleep through the train's arrival."

Maggie sighed. "I feel for the man, and I do hope Mr. Wood makes some changes in his life."

"So do I."

In front of the saloon, a cowboy dismounted from his horse. He saw them, touched his hat to Maggie, and headed inside.

"The bathhouse is on the street behind the saloon. This is the worst area in Sweetwater Springs." Caleb steered them along the side of the building, past malodorous outhouses. As they walked by, he held his breath at the reek. From the corner of his eye, he saw Maggie do likewise. "You'll have to be careful not to be out after dark and remain vigilant during the day."

She swallowed but said nothing.

Once past Hardy's outhouses, he guided her toward the bathhouse, a shabby, false-fronted wooden building with a narrow porch. A rickety bench was propped against the wall on one side of the door.

A sign hung crookedly next to the entrance, the letters so faded he could barely see the words, although the last line looked shadowed as if Wood had blackened the letters with ink to make them stand out more.

BATHHOUSE

BILL OF RATES:

Baths .25

Hot Baths .50

SOAP .10

TOWEL .10

CLEAN TOWEL .15

HOT WATER .25

TONIC .10

SHAVE .50

CLOSE SHAVE .75

HAIRCUT 1.00

NO MORE THAN 30 MINUTES PER BATH

WHISKEY .50

One of the two windows in the front had cracked glass. Dust coated both panes.

Caleb stepped onto the porch and pulled open the screen door that had a rent in the bottom as if someone had kicked it. He turned the rusted handle of the door and pushed it open, gesturing for Maggie to enter, and then followed her inside.

The first room was set up as a waiting area with a settee with faded, dusty cushions and a desk that held smudged glasses and whiskey bottles, most of them empty. A bentwood chair with a cane seat was pushed into the corner.

"I'll wait right here while you look around." Caleb figured Maggie needed to see the truth for herself without having to pretend to him that everything was all right. He also sensed his pointing out all the problems would get her back up. So as much as he wanted to watch her expression, he turned to look out the window, not that he could see much, and listened for the sound of her footsteps as she slowly moved from room to room.

When he'd first moved to Sweetwater Springs, Caleb had rented a small cabin while his house was being built. He'd frequently used the bathhouse and knew how Mrs. Wood had taken pride in the cleanliness and service of her establishment. He touched one of the tattered, dirty lace curtains hanging from the windows, remembering them as crisp and pristine white. *The poor woman must be turning over in her grave.*

He'd already seen what Maggie would find in the rest of the establishment—a men's area holding two claw-footed tubs with dirty rings around the sides and a smaller ladies' room with only one. That tub, at least, was cleaner—probably because any woman who used it tidied up after herself.

He heard the thudding of pipes and the gush of water and knew Maggie was smart to test the plumbing. That feature, fortunately, remained in good shape.

Behind the bathing rooms was the living quarters—one big room, smelling of dust and stale food, with a small kitchen area along one side. The furnishings consisted of a bed with a stained mattress—for he'd sent the bedding along with Wood—and two chairs around a small round table, the surface dusty enough to write on. A pile of graying towels sat next to a wooden washtub.

Rapid footsteps approached. *Good. She can't wait to get out of here.* Relieved, he turned.

Maggie wore a serious expression. "How is the water heated?"

"We're sitting on one of those hot springs I told you about."

"Ah." She gave a decisive nod. "This business is in better shape than I thought. Nothing some elbow grease won't fix—mostly scrubbing and paint. I'll buy the place from you."

What? He couldn't believe his ears.

Maggie smiled, although the wary look in her eyes told Caleb she expected him to challenge her.

Over the next several minutes, he tried to make her budge from her position, marshaling the arguments he'd been thinking of all day.

To each of them, Maggie remained adamant. Finally, she made a slashing hand gesture, cutting off the debate. With a cross expression, she reached up and removed her earrings, holding them out.

"Is there *nothing*—" he put special emphasis on the word "—I can do to change your mind? Will you not remain under my protection?" *My love?* He dared not say the words and expose his heart to more hurt.

Maggie would not meet his gaze. She shook her head and left her hand extended.

Defeated, Caleb took the earrings. He lowered his arm and fisted his hand until the metal pressed into his palm.

"I'd best get started cleaning." Maggie opened her satchel and pulled out an apron. She dropped it over her head, tying the strings behind her back.

He gazed at her, dumbfounded. It was all he could to do keep his mouth from dropping open. *She'd prepared for this before we even left the house.*

Maggie started to roll up her sleeves. "I want to make the most of the next hour while Charlotte is still sleeping." She gestured with her chin toward the door. "Go on with you, now, Caleb, and let me get to work so this place is livable by tonight."

✻ ✻ ✻

Three weeks later, Caleb sat in his study, drinking tea and staring at the stack of newspapers and letters he'd just collected from the post office at the train station, after being away on the belated visit to Morgan's Crossing. He took a letter opener from the top drawer and slit the top of an envelope without even looking at the return address. Usually, he enjoyed the ritual of catching up on his correspondence and reading news—local, state, and national. Today, he was conscious of a feeling of malaise, for he'd gone these weeks without speaking to Maggie beyond an exchange of polite greetings after Sunday service.

He'd hoped the reality of fixing up and operating the bathhouse would quickly bring her back to him, but word was, she'd already established a thriving business. He and Sheriff Granger had put out a warning that Maggie was running a respectable establishment, and any man who took liberties would face serious repercussions.

Sheriff Granger had also promised she'd keep a close eye on the place, especially since she was a frequent customer of the bathhouse. She kept him apprised of Maggie's doings, although she wouldn't share any confidences. But the lawwoman was grateful to have the place clean and respectable again.

Caleb sorely missed his warm exchanges with Maggie, her commonsense advice, the way they laughed together, her feminine appeal. *And oh, how I miss that sweet baby.*

He took a sip of tea. *I need to come up with a new plan.*

The door to the study opened, and Edith rushed in without knocking. She waved a letter.

Startled from his dark thoughts, Caleb was about to give her a sharp reprimand but saw she was as white as a sheet, and the hand holding the letter was shaking. "Sister!" He leaped to his feet and hurried to steady her. "Come." He walked her over to the wing chair and sat her down. "What's wrong? Are you ill?"

She clutched his sleeve, opened her mouth to speak, but nothing came out.

"Edith, you must tell me what's wrong," Caleb used a tone of command that hid his growing apprehension.

She burst into tears and blindly thrust the letter at him.

He flipped the envelope over to see the missive was from her late husband Nathaniel's parents. His gut tight, Caleb began to read.

Dear Edith,

It is with deep sadness that we regret to inform you that our son George was killed in a riding accident. As you know, he leaves behind a wife and three daughters. With Julia's latest pregnancy, we had hopes she'd finally deliver a son, but the stress of George's death was too much. She miscarried the baby, which turned out to be a boy.

Our granddaughters will receive generous dowries. As our only grandson, Benjamin now stands as the heir to the family business.

Mildred and I know we were not as accepting of you as we should have been. We were stubborn and tried to force Nathaniel down a path of our choosing, and so we lost him long before he passed away. We were wrong and paid the worst possible price for our decisions. Thus, we must ask your forgiveness for our treatment of you.

Over the years, we have suffered from not seeing Nathaniel's son and watching him grow up. But we were too stiff-necked to bend. Unfortunately, we did not heal the breach we had caused and were punished for our own pride.

We appreciate that your letters have kept us informed of Benjamin's progress. Thank you for writing, even though you received no response. Benjamin sounds like a fine young man. I'm sure his father would have been proud. You and his uncle have surely done a good job in raising him.

The passing of George has humbled us. We are brokenhearted by the loss of our two beloved sons. Thus we come, hat in hand, to beg for you and Benjamin to return to live in Boston. Both of you will be most welcome.

Sincerely,

Henry Grayson

Caleb finished the letter and stared at the words a moment longer. The letters were written in a quivery hand and some tiny blots told of the emotion of the writer.

"Humble, indeed." He dropped the letter and the envelope on the table beside the chair. Setting aside his own sadness, he turned to crouch in front of his sister, taking her hand and patting it. "You've had a severe shock, dearest. If I pour you a little brandy, will you take some?"

Still weeping, shoulders shaking, she clung to his hand. Finally, she nodded and released him.

Shaken by the sight of his formidable sister reduced to such a state, Caleb set out two brandy snifters, for he, too, was in need of liquid fortification. He walked back and handed one to her. "Drink this, and then we will discuss the situation."

Edith sipped the brandy and gradually color returned to her face, but her expression still looked haunted. She pulled a handkerchief from her sleeve, patted her face, and blew her nose. "Such a shock. Both the letter and George's death."

"I remember he and Nathaniel were close."

She nodded. "George was supportive of our relationship, but he wouldn't go against his parents and stand by his brother. He didn't have Nathaniel's spine."

"Ben has that spine," Caleb said gently, crouching to take Edith's hand. "The changes in him have been astonishing and so gratifying to watch."

She released his hand to dab at her eyes with the handkerchief. "I'm afraid for my son. I know how difficult it was for you and I to go back and forth from the West to the East—how we didn't fit in."

He took a seat in the other chair. "The adjustment won't be easy. But there are differences in Ben's case. Think of it, Edith. We spent the majority of our formative years in the West, only returning to Boston for long visits. Just about the time we started to fit in, we were whisked away again. When we were there, Mama had no idea of proper Boston life. She was miserable, and Black Jack didn't care what anyone thought. We were ill-prepared for society."

"That's right," she murmured, twisting her handkerchief.

"On the other hand, Ben grew up in Boston. I imagine you and he could easily slip back into the same social circles you had before—and Ben would remember his school friends."

"Oh, Caleb," Edith wailed. "What am I to do?" She sniffed back tears. "The Graysons caused Nathaniel such pain and strain. Such heartache we endured. Yet, my dear husband *always* stood steadfast by my side. *Now* they are sorry when it's years too late."

"What do you want to do?"

She shrugged and turned her head. "I don't know."

"Let's set out the possibilities, shall we?"

Edith nodded.

"You've never been happy living here."

She twisted her handkerchief some more. "I don't know that I'd have felt happy anywhere after Nathaniel's death. But at least here Ben and I had you."

Caleb swallowed down the emotion that lodged in his throat. "We had each other." *Difficult though that's been at times.* "As I see it, you can stay here, or you can return to Boston. You can also *visit* Boston to see if it suits you and Ben. And I would urge you to do that for Ben's sake, both to bring Nathaniel's family some comfort and for your son to become familiar with the company he will someday inherit. If Boston does not appeal, then you two can return. This doesn't have to be a decision that is set in stone."

"Yes, yes, you're right." She straightened her slumped posture.

"There is another possibility, not one I'd suggest. But if we are to consider all your options...."

She raised her brows in askance.

"If you think you could find happiness someplace else, move to a different city, anywhere in America, or abroad for that matter."

"I don't look to find *happiness*, Caleb. If Ben is happy, then I'll be well pleased."

"Perhaps you should consider your own happiness," he said with deliberate sharpness. "I do respect your grief for Nathaniel's death. However, I think you've cut yourself off from the possibility of finding love again."

She flinched as if he'd slapped her. "I could *never* love another man like I did him."

"Of course not, Edith. Marriage with someone else would be different than what you had with Nathaniel. But that doesn't mean the relationship wouldn't be just as rich. As long as you close your mind to the possibility, a new love won't happen for you." He waited for a few minutes, watching her face to see if she absorbed his words. "Think of the happy second marriages we know of, where one or both spouses suffered previous bereavement. Just off the top of my head, I can think of the Thompsons, Barretts, Muths, Dunns. With a little thought, you'd come up with more."

She bit her lip.

"Frankly, your chance of finding the type of man who'd interest you is minuscule in Sweetwater Springs. In all the time you've been here, only Wyatt Thompson mildly attracted you. In a few years, Ben will be off to school, and you'll be alone. If you marry again, you might even have another child. You're not too old."

"Are you just saying this because you'd like your home to yourself... because you want to take a wife...a *certain* wife?" she asked in a grudging tone.

"Is that what my advice feels like?" he asked gently.

She sighed. "Actually not. I feel how sincere you are."

"There will always be a home here for you and Ben, regardless of whether I marry." *Although that doesn't look like it will happen,* he thought in despair.

"I thank you for that, brother."

Then he remembered Maggie's Gypsy background and held up a hand. "Perhaps I should qualify what I'd just said. You might not approve of my choice of wife, but I would expect you to treat her with politeness and consideration."

"I'm used to managing my home, Caleb. If I choose to stay in Sweetwater Springs or return here after you marry, it would be best if I had my own house built."

"Well, the construction crew is almost done with the Norton house, and they'll soon be available to work on another. Would you like to have plans drawn up?"

Edith tapped her chin in thought. Her mouth broadened into a smile. "I think I will. Even if we live elsewhere, we can still return for the summers—to avoid the Boston heat and humidity."

Caleb forced a smile, hiding his sadness and the thought he might be rattling around alone in his big house for a long time. "I think, sister dear, we have a plan."

❋ ❋ ❋

That night after a shocking talk with his mother, and after reading his grandfather's letter, Ben glumly sought out his uncle, who'd retreated to his study. The contents of the letter had shaken him, and he didn't know what to feel. He needed his uncle's counsel.

His stomach ached. Ben hadn't been able to eat much supper. Not that Mother and Uncle Caleb noticed. They, too, had been quiet and had pushed their food around on their plates, probably for the same reason.

One thing's for sure—if I'm to leave Sweetwater Springs, I have things I want to do first. Ben knew he needed his uncle's permission for some of them, because his mother would automatically say no.

After he knocked on the door and was told to come in, Ben entered the darkened room, lit only by the fire and a single oil lamp burning on the desk. His uncle hadn't even turned on the gas lights, but he sat by the fire, staring into the flames, obviously brooding. A snifter of brandy sat on the table next to him. He looked up and waved Ben to a chair. "I can tell by your expression your mother told you the news. What do you think about your grandfather's proposition?"

Ben shrugged, staring into the fire in the same way his uncle just had, trying to find words to express his feelings.

The silence lasted for several moments as Uncle Caleb allowed him time to gather his thoughts.

Finally, Ben looked up. "Can you feel good and bad about something at the same time?"

"Yes. You can also *think* one way and *feel* another at the same time. Very disconcerting when that happens."

Encouraged, Ben started with what was foremost on his mind. "I don't want to leave my friends. Leave you. Leave my horse."

"I'll miss you, too."

Ben gave his uncle a direct look, and his throat tightened. He swallowed. "Matthew and I have planned some fishing trips, and Hunter is going to teach me to track game. Mark Carter invited me and Matthew to spend a few days at their ranch this summer being a cowboy."

"All those activities sound appropriate." Caleb settled back in his chair. "As I see it, there's no hurry for you and your mother to leave right away. Might as well finish the school term and spend part of the summer here. She and I also talked about the two of you returning every summer, although maybe to a home of your own and not this house."

Ben felt as if a weight had lifted from his chest, and he let out a long breath of relief.

"Boston will have many compensations, Ben. In fact, you might want to talk to Peter Rockwell about working at his family's hotel like you've been doing here. If you're interested, I'm sure he'll write a letter on your behalf. Then again, there's the Grayson retail business, which you should learn."

Ben thought about those ideas, and excitement quickened. "I'll talk to Mr. Rockwell tomorrow." He remembered his original purpose for seeking out his uncle. "I want to go along on the next expedition to the Indian reservation. Matthew is going. Hunter Thompson and Mark Carter, too."

Uncle Caleb steepled his fingers. "I don't think that's a good idea. I don't know how safe that trip will be for someone your age without the guidance and protection of a parent."

"The sheriff will be there, and Hunter's gone *twice* without his father."

"Hunter Thompson's situation is different, as well you know. Hunter is a Blackfoot adopted into a white family. He can understand the Indians and speak their language. That young man played a vital role in the success of those two missions." He tilted his head. "What do you boys think you can accomplish?"

"I don't know," Ben said honestly, still hoping for permission. "Hunter thinks we're building peaceable relations with the tribe."

"Sounds like the sheriff's words, although not a bad sentiment and a worthwhile goal."

Ben shrugged. "Hunter told us some stories. How hungry and skinny the children are."

"We have some hungry and skinny children in Sweetwater Springs. Certainly with wealth in your future, you must consider the needs of those less fortunate."

"No one here is dying from lack of food," Ben protested. "If things get that bad, they have other people to help them. The Indians don't."

The brown-eyed gaze settled on him, seemingly speculative. "Are Wyatt Thompson and John Carter going along with their boys? What about school?"

"Mr. Carter, yes. Not Mr. Thompson, though, with the baby and all. Mrs. Gordon will work out lesson plans we can take with us so we don't fall behind."

"Your mother will be against your going on this expedition."

"I know. But you can overrule her."

His uncle grimaced and shook his head. "Those conversations are never pleasant." He stared into the fire.

The melancholy expression on his face prompted Ben into a more delicate topic. "You're going to be alone, here, Uncle Caleb." Ben voiced another of his worries. "I don't think Mrs. Graves counts."

Caleb gave him a wry smile. "You've quite the list this evening, Ben. I don't want you worrying about me. I will manage just fine."

"What about Mrs. Baxter and Charlotte?"

His expression closed up. "What do you mean?"

Ben crossed his arms and rolled his eyes. "I know you're sweet on Mrs. Baxter. She made you happy. You doted on Charlotte. Yet, you let them go."

His uncle sighed. "I had no choice. Mrs. Baxter didn't want to stay with me, and I couldn't keep them prisoner here."

My uncle is square on the logical side of the emotional scale. Ben narrowed his eyes and asked the question he'd been wondering ever since Mrs. Baxter had up and left. "What did she say when you asked her to marry you?"

His uncle frowned, and his eyes grew cold.

Ben knew that look, and his knees trembled. But he forced his legs to still. He hadn't done anything wrong, and this topic was too important to allow Uncle Caleb to intimidate him into silence. "Well?"

To his surprise, his uncle backed down. He looked away and fiddled with the brandy snifter, moving it six inches to the left. "Mrs. Baxter made her feelings quite clear. She'd rather work at the bathhouse than marry me."

That doesn't sound like something she would say. "Those were her exact words to you?"

He hesitated. "Well, no."

Ben lost his patience and threw out his hands. "Uncle Caleb, did you actually *propose*? Down on one knee, diamond ring, and all?"

"I never got that far."

Ben lowered his arms. "I think Mrs. Baxter loves you. I saw her feelings in her eyes when she looked at you and wasn't aware anyone was watching."

The man shook his head. "No. She would have given me some indication."

"Meaning no disrespect, sir, but…. You're good with money and business, but you stink when it comes to love and women."

"Bordering on disrespect, young man," he warned, his mouth tight.

"Yes, sir. Beg pardon. But I pay attention," Ben retorted. "And Papa used to give me tips." He deepened his voice to mimic his father. "'Son, someday when you grow up and are courting a lady…'"

His uncle laughed, but his expression quickly sobered.

The pain in his eyes goaded Ben to give him another push. "Maybe Mrs. Baxter left because she didn't think *you* loved her, or because she thought people would gossip. Might have gotten too hard for her to stay under those circumstances."

Uncle Caleb's eyebrows pulled together.

Ben thought some more about the situation. "And another thing. Frankly, Uncle Caleb, you're a snob."

His uncle looked taken aback.

Before he could respond, Ben plowed on. "So is Mother. So am I, but I'm trying to change. Everyone knows this about us. However, you *weren't* that way with Mrs. Baxter. Not that I saw, anyway. Quite a shock that was at first, actually. But what if somehow she felt judged, or someone said something to make her think she wasn't good enough for you?"

His uncle picked up the brandy snifter and took a sip. "Your mother did act that way at first."

"I know. And Mrs. Baxter's gotten awfully close with Miss Bellaire, uh, I mean the new Mrs. Norton. You won't tell me what happened between you all, what the Bellaires did. But I bet you and Mother weren't blameless. What if Mrs. Norton told Mrs. Baxter what happened?"

Uncle Caleb set down the glass with a snap. He rubbed his forehead and let out a tired sigh. "You may be right."

"You'll never know until you talk to Mrs. Baxter. *Propose* to her." Ben patted his belly. The ache had eased, and suddenly he felt hungry. "I seem to recall a lecture on taking risks and trusting your gut. She says no, then you're no worse off than you are now. *And* she might say yes."

His uncle stood, walked to Ben's chair, and placed a hand on his shoulder. "I will think on what you said, wise counselor. I'll also think about you going to the Indian reservation and let you work your wiles on the natives." He said the last words in a playful tone.

A bittersweet pain went through Ben. He'd never thought the two of them could grow so close. Although he felt good that his uncle had taken his words to heart, he was sad at the thought of leaving. He hid the emotion under a bantering tone. "Well, don't think too long. Mrs. Baxter's a mighty pretty lady, and some other man might snap her up while you're dillydallying."

✳ ✳ ✳

When a customer walked in and rang the steel triangle she'd hung by the door—a sound that would alert her but not wake the baby—Maggie, on her hands and knees scrubbing the floor of her living area, rocked back onto her knees. The pungent smell of lye had made her eyes water, and she swiped an arm across her face before tossing her scrub brush into the bucket of soapy water. Then she rose to her feet, suppressing a groan from her sore muscles, wiped her wet hands on her apron, and went to the doorway of the waiting area.

Caleb stood there, his hat in his hands.

Her heart in her throat, Maggie watched him take in every detail.

He didn't see her at first, and his gaze moved from the white paint on the walls and floor to the polished furniture, to the sparkling glass of the windows and the crisp lace curtains that gave privacy but let in light, and finally to the neatly printed sign that didn't make any mention of whiskey.

Maggie stepped into the room, wishing she'd taken off her apron and washed up. She wanted to press her hand to her chest to calm her breathing, but instead clenched them around the folds of her skirt. "Good afternoon, Caleb."

"You've done a fine job, Magdalena Petra." His smile was warm, although his eyes looked sad. "Word is that your business is booming."

His use of her given name made her heart lift. She tried to yank the organ back in place where it belonged. "Yes. I've plowed almost every penny my customers have paid, except for necessities for us, back into the bathhouse."

He walked over to the cradle and crouched to view her sleeping daughter. She'd moved the cradle into this room while she scrubbed the living area floor.

"She's grown and it's only been three weeks." His jaw clenched as if he held back emotion. "I've missed her so." He glanced up at Maggie, his dark eyes forlorn. "Missed you both."

I've missed you, too. So very much. She couldn't say the words for fear of starting to cry. When Maggie thought she could speak without her voice trembling, she commented, "I heard you went to Morgan's Crossing."

"Only a month or so later than I'd planned. Your friends all wanted the latest news of you and send their greetings. But I'm glad to be home."

Home. "Why did you choose Sweetwater Springs when you could live anywhere in the whole country?" This was a question she'd long been wondering. "There's probably plenty of places where you'd make far more money."

Caleb took in a deep breath. "I wanted the freedom of the West."
He ticked off the list on his fingers. "I wanted a town small enough to
make my mark. I wanted a place where the citizens were law-abiding
and the leadership included men of integrity. I wanted to live among
scenic beauty. I wanted a town that needed a bank and whatever other
businesses I could provide. I wanted a community where I could feel at
home—as much as that is possible for me anywhere."

"Did you find those qualities here?" Maggie thought she already
knew the answer, for she, too, had discovered all of those special aspects
in Sweetwater Springs.

Caleb glanced down at her. "I thought I had." With a tender smile,
he brushed a wayward curl from her forehead. "But then I met you."

Maggie couldn't breathe. "What are you saying, Caleb?" The question squeaked out.

"If you think I'm saying *I love you*, you'd be right."

Can this be true? "Oh, Caleb." She nearly said, *I love you, too*, but
she held her tongue. *We couldn't possibly be suited.* "Have you forgotten
that I have Gypsy blood?"

"My memory is not so bad," he said in a dry tone.

"You…don't mind?"

"I do mind. Or maybe I should say, I *did* mind. Now, when I look
at you, I don't see *Gypsy*. I see *Maggie*. My Magdalena Petra. Your Gypsy
blood is part of who you are. Part of who Charlotte is. How can I help
but love *all* of you?" He gestured to the cradle. "All of *her*." He held out
a hand. "Come with me. There's something I want to show you that I
hope will prove how serious I am."

She hesitated, glancing at the cradle and trying to decide. Charlotte
had just fallen asleep and would probably be out for at least an hour.

"I'll come back in a minute for the cradle."

Reluctantly, Maggie extended a hand to him, wincing when she
saw the red roughness of her skin from all the scrubbing. She bit her
lip and started to pull back.

"No." His fingers closed around hers, and he held up her hand to the light of the window and spread her fingers, examining the damage. "You've worked hard, Magdalena Petra. You've taken a rundown business and made it a success. Be proud of this hand, not ashamed." He kissed her palm.

Tingles raced up her arm to swirl through her body.

He kept his hand around hers and led her out the door to the side of the bathhouse.

There in the path of the setting sun stood her piebald workhorses, Pete and Patty, mane and tails braided with colorful ribbons. They were hitched to her *vardo. My vardo!* The caravan looked resplendent—fresh and new in green-and-gold glory. Above the cherished scene, orange, bronze, and gold streaked across the purpling sky, illuminating the underside of puffy pink and white clouds.

"Caleb!" Maggie gasped. Emotion welled. Her free hand flew to her mouth, and tears leaked from her eyes. She glanced from the caravan to Caleb and back again, unable to believe the sight.

He brought her hand to his lips and turned it to kiss her rough palm. "Magdalena Petra, I want you for my wife."

"But Caleb—"

"The *vardo* is a gift to you, Maggie. But it's yours regardless of whether you marry me or not. I don't want you to accept me because you want that caravan!"

She gazed up at him in disbelief. "But why, Caleb? Why would you restore the *vardo*?"

His smile was tender. "Because it meant so much to you." He ticked down the list on his fingers. "Because I want Charlotte and our future children to have the experience of traveling in it. Because I figure it will be a good way for us to navigate the journey from here to Morgan's Crossing and back when I need to travel there for business. Because, if you wish, we can go along on the expedition to the Indian reservation. And…because I figured that instead of a fancy honeymoon journey, you might enjoy a jaunt in your *vardo*." He tipped his head toward the caravan. "I'd be willing to turn into a Gypsy for a week or ten days. I rather fancy being all alone with you and Charlotte out in the wilderness."

Maggie released a sigh that seemed to come from the very depths of her being. Speechless, she stared up at him, seeing the vulnerability in his eyes. With a whisper of movement like the slightest breeze, she felt the spirits of her family reassure her and nudge her toward Caleb.

He seemed to understand, for he guided her toward the *vardo*'s door. "Go see. I'll get Charlotte."

Maggie first went to the horses and petted and murmured to them. Once her ankle had healed, she'd visited them every day, taking along a carrot or apple slices. Jed had taken good care of the team. They'd filled out, and their coats were shiny, their feathered forelocks clean and fluffy.

Caleb returned with the cradle. "Come see the inside. We had to guess where things went."

Maggie lifted her skirts to climb the ladder. She stepped inside and drew a quick breath. The interior was completely redone—the table and cabinets sanded and stained a rich mahogany. The bed had a new, floral-patterned covering and pillows that matched the curtains.

Caleb set the cradle inside to the right of the door and climbed in after her. He gestured toward the bed. "There's a new mattress, too."

Maggie ran a hand over the soft coverlet and glanced at the shiny walls. Someone had brightened up the faded folk art. She reached to touch the ceiling.

"Pepe Sanchez from the livery did that and the detail work on the outside. Phineas O'Reilly and Gid Walker did all the restoration."

"They did such fine work. I wish my grandparents were here to see this." Slowly, Maggie turned, taking in everything, her heart swelling with each loving detail she noticed.

On the kitchen counter sat a small, enameled box. Maggie picked it up and looked inside. "Oh, my," she said at the sight of her earrings, the gold looking shiny and new.

"No more hiding who you are, Magdalena Petra."

She picked up an earring and tried to put it on. Her hands trembled, so it was a moment before she could hook it into her earlobe. The second was just as difficult. Once she had both in, she swung her head, feeling the hoops move—a sensation she'd missed in the last few weeks.

"Caleb," she whispered to herself. "You're so *very* kind." Remembering her grandmother's silk dress, she gasped and hurried to the bed, attempting to fold back the mattress, but the new one was stiff and didn't bend like the old one had. She struggled to lift it.

"What are you doing?" Caleb grabbed the edge of the bed.

"There's storage underneath. Can you please hold it for me?"

He picked up one side of the mattress and held it in place. "Go ahead."

Maggie leaned underneath and was relieved to see the familiar cedar box. She hefted it out. "You can put the mattress down."

Once he lowered the mattress, she set the box on top and lifted the lid. At the sight of the folded pink silk, Maggie was so pleased that she placed a hand to her chest and let out a sigh. She glanced up at Caleb. "This was my grandmother's." She touched the fabric, blinking quickly. "The gown is very special to me." She closed the lid and motioned for him to lift the mattress again while she replaced the box underneath. "This is a dream come true! No, more than a dream. For I couldn't even imagine the *vardo* looking so grand. Caleb, thank you from the bottom of my heart."

He grinned. "My pleasure, darling."

She whirled, spinning so quickly her skirt belled. "Come," she demanded. This time, she was the one who held out a hand.

Caleb allowed her to pull him toward her before taking her into his arms and kissing her.

Maggie stood on tiptoe and answered his kiss with a deeper, hungrier one of her own. The kiss ended, and she placed a hand on his chest. "I love my *vardo*. Before, I thought I wanted to live in here more than *anything*." She patted his chest right over his heart. "But I've found my home is here, in your arms. *This* is where I find shelter and contentment. *You* are my sanctuary."

He tenderly brushed her cheek with the back of his hand. "And you are mine, my love."

Maggie took his hand and towed him toward the bed. She reached up and clasped her hands around his neck, leaning backward. Giggling, she toppled them back together onto the mattress.

He braced himself to land with his hands propped so as not to squash her.

Maggie wiggled sideways to make room for him.

Caleb sprawled on his back, encircling her waist with his arms. He lifted her on top of him. "Now that you're compromising me, you'll have to make an honest man of me, Magdalena Petra soon-to-be-Livingston."

Maggie laughed. "And so I will, Caleb Charles Victor Livingston. But I want a *two*-week honeymoon. For we'll need plenty of time for this." She pressed her lips to his in a passionate kiss.

My Gypsy bride. Caleb's arms tightened around her, and he deepened their kiss. *Forever.*

Dear Reader

Thank you for reading *Mystic Montana Sky*. I know a lot of you have waited many years for Caleb Livingston to fall in love. But you haven't waited as long as I have, for the opening scene came to me in 2004. I'm so glad the time was finally right to bring Caleb's story to life and give him the exact opposite wife from the kind he wanted, but who was really the one he needed.

Charlotte was a bonus. I based the baby on my niece Christine Holland, who is now old enough to be my assistant. As an infant, she and I shared a bonding look, and I also watched her do that same exchange with my grandmother—her great-grandmother. I experienced that rare and mystical moment when a little old soul peeked out and connected, only to slide away, and once again, she was only a newborn.

Like all my books, *Mystic Montana Sky* is a stand-alone story, but familiar characters from other books weave throughout—Joshua Norton and Delia Bellaire in *Glorious Montana Sky*; Erik and Antonia Muth in *Healing Montana Sky*; Ant and Harriet Gordon in *Stormy Montana Sky*; Wyatt and Samantha Thompson and their children in *Starry Montana Sky*; Gideon and Darcy Walker in *Mail-Order Brides of the West: Darcy*; Michael and Prudence Morgan in *Mail-Order Brides of the West: Prudence*; Sophia Maxwell and Kael Kelley in the upcoming *Singing Montana Sky*; Peter Rockwell, Blythe Robbins, and the Salter family in *Sweetwater Springs Christmas*; Howie Brungar and Bertha Bucholtz in *Mail-Order Brides of the West: Bertha*.

This was my third book in a row with childbirth scenes, but the first one from the point of view of the woman giving birth. Katharine West, a labor and delivery nurse, generously read those scenes and gave me so much new material that it took me a week to incorporate it all into the scenes. Look up "baby crawl" (which I'd never heard of) to see the natural movement newborns make when placed on their mother's chests directly after birth. Katharine and I figured Maggie might have some Gypsy knowledge of this practice, and I incorporated it into the story.

Katharine is also very knowledgeable about musical history and helped with the wedding and reception scenes. Did you know Bach's "Ode to Joy" was considered secular until the 1960s and "Pachelbel's Canon" was lost to history until rediscovery in 1929, and then reintroduced by the Boston Pops in 1940s? Me, neither.

Still to come is Sheriff K.C. Granger's story in *Montana Sky Justice*. If you have read all of my Montana Sky series books, which include the Mail-Order Brides of the West stories, and want more of my characters while you're waiting for my next one, go to my Montana Sky Kindle World, http://debraholland.com/kindle-worlds.html, to read fan fiction Montana Sky stories written by other authors. I'm sure you'll enjoy their books as much as I have.

Keep in touch by joining my newsletter list, http://debraholland.com, and receive access to a secret page on my website. Also, please follow me on Facebook and Twitter.

Debra Holland

Acknowledgments

In gratitude to:

Louella Nelson—editor, teacher, and friend—with many thanks for the love and support, as well as the days of welcoming me to her house, while I wrote and edited *Mystic Montana Sky.*

To my readers, who love the Montana Sky series and who've been asking for Caleb Livingston's story for years! With many thanks for your reviews, e-mails, and social media posts about my books. Every day, you inspire me.

My Montlake Romance editor, Maria Gomez, whose support throughout the process of writing *Mystic Montana Sky* has been so important to me.

My editors—Linda Carroll-Bradd and Adela Brito—who always make my stories better.

To Delle Jacobs, who designs such beautiful covers for my books, and her brother John Mitchell, who also contributes. We went back and forth for days before finding the right images—especially the sky—for *Mystic Montana Sky*. But we ended up with exactly what I wanted.

My mother, Honey Holland, and Hedy and Larry Codner (my aunt and uncle) for being my beta readers.

Katharine West, labor and delivery nurse, for help with the childbirth scenes

To my Facebook friends for suggestions and research help.

To all my friends at Pioneer Hearts, a Facebook group for the authors and readers of Historical Western Romance, for answering my questions, making suggestions when I asked for help, and for their eagerness to read more Montana Sky stories. I'm truly blessed to "know" you!